FLASH OF FIRE

A Firehawks Novel

M.L. BUCHMAN

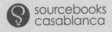
sourcebooks
casablanca

Published by Sourcebooks Casablanca, an imprint of Sourcebooks, Inc.
P.O. Box 4410, Naperville, Illinois 60567-4410
(630) 961-3900
Fax: (630) 961-2168
www.sourcebooks.com

Printed and bound in Canada.
MBP 10 9 8 7 6 5 4 3 2 1

Also by M.L. Buchman

The Night Stalkers

The Night Is Mine
I Own the Dawn
Wait Until Dark
Take Over at Midnight
Light Up the Night
Bring On the Dusk
By Break of Day

The Firehawks

Pure Heat
Full Blaze
Hot Point

Delta Force

Target Engaged

Praise for *Hot Point*

"You don't just read; you devour each and every word, savoring them until the end, when you can go back for seconds. Like Suzanne Brockmann and Catherine Mann, Buchman's work has catapulted him to the top of the military romance genre pack, and the honor is well deserved. With high-octane action sequences throughout, three-dimensional characters to love, and another sigh-worthy romance."

—*RT Book Reviews*, 4½ stars, Reviewer Top Pick

"As always, Buchman excels at character development and romantic chemistry, his leads sympathetic and compelling. His writing borders on poetic, rich with emotion and depth, and he fleshes out the story with attention to technical details."

—*Publishers Weekly*

"'Signature Buchman': great characters, a wonderful love story, strong and accomplished women, good action plotting, great technical details, suspense, and some cameo appearances by characters from previous tales. A sure bet for all of his regular fans as well as any deprived military-romance readers who haven't yet found Buchman on their own."

—*Booklist*

"This author is great at creating charismatic folks who have adrenaline-stimulating adventures and this story was another wonderful example of his talent and I look forward to reading more tales in this exciting series."

—*Night Owl Reviews*, 4 stars

Chapter 1

AN ALARM SHATTERED THE PREDAWN SILENCE. NOT some squeaky little beeper. Not Macho Man in the Morning on the radio. And, thank all the gods there ever were, not the bloodcurdling "incoming enemy fire" siren that Robin Harrow had heard a lifetime's worth of during her six years of Arizona Army National Guard service—both in practice and during a pair of six-month deployments the AANG had rocked in Afghanistan.

But it was just as strident.

Wildfire!

She lay in her bunk a moment longer, as grunts rolled out of their own racks up and down the barracks hall, feet thudding to the floor, moans and groans sounding through the thin plywood walls. With no drill sergeant to move them along, there was more shuffle than hustle, but they were moving.

Robin had been awake and glaring at the blank darkness of the bunkhouse's low plywood ceiling for hours, only now coming visible in the first light through the thin curtains. Awake and ready to go. Day One on the job, also Day One of the fire season. She'd lain there wondering just what she'd signed up for and how long it would take for the action to start. Part two had just been answered—not very long.

Bring it, people.

In the interview for Mount Hood Aviation, they'd

promised her that when it hit, she'd be scrambling. She was absolutely down with that, no matter how little she actually believed them.

After the worst of the clatter in the neighboring dormitory rooms had settled, Robin dropped out of her bunk. She'd used her dad's firefighter trick—at least her mom was pretty sure her dad had been a firefighter, so she'd watched a lot of firefighter movies and learned what she could. Her flight suit was pre-slipped with fire-retardant cotton long johns and the legs of her flight suit in turn were already in her unlaced boots. In thirty seconds flat, she went from sleeping bare on top of the covers to lacing her boots.

She'd spotted the job opening for a temp one-season piloting job and, needing to get out of her post-service life in the worst way, answered the ad. Her time in the Guard had included certifying for heli-bucket brigade on out-of-control wildfires. It was a damn sight better than her gig in her mother's truck stop restaurant playing the "Hi! I'm Robin!" perky waitress. She'd had way more than enough of that as a kid and teen.

Phoebe's Tucson Truck Stop—founded by and named for Grandma Phoebe Harrow—was one of the last big independents on the routes. A massive complex that sat on the I-10 just south of Tucson. They could fuel over a dozen rigs at a time and park hundreds. Truck wash and basic service, certified CAT scales, motel if you wanted a night out of your rig, barbershop, and—the bane of her existence—Mom's Grill.

Peddling herself as a waitress was part of the gig, or at least pretending to: tight—and too goddamn short— outfit to reveal her soldier-fit body, her light-blond hair kept short with that chopped look that men thought was so cute—and she liked for its low maintenance. She really did do it herself with a pair of scissors.

Robin double-checked her Nomex pants and her leather Army boots, now that's what a girl should wear, not some damned hot-pink mini-skort. She pulled on a white cotton tee—screw the bra, she'd never liked the damn things anyway, and on a Harrow woman, they weren't mandatory. Nomex jacket in one hand, personal gear bag over her shoulder, and she was good to go. Nobody was going to mess with Robin the firefighter pilot.

She headed out into the hall of the now-silent dormitory. Not a soul in sight. She put on some hustle down the dark and narrow hallway. But she'd gone the wrong way and hit a dead end. Turning back, she went looking for a way out of this place. The corridors weren't long, but it was a maze worse than dodging the truckers with straying hands.

Despite Robin's constant battles at the truck stop, the tips had been really good; Grandma Phoebe's pointers on how to work money out of the late-night guys' soused brains—and their deeply overinflated illusions of what was *never* going to happen—paid well, but…GAG!

Much to her surprise, when she told Mama and Grandma about the ad for a seasonal firefighting job, they'd shuffled her ass out the door and over to the airport so fast it had left her head spinning. Robin had always assumed she'd eventually settle into the traces to become the third Harrow woman to run Phoebe's Tucson Truck Stop, but maybe not. At least not this season.

Robin zagged the other direction through the MHA

camp's labyrinthine barracks after hitting a second dead-end corridor. The building was far bigger than it looked from the outside. Actually, it simply had more cramped into it than should be possible. She spotted a few guys coming out of a door, holding their toothbrushes. But when she arrived, she didn't see any women's bathroom close beside it.

Robin gave up on finding the women's bathroom and walked into the men's. While she leaned over the cracked porcelain and brushed her teeth, the guys who were rushing by half-dressed gave her odd looks reflected in the sheet of scratched steel screwed to the battered wood wall as a mirror. In moments, she was the only one there, staring idly at the "Jimmy + Theresa" inside a heart and a thousand more inscriptions carved into the fir-plank wall with a penknife over the years.

Robin pocketed the toothbrush and rinsed her face. If this were the AANG, grunts would all be formed up on the line by now, but in the civilian world…the men would still be moving slow and the women were probably back in their rooms doing their hair. She stroked a damp hand through her short hair and she was done with that. Robin headed for the field.

Robin headed down the hall and banged out the doors, ready to leap at the fire…and was staring at the gravel parking lot. Not a soul here. The lot was crowded with dusty pickups that had seen better lives a long, long time ago, an impressive array of muscle cars—enough to make a good drag race—and several motorbikes—some hot and some not. But no people.

Damn it! She'd come out the wrong side of the building.

—w—

"How was the wedding?"

Mickey Hamilton was moving too slow to avoid Gordon's cheery punch on the arm. He'd pulled in late last night and he'd been more stumbling than functioning since the fire alarm had rousted him. He'd had enough hours of sleep, but he really needed some coffee.

"Morning, Gordon." Mickey rubbed at his eyes, but it didn't help. The first day of MHA's fire season, he should have been allowed to sleep in. But no-o. Sunrise hadn't even hit the horizon yet, though it was only minutes away, and the first call had come in. Most of the team were already at the base of the airfield's two-story control tower even though it was less than five minutes since the alarm. MHA tried to hit fifteen minutes from alarm to airborne and no one wanted to screw it up on the first day.

The rising sun was dazzling off the glaciered peak of Mount Hood that loomed to the west. The air smelled ice fresh and pine sharp on the June breeze—especially after spending four days back home in the Eastern Oregon, where the grass was already going dry and dusty. It was going to be a hell of a fire season.

He breathed in deep. Here the Doug fir and spruce that surrounded the camp rolled for dozens of miles in every direction, except up the face of the mountain that spilled glacier-cooled air down through the warm morning.

The grass strip runway split the ramshackle camp buildings behind them from the line of beautiful fire-fighting craft parked down the farside. Straight across stood Firehawk One. He could almost see a frown on its blunt nose because Emily wouldn't be aboard. But his own Bell 212 was three down the row and was just as eager to get going as he was.

"Smells like a good morning to go fight a fire."

"Avoiding the question, Mickey. Tell me, was the bride hot?"

"My sister, Gordon. Get a grip."

"Right, sorry."

Vern, one of the Firehawk pilots, moseyed up looking about as awake as Mickey felt.

"Hey, Mickey. So, was the bride hot?"

Mickey sighed. "Yeah, she was…" And he left the guys hanging for several very long seconds. "But not as hot as the number-two bridesmaid."

"Yes!" Gordon pumped a fist. "Details, Mickey. We want details."

Mickey scanned the crowd gathering. MHA's pilots, smokejumpers, and support personal were all hustling up. The team's leaders, Mark and a spectacularly pregnant Emily, and Carly, their genius fire behavior analyst, were all conferring on the platform landing one story up the control tower stairs. But they didn't look ready to announce anything, so he turned back to his audience, which now included Steve, the drone pilot, and Cal, the photographer.

"Suzanna Rose. Went to high school together, but we never hooked up. Saw her at rehearsal dinner and let's just say I saw a whole lot of her after that."

"It's those blue eyes of yours."

"Nah, it's because he looks like an ex-Marine."

"Which I'm not." Mickey had started flying helicopters before he started driving cars. Actually, he'd flown his first helicopter on his tenth birthday and never looked back. It had been a ten-inch-long, radio-controlled wonder with red-white-and-blue racing stripes that he'd crashed and rebuilt a hundred times. It still ruled a place of honor on his dresser at his parents' house in Bend, Oregon. He'd been fifteen before his first real bird. Had been with MHA for eight years since graduation, all of it flying to fight wildfires.

"Women don't care."

"It's because you're so pretty." Gordon tried to pat his cheeks until Mickey fisted him lightly in the gut.

"Let's just say it was an awesome wedding."

"Seeing her again?" Vern, the cowboy-tall pilot from Washington State.

"Nah." Mickey tried to sound casual about it. A part of him—a past part—should have been pleased by how neatly it all worked out, but another part of him—one he didn't know well—was disappointed. "She's leaving for a job in Europe next week. Be gone at least a year."

"Perfect!" was Gordon's response, but Vern looked a little sad for him, only reinforcing the feeling of disappointment that Mickey didn't understand.

Of course Vern was biased. He'd gone and fallen in love with the gorgeous and diminutive MHA chief mechanic over the winter. Oddest-looking couple, but it was working for them which was…good? There'd been a whole lot of weddings lately among the MHA top staff and it was…odd. He sighed but kept it to himself. Mickey missed the rest of the guys when he'd hit a bar and pick up some hot chick with the standard, "I fly helicopters to fight wildfires."

"Oh, hey. You gotta see the new pilot. Emily's

replacement. She's amazing!" Gordon, however, Mickey could still count on.

He glanced up at the pregnant Emily up on the landing. It was still wrong that she was grounded.

So she'd finally found a replacement? Flying without Emily Beale in the lead this season was going to be like having one of your arms amputated and no one telling you. You just kept reaching out and getting nothing but air. Of course, one look at her huge belly as she stood there next to Mark up on the first-story landing of the tower, and he wondered how she'd even fit in the pilot's seat for the candidate-interview flights.

They'd gone on for weeks. Hopefuls—all guys—showing up, sometimes several a day, trooping into the Oregon wilderness and driving up to the high Mount Hood Aviation base camp. To substitute for Emily, someone was going to have to be seriously good. She was the best heli-pilot Mickey had seen in a decade of flying and eight years on fires.

In between refresher flights up and down the slopes of Mount Hood, Mickey and the others had taken to hanging out at the wooden picnic tables in front of the mess hall, sipping cold sodas, and watching the slaughter.

Mickey could see the failures almost as fast as Beale had them back out of the sky. Military-quality control but no feel for a fire—not even the flaming steel drums set up midfield. Weekend aviation jocks who thought that flying fire was just about taking the certification course—MHA wasn't a place heli-aviation firefighters started, it was where they strove to end up. Top fliers from other outfits slipped into camp quietly so their current bosses wouldn't know, then slipped out just as quietly when Emily booted their butts for not being up to MHA standards.

And then she'd hired a female pilot. If it was anyone else than Emily Beale, you could claim gender bias, but not her. Emily only cared about finding the very best. She set an amazing standard.

"So…" Mickey turned back to the other guys as Betsy the cook worked her way through the crowd with a stack of Styrofoam and a pitcher of coffee.

Everything stopped while they all loaded up, then reconvened gripping cups of Betsy's best brew.

"So, what's the new recruit like other than hot?"

———

Robin stood at the back door of the MHA barracks and stared up at the trees. She'd arrived four days ago at this funky, little camp lost in the foothills of Mount Hood, Oregon, for an interview and still couldn't believe it every time she saw the forest.

It had been six months since she'd flown, and that had been her last day in the Arizona Army National Guard. The army heliport in Marana just north of Tucson, where she'd spent most of her six years in the AANG, was three hundred acres of baking tarmac covered with long, neatly parked rows of Blackhawks and Apaches, surrounded by tens of thousands of acres of baking desert.

Mount Hood Aviation was a tiny grass strip perched at five thousand feet on the side of an eleven-thousand-foot-tall dormant volcano. A runway stuck in the middle of trees that soared a hundred feet or more high. Spruce, Douglas fir, maples, and alder. Beneath them lay a thick mat of blackberry, salal, and a hundred other scrub varieties that she didn't recognize. And moss frickin' everywhere: dripping from tree branches, mixed into the grass, clinging to the north sides of buildings and roofs. The lush biomass was so dense that it was impossible to take in, but she could taste it in the air, thick enough with oxygen that it felt like she was in an emergency ward and they were pumping it directly into this Arizona gal.

Robin had grown up in Tucson, served twenty miles away in Marana and ten kajillion away in Afghanistan—all places where oxygen was served in reasonable helpings rather than Oregonian truck stop–sized portions. She'd never been much of traveler, so Oregon was about as familiar as the moon.

The MHA base camp was the run-down remains of a Boy Scout camp along one side of the grass runway. Plywood barracks, dining hall, and a rec hall turned parachute-and-supplies loft, all of the wood gone gray with age—at least all that wasn't covered by the frickin' moss.

She decided that going back through the dim maze of the barracks would be ill-advised. Like Alice, she might slide down the rabbit hole and never be seen again. She began walking around the building.

On the far side of the runway that cut this place in two stood a line of the finest Firehawks she'd ever seen, which more than made up for the disaster of the camp. MHA was one of the only civilian outfits to run the converted Black Hawk helicopters that she'd spent six years flying for the military. That was a huge draw, almost as big as getting out of her waitress outfit.

Robin imagined taking that pretty Firehawk helicopter—painted with the Mount Hood Aviation

trademark gloss black and brilliant red-and-orange
flames like a hi-fuel dragster running out at the strip in
Tucson on a hot summer night—and lifting it smoothly
into the Oregon sky. The controls had been silky in
Robin's hands during the interview and subsequent training flights. Though it ticked her off a little that the MHA
firefighters had better-equipped Black Hawks than the
ones she'd flown for the Arizona Army National Guard.

The AANG birds were always three steps behind.
The Night Stalkers of Special Operations got the best,
of course, then the Army and Navy got the good gear.
The National Guard didn't always get the castoffs, but
it felt like they did. The Army and Navy made sure you
knew you were a second-class citizen—they were dumb
enough to think they were both first when actually neither was. But as a Guarder, she'd never met a Spec Ops
dude anyway, so they didn't affect her reality.

Now she was discovering that she'd been *four* steps
behind. This measly little civilian outfit fielded three
Firehawks with fully electronic glass-screen cockpits.
A lot of the Army and Navy birds were still mechanical
dial and gauge, like all of the AANG craft. The high
tech had taken some getting used to during her training
flights, though all in a good way. Of course she'd now
been totally spoiled.

Mount Hood Aviation also had two little MD500s and
a pair of midsized Bell 212 Hueys—called Twin 212s
for their dual engines—all of which were immaculate
and also sported the latest gear. All the aircraft looked
unusually sleek and powerful in that black-and-flame
paint job.

Robin stumbled to a halt halfway around the back of

the parachute loft—she'd clearly chosen the long way around. A service truck sat there with a seriously massive lock, and attached to the hitch was a trailer. The trailer was an odd one and so out of context that it took her a moment to recognize. It belonged to a ScanEagle drone. She'd seen them in Afghanistan. A small, five-foot-long surveillance bird with a ten-foot wingspan... that no civilian outfit should have.

Who the hell were these people and what had she gotten herself into?

It's not that she didn't appreciate the high-end gear. Didn't matter. Whatever the past, she had the best at her command now. Even if her new contract was only for a single fire season. So she'd stop complaining...soon.

Mount Hood Aviation had a one-season slot because their lead pilot was in her final trimester—for her *second* kid, like she was doing it on purpose—and would be grounded for the fire season itself. She probably shouldn't have even been flying the interview flights, but Robin guessed no one had dared to stop her. Emily Beale had been a total bitch in stretch-waist camos and a belly-hugging black T-shirt for Robin's interview flight, even if she was the size of an RV.

Robin dragged herself away from considering the launch trailer and continued around the service garage. Maybe she should have braved the barracks corridors. She hurried up her pace.

It wasn't that Emily Beale had been nasty, but rather that she'd been so damn good and corrected every tiny thing Robin did that wasn't up to her standards. Worse, she'd delivered every little tidbit as a simple correction. That left it to Robin to feel shitty for failing to meet the standards of a woman who could barely fit between the pilot's seat and the cyclic control joystick.

"You're starting your drop three seconds too early." They soared over a mind-boggling wilderness of trees so thick that the terrain was invisible beneath it.

Robin *hated* personal failure; she was a specialist in self-recrimination. Had thought about putting it on her résumé.

"If you hover two feet lower, you'll pick up another six percent efficiency on the belly tank loading pumps mounted on the snorkel." Over a mountain lake that must be twenty miles from the nearest road and just begged for her to go swimming in it.

She should have known that about the snorkel; it made perfect sense after Beale had dropped the fact quietly over the intercom. A quiet, sure voice in the roaring cockpit of the converted Black Hawk helicopter. Unlike her AANG birds with a big, orange bucket dangling unpredictably on a hundred feet of long-line, the MHA Black Hawks had been converted to Firehawks with big belly tanks that were bolted right onto the bottom of the helicopter's frame. It let her carry a thousand gallons of water, instead of the eight hundred that the bucket held, which was sweet.

The belly tank also meant she could get more up close and personal with the fire. Aiming a bucket on a long-line was like spreading your feet and trying to pee straight down into a shot glass—a good party trick in the girls' barracks during those really boring and occasionally drunken AANG weekends. The belly tank let her decide, "dump starts here, ends there," and hit it every time.

Even without the black T-shirt and camo pants, Ms. Queen Beale had that feel of ex-military that some air jocks never got over when they hit the civilian world. *You're out, lady. Deal with it.* Robin had taken enough officer shit on the inside and didn't need it out here.

Beale wasn't the only one who was all ex-military in this outfit. The lay of the MHA land was odd.

Mark, the boss man, was also ex-officer material. Handsome as hell but married to the pregnant queen bitch. Not Robin's type anyway; she liked her men still a little rough around the edges. The boss was totally AJ Squared Away. He also was always toting around their two-year-old daughter. Which was pretty damn cute — if you lived in a women's magazine world. Besides, he spent his workday circling at high elevations in his command plane as if that was really flying.

A guy who wasn't rotorcraft? Robin was definitely not interested.

Robin hadn't sorted out the helicopter pilots yet, but she would. There had to be some extracurricular recreation to this job or she'd go stir-crazy for sure just chasing after the occasional fire.

Finally, she cleared the last corner of the last building and stopped in surprise at the size of the crowd gathered around the base of the control tower. She'd seriously underestimated the size of this outfit. Forty people were gathered together, with Mark and Queen Bitch Beale perched up on the platform as if ready to deliver some military lecture.

Her two Afghan tours had been in her rookie and her third year of service in the Guard...then three more years of sitting on her butt before she bailed on them.

The stand-down of forces in Iraq and Afghanistan had turned the National Guard into a whole lot of training weekends with the tuition turkeys—in it for the free school and just praying they never deployed—and the occasional call up for a fire, flood, or some other natural mess. And she wasn't really a regular Army sort of gal.

If she spent the next six to nine months sitting around on her butt, alone, between infrequent fire calls, she was going to die of boredom.

There was hope though. She'd take this morning's alert—a fire on her very first day—as a good sign.

She'd been lying there in the crappy base accommodations—no complaints from her; they were free, but they were still crappy—bored to shit in the dark. And then that sweet alarm that could have awakened Jesus it was so damn strident had rung through the base.

And the crowd was almost entirely male, which boded very well for summer entertainment.

She tried to ease up to the back of the crowd. She was last to arrive, which she hated.

She didn't get away with it.

Emily and Mark were both looking right at her.

All forty people were.

Some still half-dressed, others were lacing their boots, but they were all there and she was delaying the entire outfit on the first day. Whatever she'd thought of the Guard, she was always first to the flight line and first in the air; anything less than her best was a personal failure.

"Now that we're all here." Boss Man Mark Henderson spoke in a normal voice. He didn't have to do that; she already felt embarrassed.

Not being the best was the worst feeling on the planet in Robin's book and it sure as shit wasn't going to happen again.

—∿∿—

Mickey had watched for the new pilot as they mustered but missed her arrival—on the far side of the crowd, all he could see was craned necks and a hint of sun-bright hair. She didn't come from the direction of the barracks, and he'd been too busy trying to pry some details out of the guys with no luck. All they'd added to "seriously hot" was "serious dose of attitude." Real helpful, guys.

TJ came down the stairs from the window-wrapped comm shack at the top of the tower with some fresh printouts for Mark. His heavy footsteps echoed over the sudden silence—he still had a limp from his last day of thirty years of smokejumping. As he handed off fresh data sheets to the others, the crowd of firefighters returned to chatting softly.

Barely past sunrise and the late spring day was already warm enough that people were shedding jackets. But the smokejumpers still kept the full suits on and zipped; the most gung-ho of the breed came to MHA. To pass the time and dissipate the tension, they were hazing each other about who was going to be eating a tree on their first live jump of the season.

Mickey had always loved his helicopters, but there were times, like now, listening to them before a big jump, that he thought about switching over. The idea never lasted long…battered by trees, torn knees, broken ribs; smokejumping was a rough life. And that was all before they started eating smoke and facing the fire up close and personal. Besides, all he'd ever dreamed of was flying. But it was fun to imagine every now and then.

"Five bucks Akbar eats the first tree," Krista, the number-two smokie, called out. Akbar, the lead smokie, was still paying for his first-ever MHA jump five years ago when he'd hung up in the very top of two hundred feet of Douglas fir. It had taken him an hour to lower himself down on a rope as he was constantly hanging up in the lower branches. Then he'd had to climb back up to top the tree so that he could recover his chute.

"Five bucks says *you* do," Akbar countered, but his voice was overwhelmed by another smokie collecting the bets for and against Akbar. Mickey kicked in a fiver for Akbar snagging a tree, knowing it was lost money. Akbar was a great jumper, but Mickey wanted him to feel the pain of the helo-jocks betting against him.

But just like Mickey, Akbar was keeping a weather eye on the four up on the platform as they conferred over the pages of new information and their faces shifted to grim. A big fire on the first day; it didn't bode well for the season. This early, it was probably California or Alaska—still too soon for Oregon or Washington to burn. At least he hoped so.

He glanced around at Jeannie and Vern. The pilots of Firehawk Two and Three had caught it as well. He'd lost track of the new pilot again. The newer pilots—Vanessa, Bruce, and Gordon—had missed the look of worry.

Mickey nudged Gordon in the ribs.

"What?" Gordon whispered.

He nodded up toward the four on the landing.

"Oh." Gordon was getting a clue. After three years, he was fine against a fire and one of Mickey's best buddies, but he wasn't the sharpest on reading situations on the ground. Gordon began double-checking his gear.

Mickey had already done that twice, so he resisted the urge to do so again. Instead, he looked around and finally spotted the new pilot again—back between a couple of smokejumpers, he could just see her face. She was watching the group on the landing intently. Sharp, she hadn't missed a thing.

As more and more noticed the leader's looks, everyone began pulling out energy bars they'd rat-holed away in their personal gear bags. Chances of having one of Betsy's generous sit-down breakfasts at the picnic tables this morning were fast approaching zero.

The newbie caught onto that quick enough. She too began stoking up for a flight.

When Mickey had left for a short vacation, the record stood at thirty-nine applicants, twelve test flights, and no hires. Mickey had been gone for four days and returned late last night to hear there was a new hire and she was already certified to be on the line. Bang! Just like that.

Even more strange, the new pilot was rumored to be the new flight *lead*. Everyone had expected Jeannie in Firehawk Two to pick up that role for the summer. At least Mickey sure had. He knew that he was a contender for the slot also, but Jeannie had a master's degree in fire management and Mickey just had an associate's degree in heli-aviation even if he had eight years of flying for MHA to Jeannie's four.

But there was no way to replace Emily. First, she was the best pilot. Second, also the best flight commander. Third, even though she was untouchable, she was an immense pleasure to look at. Even six months gone, she was a knockout. No question that Mark was one unreasonably lucky man because, damn, who knew pregnant could ever look good to a guy.

Mickey had never thought about getting serious with a girl, not really, until he'd first seen Mark and Emily together when they took over the outfit three seasons back. Joke was Emily Beale was still showing her mama bear spine of steel; Mark was the one who was so mushy around her it made you wonder if he was the one dosed with massive waves of pregnancy hormones rather than his wife.

Of course, thinking about getting serious with a girl versus actually doing it…well, that was something he'd do as soon as he found the right girl. Maybe.

He'd only been at his sister's wedding for four days but totally missed the new pilot's eval and training process. It had happened so fast. That had to be some amazing pilot to take the lead slot. He was sorry he'd missed the action; watching the candidates roll through camp had been amusing. Some of the candidates, especially the high-hour pilots, invariably male, would get really torqued when a beautiful, pregnant woman showed them the road home.

Of course Emily had never told them she was an Army Captain with the Night Stalkers Special Operations helicopter regiment. Or had she been Major? Emily and Mark rarely talked about their military backgrounds. It didn't matter. They were the two best pilots Mickey had ever flown with.

For more serious possibilities, Mickey had his eye on the lovely yet shy Vanessa, who flew one of MHA's little MD500s. But it never hurt a guy to look around.

A shift in the jostling smokies and Mickey got his first good look at the newcomer.

Her short plume of white-blond hair that shagged its way to her collar shone in the low-angle morning sunlight. She stood bone straight, which either meant ballerina or maybe workout instructor. She didn't look like any ballerina he'd ever seen on one of those TV shows Sis loved—*Nutcracker* every damn Christmas like religion. She might be long and lean, but she was no waiflike frail flower either. The pilot had shining, blue eyes and high cheekbones on an elegant face that went well with the choppy haircut.

She looked right at Mark, not shying off despite his reprimand for being late, which meant balls of steel. Metaphorically. Even though she had her flight jacket shrugged on and he couldn't see much of the figure beneath, there was no question of a hundred-percent babe.

"Told you she was hot shit!" Gordon leaned over to whisper in his ear.

"No ring or tan line on the finger." Mickey played along as she raised her energy bar to bite off another chunk.

"She doesn't walk like a married person."

Mickey Hamilton had missed her walk. He'd make sure to watch until she moved again.

He was tempted to ask Gordon how a married woman walked just to see what his friend came up with.

To pass the time, Akbar and the other smokies renewed their hot debate over which would eat a tree first. Their shifting positions exposed Vanessa standing beyond them, just a step away from the newbie.

A soft-spoken and dazzling brunette right out of an Italian travel magazine to one side.

To the other, a slender, blond Anne Heche look-alike from that movie on the island with Harrison Ford and a power stance straight from Angelina Jolie.

Side-by-side comparison of the two women during a summer sunrise, with a fire on the way. His day was off to an exceptional start.

"What's her name?"

Gordon cursed. "Thought you were after Vanessa. I was gonna have a clear shot at…"

"Buddy, she'd eat your lunch." And by the look of her, she would.

Gordon was too decent a guy at heart for someone who looked as tough as the newcomer did.

"Besides, I *am* thinking about Vanessa. She just doesn't appear to be thinking about me so much." Hurt to admit, but it was true. His attempts at charm had produced exactly no results. Yet. He could be patient when a woman looked as good as she did, and his ego wasn't ready to admit defeat. Yet. At least not in front of his buddy.

"In other words, *she* ate *your* lunch. I thought everybody fell for the Mr. Northwest outdoors guide."

"Dad is the adventure guide. And it doesn't mean that. It means—" Mickey stopped.

The leaders of MHA were done with their conference.

Besides, it meant exactly that, but he still didn't want to admit it. Not to Gordon. Not to himself. Vanessa had a real spine under that quiet exterior, which only made her all the more attractive for what good it did him. It wasn't that the vibe was off or whatever it was that women said. It just hadn't…clicked for him. Or he hadn't clicked for her?

But watching her side by side with the new recruit, he was suddenly glad that nothing had clicked. The blond was spectacular. Suddenly all of his some girl, someday talk didn't seem quite so remote.

"It seems," Mark called out over the assembled pilots and the twenty smokejumpers of MHA, "that there has been a new 'export' problem and they've asked us to stop it from happening."

Mickey looked at Gordon, who only shrugged. Even Akbar, the lead smokie, was looking a bit lost and he always had the inside scoop.

"I thought export problems was what the Customs Service was for," some wag shouted from back in the crowd.

"Next you heli-pilots will be trimming trees and inspecting power lines," a smokejumper called out, and others laughed.

"We'll start using smokies for express delivery of online shopping parcels," Mickey shouted back, and the laughter grew. "About all they're good for anyway. Real battle is from the sky."

There were a lot of tasks best done by helicopters, but not a one of them was as important or as hazardous as fighting wildfire.

Only the best of them flew to fire. And only the truly exceptional flew for MHA.

Which had Mickey looking toward the new blond again, as Vern riposted the next smokejumper tease.

Ballerina or workout instructor didn't get you in the cockpit of an MHA Firehawk. And especially not the lead ship. To do that, she had to be fantastic. So what did she bring?

At that moment, she turned to look at him.

—∿∿—

Robin concentrated on not shifting foot to foot while she waited. Would the new commander hold her first-day tardiness against her? For getting lost in the goddamn rabbit warren of a barracks? And then gawking like a schoolgirl at the trees and the drone launcher and the line of Firehawks and…

The men.

Enough time had passed that everyone should have stopped staring at her by now and she could turn to scan the crowd. Time to assess just who she'd signed up with.

And the first place she looked, there was a guy staring at her from the far side of the crowd. No one else, just him.

And then another, whom she vaguely remembered meeting yesterday, looked over the man's shoulder. No comparison.

Blue eyes, short—almost crew-cut short—brown hair, and one of those friendly faces that looked like it smiled too easily and too often.

At the truck stop, they were the one kind of guy you could never figure out. The ham-handed ones were easy to spot and all of the women knew to look for the extra pair of straws that were always dropped along the outside edge of such tables, a clear sign that "This table sucks."

Most of the truckers were fine, decent guys, and there were a lot of couples rolling down the roads, way more than in Mom's youth. She'd been able to pick out any of those types easily by the time she was ten and wiping down tables after school.

But then there were the ones like this guy on the far side of the crowd. Flying solo, looking nice…very nice, and wholly unreadable. Mr. Nice Guy or Mr. Jerk? It was hard to tell, because at the moment, he had a rather bug-zapped expression.

—⁘—

Mickey tried to look away, but that *so* wasn't working. Her eyes were a brilliant blue, the color of the morning sky now shining above them. High cheekbones and a chin that made him wonder what it would feel like to run his fingers along its lines.

"Told ya," Gordon whispered behind him.

Mickey offered her a friendly nod. She returned it. Not cautious or calculating like you'd expect from a newcomer, but a short, assessing greeting. Then she turned her attention back to Mark as if Mickey had suddenly ceased to exist.

A soft "Damn" was all he could manage. *Hot* didn't begin to cover this lady.

"Told ya," Gordon repeated himself beneath the last of the back-and-forth banter. The crew was feeling good, ready for the start of the season.

"Mount Hood Aviation sightseeing tours will be next. I've been telling Mark that's all you air jockeys are good for anyway," Akbar teased them.

Mickey had been feeling good too. A final glance to the blond and he felt even better now.

"We have"—Mark raised his voice to quash the last of it—"a little lightning-strike fire east of nowhere in Alaska. It's in an area classified for limited to no intervention. Normally they'd just let it burn, as there are no nearby towns. However, it has grown up in the last twenty-four hours and thinks that it has a passport and entry stamp to cross into Canada."

"That's *our* kind of export problem," Mickey shot back at Akbar. First fire call of the year always felt great. It wouldn't be until they'd had a month or two of impossible hours and crappy camps that the feeling would wear off. Even then, it beat the dickens out of any day job he could imagine.

"I thought Canada wouldn't mind," Jeannie asked. "They're into sustainable forest burn now." Jeannie was getting good. Of course she'd have track of all of that, what with her fire management degree and working along with Carly the Fire Witch—as the fire behavior analyst was known all up and down the coast because she was just that accurate.

Let her be the next Carly; he didn't care.

Mickey was a flyer first, last, and all the way in between. Which left him to wonder again what the blond was.

"Not when it's threatening Dawson City," Mark answered Jeannie's question. Mickey really had to focus. The new woman was already distracting him. Women didn't distract him; he enjoyed them and fully appreciated how easy it was to gather them up at bars or his sister's wedding with "I fly a helicopter to fight wildfires." But this one was making him—

"Isn't that like twenty miles into Canada?" Gordon called out.

"More like forty," Mickey answered, but Gordon's question made good sense. That was a lot of territory for a fire to cover.

"The fire burned forty thousand acres last night and is rated at zero percent contained. They want us to stop it before the strong westerlies help the fire chew up another hundred thousand acres and the only city for three hundred miles around."

Mickey had flown enough fires in the Alaskan and Canadian wilderness to be familiar with Dawson City. It had thirteen hundred people, making it the second largest municipality in the Yukon Territory—an area bigger than California. It had fallen below "city" size with the collapse of the gold rush at the turn of the prior century, so it was technically the Town of the City of Dawson. And if the fire analysts were worried about a U.S. fire reaching all the way there from Alaska, it was an early-season monster in the making.

"Canadian firefighters are heavily engaged in the Banff fire at the moment and our crews are chasing a mess outside of Anchorage. The Alaska Fire Service put out a call for our full team. So, smokies: get outta here! Helicopters will be hot on your tails."

───※───

The lead smokejumper let out a *Whoop!* that was picked up by the other smokies.

Robin froze, because the slightest movement seemed likely to get her trampled as they raced for the parachute shed and their full jump gear.

That thinned the crowd at the base of the radio tower by two-thirds and she could see the guy who'd kept watching her more clearly. He looked solid in the way of someone who'd always been fit, even as a kid. On a soldier, you could see the guys who'd been bulked up by weights and war versus the ones to whom it was just second nature. This guy had always looked this good.

He grabbed a second energy bar, which was a good idea, so she did the same. Once they were aloft, they'd need both hands for flying.

Adding to the general mayhem, Chutes—the head of MHA's paracargo operation who she'd met yesterday—fired up his forklift to run pallets of supplies across the runway to the waiting DC-3 and Shorts Sherpa C-23 jumper planes. The first load was a whole pallet of pumps, chain saws, and gas cans followed by another one of food and Pulaski fire axes. Each had a big parachute strapped on top of the tightly bound gear.

For two or three minutes, the field was alive with smokejumpers rushing to their ready racks, grabbing jump gear, and racing across the field to their two planes.

Robin estimated that for the planes, flying from Hood River, Oregon, to Nowhere-and-Gone, Alaska, would be six hours plus a fuel stop. They'd be jumping the fire by lunchtime.

It was the one thing Robin hated about helos, the long hauls. At a good solid cruise, they were over ten hours from the fire, not counting two refueling stops which would stretch it closer to twelve. And by then, they'd be too wiped out to do much more than sleep. They wouldn't be on the fire until tomorrow morning. It seemed like a crazy system to be sending them so far, but these guys seemed to know what they were doing.

—⁓—

"Helos," Mark called from where he still stood with Emily and the others.

Mickey forced his attention away from the newcomer. She was taller than he'd first thought—close to his own five ten—and he'd always been partial to tall women. Her expression was intent. Despite being last to reach the line this morning, he'd guess there wasn't a lazy bone in that fine body. She looked as ready to spring into action as Akbar had.

"This is too far away for the MD500s," Mark continued. "But fear not. Gordon and Vanessa, they have a mess up in Washington at Leavenworth that needs your services. The fire chief is in desperate need of someone able to tackle spot fires in severe terrain and the MDs are perfect for that. Gordon has lead."

"Vanessa and me," Gordon whispered to Mickey in a tone of bewilderment, completely missing that he was in charge.

Oddly, Mickey could almost see that working, the dusky Italian beauty and the tall, Wyoming rancher boy. He gave Gordon an encouraging slap on the arm.

"I'm also sending one of the Twin 212s because the fire map looks ugly. Carly thinks they're underestimating the trouble they're in." Which meant they were wrong, because the Fire Witch never was.

Mickey held his breath, wondering which he'd prefer: Washington or Alaska, a chance to rub shoulders with Vanessa or the new pilot? He was on the verge deciding the latter on the basis of no more than that shock of shining hair and her brilliant blue eyes, when Mark called for the other pilot.

"Bruce, you're for Leavenworth. I need Mickey's deep experience in Alaska."

"No argument from me," Bruce called out. Bruce

was just a two-year man. Good enough but needed close watching on the big fires. A small but messy fire would be good for him.

"Mickey, you're with the Firehawks." Mark raised his voice. "Your refuel stops are in Vancouver, BC; Juneau, Alaska; and final destination, Dawson City, Yukon Territory. There's an airstrip eight miles due east of town along the highway that will be our base of operations. You're aloft in ten. Firehawk One?"

"Yo," the new pilot called back. Nice voice. He'd expected rough and salty, or deep and throaty, but it wasn't either. It was surprisingly normal. A nice contrast to her tough demeanor—because she radiated the tough attitude that the guys had been warning him about.

"You'll have a standard config for that bird, which is Carly as your copilot and Steve with his drones in back. Denise?"

"Here." The mechanic raised her hand though there was no need. Despite her short stature, her long mane of blond hair would stand out anywhere.

"Kick your assistant Brenna and some supplies over to Bruce's bird. You and your main shop are with Vern up to Alaska. That does it. Get a move on, people; the forest is burning."

Denise and Brenna bolted off toward the service trailer.

Mickey almost left Gordon to his own devices, but he'd be bound to screw it up. Just as he was duty bound to try to cut his friend off from any attractive woman, he also had to help him if he could.

"Gordon?"

"What?" His friend still looked a little overwhelmed.

"With Vanessa, just be yourself. Don't gum it up with trying to be charming; it doesn't work for you."

"Sure it does," he protested. "I'm a charming kind of guy." He shot Mickey a grin.

Then he looked more carefully at Mickey's expression and sighed. Mickey didn't have to say a word.

"Okay, maybe not so much with the charm. Thanks, Mick." And he turned for his helo.

Mickey caught his sleeve before he could move off. "Her name?" He nodded back over his shoulder toward the newbie.

"Robin something."

"Like the bird?"

"Like," that smooth female voice sounded from close behind him, "Robin Hood, who will put an arrow in your ass if you say Robin Red Breast."

Mickey turned to face her. He decided that all of his first judgments at a distance were accurate, and at this close range, they were ten times more powerful—both the fine looks and the serious dose of attitude.

"Hi! Mickey Hamilton." He held out a hand. "As long as it's not a Firehawk you're trying to ram up my ass, I'm fine."

That earned a half smile; nice on the lips, not touching those crystalline, pure blue eyes. Her hand was fine fingered yet strong, like she did a lot of lifting with it. A lot. She glanced over his shoulder.

"He's Gordon Finchley," Mickey filled in before Gordon could speak and get a foot in the door. Helping him with Vanessa was one thing; easing his access to this pretty unknown was *not* going to happen. "Yeah, Finch just like a little Tweety Bird. Don't pay him any mind."

"Hi, Gordon. Good luck in Leavenworth." She leaned around Mickey and reached out a hand, which Gordon shook as he mumbled something unintelligible. Or perhaps it was intelligible and Mickey just couldn't hear it.

He was struck by several things at once. It was the first time he'd actually seen Robin move, and both of his first guesses of ballerina and workout diva were equally justified. Her simple move was both lithe and powerful. Martial arts student perhaps. If so, it was a different form than his Taekwondo, something with more grace and flexibility.

Also, her lean toward Gordon had placed her so close that he could smell her. Her Nomex flight suit was brand-new and the woman wearing it smelled of clean soap and…cool ice—that impossible clarity of air when snow skiing. As if—newborn was the wrong image—newly wrought.

Gordon actually wasn't fluttery like Tweety Bird, but he was also clearly a sweet man—a major mark against him in Robin's book.

She knew from past experience that she tended to scare the shit out of men like him. They wanted her, but she would run over them roughshod, even on the rare occasions when she was trying not to.

This Mickey, on the other hand, she had been able to feel him watching her from the moment she'd hit the line. He hadn't shifted away as she reached past him to greet Gordon, letting her lean right into his personal space.

Guys named Mickey were supposed to look like hoodlums or something. Instead, Mickey Hamilton looked like a cop…or a firefighter. The trustworthy kind, not the sneaky shit she'd always pictured slipping from her mother's bed in the dark of the night and never coming back.

Up close, she could appreciate how nicely broad his shoulders were. And he had the kind of blue eyes that could see through any fog or other BS—far away the best feature on a very handsome face. He was an inch taller than she was but looked bigger and more solid than his taller finch friend.

Robin knew that—because her heritage was half firefighter and half truck-stop mama—she was a pushover for Mickey's type. Now she had to ask if she *wanted* to be a pushover this time or not.

She rocked back onto her heels and Gordon slipped out of her attention. Mickey didn't fade in the slightest. He had a slow smile, a real one that showed beneath the quick grin he'd been using to tease his buddy.

He didn't blink, squint, look away…or look down toward her chest. Mickey faced her eye to eye and offered that slow smile.

Summer is definitely looking up, she thought to herself. *Most definitely*. Didn't mean she was going to make it easy for him.

"Mickey? Like the mouse?"

Gordon snorted out a laugh, slapped Mickey on the back, and headed away.

"Not Mickey Rooney either," he offered in an unperturbed tone, showing no desire to hurry off to his aircraft.

"Not short and round?"

"Nor likely to break into a song-and-dance routine. And Mickey Mantle died about the time we both entered grade school, so I'm not him either."

"How about *Mickey Blue Eyes*?"

"Well, my name is Mickey. Eyes are blue."

"You don't strike me as the Hugh Grant romantic comedy type."

He shrugged noncommittally. "You the type to watch them?"

"Not so much," Robin admitted. Astute question. "So, Mick Blue Eyes it is."

At that, he smiled and those blue eyes lit and sparkled with laughter that was only suggested by the sudden curve of his lips.

Then those deep blue eyes shifted over Robin's shoulder for a moment and she could feel someone coming up close behind. Give her one guess and it was an easy one.

But rather than scooting away from the incoming Queen Bitch Beale, Mick—no, she did like Mickey better—turned back and took Robin's hand again for a moment. Instead of shaking it, he just held it for an instant and she rather liked the warm, steady feeling.

"See you in the air." Then he nodded to the woman behind Robin. "And we're really going to miss you, Emily." He addressed her much more easily than Robin would have dared.

"I can see that." The Queen's tone was dry enough to make the Tucson desert look well irrigated.

Mickey, looking not the least abashed, squeezed Robin's hand a final time and headed over toward his smaller Bell Twin 212—a respectable enough machine, though it couldn't carry half of what the pretty Firehawk hauled.

Robin braced herself before turning to face Queen Beale. Even pregnant, she was fit and beautiful. Her straight hair was a perfectly trimmed fall of gold to her shoulders. It caught the morning sun like a maiden Viking's helmet.

"You're a fine pilot," the Queen launched in without preamble.

Robin opened her mouth and then shut it again when the unexpected compliment registered.

"You also think you're the *best* pilot, which you aren't. But you have the potential to be or we wouldn't have hired you out of the forty applicants that we accepted for interviews and tests or the two hundred that we didn't accept at all."

Forty? Shit! Robin had kind of assumed she'd been the only one to apply. She sure hadn't seen anyone else around and had been hired right in the middle of the interview flight. Which meant QBB knew exactly what she was looking for, even if Robin had no idea why she was it.

Queen Beale had her take runs at flaming barrels with tanks full of water dipped from narrow streams. They'd flown tortuous routes among the crags and peaks of Mount Hood, right up past the tree line, to where the air was thin enough to drastically change performance profiles, and down into forested valleys so thick with fir trees that there was no sign of the land beneath.

She'd been sliding up to hover close beside a cliff when Beale's voice had shifted. Suddenly there were no longer instructions of "Do this! Go there!" It all became "When you're flying in this situation, you'll find…"

Robin had only needed to glance at Emily to be given the nod, "Yes, you passed. Now let's work on skills." And they had done nothing else for the last three days.

Robin was good, but the amount Queen Beale knew about helicopters and fire was astonishing.

"Bruce, Vanessa, and Gordon are good pilots," QBB told her as they started across the runway. "They're coming up nicely, but they're on the Leavenworth fires, so you won't have to think about them yet. Jeannie, Vern, and Mickey, the three that you'll be traveling to Alaska with, are all exceptional. Jeannie has a degree in fire management and years of fire, Vern's years of flying Coast Guard makes him our best pilot, but Mickey is your fire specialist. He has more years flying to fire than the others combined. He's the best fire pilot I've got. You've met Carly and Steve?"

She had, barely, and offered a cautious nod. She was pretty sure Carly was the one who'd gone up to meet with the other leaders on the radio tower platform, but maybe not.

Emily slowed down her pace midfield with a curse and a hand on her belly. "This one kicks even worse than Tessa did. Carly flies left seat on Firehawk One. She is the top specialist there is on fire behavior. Her recommendations are gold; doesn't mean you have to follow them, but you'll want a good reason not to. Steve flies a spotting drone, typically from the backseat of my bird."

"Why do you people have a drone?"

Queen Bitch Beale's smile was chilly, enough to make Robin's blood freeze in her veins despite the warm spring morning.

"*We* have a couple drones and they are very useful." She backed up her words with a look that left no doubt Robin had damned well better take ownership of the team right fucking now.

"Got it!" *Don't need to beat me with a stick. Soldiers know the importance of teamwork.* And even though she was six months out, Robin knew she had a lot of soldier still in her "*We* have a drone."

"ScanEagle with infrared heat imaging for fires," Beale continued without acknowledgment. "Steve has a few other tricks up his sleeve as well. He'll mostly feed to Carly and she to you, but be ready for it."

They reached the Firehawk that had been Beale's but would now be hers for a season. It was in the middle of the line of aircraft parked along the far side of the narrow grass runway. Place of first choice. Yet another sign among the hundred Robin had seen that said, pregnant or not, QBB ruled. Robin liked that in a woman.

"I can see you discounting Mickey's smaller helicopter. Don't. He has more hours in it aloft against fire than you have in your entire National Guard service."

Robin nodded. Partly because that was interesting information about Mickey and partly because the Queen's attitude was one hundred percent that of a commanding officer, which made Robin's nod a self-preservation instinct. Of course, if Robin had run into a few more officers like this one, she might still be in the Guard.

"You'll be carrying the launch trailer for Steve's drone to Alaska with your Firehawk."

Her Firehawk. Just that simply Queen Beale was handing over the reins. It felt…weird.

"He'll make sure you have the information you need. Information's going to come at you fast and hard over a fire."

"I'm used to that." Robin patted the nose of Firehawk One. *Hers?*

"Not like this. Trust me." And Emily Beale smiled for perhaps the first time.

It was a powerful, engaging smile that made Robin feel as if she'd just crossed over some line. Unworthy to trusted? Outsider to insider? Most likely heathen out-cast to razor-thin tolerance until her initial screwup, then outta there!

"In the Guard, when you were on a fire," Beale continued, "you heard from one source, Incident Commander—Air, which is Mark for us. But you're seated in the Number One bird for Mount Hood Aviation now. I almost gave it to Jeannie and pushed you into the Number Two slot, but your commanders convinced me to keep you front and center."

"My..." She trailed off. Of course MHA had called her former commanders. What was surprising was that they'd given her good reviews.

"They said you were an exceptional pilot and a royal pain in the ass."

"I expected the second part of that." Robin did her best to hide her shock at the first part, because while she'd done her best to prove it, they had sure acted like they didn't notice.

Then the Queen Bitch Emily Beale held out a hand that was warm from resting against her rounded belly.

Robin shook it tentatively, unsure of the message.

"Welcome to the club. My last commander was always saying the same two things about me." Again that radiant smile that was even more of a surprise the second time.

"Did he give you a good recommendation when you needed it?"

Emily looked amused, an expression that Robin had never expected on her face. "I don't know about that, but he did give me a wedding band and two children. I have yet to decide if the second child is a blessing or a curse." Though the way she kept a hand resting lightly on her belly, there was little question of her true feelings.

QBB had married her commanding officer, Mark Henderson. Which would explain why someone so military was out in the civilian world. Though it was clear this woman had plenty of backbone. If the military had been so important to her, why did she leave the service to marry her commander? What's more, why didn't he stay in anyway? Something in her story didn't make sense.

Three airplanes along the line fired to life with a distracting roar of large engines and the sharp buzz of accelerating propellers beating the air: the two smoke-jumper delivery planes and the Incident Commander's Beech King Air.

Emily turned to watch the Beech King Air but kept talking to Robin. "I can't wait to see how he flies that observing plane with two kids in the cabin. We're going to have to find a nanny willing to travel at high elevations." Then Emily's face shifted in a way Robin couldn't quite interpret and she turned away from the plane, now resting a hand on the nose of her Firehawk as if saying good-bye.

"Get aloft." Emily didn't look up but kept her focus on the helicopter or something beyond it. "Be safe. Listen to Mark from above and Carly from beside you. Vern doesn't speak much more than Denise, our quiet mechanic. Jeannie is an exceptional wildland firefighter, reads the flames almost as well as Carly. Vern is a masterful pilot. If you need someone to explain *how* they do what they do, listen to Mickey. In addition to being very skilled, he's highly observant and knows how to turn it into words."

And without another word or gesture, Emily Beale was gone.

Robin was left standing beside Firehawk One trying to remember who she was supposed to watch for what.

She looked down the line.

Firehawk Two was another husband-and-wife team; the woman must be Jeannie. The pilot sported an Australian accent and a fire-red streak in her dark brown hair. Her hubby was a world-class fire photographer. Hell, Cal Jackson was *the* wildfire photographer; didn't need to be on the outside to know that either. Over the years, he'd taken enough photos of the National Guard helos flying to fire to satisfy anyone. There were even a pair of shots—Colorado two years ago and California three years back—that Robin was fairly sure were her bird high up and making a drop. One had hit *Time* magazine the other the *LA Times*. Seriously cool.

Firehawk Three had a long, tall drink of water for a pilot, Vern. He was married to a tiny blond who barely reached his shoulder. Robin had been eyeing him for a little summer fun, but the blond was the chief mechanic. Denise, maybe? And you never *ever* pissed off your helicopter mechanic. Robin had never actually tried the married guy thing anyway, but Vern almost made it look tempting to try.

But having met Mickey Hamilton, maybe she'd no longer need to.

Parked beyond Firehawk Three, Mickey noticed her

attention and shot her a cheery wave. She started to wave back just as Jeannie wound her Firehawk's Auxiliary Power Unit to life to start her engine; the APU had a high-pitched whine that sliced into Robin's ears.

Crap! She was behind again.

A redheaded woman from the kitchen pulled up close by in a battered golf cart and began wrestling a large cooler into the cargo bay of Firehawk Two. "Sandwiches, snacks, soda, cold water. Y'all are going to need it when you land because I won't be set up yet."

Robin nodded, but the woman was too busy unloading the rest of her supplies into the back of the Hawk to notice.

She shook her head to clear it and began working her way around Firehawk One, doing the Preflight Check to prepare the helo.

Her Firehawk.

Nope. Still no reaction. The reality simply hadn't sunk in. No real surprise either—only her first day.

She was last in the whole line to climb aboard her helo. She scanned the Preflight Checklist to be sure she'd remembered it all. *Yes!* She'd gotten everything. Robin flipped to Before Starting Engines and checked the collective position lock, the seat belt harnesses setting, and strapped in, then the parking brake. She began throwing circuit breakers from memory. After that, she chewed through the Cockpit Equipment Checklist, ignoring the fact that everyone else's rotors were already churning air when she glanced down the line.

At least this time, being last wasn't her fault, at least not entirely. Emily had escorted her across the field and given her far more advice than she'd wanted.

But Robin had also stopped to meet Mickey and, while hard to regret, he had slowed her down.

Just roll with it. Nothing else to do.

The engines both fired off cleanly and the high whine of the APU had given way to the throaty roar of the twin turboshafts by the time Carly Thomas, the fire behavior analyst, hurried across the field toward her. The woman slipped into the copilot's seat.

"Do you fly?" Robin asked in the least-irritated voice she could muster. It was a lot of work to start a Blackhawk on your own. She'd seen Denise helping Vern and Cal helping Jeannie. Though she hadn't spotted anyone with Mickey on his Twin 212.

The fuel flow was good and the temperature was rising right along with Robin's.

"I have my basic rotorcraft ticket finally," Carly admitted. "But not much more. Emily always handled everything. I'm really in this seat because it gives me the very best view of the fire. I only got my ticket in case of emergencies, so please don't have one. We're picking up Steve's gear on the far side of the bunkhouse." Carly slipped it all out in one breath. She was a softer version of the Queen Bi—no, that didn't fit anymore.

Emily Beale was the Queen…Bee. How hard had that been for her to relinquish her helicopter just now? And…

Robin laughed aloud as she shut off the APU and finished the Engine Run-Up list.

"What?"

She shook her head. Soon the high-pitched whine of the Firehawk's twin turboshaft engines overwhelmed the cockpit. They both pulled on headsets.

As soon as the intercom was live, Carly repeated her question.

Robin could only shake her head again in wonder. "I just realized the seat I landed in."

"Emily's." There was both reverence and doubt in Carly's tone, and it didn't take a genius to determine which part was allocated to Robin.

She understood now.

Emily clearly ruled the hive that was MHA's helicopter pilots, no matter that her husband was the outfit's boss. And now that Robin was in Emily's seat, she was going to have to figure out what to do about that. She'd led plenty of multi-aircraft flights in the Guard, so it shouldn't be a real problem.

Robin looked up and down the row. The other six helicopters were ranged to either side of hers. They all appeared finished with their preparations—rotors were turning above all of the birds. They each shot a thumbs-up to show they were ready. There had been none of the arrogant swagger that most National Guard pilots displayed, used to cow those around them, but neither was there the disorder she'd always observed among civilians. MHA pilots were organized and well practiced and had displayed no overt signs of ego.

Mickey had shown plenty of interest and enough ego to think she'd simply swoon over him. But he had carried none of it to the line that she'd seen.

Robin thought through the hundreds of pilots she'd served with at the AANG. Those who were the very best rarely bothered with ego. They were a cut above and knew it. They didn't need to flaunt it. Was all MHA at that level? Was Mickey Hamilton? If so, the summer was looking even better if possible.

That had been one of the big challenges for Robin in the AANG. When you deployed into a war, your crew and your flight turned into a cohesive team so interdependent that an injury felt personal and a loss of personnel was a guilt trip from hell for not being the one to go down instead.

Then, back stateside, weekend warriors were always trying to one-up each other, and the tight camaraderie that she'd so depended on in theater slowly dissolved. It ultimately shattered under the departure of those who had served overseas and the arrival of those who didn't have a damned clue.

MHA was the first time she'd seen a civilian team that felt like a team, rather than a clusterfuck of colliding egos.

The three planes had finished their run-up and taxied to the far end of the grass runway. The Sherpa and DC-3, their bellies full of smokejumpers, roared by the line of helicopters and wallowed aloft. The King Air followed close on its tail with Mark Henderson at the controls.

Directly across the narrow runway from her Firehawk, Robin could see Emily Beale standing at the base of the radio tower, holding her daughter's hand and waving at the twin-engine plane taking her husband aloft.

Now Robin understood the look she'd seen on Emily's face the moment she'd turned away from issuing her final instructions to Robin. It was the look of a woman left behind.

She wouldn't be for long. Robin was willing to bet good money that Emily would set records for returning to the flight line after she delivered, but still, the sadness struck at her heart.

Well, Robin was the one here now, and she was going to make the most of it while she could.

Over the radio, Robin cleared with a gruff guy named TJ in the field's small tower and was first aloft. He sounded like someone else sorry to be left behind.

Vern in Firehawk Three cleared aloft next to fetch his wife-mechanic's trailer. He'd be carrying it on a long line. Everyone else still sat on the ground while he and Robin picked up their gear.

She could feel Mickey's eyes tracking her across the field.

Robin was rarely self-conscious about her flying skills. When QB Beale had been critiquing them had been an exception.

With Mickey tracking her from the cockpit of this Twin 212, she was aware of the tiniest variations from an ideal flight path. She was flying a couple hundred feet across a field, for crying out loud.

She did her best to shake off the feeling, but it followed her anyway.

Mickey had eyes for nothing else as Firehawk One lifted from the line and shuffled across the field to pick up Steve's drone equipment. He'd watched Emily do the same thing every time there was a fire that couldn't be fought from right here at the base camp.

Robin made the flight completely differently. She flew like she moved, with power and grace.

And he still wasn't sure how he felt about it.

Emily Beale always flew the most perfect, most efficient path. You could feel her control and confidence in the slightest maneuver, which in turn instilled it throughout the team.

Robin flew well enough…but it was still somehow wrong.

He tried not to fault her for not being Emily Beale, but it was hard.

The Leavenworth flight called for clearance and headed aloft.

"Good luck, guys," Mickey sent over the radio.

They rocked side to side as a wave good-bye and headed northeast. Bruce in the lead with his Twin 212 and the Number Two mechanic beside him. Vanessa and Gordon side by side in his wake in the little MD500s.

"Best of luck, buddy." Mickey didn't hit the transmit switch as he sent a good thought aloft with Gordon.

Then he turned his attention back to Robin in Firehawk One.

It might feel wrong to have her in the air, but that wasn't her fault; she was just the unknown.

But on the ground, there wasn't a single thing wrong with her.

His twin T400 engines were at full roar, his two-bladed rotor was pounding the air. He was so ready for this fire season to kick off.

Yeah, he'd get over Robin being in Firehawk One fast enough.

~~~

Robin hovered to the farside of the runway, around the back side of the scattered buildings, and landed lightly.

Steve, the handsome drone pilot with the bad limp, slid several cases—each two yards long and a half yard square—into her Firehawk's cargo bay. They must be the drones themselves. She picked up the hook on his drone's launcher, about the size of a small fishing boat trailer, and he climbed aboard.

They were ready.

As she climbed aloft and turned north, she rocked the controls side to side to wave good-bye to Emily. It was the best comfort she could offer.

Robin climbed up out of MHA's base on the side of Mount Hood in Oregon, turned north, and tipped the nose down. The Firehawk leaped for the horizon like an unleashed thoroughbred—or at least what they always looked like in the firefighting videos; she'd watched hundreds to prepare for the interview.

A quick glance back showed the others forming up around her. Diamond formation, Vern and Jeannie slightly to the rear and off to either side.

She couldn't see Mickey. After a moment's panic that something might have happened to him, she spotted him on the radar, flying just a little higher than she was and dead astern.

That moment of panic wasn't like her. Since when did she worry about a man that way? She hadn't thought of the helicopter or the pilot, she'd been thinking of the man.

As Mount St. Helens reared her pretty, glacier-capped head, Robin vectored the flight west to avoid the cluttered airspace around Joint Base Lewis–McChord and the Seattle–Tacoma mayhem. She'd give this part of the country credit for having some character. Thick with green everywhere she looked, towering volcanoes, island-dotted Puget Sound—the Pacific Northwest was living up to its reputation for amazing geography. Maybe she'd take some time to explore it after the fire season, before she returned to the Arizona desert.

Robin's reputation was for being a ball buster, not someone who thought about a man's feeling. It wasn't by choice—not really. In the AANG and even more at the family truck stop, it had been a survival trait.

More than a few overly macho National Guarders had found out just how fast her counterstrikes were. Another gift of her grandmother's insistence on a dozen years of kung fu lessons. Robin and Mom had earned their black belts together, which had totally rocked. It had also provided a great deal of help during Robin's angry-teenager years. They'd worked out a lot of their problems on the sparring mat. Better than therapy.

In exchange, for her mom's sake, Robin managed not to threaten to rip the nuts off the truckers who palmed her ass. At least, not too often. Somehow, her section never drew the decent guys trying to make a living driving the long road. Her tables either drew the saccharinely happy married couples—which was never going to happen to this Harrow girl as long as she had any say about it—and the shits who *did* deserve a slow and painful castration.

Problem was, after one time having come pretty close to doing precisely that, she got a reputation down the line. Now, the worst of the truckers would come in to see just how tough she really was. A long line of bloody noses and broken fingers oddly hadn't hurt business or discouraged those trying to breach the femizon Iron Maiden's bastions.

Maybe she'd have been better off if she hadn't chosen

to worship the bad girl who only survived for sixteen comic books, but what was a preteen girl seeking a role model supposed to do?

Sue Storm the Invisible Woman?

"Hi, I'm all-American and sweet at heart!"

Shit, woman. No way!

Wonder Woman?

Chick in a too-tight one-piece. That's supposed to be a girl's role model?

Iron Maiden, cloak of shadowy chain mail that clung to every sexy curve, deadly assassin of Earth-616 series.

She at least had some moxie.

If she was Iron Maiden, what did that make Mickey? Iron Man?

Chapter 2

"NOT THERE," MICKEY CALLED OVER THE RADIO AND watched as Robin pulled to a hover a hundred feet above the airport.

The Dawson City Airport in the heart of the Yukon Territory was a mile-long strip of gravel beside the Klondike Highway, which was itself alongside the Klondike River. The airport was the one flat stretch in a bowl of rounded, pine-covered hills. The field had two white soft-sided, half-cylinder hangars, a Dumpster, and an airport terminal that couldn't hold more than a dozen seats. At the far corner of the field was a fueling station.

The Sherpa C-23 and the DC-3 smokejumper planes had already delivered their cargo to the fire and were parked along the side of the airstrip between the terminal and pop-up hangars.

"Why not?" Robin was in the lead as they arrived and had started to settle next to the jump planes.

"Look at them. What do you see around them?" If it was anyone else, Mickey would just explain, but Robin had preoccupied enough of his thoughts on the flight that he felt the need to get back at her somehow. He'd been in straight-and-level flight close behind her for the last twelve hours, with only two half-hour breaks for fuel and food. The only one of the team flying solo, that had left entirely too much time for his imagination.

"A bunch of nice, open, paved parking area," she snapped back at him, the irritation clear over the radio.

"Paved is the issue. We want to be on the other side of the strip by the fuel depot. Trust me."

You met her for only about eighteen seconds. She really shouldn't make you feel angry.

But Robin did, even if he couldn't pin down why. And each stop had only made it worse.

On a long haul, most pilots climbed out of their aircraft and moved around like they were in their dotage, doing twists and turns to try and shake out the kinks.

Robin climbed down in the fluid, dancer-like way of hers, and then began a series of stretches that reminded Mickey of his martial arts training. At Vancouver, he'd been too mesmerized and merely watched from a distance as she bent and twisted, completely forgetting to flex his own body.

At Juneau, he came up beside her and they silently went through the stretching routine together. She was right, of course, he felt better on the final leg of the journey than he had on the second. She'd also completely fired his body's imagination, and his body had a good one. Limber, powerful, and probably plenty dangerous.

He didn't even know her last name. Hood, she'd said. Robin Hood. No, that had been a joke. Hadn't it? And maybe he should have just explained rather than teasing her.

He tried to clear his mind, but it was all blurred after the long flight.

Dawson City Airport was blurred as well, and the sting of smoke on the air told him it wasn't only the long flight that was affecting him. It was wood smoke. Enough to haze the sun.

Wildfire was coming and Dawson City was still directly downwind from wherever the burn was happening. After eight years flying to fire, the smell always edged up his nerves until he could attack the flames. So instead, he was attacking the newbie.

Robin hovered there, a hundred feet from putting them in the wrong place. He was about to explain, when, without any further question, she slammed her Firehawk across the field and landed on the grassy strip on the far side of the empty gravel strip.

The others lined up beside her in a neat, evenly spaced row. They left little more than a rotor between aircraft. It was the best way to measure a distance with a helicopter, one "rotor diameter"—sixty feet on a Firehawk, forty-eight on his 212. Three rotors was a safe minimum distance if flying in clear air. Double or triple that in rough air.

"Oh, my aching butt!" Mickey griped as they deplaned. Rubbing it brought little comfort. The Twin 212 seat was meant for shorter hauls.

The Firehawk pilots looked fine as they clambered down out of their comfortable craft. One of them looked especially fine and started moving his way.

Damn! He could see what Gordon had meant about her walk. She was pissed, and every stamp of her stride practically shivered the earth beneath her feet rather than the shock of her steps jarring her body. She walked like she totally owned the planet.

He tried stretching again.

"Hey, buddy." Vern came over from the closest Firehawk—Oh-Three—and clapped him on the back. Denise was already busy checking over her

containerized helicopter maintenance shop that Vern
had carried north slung beneath his Firehawk. "Looking
all gimped up there."

"Says the guy with the cushy seat." Mickey had
always liked him. They were two Northwest boys, he
from Oregon and Vern from an island in Washington.
They'd been flying together for years. Someday, he
might have to try a Firehawk, but his whole career had
been in the 212, and other than his sore butt, he'd never
found the desire to change his platform.

"Beats being shuffled off to spot fires in
Leavenworth." Vern had started out in the MD500s and
jumped up to the Firehawk last season—the season that
had seen him marrying Denise, the cutest mechanic on
the planet. Even now, as she began checking out the first
of the helos, the soft, smoke-laden breeze was teasing
her long, blond hair into a banner.

"Agree with you there." Mickey decided that he'd
much rather be on an Alaska wildfire than fighting spot
fires in Washington.

He kept an eye on Robin, but she'd stopped to check
in with Jeannie at Oh-Two. A smart move as a leader.

Vern nodded and headed back to help his wife. He'd
become her assistant mechanic somewhere over the
winter. Mickey didn't know quite how that happened.
It had been pretty clear that they were hooking up
as a couple toward the end of last season, which had
been beyond strange in itself. Denise was pretty as
could be, but she'd been such an odd duck—total nerd
mechanic—that Mickey had never thought twice about
her. Clearly Vern had.

Then half of MHA had gone to Australia, including

Mickey, to fight bushfires for the southern hemisphere summer, and the other half, including Vern and Denise, had gone somewhere else. Somewhere that none of them were talking about, which was seriously strange.

He caught references to Central America, which had plenty of fire problems, but what was so odd was their joint silence about the fire season. They should have returned with plenty of good stories, but none had been forthcoming. He'd have to corner Vern on that at some point.

Mickey had stood best man at Vern and Denise's wedding just a few months ago. Other than parents and one guy from the Boeing restoration museum, it had been strictly an MHA event. No willing bridesmaids for him that time: Emily, Carly, and Jeannie had stood beside Denise—all married. Though they made a stunning array of womanhood when the four of them lined up. Not a guy in the outfit could do anything but stare when they stood together in those sleek dresses.

So while the warm breeze teased Denise's long hair, as if the winds had traveled across the Alaska and Yukon wilderness solely for that purpose, for Robin, the wind was busy getting out of her way.

After Jeannie and Cal at Firehawk Two, Robin stopped with Vern at Firehawk Three, though there was no question that he was her final target. However nice she was being to the others, he wouldn't be receiving similar treatment. He liked that about her. No games. He could see exactly what she was thinking.

Betsy was dumping the supplies out of Firehawk Two to set up her kitchen. For the moment, there would only be the pilots to feed, but she'd soon be feeding the smokies when they rotated back into camp for a break, or sending food in for them.

Robin was still chatting with Vern and Betsy.

During the long transit to Alaska, Mickey had come to terms with Vanessa drifting out of his summer romance flight pattern. Not that she'd ever really been in it except for a few private daydream fantasies. Beautiful women flying heavy machinery was always a good combo.

Robin of the Hood flying a Firehawk, well, that definitely fed that corner of his libido.

He began pulling his camping and personal gear out of the Firehawk. Robin would be arriving soon enough. Then he'd see what was what.

He inhaled a deep lungful of the wood-smoke air, still lighter than a cabin woodstove on a fine winter's night. Mickey loved flying to fire, and now that the transit was done, he was feeling damn good about being here—other than his aching butt. The fact that he'd bagged the Yukon wilderness assignment rather than the Washington tourist town completely worked for him. He'd spent every spare moment of his youth outdoors with his dad.

Dad was winter ski patrol at Mount Bachelor in the winter and a raft-and-river guide when the water was running. In between, he picked up odd jobs leading hikes and bicycle tours. Sis had joined them about half of the time, but Mickey simply couldn't get enough of it. Still couldn't. He'd never flown a fire in the Yukon and couldn't wait to see what lay out there to be discovered.

Though looking around the barren field, maybe he shouldn't have been quite so eager. He'd flown Leavenworth-area fires before. The scenery was astonishing. By definition, wildland firefighting was mostly fought in the remotest places that others rarely saw. He never tired of discovering new places, not even when they were on fire.

And in Leavenworth, the locals made sure you were fed, often put you up in a spare bedroom even if you stank of flying through fire smoke all day. The terrain was harsh, but the accommodations were...more lush. Most tourists who hit Leavenworth did it as a couple; the Bavarianized mountain resort town wasn't geared to attract singles. But there was always some cute girl glad to share her time with a firefighting helicopter pilot—a line that *always* worked well in the local bars.

Here in Dawson City, however, the accommodations for both sleeping and recreation were going to be far less impressive. Betsy was already setting up her cook tent, and their sleeping tents would soon join the lineup.

"What the hell are we doing on this side of the field, Hamilton?" Robin stormed up and stopped well within what most folks would figure to be his personal space. Robin clearly had no problem walking right into it.

"You'll be much more comfortable here, honest." Mickey wondered if she did that to everyone or only when she was mad. No, she'd done it at the airfield as well. Maybe he was just extra lucky somehow. Or extra in trouble.

"I didn't just fly a dozen hours for comfort." Fists clenched and ready to strike, she glared at him. She'd left her jacket in the helo, and her thin T-shirt left much to admire, but he didn't do so actively. He was tempted—not to see if his peripheral vision was returning truly accurate reports of strong shoulders, trim waist, and all the nice shapes in between, but to see what her reaction might be. He decided against it, partly because those blue eyes, sharp with irritation, were so intriguing, and partly in case her martial arts training turned out to be better than his.

"No, it's after you've flown sixteen-hour days on a fire that you'll appreciate it." Mickey waved toward the small airport terminal that was the only permanent structure on the far side of the field. "No hotels here, no town nearby. This is our fire camp and instead of hard pavement, we'll be sleeping on this ground." He thumped a heel down on the deep, springy grass and soft dirt for emphasis. "You'll thank me."

"We'll have plenty of time after a flight to find decent beds."

"If we do"—Mickey did his best not to laugh in her face—"that will be a first."

~~~

Robin could feel she was being a little stupid, right up in Mickey's face, but she couldn't bring herself to back down. She felt a need to push against someone, and Mickey Hamilton presented a very tempting target.

Moments after takeoff from MHA's base camp, Carly had crawled into the back of the Firehawk; she and her husband had spent most of the flight studying the fire maps. Robin had been alone the whole way. The short night's sleep hadn't been a problem for the first six hours of the flight, but the second half of it had been increasingly done on nerves—by now they were *raw* nerves. Eleven hours at a helo's controls was a long day by anyone's standards.

The one fact that had done the most to keep her on point was that she was flying in Emily's seat.

At first, when they all fell in behind her, she'd thought it was because they were all evaluating her, watching her fly, judging every little bob and weave. Then, after the refueling in Vancouver where no one paid her any special mind, but re-formed into the same flight pattern for the leg to Juneau, another possibility had dawned on her.

They were letting her fly in the point position because she was in Firehawk One. Because they were used to flying in Emily's wake. She'd spent that whole final leg of the flight trying to unravel how in the hell she was going to live up to that standard. *WWQBBD* had become a mantra in her thoughts: *What would Queen Bee Beale do?*

Robin had finally gotten so pissed about how little information she had to go on to answer that question that the phrase had shifted somewhere over the endless forested islands of the British Columbia coastline. But *What would Queen* Bitch *Beale do?* didn't offer any greater insight even if it did make her feel a little better.

What had the woman been thinking when she put Robin in the lead helo's seat? Put her there and then given her absolutely no guidance. Emily had signed off on her training yesterday afternoon, and this morning, she was leading the flight north and she couldn't even be sure of all their names. Tweety Bird Gordon, the other 212 pilot, the darkly Italian and far too pretty woman pilot, and the other female mechanic had all gone off to Washington, which had spared her some of it.

By the time they'd blown through Juneau and started

slicing over the unending forests of the Yukon, she'd given up on trying to remember QBB's final list of instructions. She'd watch everyone and listen to everyone and goddamn fake it until she made it.

She'd had to remind herself of that when Mickey directed her to land at the apparently much less desirable side of the field. "Listen to Mickey." That was the only one of Emily's final instructions she could remember with any certainty. He could explain what the others did and why. Like maybe he had some sort of stupid crystal ball.

So why did she still want to attack him even after he explained why the grassy side of the field had been best? And why did she want to jump his bones after the way he'd slid so easily into her kung fu stretching routine? Maybe she could ask him and he could explain both to her.

Good luck with that, Robin. You can't even explain you to yourself!

She certainly wasn't about to ask Carly and Steve. After sleeping for most of the flight—leaving her to do the whole thing solo—the instant they hit ground, the two of them had jumped to life like newly batteried bunnies, fussing over the trailer and their equipment.

And now Mr. "You Need to Listen to Him" Hamilton was saying that real soon now, the crappy Mount Hood Aviation base accommodations were going to look like a luxury.

She'd camped plenty before joining the Guard. Sleeping out in back of the truck stop to watch the desert's starry sky. Sometimes driving up into the Tucson Mountains to get away.

In the Guard, helicopter pilots always made it back to base because that's what pilots did each night—got themselves back for equipment service and security perimeters. Pilots slept in their bunks, not out in the dirt; it was part of the gig.

Robin glanced down the flight line. Denise the mechanic's portable machine shop was already open right where Vern had parked it on the line. The little blond was hustling out of the container wearing a tool belt. As if this was all completely normal.

A rusty red fuel truck had ground to life with a black puff of diesel and was headed to the first helo in the line with a loud grinding of gears.

Well, if they were camping, this *was* a better place to park the helos.

"Okay," she told Mickey to show that she'd accepted he was right and would just swallow the bitterness of her initial irritation.

He waited a long moment, with that half grin that she was tempted to wipe of his face with a quick right jab.

"What?"

His grin widened. "I wasn't expecting you to wind down so fast. Thought you'd want to beat up on me some more about parking us here." He was busy assuming all kinds of things about what sort of a person she was. Next he'd be judging what kind of a woman she was.

Robin shrugged and felt the tightness across her shoulders. Tried cricking her neck but the tension of the flight wouldn't release.

He made a twirling motion with his finger.

Robin scoffed at him.

He made it again.

"What?"

"Can't you even turn around without an argument?"

It was either paste him one in the grin or turn for him. Since it was her first day on the job, she opted for the latter. Though she certainly reserved the right to land one of the former.

When they faced each other once more, his eyes still hadn't drifted downward—which was what she had expected him to be doing.

"Halfway around, Robin. Halfway."

She turned her back on him; that was easy.

Then his fingers dug into her shoulder blades. She hadn't really noticed his hands, not separately from his general form. But—oh God—they were strong, and he knew exactly what to do with them. She braced a foot forward to keep herself in place as he dug his thumbs into her tight muscles.

Mickey gave the impression of being a solid guy. Not heavy or anything, just…solid. She didn't have a better word for it. Like he was anchored right to the earth. And his hands—she could see them clearly in memory even as she closed her eyes in appreciation of the deep massage—were strong, powerful.

Working man's hands. Yum, Mom would have purred.

Grandma Phoebe would have agreed.

Robin was caught between purring herself and complaining loudly as painful knots released. She could finally feel her shoulders let go and slope more normally. Robin pushed back against the lovely pressure, ignoring the unexpected intimacy in the sheer relief from the aching tightness.

Good hands were one thing. Knowing what to do

with them, oh, that was something special. And Mickey was good at it.

When he finally stopped, her head was spinning slightly. She cricked her neck left and right. There was a freedom of motion that she hadn't felt…perhaps since showing up at MHA's base for the interview flight last week.

She didn't turn or open her eyes, just stood for a moment relishing the loose feeling.

"Damn, Mickey. If you can do that, it makes a girl wonder all sorts of things."

———

Mickey was wondering too. His hands tingled with the memory of her. And all he'd touched were her shoulders.

"You work out." He'd found some splendid muscles and used that as a subject change before he simply grabbed her around the waist and dragged her down into the tall grass.

"Lifting dishes." Her voice was soft and a little dreamy, though he was sure she'd shake that off in a moment.

"Dishes?"

"Mom owns a truck stop. Actually Grandma still owns it, but Mom had taken over most of the operation. I'm a soldier-pilot turned waitress."

"Duh, that explains it." Soldier. Of course. That explained the way she moved, and soldier-pilot would explain why she flew a Black Hawk.

Robin turned abruptly. "Being a waitress explains what?"

Mickey laughed right in her face; he couldn't stop himself.

The blow to his gut was good, solid, and would have winded him badly if he hadn't spotted it coming and tightened up his gut muscles in time.

"Hell of a way to say thank you for a massage."

"Thank you for the massage," she said in an overly sweet tone. Then she stepped in until their noses were almost touching; her voice went low and dangerous. "Now what does being a waitress have to do with anything?"

Mickey glanced down the line. The other pilots were all moving about their craft. He heard the sharp buzz of Steve's little drone's engine. It was a distinct whir on the otherwise abandoned airfield, followed by the sharp *whoosh-snap* of the launcher and the six-foot-long bird shot aloft at ninety miles per hour.

Robin also spun to look up at the sound.

"C'mon." He started walking. "They'll have pictures for us soon."

He bet himself sixty-forty against her following.

He lost the bet—or perhaps he won—when she followed along, trotting quickly to catch up and then unexpectedly stuck out a foot to trip him.

Mickey let his martial arts training turn it into a forward roll and made it back up onto his feet, barely breaking stride.

"I must have tripped on something." He spoke as if in surprise.

She grabbed his shoulder and jerked him around to face her. "Answer what's wrong with me working as a waitress, Mickey, or I'll make sure you don't get up so easily the second time."

He faced her, waited a moment as Denise circled around Firehawk Two, which they were now alongside.

Robin was ready to take on the world, challenge it mano a mano—or rather womano a womano—and it looked damn good on her.

"Waitress explains the strong arms and shoulders—very nice shoulders, by the way. Pilot explains the Black Hawk. I'm guessing National Guard because Emily wouldn't have sent you out solo unless you had flown to fire before, at least on occasion."

"I've done it plenty."

Mickey decided he'd wait a week and see if her response was the same.

His Dad had told him to *always speak truth to power*. Mom was one of the head brewmasters at Deschutes Brewery and one of those amazing-women role model types, so Mickey figured Dad knew what he was talking about.

"Soldier," he continued, "was the last piece I was missing. It explains the awesome posture and fitness that makes you so incredible to look at. A capable, strong, beautiful woman. What's not to like?"

Then he walked away to see what Steve's drone would show of the fire.

No steps rustled through the knee-high grass behind him—neither the run-up to an attack or any sign that Robin was following at all.

He'd have to remember to tell Dad that he'd been right.

For a moment, Robin wished she'd flown to Leavenworth with Gordon. Him she understood: nice guy, too polite for his own good, probably shy, and if you dug deep enough, plenty smart.

Mickey Hamilton she didn't understand at all.

She had hit him, failed to thank him, and tripped him—and he'd told her she was strong and capable. He'd seen her in a state of tired, sweaty, disheveled mess at the end of a long flight—and he'd complimented her on her posture and called her beautiful.

If he was messing with her, she couldn't spot it. If he was trying to bed her, giving her a brief shoulder massage without the slightest inappropriate gesture was an odd way to let her know it.

The man was a puzzle, which only made him more intriguing. Maybe that was his nefarious plan...but she wasn't buying that explanation either. The man hadn't played a single game that she could spot yet. He either had a masterful poker face or was genuinely decent and plainspoken.

Yeah, right! Since when had there ever been a man like that?

Fire. She'd focus on the fire.

Sure, it was clear she didn't know MHA's routines, but she'd seen plenty enough burns to know she understood those. Even if Mr. Smug Hamilton's expression had warned her she was in for some surprises.

The sun was headed for the horizon. Time to learn all she could tonight, so that she'd be ready for tomorrow's flight.

She hurried to Firehawk One to see what Steve and Carly could teach her. Another piece of Emily's instructions clicked back into place; they were part of her information flow.

And while she was learning what she could about the fire, maybe she could figure out a little more about Mickey Hamilton.

Chapter 3

ROBIN ARRIVED AT THE OPEN CARGO BAY DOOR OF HER Firehawk One in time to hear Steve cursing.

She stopped and stared at the setup. She hadn't paid as much attention as she probably should have to what was in the back of her helicopter—as in none at all other than chucking in her gear bag.

The cargo bay on a Black Hawk was six feet wide, a dozen long, and four and a half high. The two big side doors slid backwards on each side to expose the center of the bay, making it almost feel like outdoors. The rear held about what she'd expected: fire safety gear, spare supplies, and some camping equipment. She'd seen Mickey dump his own camp gear behind his bird, so she snagged hers and tossed hers to land clear of her tail rotor.

It took her eyes several moments, and a lot of blinking, to focus on what Steve had set up in the forward four feet of the bay. In the AANG birds, that was where the two crew chiefs sat in sideways-facing chairs close behind the pilot's and copilot's seats. From those, they each controlled an M240 machine gun sticking out of the side windows.

Instead of nine hundred rounds per minute of flying 7.62 mm death, Steve had a pair of keyboards with a joystick to one side and a trackball to the other. Bolted to the sidewall and the back of Robin's pilot seat was an array of four laptop-sized screens. Like the Firehawk's cockpit, it was an electronic wonderland.

Carly sat intently in the only other chair close beside her husband.

Mickey squatted—which was necessary in the low cargo bay—easily behind Steve.

Robin's shoulders felt fine, but her legs were still stiff enough from the long flight that she didn't want to squat. Maybe Mickey gave leg massages as well. Now there was an interesting thought.

She opted for leaning on the door frame and looking over Steve's shoulder.

In moments, Jeannie, Cal, and Vern had gathered around, kneeling or sitting on the steel deck of the cargo bay. Only Denise was missing, still tuning up their helos.

Vern must have seen the question on her face. "She's making sure that we didn't damage her precious birds."

"All those hours were straight-and-level flight. What could we have possibly done to them?" It had been ideal flying weather. Nothing but clear air and sunshine, visibility fifty miles plus the whole way. Flying north along the Inside Passage had actually been one of the prettiest flights of her life. She'd like to do it again someday when she wasn't stressing about first-day-on-a-new-job performance anxiety.

She also wished she'd had someone to share it with. Like…her mom. Robin finished the thought lamely, not knowing who she'd really want beside her.

Vern chuckled at Robin's question. "You'll learn. Denise is like that. She's still pissed at herself that I actually had one of her birds break on me last year."

"Last year?"

Someone had arrived with a fuel truck and began working along the line refilling tanks.

"She's convinced that it broke her hundred-percent flight-availability record, even though I was able to fly back to base and land without a problem. I've given up trying to convince her that it doesn't count."

Robin opened her mouth and then closed it. A hundred percent? No one ran a hundred percent except the Marine One geeks—and if you were flying the President, you sure as hell had better be at a hundred percent. Hell, she'd thrown a party for the mechanics back in the Guard when they broke eighty percent aircraft availability.

If that was true about MHA's mechanic, then... Maybe she'd just keep her mouth shut.

"Tell me what I'm seeing." She turned from Vern back to Steve's displays. They looked as if she should know what was happening, but Robin couldn't make sense of all of it.

It was enough to distract Steve from his ongoing stream of quiet curses. He tapped each screen, moving clockwise from the bottom left. "ScanEagle flight controls."

That one she recognized, a very simplified version of her own displays.

"Top left screen, visible light." He traced a finger along a line. "You can see the main fire line here. Top right, same view in infrared light. We can see the core temperatures of the flames." He tapped a key on one of his keyboards and numeric labels spread across his screen.

They were helicopter-melting numbers—some of the temperatures were four digits instead of three.

"Not too hot in this area."

Robin did her best to nod wisely. As a Guard pilot certified to fly to fire, she'd been trained in the use of a last-resort emergency foil fire shelter. If she was knocked out of the sky over a fire and had to ride out a burnover, she had one tucked in the pocket of her Firehawk's door. The little one-person shelters were typically good to around fifteen hundred degrees, but to think of a thousand degrees as "not too hot" still boggled her mind.

"Here"—he tapped a line of faint dots well in front of the fire—"are the smokejumpers cutting their first line of defense."

Robin looked back to the visible light screen but could see no sign of the smokies. Then, even as she watched, she spotted a tall tree fall over like a needle falling among a haystack. Once Steve superimposed their heat-signature images on the visible-light display, she could see the impossibly thin lines through the vast forest.

She'd never been a part of this side of the firefight. She'd arrived on a fire and the Incident Commander—Air had told her where to drop. This setup provided a great level of detail, which would make it much easier to keep the ground crew safe. "That's sweet."

"The bottom right screen is the kicker."

Kicker? Once she focused on it, Robin sure enough felt like she'd been kicked in the stomach. It was a wide area view and what it showed was a freaking huge fire. There was a scale across the bottom that she had to study several times before it made any sense. The numbers were way too big.

They were facing a fire that had traveled over thirty miles, starting from a narrow strip of Alaskan forest, expanding as it moved, and was now a front five miles wide. A thirty-mile-long, expanding teardrop shape of wilderness had been scorched into burned black.

A hundred spot fires burned within that scorched area, seeking to kill the few scattered spots of green in the mile upon mile of black char. Flames danced along both flanks, still burning sideways into fresh forest.

"The Black," as the area of smoking wasteland was known, had about a tenth as many trees as stood ahead of the flames.

And the front of that five-mile-wide fire was moving over the landscape like the blade of a massive orange bulldozer. In front of it, a hundred thousand spires of green trees and groundcover already gone brown climbed rolling ridges and clogged valleys. It was a world of startling shades being eaten by a mile-wide blade of orange-colored hell mostly hidden beneath a shroud of black-and-gray smoke.

It was only upwind that the fire was truly visible, for all the smoke and sparks were being blown downwind— eastward by the strong westerly winds.

Now she understood Steve's earlier stream of profanity.

"How much…" was all she could manage from a throat suddenly gone dry.

"We'll crack a hundred thousand acres in the next hour or so."

Robin was glad she was leaning against the door frame so that she didn't collapse outright.

She caught Mickey and the other pilots exchanging glances. Not worry, rather, determination showed on their faces. They'd obviously faced things like this before, but she hadn't.

"Once we get some more data—I've only had the drone over the fire for fifteen minutes—this will look more impressive." Having spent his anger, Steve now continued with all the passion of someone watching *Jeopardy!* on TV. He did something with the trackball and the fire shrunk a little, then expanded again when he reversed the gesture. "Watch the clock in the upper right corner." He did it again.

He was going backward and forward in time. She didn't know whether to be impressed by the technology or to be terrified that the fire had moved enough for them to see the change in the last fifteen minutes.

"Not much help to you yet. Sorry, honey." He addressed the last to Carly, who didn't appear the least bit put out. "The smokies are here and here." He again did something on the keyboard, and two thin, red lines showed up on the wide-area view. They were a miniscule presence against such a beast.

"See." Carly pointed to the fire. "They did a smart initial set. If they can cut these two firebreaks in time and then hold the lines, we'll be facing three miles of flame, not five, when it clears the next ridgeline. However, in a few hours, there will be a wind shift, so they'll have to watch for the northern edge slipping around behind them."

Robin glanced over her shoulder at the sun; it was already heading down to the horizon.

"Shit!"

"What?" Mickey was still squatting with some form of perfect balance.

"I wish we had time for a couple of runs before sunset to help them out."

"We do."

She waved her hand at the sun to indicate that he was an idiot.

"We're in the Yukon Territory," he countered with that irritating complacency of his.

"Which means?" She could see that most of them understood something that she was missing. Jeannie didn't either. At least that was one less person she needed to be pissed at.

"Pretty much the same latitude as Fairbanks, Alaska."

"Mickey." She managed to not go for his throat. He was clearly having too much fun, which she'd make him pay for later.

"The Arctic Circle is only a hundred and fifty miles that way."

The lightbulb went on for Jeannie.

Now she was the only one who didn't—"Wait a minute."

"Ding!" Mickey called out, terribly pleased with himself. She shoved against his shoulder, but he was so stable in his squat that he merely rocked to the side and then re-centered.

She recognized that type of training. When Mickey had joined so smoothly in her stretching routine, she'd figured him for having been a soldier or an athlete. Not a soldier, she'd decided. He didn't have enough attitude.

But now she could see by the way he let her shove ripple through him and the way he twisted that he too had martial arts training. For just a moment, she wondered what it might be like to spar with him. It also told her that frontal assaults were not going to affect him.

"Arctic Circle." Robin spoke aloud to show that she wasn't a total idiot. "Today is June 18th, four days to the summer solstice. So when the hell is sunset around here?"

"Twelve forty-eight," Steve read off one of his screens.

"Hold it! The sun doesn't set until after midnight up here?"

"And sunrise is just three hours later, shortly before four a.m." Steve look amused. "Twilight in between. No true darkness."

"Four a.m. I'm going crazy." Robin's head hurt.

"Then you'll fit right in at MHA." Mickey looked beyond amused.

Robin surveyed the group of pilots crammed into the back of the Firehawk. They'd just done a punishing flight lasting a dozen hours and not a one of them was showing it.

Not when there was a fire waiting.

Not when their friends were already on the ground facing the beast.

They were all watching her. Waiting for…what?

For someone to take control. Robin suddenly wished that Emily Beale was here and she was still chasing tips at Phoebe's Tucson Truck Stop.

Well, Emily wasn't here and she was.

"Mickey?" She did her best to make her voice all sweetness and light.

"Yes, Robin?"

She leaned into the cargo bay until her face was mere inches from his. His easy and open expression almost invited her to lean in the last inch or so and kiss him. She would have if she thought it would shock him, but he'd been a step ahead of her since the MHA airfield back in Oregon and she'd had enough of that.

Robin rested a palm against the center of his chest.

Then she shoved fast and hard.

He tumbled over backward and landed against the rear cargo net, snagging his foot high in the net and getting stuck there.

"You have five minutes to get that cute ass of yours in the air. People"—she turned back to the others—"get calories from Betsy's cooler and double-check your safety gear. We're going in."

There was no answering cheer.

No calls of any kind.

Instead, they scrambled out of the cargo bay, grabbed a couple of sandwiches out of the cooler, and hit the ground running. Carly shifted forward into the copilot's seat and began setting up a laptop where it mostly blocked the woman's access to the flight controls.

Robin decided that Carly hadn't been kidding when she'd told Robin not to have an emergency that required the copilot to fly.

Mickey untangled himself from the cargo net and rolled out of the cargo bay, landing on his feet close beside her on the grass.

"How did I do?" she couldn't help asking and then felt like an idiot for doing so. That wasn't how leaders led.

Mickey looked her up and down like a man suddenly turned greedy, but his big smile wasn't a leer. Not quite.

"Picture just keeps getting better and better, lady." Then he placed a hand on either side of her face and kissed her hard and fast.

He'd sprinted halfway to the next helicopter before she managed to recover.

"Hamilton!"

He stopped and turned. "What?" He had to shout over

the sound of the grinding fuel truck as it finished fueling the last bird.

"What the hell?"

"Hey, lady, I got a fire to fight. You can pay me back later." His cheery wave explained exactly what kind of payback he was hoping for.

That little shit! If he thought he was going to get that, he was in for a major wake-up call.

Of course, Robin couldn't help noting that she was grinning as she stuffed a sandwich in her mouth and started pulling on her Nomex gear.

Bastard!

The others were going over their birds, still warm from the long flight. Now Robin could appreciate Denise's tending to the helicopters immediately. They'd been on the ground under half an hour and they'd be aloft again in minutes, yet impossibly, they'd be ready.

She turned to track down the mechanic only to find her standing beside Robin's elbow.

"I've signed off on all four birds' flight readiness as cleared for operations." Denise held out a clipboard with the forms on it. There was a place for Robin's counter-signature just like in military operations.

"Really?" She glanced over each sheet before scrawling her initials across the bottom. The list of inspections she'd done in the last thirty minutes made it all the more impressive. "You must be some kinda hot shit to get all this done."

"I am."

Robin stopped looking at the forms and looked at the mechanic instead. She was maybe five-four and could easily be mistaken for a former cheerleader type. Except her few interactions with the woman had all been simple, professional, and hadn't had a single wasted moment.

There was no tone of arrogance or cockiness in Denise's "I am," just a simple statement of fact. As if she was so clear about who she was and how she fit into the world that there was no doubt.

Robin handed back the clipboard with the last form unsigned.

Denise tried to hand it back to her.

Robin just shook her head. "In the future, if you tell me an aircraft is ready, that's all I need to know."

Denise looked up at her for a long moment and then offered a simple nod. "Emily was right about choosing you. Good flight."

And the little woman turned and was gone back into her service trailer, rather than climbing aboard Firehawk Two as copilot.

Robin was smiling as she finished her own sandwich while going through the preflight inspection and preparing herself for flight.

Mickey followed the others aloft.

They might have their big fancy Firehawks that could carry double what his 212 could manage, but the 212 had an agility that the bigger Black Hawks lacked. The Twin 212 Huey was one of the many birds based on the venerable Huey, the helicopter that had changed the face of warfare in Vietnam.

His mom's dad had flown them there and given him his first radio-controlled helicopter. He like the connection with Pops. He was always asking about Mickey's flights whenever he was home. The Huey was part of Mickey's family.

In his 212, only Emily Beale could outfly him—because what that woman could do with a Firehawk was unreal.

Why had he kissed Robin? Mickey didn't usually spend a whole lot of time dissecting his own actions, but that was definitely out of the norm for him. Sure, he'd picked up plenty of women with the old "I fight wildfires from a badass helicopter" line. Had cheerfully kissed and bedded them within hours of first meeting.

But kissing Robin, however briefly, without her invitation or permission was something he simply didn't do.

So why had he?

They followed Route 2, the Klondike Highway, along the Klondike River, west toward town. Massive moraines of gray dirt lined a whole section of river. Dawson City had been a gold town, and they'd dredged enough river gravel to cover the entire town of Hood River, Oregon, and more. From the air they looked like the sinuous tracks of Oregon-sized banana slugs.

He'd kissed her…because he couldn't help himself. *Flimsy excuse, Hamilton.* He'd done it because the woman was irresistible. A level of energy, of life, just poured off her. Damn, he felt better just for being around her. Still, it was going to be interesting to see what retribution she worked out for him next time they were on the ground.

No matter what it was, he'd bet good money that it was going to be fun.

He couldn't wait.

At a cruise speed of 130 miles per hour, they crossed over Dawson City just three minutes from the airport.

There were few outlier neighborhoods. The town was a small cluster of buildings on a grid of eight blocks by a dozen, where the Klondike ran into the Yukon River. Even as they flashed by, he could see that the town was filled with turn-of-the-century buildings. There were fake storefronts like the Old West towns of Colorado and a big, brown-trimmed white church that dominated the waterfront. A broad dike and a green grass park separated the town from the river. The park was clogged with…motorcycles. Hundreds of them.

"Well, folks," Mickey addressed them from his solo cockpit, "if you all came for a fire show, it's happening a dozen miles west of you. We'll be doing our best to keep it there for you."

The highway ended abruptly at the north end of town. There a small ferry, currently out in mid-channel, crossed over to Highway 9, the Top of the World Highway, headed west toward Alaska.

Or where it *had* headed west. On Steve's map, Mickey had seen that the highway had been cut in four or five places by the fire and must be presently closed.

They all hit the Yukon River and dropped their hose snorkels down into the clear water. Even in July, he'd wager it was plenty chilly.

Once the twenty-foot-long hose was well in the water and Mickey was hovering stable at fifteen feet, he kicked on the pump. With a muted roar, water flooded into his belly tank and he had to slowly ease up on the collective in his left hand so that he didn't sink down into the river as he picked up two tons of water.

"Apparently we're quite a hit," Vern called out over the radio.

People and motorcycles were gathering on the top of the dike to look out at the four hovering birds sucking up river water. Mickey knew from experience that a flight of the black MHA helicopters painted with drag-racer flames left a big impression. It consistently filled the post-fire bars with hot and eager women.

"Looks like a ride or a rally. Makes me wish I had my bike here," Mickey answered. Thirty seconds of pumping—he kept an eye on the fill gauge.

"What's your ride?" Robin radioed back. He glanced over at her hovering just a hundred feet to his right. Beneath each of their helos was a circle of small white waves racing away from the center of the downblast of air driven by their rotor blades. It looked as if they were each creating their own circular white landing pads. If they shifted around a bit, they could do four of the five Olympics logo rings.

"A Gold Wing." He hadn't thought of picturing Robin on a motorcycle, but it definitely fit.

What he got back was a snort somewhere between laughter and derision.

At forty seconds, he'd hit his load limit and began lifting up and out of the water. He nudged the pump switch off, reeled in the hose, and started flying west. He could see Robin lag significantly behind. She was doing one thing at a time: killing pump, reeling in hose, and then focusing on her flying. She'd figure the shortcuts out fast enough or he'd underestimated her.

Actually, he'd bet that even being careful not to underestimate her, he'd still be coming in below the bar. This was the pilot that Emily Beale had chosen to take her place. That meant something way more than merely being a kick-ass fire pilot.

The others held back to let her take the lead again, but Mickey didn't bother. He knew where he was going. Besides, that scoff hit his pride a bit. A Gold Wing wasn't some flashy crotch rocket of a machine. It was safe, reliable, and comfortable. He'd done any number of long-distance road tours on it, and it was far more comfortable than the seat of his 212, even if it wasn't flashy.

"An Indian Blackhawk isn't all that much sexier a bike." He made a guess in the dark that a Black Hawk pilot would ride a Blackhawk motorcycle. They left the Yukon River behind as the flight turned for the fire.

Mark would be circling high over the fire waiting for them. As ICA, he would feed Mickey what he needed to know soon enough.

"No, it isn't," Robin replied over the air. "But my Kawasaki Ninja certainly is."

Damn! Robin on the fastest production street bike made. Somehow it both made and broke the image.

Hot lady on a hot bike, sure.

But it was also a woman on the far side of some dangerous edge, way on the far side. A racing bike that the manufacturer had to electronically limit to under two hundred miles per hour just to make it street legal.

He made sure that she was still flying a safe distance behind him.

A Ninja wasn't a motorcycle; it was a death wish.

At least a Ninja is what Robin always wished she had, rather than a twenty-year-old Toyota Camry hanging on by a thread—that particular life choice she could only attribute to her mother's conservative spending advice.

Mom was eminently practical, but at times she was a bit of a killjoy—even Grandma said so—but she was also right.

Robin had left the Guard with a nicely padded bank account. And due to following her mother's advice all these years, her account still was. It had actually grown with all of the waitressing money, despite the car purchase and having a little fun.

Maybe after this summer of flying she could justify a bike. Though no way would it be a Gold Wing. That was an old fogey's machine. Mickey made less and less sense to her with time.

She shook her head to clear it; she was flying to fire in a twenty-million-dollar machine. This was something she definitely understood and could never get enough of.

To get back in the air, she'd almost have paid MHA. To get out of waitressing, she definitely would. She'd certainly have taken any wage close to what she made at the truck stop.

In among the huge stack of paperwork to sign aboard with MHA—including a few curious documents like a nondisclosure agreement and a form to authorize a high-level governmental security check, both of which she'd signed with a shrug of indifference—Queen Beale had handed her a payment schedule that had shocked Robin right down to her boots. Base pay as a civilian Firehawk pilot was high living by Robin's standards, a number that acknowledged hard-learned skills and then some. But if she spent even a few weeks over the summer collecting the hazard pay for each day spent on a fire, it would be life changing.

There was another payment category labeled "Special

Projects," but that number was ludicrous, double the hazard pay number, so she'd ignored it. Obviously it was meant for someone else. There were also nice bumps with each additional year of service, though that wouldn't apply, as she was under a one-season contract.

Standard hazard pay was plenty sweet.

Of course *wishing* for fire was…bad. But at that pay rate, even a reasonable amount of fire and she could afford any bike she wanted.

Meanwhile, she'd let Mickey and his Gold Wing touring bike suffer under the image of her ripping past him on the fastest street bike made. What sort of a guy under sixty drove a Gold Wing anyway?

The smoke was thickening ahead of them.

Somehow Robin had ended up at the rear of the flight, and she wasn't quite sure how that had happened. Well, QB Beale had told her to watch and learn. So, like a good soldier, she stayed where she was and watched.

Carly looked at her oddly from the copilot's seat, which Robin chose to ignore.

"Incident Command—Air, this is MHA Firehawk One," Carly called over the radio. "Flight of four, inbound from Dawson."

Oh, that's what Carly had been waiting for. They were the flight leader, no matter their position in the air.

"Wondering when y'all was gonna show up out he-ah." Emily had said Mark was from Montana, so why was he talking like Texas?

"That thar"—Robin put on the thick drawl she'd picked up from a thousand Lone Star State truckers passing down the I-10—"is about the worst damn fake Texas it has ever been my burden to have-ta listen to."

Steve snorted with laughter over the intercom.

"What have you got for me, Carly?" Mark actually sounded sullen as he spoke normally over the radio from his spotting plane circling high overhead. He'd be up around six thousand feet, and the helos would only rarely be above five hundred and never above a thousand. All other air traffic was forbidden from the zone except Steve's drone.

"Sorry for hurting your feelings, boss." Robin really was. It was only her first day. "But that accent sucks, mister."

"Thanks, got that message. Carly?" And now his tone had the snap of command that made Robin wish she'd kept her mouth shut.

Over the next minute, Carly spun out an amazing analysis of the fire and its predicted behavior. In sixty seconds, she'd spilled out more words than Robin had heard in the long flight to get here.

Robin had nothing to relate it to in her past experience. As part of her firefighting certification in the Guard, she'd studied fuel mixtures, importance of relative humidity, the effects of world winds versus fire-generated winds caused by the intense heat over a fire, and a hundred other factors. But this was a whole other level of information.

Beale had said that Steve and Carly would be huge sources of information and she hadn't been kidding. Now she just needed to understand it all.

"Roger that," Mark said at the end of Carly's info dump.

Robin was still catching up with just how bad the situation was.

"Okay, gang," he continued. "Canadian and Alaskan forces are fully involved elsewhere, so we're it. Let's

stay focused and make sure that we don't have to esca-
late them to this one. I want to keep this an MHA fire.
To start, we need to clean up the line and the spot fires,
as well as the attack line that Carly suggested."

There was a sudden silence on the air.

"That's your cue, Texas," Mark said over the air like
he was glad to get some of his own back.

"Arizona," Robin shot back but didn't know what it
was her cue for. She'd barely followed the huge dump of
information in Carly's report. And now she was looking
out at the fire front and trying to even process what was
going on in front of her.

The line of smoke and orange on Steve's screens, fed
from a drone flying ten thousand feet above them, was
now a massive reality less than a mile away.

The real-life wall of flame towered far higher than
the fuel it was burning. Individual flames shot three or
more times the trees' heights. There was no way to tell
how much higher because the orange disappeared into the
dirty black of thick smoke, which climbed to gray and was
almost white at the tops, once it had shed all of the heavier,
cooler ash—which fell as sparking embers, igniting the
unburned forest in front of the conflagration. The sun
made the very tops of the smoke cloud blinding to look at.

"Where are the smokies?" She couldn't spot them.
They were making a firebreak somewhere, weren't they?

She must have spoken aloud for Carly tapped a few
keys and then pointed to the center screen on the console
that swept side to side across the front of the Firehawk's
cockpit. It was the graphic from Steve's drone overlaid
on a terrain map. The two red lines of smokies were
almost directly below them.

Robin looked over the console, but they were now too close to the flames, so she looked below the console, out the glass-laminate view windows down by her feet, in the very nose of the helo. She could just make out the line, a narrow break of only a hundred feet, that was supposed to stop the approaching inferno.

No! It was supposed to narrow it. Cut off the sides.

Pieces of what Carly and Mark had said began fitting in. Encroaching edges, shifting winds, spot fires in the Black reigniting new areas. Edges of the fire still growing sideways, expanding the width of the leading edge. And that expansion was going to put the smokejumpers at risk.

"Robin? You still with us?" She could hear that Mark was on the verge of pulling her off her first command.

She still didn't know what to say. Below her there were twenty people spread out across miles of Yukon wilderness armed only with chain saws, axes, and small water pumps. Aloft were four helicopters that could disappear in a single errant lick of the oncoming conflagration.

"Hey, Ninja Girl."

Mickey, thank God. Emily had said to ask him, but she was going to have to keep her cool, or Mark would shove her aside in a second.

"Talk to me, Gold Wing. How would Emily attack this?" She'd almost said "the Queen Bitch," but Robin would wager they wouldn't take it as the compliment it was rapidly becoming in Robin's mind. Though not too complimentary—the amount Emily hadn't prepared her for was staggering. Robin didn't even know how specific her directions had to be worded for this crew: every little step, general tasks, or broad sweeps and let them do it? She decided it was the latter now that she'd thought it through.

"Let me tackle the Black," Mickey replied. "I'll go in and beat down the spot fires; keep the three heavy-hitting Firehawks on the main fire. Send Jeannie down the south edge of the Black, and you take the north. Let Vern start soaking the line in front of the smokies."

Robin almost agreed out of sheer relief at having a plan. She hesitated just a moment to picture it in her brain as if it was Emily's strategy.

Mickey making sure old fire didn't re-erupt. Check.

She and Jeannie stopping the fire from expanding sideways. Uh-huh.

Vern facing the beast head-on. There was a pinch there.

But if Robin sent the two more experienced pilots down the fire's flanks, they'd get the job done just that much sooner. Then they'd all be up at the fire's head together.

"Do it, Mickey. But Vern and Jeannie, you take the sides, call Mickey if you need extra help. I'll start the main line. Get your jobs done and join me at the head of the fire." *And be damn quick about it*.

That was how Emily would do it. And she'd face the head of the fire personally.

Without a word, the helos split to their differing tasks.

Steve began calling down the locations of the closest rewatering spots to the individual pilots. Ponds, a few small lakes, and the closest to her was a wide bend in a big creek that wandered out of the burning hills and headed for the Yukon River.

Carly marked it on the display on the central console for her. Or maybe Steve did. More information flow, but somehow it was starting to make sense.

"Which side of the smokies am I dumping on, Carly?" Upwind, she'd be soaking the wood before the fire reached the smokejumper's firebreak, hopefully easing the heat. Downwind of the firebreak, it would help kill off any embers that tried to jump their line.

There was a long pause as Carly flipped through several screens on her laptop.

"Downwind." She didn't sound totally convinced. Then she kicked on the radio. "Mark, find out if Akbar is planning a backburn."

Moments later Mark called back with an affirmative on the north, but the south wasn't ready yet.

"That's it." Carly sounded more certain this time. "Downwind of the smokies' firebreak on the north leg. Hit the outer end first to make sure they can maintain a clear escape route."

Robin rolled right and slid her Firehawk down to tree level. No, she was a hundred feet too high, no bucket on a long line dangling far below her, ever so eager to snag a tree.

She slipped lower until she was flitting only a dozen yards above the tallest trees. No fire here yet. She could get right down on them with her load of water.

There was an instinct that said to turn on the landing lights, even though she knew the sun was still well above the horizon. The shroud of smoke billowing above her made the world darker than any thunderstorm that had swept over the Tucson desert to shed a hail of fire-starting lightning.

Safety first. "Lights on, everyone," she called out before starting her final run.

By her own drifting flight path, Robin was able to

judge the wind speed and shifted her path to compensate. She sighted and chose a tree to initiate her drop. A quick check to make sure that her airspace was clear and also that she wasn't going to drop right on any smokies.

Traveling at a hundred miles per hour. So, one second before she reached the tree she'd chosen, she hit the release switch and a thousand gallons of water sprayed down on the dry trees. Three seconds and five hundred feet later, her aircraft was a thousand gallons and four tons lighter.

She wanted to turn back and admire her handiwork. But the fire wouldn't wait. Still, she felt terribly pleased as she turned toward her designated snorkeling point along the nameless creek. She could do this job. She could.

The smokejumpers might or might not be cheering as she made her first drop on the trees, but she liked to think that they were.

Chapter 4

THREE HOURS LATER, MICKEY'S FUEL LEVELS WERE down as far as his blood sugar level.

Right on cue, Robin called for return to base and refuel. Bless her.

He killed one last hot spot with his current load, a circle of fire fifty feet across and equally high right in the heart of the Black. Four hundred and fifty gallons released in a slow circle of spray was enough to convince it to retire from the fight.

He climbed and then looked down at what he'd achieved. When he'd arrived, the wide expanse of burned-over hills had looked like those Earth-at-night photos showing all of the glowing cities, flaring and spitting fire in a hundred locations.

Now it was just the char of burned-over forest. The little patches of green left behind by the fire would do their best to regerminate the Black. At the temperatures Steve had been reporting to him, this was a hot fire but not a soil killer. Some of the standing timber could recover. Fireweed and alder saplings would begin filling in soon.

Here, behind the fire, the sun now shone bright and clear, with only the occasional wisps of smoke to momentarily cast a dim shadow.

He swung wide around the head of the fire and saw that Jeannie and Vern had indeed stomped hard on the edges of the Black that had been trying to creep north and south.

Then he circled back around the front, keeping low beneath the smoke.

Working in the Black through the early evening, it was easy to forget that the main fire was undiminished.

Hundred-foot flames were hammering toward the smokejumpers' firebreaks. Escape routes had been cut to the sides, but the battle was definitely about to be engaged.

Now it was back to the airport for fuel, food, and back to the fire as fast as possible.

Mickey laid down the hammer on the 212 and, tight on the tail of the three Firehawks, raced for the Dawson City Airport.

When they hit the airport, he saw that things had definitely changed.

Their tents were up in a neat little line between the cook tent and Denise's service container. Betsy had done her usual magic of turning a pile of gear and coolers into a kitchen tent that always managed the best food even under the worst conditions.

Stacks of more supplies had been flown in and delivered. They had left their cook and mechanic alone at a deserted field and they'd taken care of business. Normally a couple of locals would have shown up to get camp fully squared away. Didn't look like it this time. And looking across the field, Mickey could see why.

On the *other* side of the runway, mayhem reigned.

A big crowd had gathered there. Most of them were on motorcycles. Over a hundred, with more pouring in through the gates.

And all on the other side of the field.

Tents had been set up, smoke rose from grills. Souvenir stands probably packed with local crafts lined the runway. Every motorcycle rolled up to check-in stands…

It made no sense.

What also made no sense was that everyone except Denise and Betsy ignored the helicopters as they settled down to park in the grass alongside the gravel strip.

The team gathered back at Firehawk One. Denise had rolled over one of her service carts as a table and Betsy delivered a tray of burgers, hot dogs, and big bags of chips as they walked up to it.

"What the hell?" He waved a hand toward the far side of the field.

"It's one of the biggest annual fundraisers for the town: Dust to Dawson Motorcycle Ride." Betsy took a burger for herself and bit down. "The locals put everything they have into it to support the town."

Her last words were partly muffled by food and partly by a half-dozen motorcycles using the runway as a drag strip racetrack, despite the unevenness of the gravel surface.

Then they scattered as Mark Henderson slipped down in his King Air. He didn't make a pass first to clear the way. He just came in at a hundred knots with his big, spinning propellers clearly saying, "You're moving, not me."

Several of the motorcycles tried to match his speed. Then he slowed enough to turn onto the taxiway and return to MHA's midfield camp. That sent the riders skittering off into the grass to get out of his way. As soon as they recovered, they returned to racing on the runway.

Henderson climbed down and walked over to join

them. Clearly pissed, he grabbed a burger. He turned to Robin and pointed a finger so close to her nose that Mickey wondered if she was going to bite it.

"You ever do anything that dumb with your Ninja and I'll boot your ass no matter what Emily says about your potential."

QB Emily said she had potential? Right, another piece of her last-minute, confusing deluge of instructions. Still, Robin found the phrase surprising.

"No need to worry, Mark. I won't."

"Glad to hear you aren't that stupid. Damn it!" He lifted the edge of the bun. "Is there any ketchup?"

Betsy handed him a bottle that had been sitting in plain view, which he used to drown the poor burger before taking his next bite.

"No, I'm plenty stupid." Robin glanced over to wait for Mickey's reaction to her next line. She waited until he'd stuffed a handful of potato chips into his mouth and had crunched down. "I just don't own a motorcycle. Mom made me buy a used Toyota Camry instead."

Mickey eyes bugged, and then he tried to inhale and breathed in a mouthful of potato chip crumbs. In moments, he was hacking and coughing out potato chip bits until his eyes watered.

Robin reached over and pounded him on the back. Hard. Hard enough that she was surprised when he didn't drop to the ground. That would teach him to kiss her without asking.

The fact that she'd decided during the firefight that she'd enjoyed it and was looking forward to doing it again didn't mean he didn't deserve the pounding. Next time it would be on her terms though, not his.

"Camry?" Mark sounded almost as disgusted by that as by the motorcycle.

"We have got to upgrade your ride, girl," Vern insisted over a hot dog buried under enough relish to make it rate as a salad rather than a meat product.

"He'll try to talk you into a Corvette," Denise said as she zipped by to check something on the next helicopter.

"That's only because it's a real car," he called after her. "Which," he admitted in a much softer tone, "she drives way better than I do even if she is more of a classic sports car kind of gal. Drives a 1973 Fiat 124 Spider that she restored herself, of course. Has her eye on a 1960-something AC Ace."

"The six cylinder, not the eight," Denise said, going by in the other direction with an ash-clogged intake filter in her hand. "Preferably the two-point-six liter, but there were only thirty-seven of those ever built, so it's probably out of my price range." And she was gone again.

"If I could find one, I'd buy it for her," Vern whispered. "But it's probably out of my price range too."

Robin's first assessment had been right; Vern was a sweet man. Her second assessment was that Denise was a lucky girl.

"F-250 Ranch," Mark said like he was laying down the law.

"Firebird Trans Am," Steve said when she glanced his way.

"Idiot drives a stick shift despite his leg." Carly was clearly resigned to it though. "I drive my dad's Jeep."

"Which is about to rust out from old age."

"And I'll drive it until it's scrap metal bits held together by duct tape." Her defiance said just how deep that choice went.

Robin let the talk swirl around her. She wasn't even sure if they remembered that this had all been started by her old Toyota, which was still parked out back of her mom's truck stop. She'd flown to Oregon and been picked up at the airport by Beale behind the wheel of Mark's big Ford pickup truck.

Interview had slammed straight into hired, and now she stood in the Yukon wilderness on her first day on the job. She did need to call Mom and let her know she was okay. Mom wouldn't be worried. It's not like she'd been redeployed to Afghanistan, but so much had happened since they'd spoken just last night.

The roar of the racing motorcycles forced their talk into cut-up sections, but she was used to that. They did the same thing on a flight line in the Guard or the truck line when fully loaded big rigs were trying to get moving again after they'd consumed a couple hundred gallons of fuel and their drivers had loaded themselves with a three-egg western omelet and one of Phoebe's renowned deep-dish apple pies with homemade vanilla ice cream.

Everyone else was doing the same: half a sentence, pause for deafening roar, curse if it was a particularly bad one, then continue the same sentence in the same place.

One cyclist, clearly a particularly dumb one—which was rare based on the groups that hit the truck stop— rolled right up to them.

"Hey, do you guys do scenic flights?"

"Sure," Mickey told him.

"Five hundred." Vern picked up the line.

Robin was about to protest, but Jeannie strolled up to him until she was only inches away. Her jacket open to her waist. Her T-shirt clinging tightly to curves more generous than Robin's own.

"We'll take you up," she said with every hint of the working girls who also often hung out at the truck stop. "And we'll dump your ass in the middle of a wildfire from a thousand feet. Dropping you from two thousand so you have time to admire the flames you're about to die in costs an extra hundred."

He got out fast.

Jeannie's laughter followed him across the field, then she turned back and mentioned how she was wanting a Mini Cooper someday and, no, Cal didn't get to have an opinion as he didn't actually own a car.

"I do. I left it at Redding jumper base before a photo shoot a couple years back. Or maybe it was Redmond."

"Maybe it was Rio Bravo," Vern suggested.

"Or Roosevelt out in Colorado," Denise quipped as she joined the group and grabbed a hot dog—which meant all of the helos were ready or she wouldn't have stopped.

Denise glanced her way and nodded a confirmation to that.

There was a comfortableness to all this that Robin was starting to get a feel for. She took another bite of her burger and appreciated being out of the helicopter. The sun wasn't that much closer to the horizon, but it was hazed reddish by the fire to the west.

She checked her watch.

Eight p.m. Four hours to sunset. Only four more after that to sunrise.

It had been an amazingly long day. Five a.m. had

rung in the day fifteen hundred miles to the south of
here with a blaring alarm. Despite the cabin air filters,
everyone's eyes were red with smoke and exhaustion.

"Who here is nighttime-drop certified?"

Her question silenced the chatter.

Jeannie raised a hand.

One.

Emily must have been the second one. The National
Guard didn't fly nighttime fires, at least hers never had.

You couldn't send one pilot in alone—helicopters
flew in pairs for safety. Not everyone did that, but the
military did, and Emily had told her that MHA did the
same. If the answer had been otherwise, it would have
made her hesitate before signing. Robin liked flying,
had always enjoyed the rare wildfire call. But if her
helo went down at a fire line, she wanted someone really
close by to fish her ass out if she survived the landing.

Mark was eyeing her closely, but it was Mickey
she was watching. Mark would be testing her. Mickey
would let her know if she got off track far sooner.

"We need fresh crews at sunrise. And we each need
eight hours of downtime for safety. Jeannie and Vern,
you're down for the next eight unless there's an emergency." The two of them practically sagged with relief.

"Jeannie, when you're back aloft tomorrow, I want you
to start working with Vern to get him night-drop certified.
Emily can sign off on him next time we're in Oregon."

"I can do that too." Mark's deep voice was absolutely
neutral. Carefully neutral, as if it hurt him to speak.

"You fly rotorcraft?"

His nod was steady. The others were now equally
careful not to look at her.

"How can *you* certify him?" Robin couldn't read what was going on around her.

"I can." Mark's flat statement sliced through the air like a Firehawk drop.

Robin wondered if she should push because it was up to her to understand or to back the hell off and trust the boss. Robin made a habit of trusting herself first, her copilot second, and no one the fuck else.

There were a hundred little signals swirling around her in calculated looks and shifts of body language. Whatever lay behind this was not going to be pretty or fast. And that was the deciding factor; she didn't have time for whatever shit was going down among these people.

"Fine! Mark, you're down for the night as well. Tomorrow you oversee Vern's cross-training. With such a small team and Steve's drone, I want you in the seat beside Vern until he's got it."

She didn't wait for his response but turned to Steve.

"Steve, you make sure that Mark has whatever feeds he needs from you or Carly in Vern's helicopter to also do his ICA tasks."

Another nod.

"That leaves you and me, Gold Wing Boy. You ready to go another round with the fire? Back here by midnight, then we're down for eight hours. That leaves the smokies on their own for just the four hours of nighttime."

"Bring it on, Camry Girl."

"That's Ninja Girl to you, Hamilton."

"Yes, sir." He saluted, looked abashedly at Mark for a moment, then grabbed another burger and headed for his helo.

She faced Mark Henderson. His mirrored aviator

shades revealed nothing of his thoughts, but it felt as if he carried his own personal shadow hanging over him.

"You got some explaining to do, mister," she announced right in front of the others. "But I don't have time to be your therapist right now." She turned for her helo.

She finished the quick circle of a fast Preflight Check and found Mark standing close by her pilot's side door as if teleported into place; he moved very quietly for such a big man. The others had already headed for their tents.

He didn't say anything, didn't move to open the pilot-side door that he casually lay back against with his arms crossed over that big damn chest of his.

"What?"

Still no response.

"I don't have time for this, Mark. Take it up with Emily."

That elicited the smallest quirk to his lips.

It was clear he wasn't moving until he was damn well ready. And unlike Mickey, who was only one inch taller than she was, Mark was closer to six—not much chance of her getting him to move by force either.

"Someday you'll have to rethink threatening me with my wife."

"Why? Seems like as a good a strategy as anything else I've got. Is it working?"

"Not in the way you think."

"Figures." Robin sighed. He also didn't go on to explain what it was doing.

"However, I think she might have been right about you and I need to revise my initial assessment."

"Which was?"

"That you're a pain in the ass."

Robin managed not to laugh. If the man didn't see

that she and Emily had that in common, it was his problem. It also made her feel closer to Emily, even though she was far away.

Again Mr. Silent.

"So you're saying I'm no longer a pain in the ass? I'll have to work on that." She could hear Mickey down the line start winding up his engines, but she couldn't get to her controls. Mark's substantial frame continued to bar her from the cockpit.

"No. I'm saying that she may have been right despite that." Then his tone shifted, deeper, more serious. "You did well back there, both what you just did and out on the line. This evening keep Mickey near you at the front of the fire. Pay attention to his drops. Your altitude is climbing as you unload and your rollouts at the end of the run are inconsistent. Up, then turn. This fire isn't hot enough to create the big downdrafts off the leading edge, but you don't want to be heeled over forty-five degrees when one hits."

Then he pulled open the door for her.

She climbed in.

And when she turned to ask what the hell was up with him anyway, he closed the door in her face and walked away.

Chapter 5

"WHAT IS THAT MAN'S PROBLEM?" ROBIN'S VOICE practically cracked Mickey's eardrums over the headset the minute they were aloft. Robin ticked off had been pretty formidable. Robin seriously pissed sounded fierce. He was glad he was flying safely a hundred yards ahead to her starboard side.

"He likes running roughshod over recruits. See how they take it. You do know that he could be listening?" It was the open command frequency and Mark had a portable radio that was never far away from him on the ground.

"Like I care. He can go f—" She cut herself off.

It was good that she bit that off. The FCC was terribly fussy about profanity on open frequencies, even if they weren't likely to have inspectors in northern Canada.

"Seriously though, what's his issue?"

Mickey decided that it was…interesting that she was asking him on an open frequency when Carly was seated right behind her in the Firehawk. They'd left Steve on the ground to get Mark set up for tomorrow morning in Firehawk Three. As a fire behavior analyst, Carly was also now their incident commander for the night. She could be preoccupied with communicating with Akbar about ground conditions, or more likely pretending to be: "I'm busy being FBAN and ICA. Please bother someone else, lady."

"Well…" Mickey dove down on the forest strip that Carly had identified for them to start on while she worked the drone to determine what had changed while they'd been on the ground. "I think it's his old Night Stalkers training. It comes out every now and then."

There was no response from Robin. Mickey flew in silence for the five miles and two minutes to their watering station. He and Robin hovered low over the small lake and scared the shit out of any fish stupid enough to live there in the Yukon wilderness, where they probably got frozen solid every winter.

They were most of the way back before she whispered to him, a funny thing to do over a radio. "Night Stalkers?"

"Uh-huh."

"Like the U.S. Army's 160th Special Operations Aviation Regiment Night Stalkers?"

"I'm not that big on details of the military, but that sounds right. Mark doesn't talk about it much." Mickey lined up for the next run on the fire.

Akbar had started a backburn, a fire set up against the burn's side of a cleared firebreak in the forest. The smokies had made a track a hundred feet wide by cutting down everything and hauling it to the side away from the fire—trees, saplings, brush, all of it. They'd even scraped and hauled away most of the soil's organics, removing anything from the firebreak that could ignite. Backbreaking hand work, which made Mickey deeply appreciate his flying job every time he saw them doing it.

Then, by setting the forest alight on the burn's side of the firebreak, it would chew up fuel as it moved back toward the fire, making the break even wider and more secure.

Of course, fire didn't always behave the way it was

supposed to, so they were chasing the backburn with lots of water this time. Every time it managed to burn another hundred feet back toward the main blaze, the helicopters would dump water to snuff the part of the backburn closest to the firebreak.

They made four more runs before Robin spoke again.

"I never met one before."

"Really? Why not? Don't all you helicopter folk hang out together?"

"Sikorsky has built about four thousand Black Hawks over the years. That's eight thousand pilots, not counting backup and changeover crews. So at least double that. And that's only one helicopter type. Then there's Little Birds, Chinooks, Apaches, Cobras, and that doesn't even get into things like the Marines' Sea Stallions and Ospreys or the military versions of your Twin 212. And we're spread all over the face of this little thing called *The Earth*! So, no, we aren't all buddy-buddy."

Carly cut in. "I'm seeing a heat signature in the burn-over area of the backfire." She read out a set of coordinates.

"I'm on it." Mickey peeled off. It was one of those instances when he'd come to really appreciate the drone. It saw heat, even if there wasn't any flame erupting yet. He aimed for the coordinates and punched it with a load of water.

"Bull's-eye," Carly announced.

Mickey used it as an excuse to fall behind, let Firehawk One and Robin take the lead. He liked flying behind her. She had a sure hand. She had technique to learn, but she flew well. Neither a textbook-perfect line like Emily nor a slight dance like Jeannie. She moved across the sky with powerful strokes, like when his big sister had discovered how to hold a crayon in her fist and make those clear, strong lines that he'd never really matched.

"And actually, you haven't met just one Night Stalker."

"I haven't?" Robin sounded totally confused as they both settled over the lake to reload their tanks.

"No." Mickey could practically hear Robin's brain shorting out and wished they were close enough for him to see it happen. "You've met two Night Stalkers. Both he and Emily were in before they came over to MHA. He always says that Emily was the best pilot they ever had. Both were majors I think. That's a pretty high-up rank, isn't it?"

Robin was silent for so long that Mickey keyed the mic to see if she was still there.

—⁓—

Robin was still there, but her brain wasn't.

She flew down, dumped water where Carly told her, and turned back for the lake.

Majors. She'd heard rumors of women flying for the Night Stalkers, the most elite helicopter unit on the planet, but she'd figured those for rumors gone bad— which the military abounded with. Apparently not. Emily had been a major of the 160th SOAR. No wonder she was so damned good!

And Henderson? Had she just scoffed in a Night Stalkers' face about whether or not he could fly rotor-craft? She was pretty sure that she had; she wanted to curl up in her seat and die. If this was all true, then there wasn't much that Henderson *couldn't* do with a Firehawk. And Emily was their best? She had even less idea what to think about that.

Her name was Robin and her merry band of wildfire pilots included SOAR professionals.

For the next two hours, Robin did little more than fly.

Big flare-up past the southwest edge of the firebreak, she dumped a couple thousand gallons on it.

Fire broke through the line and made a stab for the smokejumpers, she and Mickey pounded it back.

They fought and harassed the fire back and forth across the smoky landscape until, shortly before sunset, they had the fire well trapped. A five-mile-wide front had just been chopped down to three. Those three miles were racing ahead, still holding Dawson City tight in its sights, but it was progress.

After a lot of consulting between Carly and Akbar, they decided to move most of the smokejumpers and the bulk of their gear well ahead of the fire before quitting for the night.

They switched over to helitack—rather than dropping water, they were shifting and moving manpower. They took turns setting down into a cleared helispot where anything over three feet tall had been leveled into a confused heap of slash to make room for helicopter operations.

The moment the cargo bay doors rolled opened, there was a flush of smoky char stench that flooded into the helo. She twisted around in her seat to watch as a half-dozen soot-blackened men piled aboard. The smallest guy of them all came up beside her pilot's door, and she swung it open to talk to him while the others loaded their gear into a sling.

His face was dark beneath the soot, but his grin was bright. "Just wanted to say thanks. You guys are kicking

ass. We'll get this beat in another three or four days at
this rate. I'll start cycling out my crew tomorrow night.
Eight hours R&R at base camp. Warn Betsy so she can
be ready for us."

Robin could only nod. Until then, if they slept at all,
it would have been by "coyoting"—collapsing in place
and sleeping in their full gear for an hour or two rolled
up in a tarp. They were paid a small hardship bonus for
doing that, but it still didn't sound like fun.

She flew them to the spot chosen for the next stage of
the battle. Everything was still quiet and green here, still
fresh—unaware of the burning hell coming in its direction. Unaware of the chain saw–wielding firefighters she
was delivering into the forest's midst.

There weren't any openings among the thick trees, so
she hovered low until the sling load of gear rested on the
forest floor and released the cargo hook. Once the line
had slithered out of sight, Akbar and his crew rappelled
down ropes hung in the after cabin.

Mickey dropped his load, and then they both turned
back for camp.

Robin was flying in a very elite group. Their equipment said well funded, but their people said far more.
For the first time, Robin was surprised that she was
actually here.

She had to consider how she'd speak to Mark and
Emily next time they met. Respect and "yes, sirs" weren't
exactly her style.

A total fangirl moment—unable to speak in the presence of living, breathing Night Stalkers—was a real possibility. These were the guys that every helicopter pilot
wished they could be but none of them were.

They might have been thrown out on their golden oak-leaf insignia, but she doubted it. These two breathed the service. Then why were they no longer in it?

Emily's first child.

They'd traded in the Night Stalkers to have a kid. But they were young enough to have waited…unless they got surprised. Another piece of their story filled in. And only Emily had to be grounded, yet another unfairness in the whole gender structure.

But Mark had left as well. She didn't know any man who would leave the service just to protect his family and to make sure that he would be there for them long term. Yet Mark Henderson had.

Where the hell did they breed men with that level of honor and integrity? And where did she have to go to order one of her own?

She laughed—as if she'd ever want such a thing. She was a Harrow woman and they'd long since proven that they didn't need anyone.

As they flew over Dawson City, Robin decided that the right way to treat Mark was exactly as she had been so far. He expected a pain in the ass, she'd be glad to give him that. She half suspected that he'd be disappointed if she delivered anything else.

How she'd treat Emily the next time she saw her, Robin couldn't guess.

A female Night Stalker?

Shit, man!

Mickey finished his shutdown by himself. The camp was quiet, despite the recent roar of their descending helicopters. Whatever motorcycle-madness event had been going on across the field was over and done. Or at least shuffled back into town.

Denise was probably struggling to wake up and check their machines right away. But she didn't appear from the line of tents—a neat line of nylon pop-ups with the individual colors lost in the slow Arctic twilight. If Vern was smart, he was keeping an arm tight around his wife's waist, keeping her close beside him. Vern had always struck Mickey as a smart man.

Mickey leaned back against his helicopter and let the exhaustion wash over him. Now that they were done with the day, he could let it in, and it was a tidal wave. If he were a different man, he would seriously consider weeping. Or at least whimpering.

He didn't know what he was waiting for until he saw the silhouette of a woman walking toward him through the twilight. Despite the impossibly long first day, she still moved the same as he'd initially seen her.

Dancer.

No, soldier.

But her motion was like a dancer too, sliding easily through the grass. Not one of his sister's delicate ballerina types, with their waiflike bodies and impossible flexibility, but like those modern-dance types. All strength and fluid moves.

He was still puzzling at dancer or soldier when she stopped in front of him. There was just enough light to see her clearly this close up.

"You look like I feel." Her voice rough with exhaustion.

"I look like a beautiful woman? Aw, shucks, Robin. Though, actually, I haven't had a chance to figure out if you feel as fine as you look." Yet. But he didn't want to wait too much longer before finding that out.

She jabbed her finger into his ribs, but there wasn't any heat behind it. Then she collapsed back against his Twin 212, so that they were leaning side by side and staring up at the sky.

The sky was a glorious blood red. The plume of smoke high above them glowed as if the sky itself was on fire.

"Not a lot of stars tonight," he managed.

"I always wanted to see the Northern Lights," she replied a comfortable time later.

"Need to wait for winter. I don't think it gets dark enough in midsummer here." Mickey was pretty sure that was right.

He'd flown fires up here before with MHA, but he was too tired to trust his memories. And maybe the last time he'd seen the aurora had been in…August maybe, so there'd be more dark. Though wasn't the Alaska fire season over by then? But he couldn't be sure.

"It might be—"

His thought was cut off by the woman, who rolled off her shoulder and lay against him, pinning him between her body and the helicopter. He was suddenly paying very little attention to the sky.

If she was going to offer, he wasn't going to be dumb enough to hesitate.

He slipped his hands around her and pulled her tight against him. Yep! Definitely felt like he was holding on to a beautiful woman.

She offered a kiss and he leaned into it. She tasted of fire smoke and very faintly of grilled hamburger.

But mostly she tasted of the impossible high-mountain freshness that so reminded him of home.

Because Dad was ski patrol, Mickey had often done last runs of the day with him. The whole ski patrol would take the lifts to the top, last up the mountain. Then they'd disperse to ski down every trail to make sure the mountain was clear. Sometimes, there was some hopelessly over-challenged beginner who had wandered onto a black diamond trail, but usually the slopes were empty and silent except for the slick sounds of their skis. The air blown in on the twilight breeze so clear and fresh that it was always a surprise.

Robin was like that.

It wasn't just the wondrous slopes of her back and shoulders that he discovered as he trailed his hands over her. It wasn't the unexpected softness of her hair or the roughness of her kiss. It was the freshness of her.

He wanted to roll her so that her back was to the helo and he could press himself more deeply against her, but her feet were planted wide and it didn't seem worth the extra effort.

His hand was half down her pants, on the inside, before he caught what it was up to and reeled it back in.

Instead, he concentrated on appreciating her waist until she finally chose to break the kiss.

She lowered her head and he kissed her forehead.

"Damn it, Hamilton!"

"You seem to be cursing me a lot today, Robin of the Hood."

"You seem to bring out the worst in me."

"If that kiss was the worst, I can't wait to try the best."

That earned him a soft laugh. On most women that

would have been a giggle. On Robin it was a friendly laugh, the kind that invited you to join in, so he did.

She placed her palms on his shoulders and pushed back until she was standing upright once more.

He let his hands slip from her waist and then didn't know what to do with them. They'd felt so good placed on that nice dip between ribs and hip.

She blinked like an owl in the twilight and looked around. "I'm, uh, not sure which tent is mine."

Mickey was, opened his mouth, and then thought better of it. If she could fib about motorcycles, he could fib about tents.

"Got me."

"Which one is yours?"

He pointed. Afraid that if he said, "the one on the end," she'd be smart enough to figure out that they were pegged in the same order that the aircraft were parked. Betsy was good about doing that, knowing how exhausted a helo pilot could be after a day on the fire. *Keepin' it simple for you brain-dead dolts*, she'd say time and again.

"I don't really want to walk in on Mark."

"Or Carly and Steve."

"Or Carly and Steve," she acknowledged.

He was about to run the list—"Or..."—when she continued.

"But definitely not Mark. I'm still a little freaked by the whole Night Stalker thing."

"Well, I know where *my* tent is." He tried to make it sound like her problem and not like the invitation he wanted it to be.

She looked back and forth along the tents once more.

He considered relenting, but he was rather enjoying teasing her.

"Okay."

Now it was his turn to blink at the woman slowly disappearing in the fading light. "Okay what?"

"Hamilton." She sighed in exasperation. "You can't be *that* tired."

"Oh." Well, maybe he could. But he'd get over that right now. He placed a hand in the small of her back, again resisting the urge to slip it down lower, and guided her toward the closest tent.

He let her crawl in first. By the time he had zipped up the mosquito screen and pulled off his boots, she was sprawled out across his sleeping bag. Dead out.

He undid her boots and then tried to decide just how much of a gentleman was he. Normally he was pretty good about things like that.

Whether it was exhaustion, the brief teaser of her incredible shapes and tastes, or that she'd lain right down the center of the double-wide air mattress, he didn't know, but he decided that this once, he also didn't care about being *too* decent.

He wrapped himself up close behind her, spooning her against his chest.

She hummed a little in her sleep as he wrapped an arm around her waist. She slid her hand over his and then pulled it up toward her chin, as if he was a sheet and she was tucking herself in.

But she didn't quite complete the gesture before falling back asleep with her hand lightly pinning his in place.

Mickey lay there with her back against his chest, his

nose tucked into the soft wood-smoke-and-mountain-air wonder of her hair, and his hand full of a truly exceptional breast with nothing but a thin cotton T-shirt separating them.

Well, if Vern was smart because he'd kept Denise tucked tightly under his arm, then Mickey was feeling pretty smart too.

Wide-awake and turned on as hell but very, very smart.

⸺◦⸺

Robin woke slightly when the other two helos took off down the line—just far enough to determine that she wasn't supposed to be on this flight. This was the second crew: Mark and Vern, Jeannie and Cal, all headed aloft.

She snuggled back down, warm and cozy in the morning twilight.

Warm, cozy, and pinned against a man's hard body by a hand clutching her breast.

Mickey.

At least that much she was sure of. She'd crawled in with Mickey with the intention of… But that's where it all went astray. Robin remembered entering the tent and seeing that beautiful expanse of somewhere to sleep.

And she'd woken up to find Mickey taking advantage of her.

She was about to shoot an elbow back into his ribs when she realized that she couldn't, as her fingers were interlaced with Mickey's. And he appeared to still be asleep.

Well, even if her conscious mind wasn't welcoming him, her unconscious one certainly had. And she was still clothed. Beneath her own fingertips, where they

curled through Mickey's, she could feel her T-shirt.
Becoming aware of her legs, she felt that they were still
in the heavy cotton underwear and Nomex pants. Even
socks, though no boots.

The man had the thoughtfulness to take off her
boots but had left her in her day-old, sweaty gear rather
than… No, he wasn't taking advantage of her—at least
not too much.

Mickey shifted ever so slightly. His face was in
the back of her hair. As he woke, the first thing he did
wasn't go for his handful of her breast. The first thing he
did was nuzzle more deeply into her hair.

That was her undoing.

It was a kind, thoughtful, gentle motion that was not
something Robin Harrow was used to. Men—when she
chose to take one into her bed—wanted her hard. She
was dangerous enough herself to make sure it never got
too rough, but she wasn't the sort of woman who made
men think gentle thoughts.

Mickey moved the hand on her breast, not to fondle
but to draw her in more tightly against him.

That simple move of effortless strength left her
breathless.

Then he shifted the arm she hadn't been aware she
was lying on. His bicep rippled beneath her ear as he
wrapped his forearm across the front of her shoulders
and pinned her back against him.

*Decision point, girl. You stop him now, or you don't
stop him at all. Otherwise you're just a goddamn tease.*
Something she'd never had patience for.

You either wanted it or you didn't and it wasn't fair
to the guy to pretend otherwise. She'd never even done

it with the truck stop hopefuls. If they chose to think they had a chance, she didn't stop them, but she never led them on.

"Robin?" Mickey's voice was a ripple of chest down her back, a whisper by her ear.

Even wrapped inside his strong arms, he was asking if she was sure.

As long as it was sex, she was. She definitely wanted more of this man. If it was more than sex, well, there was a laugh. If he was thinking about more than sex, he'd be just as wrong as the truck stop long haulers.

In answer, she pressed her hand against the back of his, easing it more strongly against her breast.

He responded with a kiss on the back of her neck and a slow swirl of his palm that had her shifting to press harder against him. When she tried to retrieve her fingers, he kept them trapped between his. That's when she realized quite how unusually strong he was.

She wanted to ask why, but he slipped their joined hands upward until he could rest a single finger against her lips. When she quieted once more, he began an exploration that was pure, exquisite torture.

He traced his fingertips, their fingertips, over her lips. She opened her mouth enough to nip one of his. Then he traced a thin, cool line down, over chin and along her neck. Still, her hand moved with his as he rode over shoulder, breast, and belly.

But it wasn't her own body that she was so aware of beneath their shared touch. It was the feeling of her hand locked in his. Of their fingers on a journey together, laced as one on some voyage of discovery. She could feel every slow flexing of his fingers, both against her skin and against her palm resting on the back of his hand.

His destination was wholly predictable. *Such a guy.* But then he turned aside to trace the line of her hip. With her fingers still trapped—she could have shaken him off if she wanted to, but he made her not want to—she could feel every line of her body that he followed. Hip, around to investigate the firmness of her behind. That behind had earned her a lot of tips, it was a good one, but she'd never felt like a man had ever so appreciated it before.

Down her leg and back up the inside.

If she were a narcissist, she couldn't have done a better job of self-love. It was as if Mickey's simple gestures were teaching her things she didn't know about her own form.

He returned so often to the rise of her hip that she began to think of that particular curve, from narrow waist to rising round, was especially spectacular. He was making her goofy in the head and she didn't have the energy to stop it. Instead, she let herself simply enjoy the movements of his hand as he teased her body to burn.

When at long last he slipped their hands beneath her T-shirt, it was such a shock that a gasp was forced out of her lungs. The impact of the lightest brush of his flesh directly on hers left her shaky, feeling trapped.

"I—" she managed to gasp out. "I don't—"

Mickey froze with his palm flat against her stomach. She could feel the tension in his fingers pressed against her skin.

"I'm not a tease. It's not that I want you to stop."

He eased off a little.

She became aware that both of them were breathing hard. She wasn't the only one feeling affected here.

What?

"I—" was all she managed on her next effort.

No man had ever made her feel so much.

"Can't we just—" *Do it!* she wanted to cry out. She didn't want to have to think; she just wanted to fly. "Just take me up, Mickey. All the way into the sky."

When he hesitated, she pulled on his hand. Pulled it from beneath her shirt, placed it over her pants' crotch, and clamped her legs together, pinning his hand there and slipping hers free.

A faint cry sounded in the tent as she pressed against his hand.

And the sound came from her.

She never cried out during sex.

Bring it on! Get it done! Let the release roll through and have a good time. Thank him for a good time. Standard operating procedure.

But not with Mickey Hamilton.

Hell no.

His merest touch left her breathless.

Even with her awkward demands and still fully clothed, he began to manipulate her body with all the art he flew a helicopter.

Emily had been right; he was a masterful pilot.

What Robin had no way of knowing was that he was also a masterful lover. He followed her instructions implicitly.

He took her up.

That powerful hand made not one ungentle move as he slowly drove her mad.

At first she opened to him, spreading her legs to allow him to do more.

She curled one arm over her head to dig that hand into his hair. The other, Robin reached back and latched on to his pants pocket. He was spooned hard against her butt, and she didn't want him going anywhere. She held on at first to keep him close and to ascertain that he didn't stop what he was doing to her body. Then she held on because there was nothing else she could do as her body finally bucked harder than the worst turbulence she'd ever flown through.

She pitched and yawed against his confining hold on her shoulders and the front of her pants, and felt like she was flying freer than she ever had in her life. She drove back against his hardness, and he pinned her there, writhing himself. Despite the intervening layers of cloth, it felt as if he was driving right into her.

At some point, her mind simply blanked as the waves washed through her—hard, hot pulses that made her want to moan. But she didn't have the breath. To cry out. She'd forgotten how.

When she finally came back to herself, she'd gone fetal. Curled into a tight ball inside the curve of Mickey's body. Her hands and her legs pinning his arms about her so that they'd never let go, never unwind.

She was going to wear this man's hands on her body like a strap-on for the rest of her life. A woman's best sex ever should definitely not occur while fully clothed.

"Where the hell…" No, she didn't want to learn where he learned how to do that.

"Made it up as I went." His voice was still hard and breathy.

"I like your imagination."

He grunted something she didn't quite follow. Then she became aware that though his hand was still pinned between her legs, he was still pressing her back against him. Against...

"Do you have any protection in this tent?"

She could feel his nod against her neck. Awkward moment, *Yes, I carry around protection, just in case*.

"Well, this is one of those just-in-case moments, Hamilton. Don't try to explain it prettily; no need to with me. Get it."

Their slow unwinding from each other was almost painful. Her body didn't want to move, didn't want to let go.

She began peeling down: T-shirt, bra, Nomex pants still smelling of wood smoke, socks, long cotton underwear—the standard beneath Nomex. About as sexy as a doornail.

———————

Mickey couldn't stop staring at her. Robin undressed as if she were a bird preening but with none of the ego. Each bit that was shed simply made the whole more delectable. Those shapes he'd been studying through her clothes were amazing in the tent's shadowy twilight. He wished he had bright lights to see how incredible she was, or a row of candles to show how soft.

"You're staring," she said when she had the long johns off all but one leg.

"Damn straight!" A firestorm wasn't going to make him look away.

"You're also still fully dressed. If I'm the only one

naked in this tent, then there sure as hell isn't going to be any more sex."

"Right." Mickey got to work and was soon out of all his gear.

"Oh, yum." Robin pushed him down on his back before he could maneuver for position. She put her head down on the middle of his chest and rubbed her face there so hard that it tickled.

She pulled the protection from his hand and slid it over him.

"We can be slow next time. Right now, I'm afraid slow might kill you." Then she straddled him and took him in.

He wasn't in any condition to argue with her. So much need had flared through him as he had given her a release that he had little control and no patience for finesse. The moment he entered her, he was arching his hips up to drive deeper, as deep as he could. Lifting her until her hair brushed the low ceiling of the tent.

He grabbed her hips to drag her down against him.

She unleashed her full body weight to press them together at the same moment. Her torso arched over him made him pray for a thousand wishes. He wished for time to admire and taste those enticing breasts. He wished to nuzzle her neck for hours. To discover the texture of her skin and how it varied over every inch of her powerful torso.

But all he could do was hold her tight against him and drive into her. She was like her helicopter, powerful. Like that stupid motorcycle that she didn't own, fast. And most of all, the mountain cool scent of her had shifted; a wildfire's worth of heat now wrapped around him until—with one final upward plunge—he was gone.

"Oh, yes." Robin's sigh of contentment was soft as she slowly melted down to lay full upon him. "I knew this was going to be a good summer."

Mickey hadn't known, but he couldn't agree more.

There was only one problem. And it was not a good one. Only way to address it was straight on…he supposed.

He managed to wrap his arms over her back to delay any attempt at a quick getaway.

"Robin?"

"Hmm?"

"I have a really stupid question."

"Ask away." She nibbled at the skin along his neck.

Mickey looked up at the ceiling of the tent, tinted gold through the flyaway edges of her hair.

"C'mon." She squirmed slightly, settling even more comfortably in his arms.

"Okay. I hate to be cliché, but…"

"What, Hamilton?"

And there it was.

"You're being awfully evasive. Not like you."

She already knew that about him? Fine.

He took another breath. "What the hell is your last name?"

There was a pause, during which he braced his arms to keep her close.

Then she laughed that delightful, soft laugh into the crook between his shoulder and his neck. He could feel it start in her belly and ripple through her.

"You bedded a woman and don't know her—"

"No, I don't. I'm sorry. Okay? I have lousy sources.

I'll kill Gordon later, but he didn't know your last name either."

Again the delighted laugh. She pushed up just enough to look down at him. Though he kept his arms around her to ensure that it wasn't a fake to an abrupt departure.

"Robin Harrow, pleased to meet you." Then she shifted her hips delightfully where he was still deep inside her before collapsing once more to laugh against his neck.

"Very pleased to meet you." He did his best to make it sound proper, but it was a hard thing to do in their current positions.

Robin Harrow.

Robin of the Hood's Arrow.

Pierced him straight through the heart.

He wasn't in love. That didn't happen in twenty-four hours, no matter what anyone said.

But if he had to pick one woman out of the crowd to fall in love with, he knew that he'd never find another like the one presently convulsing with laughter in his arms.

Chapter 6

THE FIRE FOUGHT BACK FOR FIVE MORE DAYS. THEY would block it to the north, and the wind would turn south. They'd airlift a team of shattered smokejumpers back to camp, only to have to roust them four hours later because of fire breaching the hard-won fire line of cut and backburn.

Robin had flown hard fires, but this was getting ridiculous. She started juggling crews not based on how she thought their skills might be best applied, but rather by whose eyes were least bloodshot with fatigue. It was a good thing that there wasn't a mirror anywhere on camp—she wasn't willing to see how she herself was faring.

Sometimes she'd crash in her own tent, which she had eventually found. Not because she didn't want to sleep with Mickey, but because it was fifty steps closer to where she parked Firehawk One.

Last night, she stumbled on him asleep in the grass close by the food tent. Someone, Betsy probably, had spread a blanket over him. Robin ate the rest of the barely started deep-fried chicken breast on his plate, even though it had gone cold, before slipping under the blanket beside him.

She'd woken six hours later with Mickey and the Twin 212 gone, but the blanket neatly tucked around her and a sliced orange sitting on a fresh plate under an inverted bowl to keep it ash and fly free. She spent a luxurious ten minutes lying on her back, sucking on orange slices while watching the morning sky. It was dark gray with the approaching fire, and most of the town's residents were now wearing those little paper masks.

Denise came over and sat beside her. She wore a goofy straw hat and a long scarf over her hair that kept it more blond than ash gray.

"Why do you look so much better than we do?" And Denise did. She looked tired but happy tired. "You're not working any less hard than we are." Actually, she was probably doing more, flying with Vern when she could and maintaining the helicopters the rest of the time.

She shrugged. "I'm not sure. I hit a turning point last winter, a turn that changed my life and brought Vern and me together. Or perhaps it was the other way around. The events and decisions were pretty interlaced. Anyway, I'm so happy about what I get to do each and every day." She shrugged again. "I guess. And then there's Vern, who makes me feel quite wonderful."

"I knew there was a reason I liked you," Robin confessed and realized it was true. Denise was probably the smartest person on the team, pleasant and funny— though perhaps the latter wasn't intentional.

"You do?"

Robin nodded and turned to look at the sky. She checked her watch again. She couldn't go aloft for another hour yet, and it was starting to chafe at her.

"Why?"

She looked back at the mechanic. "What do you mean, *why*?"

"Uh…" Denise adjusted her hat to no purpose that

Robin could see. "I'm not used to people doing that. Liking me. Though Vern does."

"No, he doesn't. He worships you."

"He does," Denise admitted with a blooming smile. "It still surprises me every day. We've only been married a few months and I'm still not used to it."

Robin sat up cross-legged and faced Denise. "I like you because I do."

"Okay." Denise squinted out from beneath the floppy straw brim. "But I still think it's odd."

"Calling me odd. Gee, thanks," Robin teased her.

"I suppose I was. I didn't mean to." Denise didn't look abashed, simply stating facts.

Robin laughed. She couldn't help herself. Robin leaned forward and gave Denise a quick hug. She wasn't used to having girlfriends. But if she had to choose one to start with, she couldn't imagine one better than the straight-ahead, plainspoken mechanic.

"What?"

"You're hilarious, Denise."

"I am?"

"Way."

"Is that a good thing?"

"Double way," Robin confirmed.

"I'll have to think about that."

"That doesn't surprise me."

That elicited a merry look from Denise. "I suppose it shouldn't. I overthink the daylights out of everything."

"Duh!" Robin couldn't stand it any longer. She had to get to a radio and at least find out what was going on with the fire. "Was there something you needed?"

"No." Denise shook her head. "I just saw you were

awake and I thought I'd come keep you company for a minute."

"See, that's why I like you."

Denise again squinted at her from beneath her hat brim. Robin was either going to laugh in her face or…

She stood, gathered the plates, and draped the blanket over one shoulder. "Come on. I need some breakfast and then let's find out what's going on." She reached down to help Denise to her feet.

The straw brim raised enough that Robin knew Denise was looking at her offered hand in surprise.

Then she reached up and Robin helped her to her feet. She held Robin's hand for an extra moment and then nodded.

"Food and information. A good plan," Denise stated from beneath her hat, and with that, they headed for Betsy's tent.

Now that Dawson City's big three-day fundraiser motorcycle event was over, the townsfolk had started paying attention to the firefight. *About goddamn time, people*. There were always a couple of the townies working with Betsy now. A young mechanic, with an obviously serious crush on Denise, had apprenticed himself to the team and was doing run-and-fetch tasks for her.

Despite the inaccessibility of the fire line, others had crossed the Yukon River on the ferry and driven into the wilderness on ATVs stocked with water and food that hadn't been freeze-dried, supplying the smokejumpers in the field.

Any of Robin's early thoughts of money earned had long since given way to estimates of minutes slept.

MHA's calls for more support from both the

Canadians and the Alaska Fire Service simply elicited UTFs—Unable To Fill replies. No National Guard to call out in the middle of the Yukon Territory.

Robin ate breakfast sitting alone on the beaten-down grass while Denise and her apprentice went to prepare a container of supplies to drop to the smokejumpers. It was easier to appreciate where she'd landed and harder to understand how she had.

Robin knew she was already a better pilot than she'd ever been. It didn't matter that Mickey and Jeannie had never flown into war zones or that Vern had only flown Coast Guard; they were good enough to push her. Robin knew she was a competitive bitch by nature, and drove herself to match them. It also helped her keep an edge when the tower of exhaustion had loomed even higher above her than the flames and smoke.

Denise was holding to her hundred percent availability—every bird was ready for every flight. Twice that Robin knew of, their mechanic had gone right around the clock to keep them in the air.

And then there was Mickey.

In five days, she should have had sex a lot more than three additional times, a whole lot more with how good Mickey was at it. Twice had been merely frantic couplings before they both collapsed. Glorious, hard, fast, and sweaty, just the way she liked it.

But once they'd been on the same schedule and both woken for an hour in the darkest moment of the subarctic summer night. Each time she'd tried to hurry him along, he had lightly brushed those hands over her. She was powerless before their direction, going quiet and still despite the needs building inside her.

He'd studied her, there was no other explanation for it. Sometimes digging those strong fingers into tight muscles until she moaned into their kiss. Other times their only point of contact was his fingertip tracing the lines of her face so delicately that it was more a feather brush than a touch. And when at long last he'd taken her, it had been a slow, silent, delicious journey to—

A shadow blocked out even the feebleness of the smoke-shrouded sun.

Robin opened her eyes, not even realizing that she'd laid back down and closed them again after finishing her salmon breakfast burrito. She tipped her head back to see Mark Henderson standing there glaring down at her—at least she assumed there was a glare going on behind those mirrored shades. Clearly she hadn't become any less of a pain in his ass over these five days.

"Morning!" She did her best to sound cheerful. "You know that you're upside down." Like a skyscraper about to collapse downward and crush her. A tower of handsome, frustrated male.

"If you weren't sleeping in, you'd be standing and I'd be right-side up."

"Guess I'm just lazy." Robin shed the blanket and rolled up to her feet. She felt almost as good as if she and Mickey had had sex last night.

"Noticed a lot of things about you, Harrow, but that wasn't one of them."

"Aw, gee, boss man. Was that a compliment?"

Even standing and facing him, the man was daunting. One of those officers who merely had to enter a room to command it. Again he offered that odd half smile that could mean anything.

She could see how Emily might fall for such a man. He and Robin would be a national disaster area inside a week and a declared war zone inside two — she'd never be able to resist poking at all that pride. No, it wasn't pride. It was the self-assuredness that came from knowing that he was exceptional. Probably the Night Stalker in him.

Apparently she brought out the same in him, as he began listing a new set of things she could be doing better.

She considered her reaction as she listened and cataloged. But he was right on every point.

Maybe he felt as much need to prod at her as she did at him.

About item five on the list, Robin noticed something. His language had shifted, if not his holier-than-thou tone of delivery.

When Robin was instructing a newbie National Guarder or a newbie waitress at the truck stop, she spoke to them in simple terms. Protocols, tasks, efficiency. Once they were the next level up and had their feet under them, instructions were mostly situational awareness — whether it was an approaching enemy craft or an empty coffee cup in need of a refill at another waitress's table. Third tier was fine-tuning, like telling her how to change her rollouts after a water drop on the fire line.

This was something else again. Something more.

"Your utilization of the team's resources is good on the ground," Mark was telling her. "But you need to think about their skill sets in the air. Don't be fooled by their genders. As pilots, Jeannie and Vern are natural followers. You're often pairing them together, but think about mixing that."

Robin waved down the line to indicate that her Firehawk One and Vern's Firehawk Three were still in camp. Mickey and Jeannie were aloft. *Mixed. Hello.*

"Yes, but you did that based on their need for downtime on the ground—ignoring your own, which was probably worse."

Robin had mostly kept Mickey beside her but finally switched things up because it was getting a little intense between them for her idea of a simple fling. And she'd wager that Mark could see that. She didn't like being so transparent, not even to a former Night Stalker.

"Mickey and Vern are close," Mark rolled right on. "Think about how a little friendly competition will help them keep their edge as this drags out."

"But that means—"

"Flying with Jeannie, I know."

And clearly he knew why Robin had been reluctant to pair with her. Jeannie had been the obvious choice for the coveted Queen Bee Beale's seat...the seat Robin had slid into for reasons she still didn't understand. She wasn't sure about the other woman's reaction, but it was more comfortable to keep her at a little distance.

Mark finished, again with that half smile.

Again, Robin had to resist the urge to pop him one right in the grin.

Now he was waiting for her reaction. To see if she was willing to digest yet another round of advice from on high. But it wasn't the advice given to a newbie or even someone merely skilled. It was the advice of a skilled observer to another skilled observer. No, a skilled leader to a less skilled one.

Pair Mickey and Vern? It made sense. It would also

still buy her a little distance. She and Mickey would be in the air together, but perhaps a little less on the ground. He wasn't smothering her like water dropped on a fire—

Mickey wasn't smothering her at all really. She was the one who had chosen to crawl under the blanket with him last night, but she was having feelings for him that she didn't have for men she was sleeping with. Maybe with a little more distance, she could also gain a little more perspective.

And she was more comfortable with Jeannie than she had been five days ago.

"Okay." After deciding there was nothing hard to swallow in his instructions, it was easy to digest and integrate them. She'd just have to wait for the right moment aloft to make the switch.

Mark looked at her for a long moment, then smiled that powerful smile that was as rare and as potent as his wife's. Their girl, Tessa, was already cute, but the gene pool these two kids had going for them was pretty damned impressive.

"What?"

He shook his head and then decided to reply anyway. "Sometimes I enjoy being proven wrong. I couldn't understand why Emily wanted to hire a National Guard dropout."

"That is the most backhanded compliment I've received in a long time. *Hey, darlin'.*" She put on Henderson's favorite bad-Texas accent. "*Y'all keep not fuckin' up when I expect ya to.*"

"Yep! Purdy much covers it." Then he turned for the chow tent.

"Hey, Henderson."

He stopped to look back at her.

"I notice you've flown with Jeannie, Vern, and Mickey. And I can see them getting better. I note that you haven't flown with me."

He nodded.

Damn man. Had to drag even that out of him. "Why?"

"Because they need it."

Robin almost bought it. "Nope, doesn't fly. They're all much better at flying to fire than I am. I'm gaining, but they're better."

"Their technique, yes." He went back to that silent mode. *This is a problem for the student to solve, honey.*

"Okay, asshole…"

Half smile was back.

"…if it's not my technique that's at issue, it must be because I'm seeing something they don't. Next level up."

"Got it in one, Harrow."

Thinking it. Saying it out loud. And having someone like Mark agree were three wholly different things.

She had always liked being best—it was a big part of what drove her ahead. Being best often meant being seen as "other" by those she flew with—yet another reason she didn't make friends easily. Robin had learned not to care. When other National Guard pilots had tried to drag her down to their level so that *they* didn't look bad, she'd only flown harder.

But now, to fly with these people who she could only admire, and then be told she still didn't fit in. Well, she did, but not as one of the heli-pilots, instead as their leader. She didn't know what to do with that at all.

"Nice to see that something can take your breath away," Mark offered with far too insightful perception.

Robin felt a small pinch in her head, like she was

missing something. She'd long since learned to trust that little voice. She bent down to gather her breakfast dishes to buy herself a moment to hear it more clearly.

Henderson waited. There was clearly something more, and he was wondering if she'd find—ah!

"What's the other reason?" she asked. "The other reason that you don't fly with me."

He turned his back and started to walk away from her.

"What is it, Mark?" She'd be damned if she was going to go chasing after him, then started to anyway.

"Because," he called back over his shoulder, "Em said that she'd kick my ass if I messed with your technique."

Robin stumbled to a halt as Mark continued on his way.

The ground kept changing beneath her feet and she didn't know what to do about it.

Emily Beale, the Queen Bitch herself, a Night Stalker, saw something in how she flew that she wouldn't even let her husband, another Night Stalker, mess with. They'd conspired to drop her into the command seat of four of the finest helicopter pilots she'd ever flown with and now told her she was exceptional in such company. Which didn't make any sense at all because she knew better even if they didn't. She was good, but every person on her team was better.

And Mickey. There was another piece of shifting ground. She and Mickey weren't just having a summer's fling of fun and hot sex. The bastard had made love to her.

Worse!

She'd let him.

Not only that, but she'd enjoyed it enough to be mooning over the memory of it.

That shift ranked as seismic level in her world. No one *made love* to Robin Harrow.

She looked down at the trampled grass at her feet, crisscrossed with the paths of five days of firefighting.

"You weren't thinking of going anywhere, were you?"

The grass wisely didn't reply, or she'd know that she'd totally lost it.

"Well, don't!" She needed something in her world to remain stable.

The grass merely rippled in a soft breeze that brought fresh wood smoke to her nostrils.

Right, time to get moving. After dropping off her dirty dishes, she swung wide on her return to Firehawk One, shifted from the path beaten in the grass to pass by the flattened spot where she and Mickey had slept together. It wasn't a big area, big enough for two people only if they'd been curled tightly in each other's arms.

Just keep walking.

She really didn't need this.

———∿∿∿———

Mickey was working on the techniques that Mark had been teaching him yesterday. A lighter touch on the cyclic allowed for a faster reaction in hard downdrafts. Mark had intentionally flown them into some bad areas to prove his point. And he had. Mickey might have swallowed his tongue somewhere along the way, but he'd learned.

Mickey had also tried to ask about his kid, his wife, his...

Mark had gently sideslipped every inquiry.

Finally, as they were flying back to the camp last night after a long, hard day, Mark had spoken softly over the headset-to-headset intercom and answered Mickey's real question.

"I can't give you advice one way or another on Robin, Mickey. First, I've got my own biases, right or not. But second, my experiences don't mean crap. These are your experiences." And with that he'd shut up, which left Mickey not quite believing he'd asked Mark the question in the first place.

Today, Mickey and Jeannie arrived at alternating bends in the small river they were dipping from. Beneath his helo, the river twisted north; beneath hers, it turned south. The mid-morning sunlight glared off the water, despite his sunglasses. They were moving into heavier trees— hovering at the river, he couldn't see anything but larch and spruce trees separated by a thread of river—which were only going to encourage the fire if it reached here.

Jeannie was up and out of the water several seconds faster than he was, which left Mickey wondering what Mark had taught her. He still recognized her flight pattern as distinct from everyone else's, but somehow it had become even more strongly hers after flying with Mark for a day.

They arrived back at the fire as Vern and Robin returned from their eight hours off. They soared down the line and punched at the side of the fire that was advancing too fast toward a firebreak. After five days, Akbar's team was slowing down, and they weren't ready for the fire to reach them yet. Not under the rising strength of this morning's winds.

Mickey waved by rocking his helo side to side and Robin replied in kind as she headed off to refill her belly tank.

Mickey lined up to hit the same spot with Jeannie close behind him.

These were his own experiences? *Thanks for all the help, Mark.* He didn't know how to trust them. Last night he'd sat down on the grass to watch the roiling tower of smoke that had reached up to the jet stream and was now flat-topped as it was ripped away to the east.

And he'd woken up with a woman in his arms.

As if it was the most natural thing, Robin was simply there. Mickey wasn't a leave-in-the-night sort of guy, but he wasn't ready for how much he wanted to wake up this way every day for the rest of his life either.

He wanted to call Dad and tell him that his son had found "The One"—like Dad always claimed Mom was. Mom was the more sensible one, talked about how long Dad had hung around before she'd even date him. Careful, taking her time. Mickey had always thought he'd grown up more like her in that way. Apparently he'd grown up just like his dad.

Well, if Dad was right, then he too could be persistent.

Maybe it would be an easier road than Mom had made Dad travel. After all, it was Robin who had chosen to crawl under the blanket with him last night, so carefully that she hadn't even wakened him.

Damn it!

Though he really shouldn't complain. Neither had he awakened her this morning for a little preflight sex. Yesterday her fair skin had looked almost sallow with exhaustion. This morning it had looked like the smoothest tissue paper, as if he could almost see her heart and her soul beating beneath its surface.

Crap!

He was getting all poetic. What he should be doing was paying attention to the fire, but once again he was overly aware of Robin as he and Jeannie headed once more for the double bend in the river and Robin and Vern returned from there.

"Helos," Mark called from his place once again aloft in the Beech King Air, "hold back from the line after your next drop and refill."

Mickey glanced over at Jeannie as they hovered and reloaded. Too far to exchange expressions but close enough to agree that something was about to change.

They flew hard to refill and return to the line as fast as possible. Just as he arrived to hover beside Robin and Vern, a half mile back from the drop zone, a Shorts Sherpa C-23 jump plane buzzed by at three thousand feet overhead. Paracargo supplies delivery.

The smokies must have called for more gear and the hold-back order to the helicopters was so that a couple pallets of gear didn't parachute right into their rotor blades.

But instead of big pallets, a dozen small, dark figures tumbled out and began popping standard rectangular RAM parachutes. In moments, they were swooping down into the firebreak, riding the hard winds to space themselves down the long line.

Mickey cheered, which echoed in his otherwise-empty helicopter, making it a rather strange sound. He didn't care. This fire was being a total bitch and the heart of it was still at a full roar. With only a few miles remaining to the banks of the Yukon River, it wasn't all that hard to imagine sparks flying across the five hundred feet and igniting the desperately dry town.

One or two sparks wasn't a problem. But time and

again in this firefight, they had been reminded that
the Yukon timber was so dry that embers didn't float
in ones and twos or even hundreds. When the wind
caught them right, the fire cast a thousand sparkling
bits ahead all at once. You couldn't dump water on
buildings the way you could on the forest, at least not if
you expected them to remain standing. If this reached
Dawson City, the battle was going to turn into a whole
new level of ugly.

Moments later, a fixed-wing Air Tractor AT-802F—
Single Engine Air Tanker (SEAT)—dumped a long line
of eight hundred gallons on the fire. Close behind it flew
a Bell LongRanger helicopter with a bucket on a long
line. Another hundred-plus gallons hit the fire. It was
easy to see the Bell was flown by a contract pilot, but
the extra help looked so good to his eyes that Mickey
wanted to go up and kiss the helo pilot right on the nose
no matter what he looked like.

Mickey recognized the paint job on the SEAT; the
Alaska Fire Service had finally freed up some resources.
The helo was a civilian job but bucket certified. Two
more folks in the air. It was time to get to work.

"Jeannie, you're with me," Robin called over the air.
"Alaska Fire Service helicopter, Vern, and Mickey, let's
see if you boys can keep up with the girls."

"Hey," a female voice called out, "Macy Tyler here in
the Bell LongRanger. Do I have to play with the boys?"

"Not for a second. You're with us." With that, Robin
called to Mark—up in his plane once more—for where
to drop. Then she and Jeannie dove on the spot, unloaded
a thousand-gallon rainstorm each, and the three women
turned back toward the river. The small stream they'd

been using was far enough behind the fire line now that the Yukon River was the closest resource. And just across the river lay the Town of the City of Dawson.

Across the river, the locals had set up lawn chairs and a couple of homemade banners atop the dike to watch the helicopters cycle back and forth for water.

Mickey flipped over a private frequency to Mark up in the Incident Command plane. "What the hell, boss?"

"Take it up with your lady." Mark's voice clearly ended the conversation there.

Not a chance in hell of that happening, especially not while she was on an open frequency with two other women flying with her.

If Macy Tyler was here, that meant that Akbar's former number-two smokejumper was with the team that had just jumped in. Two-Tall Tim had returned to Larch Creek, Alaska, for a vacation and ended up marrying his high school girlfriend. He took over as number-one smokejumper with the Alaska Fire Service out of Fairbanks to stay near her. Akbar had been quite put out about it until he'd flown up with Mickey and some of the others to be best man at the wedding.

Well, that was sure going to apply the pressure on Akbar and the other smokies, because they'd be forced to show Tim up, as if MHA's smokies hadn't just been five straight days and nights on this fire.

Mickey turned to take a long look at Vern, who was still hovering there beside him. And there was not a chance that Vern was going to beat him to the fire either.

Mickey continued to stare across between their helos until he saw Vern shrug. Mickey took advantage of what would be a one- to two-second delay to return to flight and dove toward the drop zone, leaving Vern to trail behind.

The race was on and there was no chance in hell Vern was going to outfly his Twin 212.

Chapter 7

THE PARTY TWO DAYS LATER IN DOWNTOWN DAWSON City was epic and Robin was totally ready for it.

The fire did reach the west riverbank, but it had lost all heart by the time it touched the river. Not a single ember crossed the Yukon.

A Canadian ground crew had shown up along with a tiny drone carrying an infrared camera to find hot spots. MHA hadn't left them many. But the Black was five miles at its widest and over forty miles long, and that was a lot of terrain to inspect.

"It's official, sports fans." Mark dropped down at the table next to Mickey and across from Robin. "One hundred and three thousand acres. So, pony up. For who is this their first hundred thousander?"

Hers was the only hand to go up at the two picnic tables butted end to end along the crowded sidewalk. The whole flight crew was packed together. They'd annexed Macy from the Bell LongRanger, who had brought her husband along, Two-Tall Tim. Tim Harada, a towering Eurasian man but powerfully built like a smokie, had dragged along Akbar, who didn't even reach his shoulder. They must have made an odd pair when they fought fires together.

Robin checked again. No other raised hands. The entire MHA crew had all flown to big fires, except her. *She would not feel out of place*, she ordered herself. *She would not!*

"Traditional punishment is you're buying first round, champ!" Mark announced happily.

Robin waved a hand at the Old West–style tavern down the block. "Diamond Tooth Gerties is footing our bill in thanks for saving the town."

"Crap, you get off so easy."

"Besides, I think that as the sole person here to never have fought a hundred-thousand-acre fire, I should get to chose the punishment."

Mark eyed her carefully. "And what might that be?"

Robin checked to make sure all of the pilots were listening. Jeannie and Cal. Vern and Denise. Mickey still trying to figure out how he'd ended up across the table from her rather than next to her. He'd looked so sad—she'd done it because watching him fly with Vern had made her wish all the more that he'd been flying with her, which meant she was becoming attached. *So not gonna happen! Harrow women didn't become attached.* But when he'd started playing footsie under the table, she took pity on him and joined in. Even that little bit of connection felt ridiculously good.

"My punishment, Mr. Mark Henderson, is being forced to watch you take the cancan dancing class up on the stage at Diamond Gerties." Its cancan dancers were one of the many tourist draws in town.

Mark's "No way, sister!" was drowned out by the cheers of the others at the table.

They were echoed by some cheers farther down the street.

It was July 1, Canada Day, and the entire town of thirteen hundred had turned out beneath the first blue sky in over a week.

The parade was starting. A very short but highly enthusiastic small-town parade. The MHA firefighters had been given a prime viewing spot as thanks from the town, so all they had to do was turn around and face the street.

Somehow in the shuffling, Mickey slid onto the bench seat beside her and slipped an arm possessively around Robin's waist. It felt far too good for her to complain, so she focused on the parade.

Tucson always had fireworks and a big deal parade on July Fourth: classic cars, multiple high school marching bands, whole troops of ever-so-pretty Air Force personnel from Davis–Monthan Air Force Base marching in their perfect dress whites beneath the blazing Arizona summer sun. People lined a dozen deep down the sidewalks to watch. Food vendors plied their trade at every corner, serving up the best gorditas and chalupas imaginable.

There were probably more people *in* the Tucson July Fourth Parade than were in the entire town of Dawson City. But Robin was surprised at how much she'd enjoyed the much smaller and more parochial affair. These people were into it.

The Canadian formation day parade consisted of a line of the town's two ambulances and four fire trucks. The couple dozen members of the high school marching band followed close behind, whacking out "Louie Louie" with a respectable enough tone. A cluster of Native Peoples danced down the street in traditional garb to beaten drums, which fit oddly well into the marching band's rhythms not far ahead of them.

A pair of old fire engines went by, old like 1930s. They had been restored to immaculate shape. And rather than firefighters, perched atop them were Gerties' cancan girls—long, curling hair; feathered tiaras; and outrageous gowns that clung tightly from the waist up and exploded into layers of brightly colored ruffles below, mostly red.

Robin imagined the look in Mickey's eyes if she was to wear one of those and then decided there were some things better left to the imagination.

A roll of laughter followed a float up the street. It looked like a small fishing boat until it pulled even with them. Atop what was meant to be a smokestack—but looked suspiciously like a chunk of old stovepipe— with a metal-bladed household fan had been mounted flat in the top of the pipe. The four blades stuck out like a Firehawk's rotors and milled lazily in the breeze. The people on the float—dressed in makeshift flight suits of bright yellow rain slicks smeared with mud like char—were tossing out packets of cinnamon Red Hots to the crowd.

Next came a beautiful draft horse pulling a restored covered wagon. And again someone had rigged a fan sideways on top. This one was a wood-bladed ceiling fan.

Some kids pulled a wagon that had clearly started out to be a bush plane with fake floats and a pair of card-board wings. Now a little boy of three or four sat in the wagon, holding aloft a broom handle, which sported four sagging cardboard flaps. One had kinked completely, making the fake rotor blade flap annoyingly against the little boy's face, but he stoically kept his hands around the broom handle to keep the rotor upright.

Everyone at the table rose to give him a standing ovation.

And they kept coming. A whole phalanx of local kids on their bicycles done up with red and white streamers,

Canadian flag capes, and beanie hats with little propellers on the top.

"That does it," Robin shouted into Mickey's ear to be heard over the cheering. "This is too cute for words; I'm moving here."

He just grinned and kissed her on the temple.

Robin looked at the people. Could see the hard edges of long Arctic nights, on the edge of desperate survival against a lean year.

But in this moment, they were perfect.

———

"I don't know if I've ever been this happy." Cal had his camera out and was snapping pictures. "I've got blackmail material for years."

Mickey sat front and center of Diamond Tooth Gerties' main floor and looked up at the stage, couldn't look away from it. Gerties' cancan girls were conducting a class and Mickey was being overwhelmed by the spectacle of the MHA women dressed in period costumes, practicing high kicks and stepping in unison.

Laced-up form-hugging bodices of black leather. Long legs flashing out from ruffled skirts. Low black heels and occasional flashes of barely discreet black underwear.

The place was packed with Canada Day revelers. The long, wooden bar with its bartenders in idealized period costumes of suspenders, straw hats, and those elastic gathers around the biceps of their button-down white shirts. The waitresses in all black cancan dresses and black feathers in their hair. Gamblers crowded about the roulette and blackjack tables.

But Mickey only had eyes for what was happening on

the stage. And if he'd never imagined her on a motorcycle, he'd absolutely never thought to see Robin Harrow in a dress, especially not a risqué piece of French frippery from the Klondike gold rush era.

But it wasn't only his Robin, shining like a golden icon, that was blowing him away.

It was the "his" that was doing it to him.

He was feeling terribly possessive and was discovering that he liked the feeling. A lot. Not that she belonged to him, but more that he was the one who could hold her close, kiss her on the temple until his senses were overwhelmed by her, and could make her laugh.

"She's laughing." Vern leaned in from beside him. "I had no idea Harrow could laugh."

Mickey did. Her joy seemed boundless when they were together. Her amused laugh trickling out at the oddest moments.

"Look at your own lady, buddy." Mickey wanted to distract Vern from the subject. He wasn't ready to share his true feelings about Robin with anyone, not even her just yet.

They'd had problems finding a dress small enough for Denise, but they had. The generally silent and deeply reserved mechanic was up there with the rest of the women on full display.

"Life is good." Vern sighed.

"And how," Tim agreed, his long legs stretched out before him.

Robin, Denise, Macy, and Jeannie were the four onstage. Carly and Steve had disappeared somewhere, perhaps to walk the town as it wound down after the day's celebration, perhaps to a quiet hotel room—definitely to escape. The group had left Akbar and several of the other smokejumpers—still stumbling from their weeklong ordeal—asleep on a patch of green grass not far from where the picnic table had stood. Only Tim Harada had remained with them, and that only because of his wife's sticking with the other female pilots.

"You're not doing yourselves any good from here, boys." Mark appeared among them.

"Hey, aren't you supposed to be up there with them?"

"Harrow may think so, but I'm not that malleable."

Mickey had to nod. With Mark Henderson, that was one thing that was for damn sure. Though he suspected that if Emily was here… But she wasn't.

In her place was Robin Harrow. She was chaotic, unpredictable, and screamingly competent. He could feel the stupid-happy grin on his face as he watched her throw herself into a stomp-knee raise-stomp-kick-stomp-knee raise routine.

"C'mon." Mark tipped Mickey out of his chair. Gave Vern a shove. "Get up there if you guys have even half a brain." He thumped Tim on the arm hard enough to dislodge an elephant. Cal stumbled to his feet quickly enough when Mark moved his way and slung his camera around behind his back.

Mickey decided that if Emily were up there on stage, Mark would have been right there with her from the first second. He was right; Mickey was being stupid. Well, no longer.

While the other guys were still protesting, Mickey ambled up to the lip of the stage. It was about four feet above the main floor. He could stand here and watch Robin dreamily as she worked on a crossover step or…

He gave a small jump and vaulted up onto the well-worn hardwood.

There was a drunken round of applause and encouraging cheers from the audience that he completely ignored.

Mickey walked up to Robin. She didn't stop her kick rhythm, but her smiling blue eyes tracked his every step in her direction. In moments, the cancan instructor, a fine-looking woman in her forties with long, dark-red hair, had him holding Robin's waist from behind to support and steady her.

The other guys, either following his lead or giving in to Mark's harangue, soon joined him and were added to the line.

By themselves, the four women had been merry, laughing, goofy, and beautiful in their blushing self-embarrassment. Only Robin had wholeheartedly thrown herself into the act, raising her skirt high for the kicks, tossing her head as if her hair was billowing waves instead of the elfin chop that it was.

With the four men on the stage, it became a quieter group. Not somber, not dampened. But more intense. He could feel it himself. As he followed the instructor's guidance on how to lift and twirl Robin, on how to lean her back when she kicked high, the instructor and the other couples fell away.

His awareness of Robin grew until nothing else mattered, not the other dancers, not the crowded bar, not even a very self-satisfied-looking Mark Henderson, who had taken Mickey's chair.

Mickey's arms were full of a beautiful woman in a stunning dress, and he was so gone on her.

The next time he laid her back in a dance step, he kissed that lovely, laughing mouth of hers.

He was far more than gone.

———〰———

The next morning, they were out at the airfield packing up the camp for the long flight back to the states.

Robin could still feel how Mickey had held her, both onstage and last night after they were alone in his tent. She'd been so relieved at surviving that first fire, at somehow belonging with these people, even having a place on that stage, in ways she'd never imagined, that she'd let the fantasy sweep her away.

Robin liked men who were strong, it made them more fun. She'd never let herself become lost in their strength. But for one single night, she had let herself do just that. Mickey's hands around her waist had lifted her so effortlessly that she felt as if she was flying. And when he had made love to her afterward, she had let him take control and submitted wholly to his whim. And his whim had been very, very good.

No rooms left in any of the hotels, they had retreated once more to his tent along the airfield, and he had made it feel like a luxury room, albeit a very small one. He had done it by lavishing her with attention and sensation so complete that it had almost redefined who she was.

In the morning sunlight, she collapsed her own little-used tent and stowed it aboard Firehawk One. Then she moved over to help Betsy restow the cook tent.

Robin continued to reconsider the prior night. The inner shift in her thinking was that she was worthy of such attention. It was a novel concept. In the past, her body had earned her what she'd wanted from a man... and nothing more.

Not Mickey. He had gone silent, barely spoken a

word to her all night. But the intensity with which he had made love to her—she no longer winced at the phrase, not totally—left no room for doubts about what was on his mind.

She'd thought to tell him to dampen down the fire a bit, but then had become so lost in that powerful need of his to hold her, to be with her, that she let him do whatever he wanted. When he beckoned her to climb atop him, she had. Later, when he chose to dominate, the heat between them had burned equally high.

"Daydreaming there, Robin," Jeannie said from close by her elbow. Her dark eyes were sparkling. "If Mickey was even half as attentive as my Cal, I can see why."

Robin scanned to make sure none of the men were close by before answering. "Attentive might be an understatement."

"Aren't men wonderful?" Denise did her crop-up-from-nowhere trick.

"They do have their moments," Robin agreed and ignored the slight blush on Denise's cheeks. Gave her shoulder a friendly rub instead.

These women were welcoming her, had welcomed her. Robin could always pick up men, but women friends had been few and far between. While she was in the Guard, she'd attributed it to being in a man's world. And once out, she'd attributed it to being a soldier suddenly caught in a civilian's world.

Last night that hadn't been the case. They had been women together, dancing in their men's arms.

And these women were accepting her, even Jeannie who had the most reason not to. Robin did her best to respond in kind.

"He made it glorious," she confessed.

"The way you two were dancing onstage would have made me really jealous if Cal hadn't come along."

"The dancing didn't stop onstage."

The other two women sighed happily. "No, it didn't," they agreed in unison.

Robin threw open her arms, and in moments, they were sharing a group hug. It was as new and different as Mickey being in her life, and somehow it felt just as important.

———

"Damn!" Mickey exhaled it on a sigh.

Vern stood close beside him. "Beautiful, happy women in the morning sun."

"Yep" was all Mickey could think to say. No woman had ever given to him the way Robin had last night. He'd never get enough of her, even if he spent a lifetime trying to please her.

Vern slapped him on the shoulder. "Uh-huh. That's exactly how it feels."

"Okay." Mickey used Robin's phrase because it was the best he could come up with. He knew what *it* was.

Mark's two-finger whistle sliced through the quiet air and he waved them all over to Firehawk One.

Everyone gathered around.

Mickey wanted to slip up to Robin, but she was firmly between Denise and Jeannie.

"Leave it alone, bro," Vern whispered over his shoulder.

"Right. Male solidarity and all that."

"Uh-huh." Vern's affirmative grunt wasn't very

convincing, especially not as he sidled up on Denise's other side and leaned down to kiss her atop her head.

Akbar's crew was mostly loaded back on the MHA aircraft. Akbar alone trotted over for the meeting. The Alaska Fire Service team were mostly loaded as well, though Tim and Macy came over to say good-bye.

"We've got a bit of a changeup here," Mark started out. "Don't know if anything's going to come of it, but we're going to divide up for the moment."

Mickey caught the change. Quick glances between Denise and Jeannie. If Robin hadn't been between them, he might have missed it, but they had leaned forward to look at each other.

Vern and Cal looked suddenly grim. No other reactions around the circle, and it looked as if Robin had missed it all. Then, after the others had all schooled their expressions back to neutral, Robin glanced at him. She hadn't missed a thing, which he acknowledged with the tiniest tip of his head.

Something was up and neither of them was in the loop.

"Akbar, you and yours are headed back to Oregon. There's a new fire out near the Dalles with your name on it. You'll take Betsy and her kitchen gear with you on the planes."

He must have already told Betsy, because she was busy shifting her pile of gear over to the Shorts Sherpa.

"The rest of you, we're going to take a couple days R&R until we know for certain what's going on. But we are on call. We'll be dropping in on your hospitality, Tim, over in Fairbanks. Though I'd rather not have four MHA helos parked out in front of the Ladd Army Airfield."

"Come on out to Larch Creek," Macy suggested. "It's

less than a fifteen-minute flight to Fairbanks. We have a field behind the town hangars where you could all park as long as you want."

"Oh, man," Akbar whined. "A chance to visit with you guys and I have to go jump a fire. Tim, why the hell did you have to fall in love with a lady up here?"

"Why did you fall for a wilderness guide?" Tim returned fire.

"Well, at least I can ride a horse with her. You looked like a stick man the few times I got you in the saddle. You know that you set the record for—"

"Boys." Mark's tone stopped them. Then he turned to Macy. "That sounds perfect. Thanks."

Mickey waited, but no other explanation was forthcoming.

Robin started to speak, then glanced at Mickey. He shook his head to stop her. She scowled but kept her peace.

"Let's go." Mark slapped his hands together and everyone began to disperse.

Robin came up to Mickey and wrapped him in an unexpected hug. He buried his face against her neck, but rather than nuzzling in as well, she whispered in his ear.

"What do you know that I don't?"

He sighed. He'd never been the most romantic guy, but it looked as if he was the romantic one in this relationship.

"First"—he shifted so that he wasn't mumbling against her neck—"Mark only ever gives out as much instruction as he's willing to. No amount of questioning shifts that."

"Asshole." But there was a laugh in her voice. "Second?"

"There's more to MHA than fighting forest fires. I don't know what it is, but there's shit that happens that no one talks about afterward. I'm guessing this could be one of those."

Robin held him a moment longer. "The nondisclosure agreement and the governmental security check."

He nodded. "I don't know what's behind that curtain, but it's possible we're about to find out."

She gave him an extra squeeze and then stepped out toward Firehawk One.

"Hey," he called to her. Not even a kiss?

She must have read it clearly on his face. "Couple days off in small town, Alaska. You just might get lucky, sailor."

That was an encouraging thought. "It's flyboy, not sailor, Ms. Robin of the Hood."

Her laugh sparkled in the sunlight and she started to prep her helo.

Mickey turned to do the same to his.

There was a third thing he knew that Robin didn't, though it was too soon to share.

Mickey knew he was completely in love with one Robin Harrow.

Chapter 8

FAIRBANKS SAT FOUR HUNDRED MILES WEST ALONG the Yukon River watershed from Dawson City—though the meandering river easily traveled twice that distance to make the journey. Larch Creek was a little town thirty miles south of Fairbanks, perched in the foothills of the Alaska Range.

It was one of the most breathtaking places Mickey had ever been. An isolated valley with a wide basin but high hills wrapping the town in a vast bowl. It stretched along one side of a small, active river that looked to be draining directly from the big glaciers of Denali. Despite being seventy miles away, the tallest mountain in North America dominated the view at the head of valley. It surprised him at every turn: driving into town from the tiny airport—whose runway was actually a chunk of the one road into town—stepping out of the small B&B that Macy had called ahead to reserve for them before stepping into the town's one restaurant/bar—a massive log structure with *French Pete's* carved deeply into the log over the doorway with a hatchet. He turned, and there was Denali's white twenty-thousand-foot peak.

But it was the river that caught his attention.

"How far upstream can you kayak?" He turned to Macy, who had landed beside him at the big lunch table.

"What?" She cupped an ear in his direction.

The interior of French Pete's was a surreal space

with caribou and moose antlers adorning the walls and
a thousand odd collectibles tacked up between them. A
massive, wood-spoked ship's wheel hung on the wall
with glass floats dangling off each spoke, even though
they were hundreds of miles from the ocean. Paintings
of dogsleds that might have dated back to Jack London
and the gold rush days. A large American flag that took
him a moment to realize why it looked wrong—it had
only forty-nine stars, made in the eight months between
Alaskan and Hawaiian statehood. Old license plates.
Even more had been stacked up haphazardly on the
porch out front, a great jumble of unfathomable content.

But what had caught his eye was the half of a kayak
bolted to the ceiling. The paddler was a dummy—at least
he hoped it was a dummy and not a corpse—and wore
a full set of scuba gear, with his flippered feet sticking
out where the missing half of the boat should have been.

Robin and Denise were chatting away like two best
friends to his other side. The table was a cheerful mayhem
of conversations and laughter in one corner of the surreality.

He pointed upward and raised his voice.

"Kayaking, how far upstream?"

"Only Class I and II rapids for about ten miles. The
same again another five miles beyond that. They're
separated by a Class III rapid that runs about a half
mile and no way on the planet to portage around them.
There's some Class IV above that, but it's probably no
good with the low snowpack this season. For the few
kayakers who make it to Larch Creek, I deliver them
upstream with my LongRanger."

"Where can I rent gear for two?"

Macy shrugged. "In Larch Creek? Wow, that's a

good question. A couple of us have canoes when we want to go hunting in the woods across the river, but I don't know anyone with a kayak except Carl." And she too pointed upward. "And that's only a half one. Maybe you could fly into Fairbanks. I think that they've got those plastic boats for the day-trippers on the Tanana River along the Fairbanks waterfront. Don't know as I'd want to run a rapid in one though."

"Shit!" Mickey looked around, feeling a little desperate. He had this image in his head: Robin Harrow in a whitewater kayak. To hell with motorcycles and cancan dresses. It was the best image he'd had of her yet and he couldn't wait for—

"Wait!" Macy gripped his arm.

"What?"

She laughed. Macy tugged and dragged him back out to the porch. You could have a big summer party out here if it weren't for all the junk—only a narrow path remained between the front steps and the entry. It was hard to make sense of the hodgepodge. There was defunct mining equipment, an old motorcycle, a dogsled with a broken runner filled with more moose antlers—they shed them every year, Macy explained, which made the local supply unending—a broken wooden airplane propeller—a lone wagon wheel, five cross-country skis, none of which matched.

And sticking out from the depths of the pile, a narrow prow of sun-bleached plastic. It took them a few minutes, but he and Macy soon unearthed a pair of kayaks with a very faded "Rent Me" sign on one of them. More digging unearthed some paddles. Sealed in bags in one of the cockpits was the rest of the necessary gear, including a pair of nylon spray skirts in surprisingly good condition considering the sun-faded state of the boats themselves.

"What are you up to?" Robin asked from somewhere beyond the mound of crap between the kayaks and the front door to the restaurant.

He waded back to her and held aloft his final find. He selected one of the hard-shell safety helmets and—after checking to make sure it had no spiders or other nasty surprises lurking within—pulled it down over her head.

"Oh, babe. You're gonna love this!"

———

"Love this" was not exactly what Robin was thinking a mere two hours later. What she had been thinking was a hot shower, a soft bed, and a couple days of restaurant food. What she *was* doing was watching her one link to such niceties take off and disappear back to the north in the form of Macy Tyler and her Bell LongRanger helicopter.

As the engine noise faded, the reality of their situation began to sink in. Except for radios currently stowed away in plastic bags, their contact with the outside world consisted of paddling tiny little boats to the next nearest human being, over a dozen miles downstream.

"You are dog meat, Hamilton."

"Uh-huh." Mickey kept organizing their supplies into gallon Ziplocs that he'd bought at the tiny general store.

"I mean it, Mickey." Something in her tone must have caught his attention and had him stop and look up at her.

"Listen—"

"I'm not feeling very cooperative at the moment," she snarled back.

"No…listen," he said softly.

And she did.

The helicopter was gone. The last heavy beats of the rotors were done echoing off the valley walls.

But there was also no roaring fire, racing helos, radio call static crackling in her ears every thirty seconds, or any of the other mayhem that had filled the last seven days. And the week of hopes and interviews, of testing and training, that had come before, that was also gone. Before that? Six months at the truck stop—pretty much without a day off.

The first sound she heard? The soft burble of the stream entering the small mountain lake where Macy had dropped them off. They were in a grassy clearing little bigger than the helicopter. Trees ranged upward on steep hills all around the lakeshore. The air was breathlessly still, making the lake a mirrored sheet that reflected the fantastic image of Denali's north face.

Some bird chirped to ask if the noisy helicopter was gone and was it safe to come out again. Another answered. A moment later there was a rustle as a squirrel raced across an overhead branch to look down at these new intruders.

More bird calls. More small critter noise.

But all of it so soft she could soon hear the beating of her own heart, her own breathing.

And the trees lived up to the river's name—Larch Creek. They were wrapped in a world of tall larch conifers, most a soft green, some yellowing with age as if it was already autumn but they were struggling on. The undergrowth was grasses and low berry bushes.

And the silence behind it all, she could only describe as…

"Wow."

Mickey came up beside her and wrapped his arms around her waist but didn't speak. He leaned forward so that his head was beside hers, chin ever so lightly on her shoulder.

She couldn't hear his heart, but she could feel it beating where his chest pressed against her back.

The silence slowly soaked the craziness out of her.

"Why did you bring me out here? You could have had your nefarious way with my willing body at the B&B in a nice, soft bed."

"Okay, I should have thought about that aspect more carefully," he joked in her ear. Then he turned her to face him, and there was something much more serious going on behind those eyes.

Uh-oh! Robin's internal alarms went off. She wasn't even sure what they were, but they were now ringing more loudly than the bird chatter in the bushes and trees around them.

"My dad is a tour guide in the summers. Raft and kayak. As a kid, I spent my summers with him out on the Oregon rivers."

"In Tucson we spent it out in the desert with a .22 rifle, shooting rattlesnakes. Personally I preferred going to the local NASCAR track. So this is about connecting with your dad? Or your inner child?"

Mickey scoffed. "You see my dad anywhere handy?" He pretended to squint into the trees, then shaded his eyes to look across the lake up toward Denali.

"What about your inner child?"

"My inner child?" Mickey looked down and poked

a finger at his own ribs a few times as if looking for it. "Trust me, Robin, there is not a single childish thought in my head at the moment." Then he turned those surprising blue eyes of his in her direction.

No, there wasn't a single childish thought there, that was for damn sure. She could feel her body heating in response, but chose to ignore it...for the moment anyway.

She slipped out of Mickey's arms and used the lake as an excuse. She wandered down to the edge of the lake and stuck in a finger.

"Yipes! That's freezing!"

"Glacial melt. I guess we're gonna be pretty stinky by the time we get back to Larch Creek."

"And how soon is that?"

"Could do it in a day if we had to. Two days is comfortable."

Then he looked away from her, and she could feel the pressure of his need for her ease as his gaze traveled elsewhere.

"I could stay right here a long time though." He spoke mostly to himself.

Robin watched Mickey watch the landscape. It was the first place he'd really made sense to her. He flew a firefighting helicopter as well as anyone she'd ever seen. As Mark had pointed out, Mickey was also a natural leader; people simply followed his initiative. Not because he ordered it, but because when he did something, it was straight from his heart.

As Mickey had jumped up onto Gerties' stage so effortlessly and stalked across the boards to take possession of her, there had been an impossible rightness.

One so powerful that the other three men followed him without any argument, possibly without any thought that they were about to make fools of themselves in front of a hundred Canada Day revelers.

Summer river guide. The strength that he wielded so effortlessly was a legacy of an active child with a paddle in his hands for hours every day.

Maybe here in this place she could understand more of who he was. Here was a place he belonged.

She walked quietly upslope to the pile of gear and fished out a sleeping bag. She spread it on the thick, soft grasses and then sat down upon it.

"Mickey?" she called to the man who still stared outward as if fitting in somewhere was the most natural thing in the world. And not the absolute impossibility that Robin knew it to be. The only place she ever truly fit was... She didn't know. Neither the truck stop nor the cockpit of an AANG bird. Maybe Harrow women were above such things.

He turned slowly to look at her.

She patted the sleeping bag beside her. There was a wildness to him that she hadn't seen before. Not of danger or loss of control, but of belonging where modern man no longer did.

He stalked up and looked down at her for a moment. She'd have felt small if his look didn't make her feel so powerful. No one had ever needed her the way Mickey Hamilton did.

Instead of patting the sleeping bag beside her again, she opened her arms to him.

As he knelt before her and then lay her back, he said her name softly.

"Robin."

It wasn't a question.

It was a statement.

A statement that maybe there was somewhere she did belong. She'd certainly never been in a place like Mickey's arms.

━━━∿∿∿━━━

Mickey had thought he knew something about making love to Robin. Finally alone and not exhausted by the firefight, he discovered that he hadn't a clue.

When he lay down over her on the grassy slope above the unnamed glacial lake, she welcomed him without any question. Her kisses had been wonderful, but now her light blue eyes were filled with something more. When she closed them to kiss him, there was a quietness about her that hadn't been there before.

Oh, he'd been able to gentle her into letting him explore her body, but now there was no need to do so. It wasn't that she was gentle; her kiss was so hard—with her arms locked behind his head forbidding his easing back—that they would both have bruised lips. Rather it was that the quiet had moved inside of her.

When he uncovered her lovely breasts and palmed them both and planted a kiss between, she hissed with pleasure and need.

And when he had removed the rest of her clothes and dragged off his own shirt, he moved to explore what was last uncovered. She rose for him in a flight so smooth, so deep, that it didn't come from mere bodily pleasure and release. Her whole being shone from her. So in tune with what was happening that even her cries didn't still the birdsong.

Robin Harrow, sprawled golden and glistening beneath the warmth of the Alaskan sun, was no mere revelation. She was a goddess incarnate—except that made her too remote and there wasn't a single thing remote about her.

Not as she held him in place until the last shudder had run the length of her delicious frame for the last time. Still not letting him move until long after her breathing and pulse had returned to normal.

Only then did she let him up to lie fully side by side against her. He should remove his pants, but was too distracted by trailing his hand over the length of her naked form. Mickey was unable to believe that she was real.

But when he leaned over to kiss her, she shook her head.

"Doesn't seem right." Her voice was a whisper.

"That I want to kiss you?"

"No, that you can make me feel that way. I'm not big on vulnerability."

"Not vulnerable?" He propped himself up on one elbow to survey the woman sprawled before him, completely naked and totally relaxed as if she didn't have a muscle left in her body.

"No." She opened one eye and looked up at him.

"Yet you just were."

"I know. And the results were out of this world, Mickey with the blue eyes. Thank you."

"You're welcome." Which sounded pretty damn stupid with what he'd just been doing to her, driving her helplessly with his own greed to see just how much he could make Robin Harrow feel. He'd wager he hadn't come close to the limit yet.

"What makes *you* feel vulnerable?"

"Me?" Mickey tried to think of something. "Watching other people fly. Emily, Jeannie, you."

"Not Vern?"

"Nah, I'm as good as he is, or near enough."

"Wait." She sat up and looked at him, completely comfortable with her nudity and his still being clothed from the waist down. "Me?"

This time he used his strength to scoop her into his lap and kiss her. That naturally led him to think about what else was there for the taking and he began working his way down her neck toward—

"Ow! Ow! Ow!" He followed where she pinched and pulled on his ear until he was facing her once again.

"You said me. Watching me fly." She let go of his ear and rubbed it in apology.

"I did."

"Care to explain why?"

—∿∿—

"Is it because we're all women and we aren't supposed to be able to fly that well?" Robin didn't like that thought at all but wasn't ready to force her way out of Mickey's lap. It was a very comfortable place to be.

"Clearly you know Emily far less well than you think you do."

"And what does that mean?"

He looked out across the lake, but his hands remained on her.

Was he even aware of them as he rubbed one up and down her back and had the other wrapped around the inside of her thigh? She suspected not.

"I figure pilots come in three categories. Some learn

to fly, just in the course of life. They make good, serviceable pilots. Gordon is one of those. Vanessa I think is another."

Robin had known a number of pilots like that, a lot of them actually. They were far and away the most common breed out there.

"There are some who always dreamed of flying and still can't believe it's really happening. Vern and I. Bruce maybe. Henderson definitely—he's just a hell of a lot better than the rest of us. Had a lot more practice."

"What's the third?"

"The naturals like you, Emily, Jeannie. Not that the learning was any easier than for the rest of us, but it just fits something in your nervous systems."

"Mark had said Emily had forbidden him to train me." Was this the final and real reason?

"Right, it would just screw up what you do. He can fix your knowledge with safety techniques and tactics, but how you fly? Probably not."

"But he flew with Jeannie."

"And she's been flying fire for close to a decade, both forest and Australian bushfire, though a bunch of the early stuff was fixed wing. She's not such raw material still."

"Raw material?" Robin protested.

"Uh-huh."

"Just waiting for the right man to come along and mold me into shape."

"Maybe." That self-impressed grin of his was back.

"I'll show you maybe." She started to struggle out of his lap and discovered she was near helpless to do so.

Mickey was wrong about himself; he was an absolute natural, both as pilot and lover.

Mickey had one arm tight around her shoulder. In a single move, he tipped her back and latched his mouth on her breast. At the same moment, his hand, which had been resting nonchalantly on her thigh, slid down and clamped on to her.

There was nothing gentle at all this time. No floating on lovemaking as soft as a breeze. No back-and-forth play.

He was taking, forcing her to give.

Robin could only think of two ways to stop him as he consumed her, launching her straight toward madness.

One was to cause him bodily harm.

The other was to ask him to stop, because she knew he would in an instant, no matter what it cost him.

She considered and discarded the first.

And no way in hell was she going to do the second.

Chapter 9

MICKEY FOUND ROBIN TO BE EXACTLY AS HE EXPECTED, as apt a student in a kayak as she was a magnificent pilot. Whitewater boats were twitchy, particularly on flat water like a lake, and some people never got used to it. Robin easily transferred that dancer–martial arts balance and flexibility onto the water.

"The direction you go as you paddle is largely controlled by your hips. Shift your hips right and you'll go right, even though it will feel as if you're leaning the other way."

"And I have such nice hips."

"I should never have told you that."

"You weren't the first," she teased.

"Who was?"

Robin tried to paddle away from him, but however natural she might be in the air, she still had a lot to learn in a kayak.

Mickey slipped up close behind her. He dipped the fingers of one hand into the cold water and flicked it at her bare back—neither of them were wearing shirts.

She didn't yelp as he'd expected. Instead, with a backward flick of her paddle, she sent a sheet of freezing water into his face and chest. Okay, maybe she was learning the truly essential skills of kayaking faster than he'd thought.

Then she carved a turn and almost went for an icy

swim, one reason they were staying within twenty feet of the shore, where the water was less than two feet deep, while she practiced.

Robin did manage to slide up to him without capsizing, their kayaks pointing in opposite directions so that they wound up face-to-face. He grabbed the cockpit cowling of her boat and pulled her in close. And as she melted into a kiss, he dipped his other hand overboard and raised it to cradle her breast with his cold hand.

It almost got out of control, and they both would have gone swimming, but they managed to stop in time. Barely. He'd never been with a woman who was so damned much fun.

"Who was your first, Mr. Smart-Ass?"

"Debra Monroe. Or maybe Debbie."

"You don't remember?" She sounded melodrama-heroine aghast.

"I was a very willing sixteen, as was she—though she was far more experienced than I was. It was on one of Dad's multiday, campout-in-the-wilderness raft trips. Trust me, if she hadn't lived in Kansas, or maybe it was Oklahoma, I would have gone back for a lot more lessons and ended up more sure of her name. How about you?"

"Davis–Monthan."

"Davis…wait a minute. Isn't that the name of an Air Force base? The one where they store all of the old planes?"

"Smart boy."

"You lost your virginity to an Air Force base?"

"Might as well have." She sounded chagrined and started into paddling along the lakeshore again. But she wasn't racing away from him, rather just continuing her practice.

He rowed after her. "Care to explain that one?"

"Not particularly."

"Hey, no fair. I told you about Debbie."

"Or was it Debra? And are you sure about the Monroe part of it?"

Well, he had been a moment ago. Of course now he was distracted, as he had been a hundred times over the last half hour, by watching Robin paddle. Those strong soldier and waitress muscles flexed and rolled beneath the creamy skin of her bare back. Her short hair left her shoulders wholly exposed, as well as that wonderful transition to her neckline.

When she stopped, he was paying attention to the wrong things and rammed right into her, again almost tipping them both into the water.

She waited for him to recover and pull up alongside her. Soon they were floating with a hand each lightly resting on the curled edge of the other's cockpit.

"You're getting pink," he commented.

"I'm not embarrassed. I just don't think I should be feeding your prurient fantasies."

"No." He pointed a finger at her breasts and then at the setting sun. "You may soon be Robin Redbreast though. And I'm a guy, of course I have prurient fantasies whether or not you feed them, which trust me, you do. Floating here next to you, they've gone right off the charts and I can't wait to get you back to shore to try out some more of them."

"Let's go."

He didn't let go his hold on her kayak.

She sighed and relaxed. "Okay. Okay. You know that Davis–Monthan is where they store the old planes until they need them again because they don't rot in the high desert. B-52s, Chinook helicopters, A-10 Warthog gunships, all of them. They call it the Boneyard."

"Right, though I've never been there."

"Then you wouldn't know that it's about five hundred yards from Phoebe's Tucson Truck Stop. Phoebe is my grandmother and she founded the place. That's where I grew up. Our house was halfway between the air base and truck stop, same side of the I-10 Interstate."

Mickey used his free hand to slowly turn them, so that her chest moved out of the sun—her back wasn't pinking yet. But her skin was so fair, he needed to get her in a shirt soon, as much as he hated the idea.

"I was fifteen. There was this drop-dead gorgeous guy. He was eighteen, fresh out of high school, and working a civilian job at Davis. It was like he knew everything about everything."

"He should be shot for touching a girl who was—" Mickey could feel the heat rising.

"I'm the one who tripped him."

"Still." He tried not to fume. At least he and Debbie had been the same age. Or Debra.

"It was over a decade ago, Hamilton. Thanks for your ire, but he's a nice guy, married now with two kids that he supports pretty well. Get over it."

He knew if he kept fuming, he wasn't going to get the rest of her story. Still, as a tour guide and later a ski instructor, he'd had plenty of opportunities with very cute young girls. And, goddamn it, he hadn't touched a one of them despite the blatant offers.

"You're still jealous, aren't you?"

"Maybe."

She leaned over to kiss his shoulder. "You really are sweet, especially when you think you're being all gruff."

Being called sweet while you're wishing to rearrange someone's face didn't sit very well.

"Were you one of those *hot* fifteen-year-olds?" he teased her, trying to find a lighter mood.

"I sizzled. Just like now."

"No argument from this boy."

"Anyhow, there's this thing called Celebrity Row at the Boneyard. One of every type of aircraft in storage is lined up there. I decided I wanted to have sex in every single make and model. Most of those are all sealed and locked, but in the vastness of the Boneyard, you can always find a model that's accessible. There are over four thousand aircraft parked there all in various states of storage or being scraped for parts."

It was a good quest. If you were going to go after something outrageous, you should really go for it. "How many different aircraft are parked on Celebrity Row?"

"Sixty-one at the time."

"What?" His shout echoed across the lake and sent several ducks aloft from where they'd been nosing in the grasses along the water's edge. "You had sex with this guy sixty-one times?"

"Jealous?" She practically crowed it out.

"No." *Desperately*. The thought of someone, anyone, ever having Robin at all other than himself was an uncomfortable thought no matter how ridiculous. "Envious."

Her laugh totally pegged him as deep green with jealousy.

"We only made it through four aircraft. The B-52 was first, because of course it had to be. But the plane was the only good part of it. It hurt like hell and I bled like a stuck pig. Scared the hell out of both of us."

"Grim" was all Mickey could think to say.

"We tried a helicopter next, a Huey as a matter of fact, the old UH-1 Iroquois Huey, the great-granddaddy of yours."

"I'll take that as a good sign."

"You'd think, but it wasn't. It didn't hurt that time, but it wasn't all that much fun. By the time we tried the big B-1B bomber, I was beginning to wonder if something was wrong with me. After the monstrous C-5A Galaxy, I decided that it wasn't me, it was him. I was seventeen by the time I tried again; turns out I was right. He still ranks as the single most boring time I've ever had."

"Most boring four times." Mickey was—

"Yep. That making you feel better?"

"Way."

"Let's get ashore and I'll make you feel much better in another way."

"No argument from me."

They were soon sprawled out in between the two sleeping bags. She was on top and doing something magic with her hips that she hadn't demonstrated before and was absolutely making his eyes cross.

"And, Mickey?" she gasped out.

"Yes?" he managed. He knew her well enough now to feel when she was rising, climbing ever so close to that breaking crest. He wasn't that far away himself, and speech was becoming a major challenge.

"Every…one of…my best times?"

"Uh-huh." He was concentrating on just how far into

her he could reach. He shifted his hips side to side to make sure there wasn't a wasted millimeter.

"Every one of them…has been with you."

Her rocketing over the top cascaded through her and sent him off as well.

But Mickey was a mental step back from his thrashing body, a single step that was a whole world away.

No one had ever told him that he was their best time. It made him feel…

Strong.

Powerful.

Incredibly male.

And it awoke a tenderness that couldn't wait to fold her into its arms as soon as the aftershocks released their control of her body. In moments, she would lay once more upon his chest, where it felt most perfect.

Chapter 10

"DOG MEAT, HAMILTON!" ROBIN SCREAMED FROM where she had managed to back paddle and save herself—an eddy current at the side of the raging river. In a pool perhaps twice the length of her tiny little kayak, it slowly whirled her in a clockwise circle every ten seconds.

Large rock.

Cliff face.

A little bit of grass.

More cliff face.

A roaring menace of Class III rapids pounding over rocks.

More roaring menace, ultimately launching itself off a ten-foot-high waterfall into more psychotic roil of Class III madness.

Large rock.

Cliff face.

A little bit of grass.

She let the kaleidoscopic whorl continue until she was starting to feel a little nauseous. With an ill-timed flick of the paddle, she almost launched herself out into the maelstrom rather than moving to the side of the current as she'd intended.

Robin managed to recover before she shot out of her safe haven. Her next attempt to move to the edge of the whorl so that she could grab on to the cliff wall threatened to launch her once again into the death-and-destruction zone.

So she sat in her toy-sized boat twirling in slow circles, contemplating the various forms of murder she would be perpetrating on one Mickey "Blue Eyes" Hamilton, if by some miracle—like maybe a *Star Trek* transporter beam—she was rescued.

Getting a helicopter in here safely would be a hell of a trick and getting back out even harder.

No way to climb the cliff even if she abandoned her kayak. Hell, a gecko with its sticky little feet probably couldn't scale this sucker.

A sharp bleat, only a little louder than the thunderous river, had her looking upward. A baby mountain sheep, still more fuzz than fur, was looking down at her from an impossible perch several stories above her. Then it laughed at her again and scampered away up the cliff.

Fine!

There was still no way to climb up the sheer—

Just to drive their casual arrogance home, a mother sheep with huge, curling horns went scampering up after her kid.

Double fine!

She glared back down at the eddy, where she was tucked into the only refuge from the mini Niagara Falls and—not being some crazy breed of mountain sheep— would be stuck here until the end of her days.

On the next spin around, she eyed the tiny clump of grass. Which was just that, tiny. Only if she wanted to live the rest of her life in fetal position would she fit there. But better that than the Rapids of Doom. She was designing her tiny grass hut, built season by season from carefully nurtured grass fronds, when another slow spin revealed Mickey coming toward her.

He'd been leading the way all day. Had graduated her from flat water to Class I, which basically meant the water was moving on its own rather than standing still.

After lunch, and some more splendidly mind-numbing sex, he'd introduced her to Class II. A little rough water, a rock to dodge, a couple of one-foot drops, just enough that she could feel herself go partially weightless.

Ah, but she had been young and naive then. After the first section of Class II, she'd foolishly decided that she could get to enjoy this sport.

Worse, she'd told that to Mickey.

They'd come out of something Mickey had called the "high side of Class II" in good shape and back into a lazy curve in the river that she now understood was a low Class I.

River savvy.

Nothing the girl couldn't do.

Fly to fire.

Screw a man until they both went blind.

Take a Class II rapid in stride on only her second day ever on a river.

…yeah right. Not anymore.

Now, she was going to kill Mickey for suckering her into this. Nothing had prepared her for what had awaited them around that last lazy bend.

Mickey had given her one of those all-knowing smiles of his as they approached it.

"What?"

"Listen."

She'd listened. And heard what sounded like ocean waves, which made no sense. The nearest ocean was hundreds of miles away, safely on the other side of the largest mountain on the whole continent.

Then it had sounded more like a train.

A freight train.

One in a big goddamn hurry.

Then, like a flight of helicopters hovering low around the corner, the pounding fusillade of sound echoing off the canyon walls. The air, which had been lazily pine scented, was now thickening with tiny water drops like when you were working close to a spraying fire hose.

They'd come out of the bend. The valley had been moseying along beside them in pleasant pull outs with charming stands of trees and brush. The occasional moose—damn, but they were huge—had watched them go by as the cute giants chewed on a handy berry bush. Around that fateful River Bend of Last Resort, the valley walls had shot upward until it looked like that scene with the statues carved out of thousand-foot-high cliffs in one of the *Lord of the Ring* movies.

As she watched the standing waves in a stupefied way for the length of three heartbeats, she was swept into the rapid. It became a blur of disconnected near disasters.

Rock! Turn hard to the right.

Another! Turn the other way and paddle for all she was worth…which only made her go faster!

Hole behind a rock. Mickey had told her holes were bad, very bad. Back paddle until her arms were screaming and then shoot around the lip of it.

Backward through the next rapid!

Dig in a blade and spin like a top.

Almost going over.

Saving herself with a quick stab of the paddle and a lucky ricochet off a submerged boulder.

Off a two-foot jump, a jarring bounce off a rock, and a face full of ice water.

She didn't remember quite how she'd finally reached the last-ditch sanctuary of the little eddy current that was destined to be her new home for all eternity, but she did.

Another gentle whirl around. Big rock. Cliff face. Future grass hut. Cliff face. Big rock. Mad rapids that she'd survived and would never ever go near again.

Mickey paddling toward her...going *against* the rapids that were waiting to kill her.

He progressed toward her, conquering the river's racing current inch by inch. His double-ended paddle whirled like a windmill in a hurricane. She twisted her head around to keep him in view for as much of her slow twirl as possible.

His arm and chest muscles were finally explained. He looked like a goddamn god driving toward her against nature's best efforts to drag him away. Well, at least the last thing she was ever going to see in this life was an example of quite how exceptional a human male could be, because...*Damn, girl!*

With a last wild effort, his kayak launched into her eddy current and stopped close beside hers.

"Hey, Robin Pink Breast. What are you doing here?" he asked, all cheery as if this was somehow fun.

He was barely out of breath.

She hit him.

—∿∿—

Mickey saw the paddle blade coming at his shoulder but couldn't dodge it in time. The blow knocked him sideways, and he was over into the icy water before he could get his paddle lined up.

He went with the roll, slashed his paddle hard, and used his momentum and a judicious dig with his blade to pop back up. He shook his head to clear the water from his ears and hair. Chill water slipped down his back and found its way inside the spray skirt. An involuntary shiver ran up his spine.

Robin was gaping at him. "How did you do that?"

"What? The Eskimo roll?" he had to shout for her to hear him over the roar of the rapids.

"Yes, the Eskimo roll," she mimicked his voice with a heavy layer of anger. "Something that looks useful as hell and you don't bother to teach to me before trying to feed me to a river that's even now gnashing its teeth at me. It wants to eat me for lunch. And not in a good way."

"No, I'm the only one who gets to do that." Not even a tiny bit of softening at the recent memory of how much fun he'd had down between her lovely legs during lunch. He also recalled how incredibly she had returned the favor.

"Well…" His guess had been right. Robin, when angry, was indeed formidable. When she hadn't come up to the chute behind him, he'd been terrified at what he might find. At first he'd searched for a flipped boat and a battered body going by.

The image of her trapped in a hole, submerged hard against a rock, had sent him racing back upstream. His relief at spotting her slowly whirling around in an eddy current like some prima ballerina had made him laugh with relief and swallow a fair amount of river water from a sudden blast of spray.

At least it wasn't fear. Anger on the river was much easier to deal with than cowering fear.

"The reason I didn't teach you the roll is that it takes hours of practice, even in a swimming pool. Doing that to you on a freezing lake would not have been a kindness. And then using it in a rapids is a whole other technique entirely. That's why I showed you how to get out of the boat if you got flipped. You do remember that, don't you?"

Without hesitation, she tapped the pull loop on the front of the spray skirt that wrapped around her body just below her breasts and was hooked over the edge of the cockpit cowling. "Pull and swim out of the kayak. Try to keep ahold of the paddle," she recited dutifully.

"Good girl."

"Stop being condescending, Hamilton, or I'll go for the throat next time I whack you."

"Safety, Robin. It's—"

"Safety?" she exploded at him as they whirled around opposite sides of the eddy current. "Safety?" It was nearly a scream. "You launch me into Class Eighty-Three rapids with no training and you're talking about safety?"

He considered his response for a moment, then answered in his best schoolroom voice. "As I explained before, there are only five classes of rapids, Robin."

He barely managed to duck in time, so that her paddle blade bounced off his helmet rather than chopping off his head. Her wild flail almost flipped her over. He saved her a dunking with a strong paddle stroke in her direction and a quick grab.

"Uh, thanks," she managed a little sheepishly once she was stable again.

"Okay." Mickey wondered how deep her reservoir of anger might be once tapped. He hoped that it had mostly run its course. "Let's talk through how to attack this rapid."

"I can't even see it with all this whirling around."

Mickey waited for the eddy to spin them to the right position, then he nudged her boat sharply forward. It slid smoothly ahead to bump lightly against the big rock that defined the downstream edge of the eddy and would offer the best view of the run. The motion had kicked his boat back-end-first past the eddy line and out into the river current. A couple of quick paddle strokes and he was able to join her.

Her scowl was back, but she didn't explain why.

Mickey decided that ignoring it was the safest policy. He pointed his paddle at the rapids.

"Once we peel out across the eddy line here, you want to aim for the big downstream V. See the clear green water?"

At her tight nod, he continued quickly.

"That will shoot you past those two big rocks, but don't worry, these rapids aren't big enough for there to be any keeper holes." He decided that his description of getting caught in one of those had been a poor choice of mid-trip stories. A keeper hole trapped kayaks, kayakers, and—if it killed them—their bodies in dangerous churning backflows that were almost impossible to escape. Rescues from keeper holes typically required a team with ropes or a river raft that was far bigger than the specific hole—the method his dad had used to save him the one time he'd thought he was strong enough to break out of one on his own.

"Thank God for small favors. But what about that?" Robin aimed her paddle at the little waterfall.

"The Tea Cup?"

"You're calling the Mighty Furrow of Death and Destruction a Tea Cup?"

"Sure. See how it squeezes between the two big rocks? And then it dumps through in a smooth line as if you're pouring tea?"

"And then it kills me."

"Let me show you a trick."

"Can I kill you afterwards?"

"Sure."

"Okay then."

"As you go off the Tea Cup—"

"Mighty Furrow of Death and Destruction," she insisted. "MFDD."

"—lean back and try to lift up the bow by kicking your legs upward. It's mostly a hip move, and I know from experience you have really amazing control of your hips." That got most of the smile he'd been looking for. "It's called a Boof."

"So you want me to Boof the Tea Cup before I kill you for leading me into the hungry maw of the Mighty Furrow of Death and Destruction?"

"Exactly!" He anticipated her swing this time, caught her arm, and used it to drag her against him. She melted into his kiss just like she did every time.

He forced himself to let go of her before he totally lost his head and ended up dunking them both. The water really was cold and hadn't stopped slithering out of his hair and down his back.

"Follow right behind me and do what I do as exactly as you can. Once I'm through the drop, I'll clear off to the side and wait for you at the bottom of the Tea

Cup just in case you bungle the Boof. But you won't. You've taken to this more naturally than anyone I've ever taught."

—〰〰—

And with one of his smarmy grins, he was off and Robin was digging in to stay in his wake. Ever so impressed with his own teaching abilities…yet he had somehow convinced her to follow him.

They "peeled out" across the eddy line and her gently whirling Pool of Everlasting Safety was lost behind her before she even had time to say good-bye to her imaginary grass hut or the sneering sheep who watched over it.

Paddle left, paddle right. Twist around the rock. Drop into the downstream V—which was like tipping a Firehawk into a steep dive. They accelerated so fast that it snapped her head back.

The MFDD zoomed into the foreground of her sight line.

She almost missed copying Mickey's little sideways jog to line up in the center of it, and then he was gone, flying out into space flat and level, paddle raised over his head in both hands like a banner of triumph.

A sound broke briefly louder than the rushing waters. It might have been a *Whoop!* of delight. It might have been a scream of terror. She knew which hers would sound like as she went over.

Then he disappeared vertically out of sight, perhaps plunged forever into the murky depths of the crystal clear waters.

Deep breath, Robin. Last moment of existence!

The roaring water was intensified…magnified…

explosively loud in the narrow cleft of rock. And then
the water went smooth, accelerating so quickly that
again she was slammed against her cockpit's back band.
At the last moment, she remembered to pivot her hips
upward, trying to kick the sky.

Her kayak shot out into space—straight and true—
and she was flying!

For an instant she hung weightlessly above the
stream. The water rushed by far below her.

Mickey paddled idly backward off to the side of the
landing pool, looking up at her with a huge smile on
his face.

And then gravity took her.

She plummeted ten feet straight down.

Hit the water so hard that the boat disappeared under-
water right up to her chest.

For a moment only head, shoulders, and upraised
arms—she didn't remember lifting her paddle in exactly
the same triumphant way that Mickey had—were clear
of the river. And spray spewed outward in a beautiful
plume in every direction.

Then, like a cork, the kayak once more lofted her
above the river, though by only a few inches this time,
before she smacked back into the water again. She dug
in with her paddle to control her line, and Mickey shot
forward to join her.

Side by side, they raced down through the lower rapids.

It took Robin a moment more to recognize that the
sound echoing off the canyon walls, a high note over the
quieting basso roar of the river, was her own laughter.

"How about we just stay here and never leave?" Robin looked up at the sunrise light glinting off Denali. The mountain seemed smaller, less daunting now than it had before. The river flowed by only a few steps from her feet, where she sat on the grassy bank.

The river had gone lazy and, except for a few little sections, was going to be an easy float into town, which lay just a few miles away.

In just a day and two nights, she had become immersed in this life. Okay, it had drawbacks. Hanging the food in a tree at night. Sleeping with a loaded rifle that Macy had loaned them—a big, nasty, bear-killing rifle. Knowing that if she left the relative protection of the valley and its constant soft breezes that she'd be eaten alive by mosquitoes.

But right now there was warm sun, amazing views, and a very handsome man cooking her breakfast over an open campfire beside a burbling river.

"You call it, Robin, and I'll build us a cabin here in the woods."

Right. Like that was going to happen. Living under a blanket of snow and ice for six months or more of the year. Her Tucson blood would freeze in her veins and she'd be a permanent icicle long before spring melt out.

"Nice thought, but I'll bet this place is idyllic for about three weeks a year."

"Longer, but I think it's more the company than the environment." He handed her a plate stacked high with pancakes drowned in maple syrup.

"How?"

"Old camping secret."

"You can tell me but—"

"—I'd have to marry you."

"Good luck with that." She took a bite and it was amazing, better than anything at Phoebe's, and breakfast was their specialty. They had the richness of whole wheat and the intense flavor of the tiny wild strawberries she'd seen him picking earlier. He'd even packed along maple syrup and butter without her noticing. "Damn, these are good, Hamilton. You should use these as an audition when you *do* find someone you want to marry. Audition, hell. Use it as a closer. Totally killer."

There was a pinch at the thought of another woman having Mickey Hamilton, but Harrow women didn't wed. But if she was looking for the perfect candidate to give her a daughter and continue the Harrow line, Mickey just might be that.

She took another mouthful and glanced over at him. He was frozen with a forkful of pancake halfway between plate and mouth. He looked as if he'd been dipped in plastic.

"What?" There was something working across his face.

For all his guyness, Mickey was lousy at hiding his thoughts and feelings—such a straight-up, honest guy. Emotions flowed easily across his features…but she had to be reading this wrong. She bit down on a sour berry.

"Oh no, Hamilton. No way are thinking what I think you're thinking."

"What am I thinking?" His voice was low, almost dangerous.

"Look here now. We've had some great sex and a lot of fun. That's all I'm looking for. A summer with maybe a few more fires in it and a great lover in my bed. That's it. That's as deep as Robin Harrow goes.

Shallow, fast-moving current, that's me." She pointed at the river, which ran slow and deep by their camp.

Mickey narrowed his eyes at her. He opened his mouth, but she held up a threatening fork to warn him.

"I'm serious. You're wonderful, Mickey. Perhaps the best man I've ever met and definitely the best I've ever bedded. And when I'm ready to have a kid, you'd be a prime candidate. But I come from three generations of single women. We absolutely do not—"

Something clarified in his features.

"We do not…" She tried to continue but couldn't find the words she'd meant to say when confronted with the suddenly self-assured look on his face.

"I love you, Robin."

She tried to answer the flat statement past the tightness in her chest but couldn't manage it.

"I didn't know it," Mickey continued in that same soft, reasonable tone that had coaxed her out of the safety of her eddy pool and back into the mad river. "But I do now that I've said it. There's only one woman for me, Robin Harrow. You're it. So I'm thinking you're going to have to deal with it."

"Deal with it! *Deal with it?* Are you fucking nuts, Hamilton? Look at me."

"One of my favorite pastimes," he said calmly. Perfectly calmly. The squint was gone and that little smile of amusement was back.

"Well, cut it out!"

"No promises on that. You're an awfully attractive woman to look at."

"Fine, look all you want. But take back that other thing you said."

He shrugged and continued eating his pancakes as if this was in any way a rational conversation. Those blue eyes studied her.

Unlike her normal tendency, she knew that striking out at him wasn't going to help a thing. Last time, she'd smacked him was in the helmet with her paddle…and he'd kissed her.

A kiss she'd quite enjoyed.

And something she so couldn't deal with at this particular moment.

"Damn you. All I wanted was a simple, uncomplicated fling. Was that too much to ask?"

"Appears so." He kept eating his stupid pancakes. She looked down at her own, missing only a few bites. It wasn't pettiness that made her cast them into the river; it was that there was no way she'd be able to keep them down if she ate another bite.

Fish began poking at them as they drifted downstream. They'd be long gone before they reached Larch Creek.

She tossed the empty plate on the grass between them.

A look of sharp pain crossed his face. He looked from the empty plate to her face and back down.

She didn't mean it that way, as if she was rejecting his delicious food just because he'd…said that thing he'd said. But she couldn't bring herself to say anything else either. So she pulled her knees tight up against her chest and turned once more to stare out at the river.

Why did it have to get complicated? Most men would be glad to have her willing body and a summer of fun.

That was Mickey's problem: he wasn't most men.

Mickey stared at the empty plate between them on the grass after Robin threw his food away.

He loved her. It didn't matter how briefly they'd known each other. What they had or hadn't done or said. It was Truth and he knew it.

He loved her…but she didn't love him.

Some great sex.

Was that really all she thought it was? Sure, it had started there. But he wasn't an overeager and clumsy boy of sixteen losing his virginity to a girl whose name he no longer exactly remembered. He knew that sex did not equal love. But Robin, the person behind that amazing sexual punch, had dazzled him even more.

Calm.

He would be calm.

He finished his pancakes, wondering where the flavor had gone. Without comment, he took her plate, his, and the fry pan to the edge of the river and washed them clean.

While he was washing the dishes, the rest of her words came clear.

"Wait a minute!" He spun back to face her.

"What?"

"You'd purposely have a kid without a family?"

"Sure. I want a girl someday. Hopefully a cute one, like Emily's kid, Tessa."

"Emily *and* Mark's kid," he managed through clenched teeth.

"Well, sure. That works for Emily, but no way am I going to marry some guy to get one. Mom didn't. Not Grandma either."

"In what kind of screwed-up world does that make any sense at all? Sure, there are single parents out there, even never married ones, but it isn't the kind of thing any idiot does on purpose." Mickey tried to picture growing up without having his mother or his father. Even trying to imagine it ripped at his gut. He'd had plenty of single-parented friends, but he could see the damage it did. "You'd raise a kid without a family?" The anger was heating up inside, and he wished he hadn't finished his breakfast, which was roiling in his gut like Class IV rapids.

"Worked for me."

"Yeah. It made you fricking crazy."

"No wedding, Mickey. No marriage. I'll be no man's wife. Crap! Now I sound like some stupid Irish ballad."

"I'd no more give you a child to raise on your own than…than…" He didn't have a worse than. "I grant that some women have no choice. But what your mother did and your grandmother before her, that was a choice. It was cruel and nasty and narcissistic."

"No!" she shouted at him. "It's because men are such assholes!"

Mickey knew if he said another word, it would be harsh and impossibly cruel and that he'd never ever be able to take it back.

It took more strength than he'd ever known he had to turn back to the cleanup along the bank. One of the plates was gone, sunk out of sight despite the clear water.

——⁓⁓——

Robin stared at Mickey's back.

She was right; she knew it. Maybe not right for his world but definitely right for her own.

It would have been better if she hadn't just called Mickey an asshole, but that boat had already sailed. She could see that she'd hurt him, but he'd get over that. At least she hoped so.

But Mickey was different every single time. She'd expect one thing and he'd be another, time after time.

If he wasn't going to get over it?

She looked upstream.

The high lake where they had made such love just two days ago was forever away from where she now sat. Beyond the uncrossable fall off the Mighty Tea Cup of Death and Destruction. That had been the idyll—near enough the closing bell of their relationship as more than fellow pilots, though she hadn't known it at the time.

A moose and her calf had wallowed along the river's edge not a hundred feet from their quiet camp last night. More birdlife than would ever visit the Tucson desert, migrated through, spending a minute, an hour, or a day before continuing their journey north. Or perhaps they were birds who had come to spend the summer. To stay awhile and breed in this valley. Even now they might be in the bushes all around them, making baby birds.

Not her. Not even with Mickey Hamilton. Ten minutes ago, she had never wanted to leave and now she couldn't wait to get away.

She tried not to think of what lay ahead.

Instead, she simply did another thing that her mother had taught her. Robin began reeling in the strings. Mentally breaking her connection to those around her.

Jeannie, Denise, Vern…she would fly with them as she'd been contracted to do.

Mark and Emily…well, at least she now knew that

the Night Stalkers truly deserved the respect she'd always had for them.

Mickey...how the hell was she supposed to cut him off? But her choices were limited, gone. Only one safe path remained down the river. She didn't help him pack up camp or douse the fire or load the kayaks. She sat like a stone as if he had petrified her into a river boulder—the kind with a lethal keeper hole just around the corner.

He set her gear in front of her, and when he began pulling on his own spray skirt and helmet, she did the same.

They entered the water together.

It was a very quiet trip to Larch Creek.

Robin spent the time slowly folding in on herself. She tried not to feel as if she was sitting in a little eddy current, spinning quietly out of control while she went stark raving mad.

Chapter 11

ROBIN KNEW SHE WAS OVERREACTING. OR AT LEAST not making sense to anyone other than herself.

Their triumphant return to Larch Creek from the wilds of Alaska should have been a time of stories and laughter. Of sitting around that big table in the town's only restaurant and recounting the saga of the Mighty Furrow of Death and Destruction. Perhaps turn it into a ballad that would be passed down through the generations.

Instead, she'd done the only thing she was capable of doing.

She'd walked through the little town, leaving Mickey to return the kayaks and other gear. A few people greeted her, but she didn't know anyone here and just kept walking with only a nod of acknowledgment.

When she reached the oddly named B&B, the Bookish Bed and Breakfast, she looked at the shower. The one that she'd been looking forward to showering in with Mickey.

Instead, though it was still mid-morning, she crawled into her room—*their* room, his pack resting on the floor reminded her. She set his pack against the outside of the door and bolted it before crawling into bed.

Robin didn't cry. Didn't believe in crying because it certainly never fixed anything. *Crying is weakness!* And though her eyes burned and her nose ran, she lay there under the covers until she finally lost herself in the oblivion of sleep.

———⁓⁓⁓———

Mickey had thought to return the gear and slink away. He'd seen Robin walk off to the B&B without a word. Maybe what he'd do was go sleep in his helo. Or call up Tim the smokejumper and see if the Alaska Fire Service needed some air drops until the next MHA call.

Maybe he'd go find Vern and get good and truly shit faced.

Maybe he'd find a bottle of scotch and do it all by himself.

They'd pulled out on the riverbank right across the road from French Pete's restaurant-bar. He carted the gear back up onto the porch, stuffed it down beneath the blue truck hood that might have dated back to the 1930s, complete with a Plymouth winged victory chrome ornament—all that was missing was the truck. Who knows, maybe it was somewhere here under all this crap.

And then he stood there without a clue what to do.

Well, if he was going to get plastered, he was standing on the front porch of a bar.

He shouldered his way in through the front door, raised a hand once in case anyone was calling his name, and went up to the bar.

A tough-looking man sat behind the bar playing chess with a girl who sat on a high stool across from him.

"Scotch," Mickey managed with a throat that had gone unexpectedly gruff with the morning's disuse. He tried clearing his throat but it didn't help. "Glass and a bottle"—he considered a moment—"without the glass."

The man looked at him for a long moment before turning back to the game and moving one of his pawns. Then he reached back without leaving his stool, snagged a heavy stoneware mug, and filled it from a nearby pot of black coffee.

Mickey looked down at the cup in front of him and back up at the bartender.

The man's eyes were clear brown, frank, and assessing. At first, Mickey thought this was going to turn into a confrontation—maybe with him beating the shit out of the guy and climbing over the bar himself to grab the bottle he wanted, that he could *see* sitting on the back shelf.

But the guy simply waited.

The little girl, maybe ten years old, waited as well. Neither one was watching the board; they were both watching him.

"That's better for what ails you, lad," the bartender offered in a laconic tone. "Trust me, I know." And then he and the girl turned back to their game.

Mickey stared at the cup for a long moment before reaching for the sugar. No packets around—not white, blue, yellow, or pink. There was only one of those old-fashioned glass jars with the silver lid. He poured a healthy spoonful and began stirring it in.

He prepared himself for sludge but instead tasted a fine French roast—that he'd pretty much murdered with a sludge-load's worth of sugar.

He set the mug down on the bar as the floor creaked behind him. Mickey braced himself for one of Vern's friendly slaps on the back, sure to be accompanied by a knowing nod and wink.

That would be good.

Because then Mickey could beat the shit out of him. He'd never actually been in a bar brawl before, but this felt like his moment. He clenched his fists in preparation.

But instead of a heavy slap, the person moved from behind him and levered herself awkwardly up onto the stool on the side away from the chess game.

"Emily? What are you doing here?"

"I flew up to visit my husband."

"You flew? In your state?" She'd gotten bigger in the week since he'd last seen her.

"On an airplane!"

"Oh." *Duh.*

"Now that the pleasantries are over. What the *hell* did you do to *my* pilot?"

"Does the whole goddamn world have to be mad at me?" He spun back to face his mug of coffee and stared across the bar at the scotch. Sitting right there, snuggled up between the Kentucky bourbon and the Irish whiskey.

Another glance at the bartender was answered with a shake of the man's head even though he hadn't looked up from his chess game. Mickey sipped his saccharine coffee.

Actually, having Emily Beale mad at him was a new one.

"You"—the ire in her tone forced him to turn back to her as assuredly as if she had grabbed his chin and yanked—"mess up my new pilot so badly that she doesn't even recognize me waddling down the street? You've earned a great deal to answer for, Mr. Hamilton."

Telling her that the way she walked had nothing to do with waddling and a great deal to do with striking

terror into people didn't seem like a good approach at
the moment.

As a matter of fact, he had no idea what was a good
approach at the moment. He was ready to take someone
apart just on general principles. But not a pregnant lady.
Where was Vern when he needed someone to pound on?

Or the fuck-'em-and-run excuse of a father who'd
messed with Robin's head in the first place? He was
gonna hunt down the little shit and break him into teeny-
tiny fireman bits and then bury his ass under a four-
hundred-gallon load of retardant.

"Mickey!" Emily's call for his attention woke something deeper. It woke the memory of Robin tossing his
food and his heart into the goddamn river and denying
who *she* was.

"I? *Me?*" He spun to face the only target he had.
"This is somehow *my* fault?" His voice was climbing
to a full shout and he was helpless to stop it. "I tell her I
love her and this is what I get?"

Emily didn't even blink, like she was studying a toad.

"Fine! To hell with her and to hell with you."

The silence that followed was deafening.

Sorry, he mouthed to the kid, who just shrugged.
Hanging out in a bar, she'd clearly heard worse language. He shoved off the stool and headed for the door.

Vern came up to him, and Mickey didn't care if it was
going to be a friend's commiseration of *What's wrong,
buddy?* or a *What the fuck, dude?* —he didn't need either
one. He shoved Vern hard in the center of the chest and
sent him flying backward into a chair that would have
dumped him to the floor if he hadn't banged hard up
against a wall first.

Mickey pounded out the door and looked up and down the street. No liquor store.

The only gin joint in town was the one behind him.

Fine.

He took a right and walked down the street.

Past the point where Robin had walked away from him, he headed out of town.

Chapter 12

ROBIN IGNORED THE KNOCK THAT HAD WOKEN HER and the rattle of the doorknob that followed. After a long moment, a set of heavy steps walked back down the hallway and thudded slowly down the stairs.

About a minute later, the heavy footsteps returned and she heard a key unlock the door.

Didn't Mickey get that his pack *outside* the door meant go away?

A chair scraped on the wooden floor and creaked as someone sat in it close beside the bed.

Go away, Mickey.

She kept her head under the covers. It was hot under here with all her clothes on, but Robin was not going to talk to Mickey while she lay in a bed. They had made love in tents and under the stars along the banks of Larch Creek in both broad daylight and soft twilight. They had yet to do so in a bed and she sure wasn't going to start a fight from one.

Go away, Mickey! Robin tried to think it louder, loud enough that he'd hear it.

It didn't seem to be working.

Well, Mr. I'm-So-Patient-And-Calm, you're just going to have to get the message at some point.

He hadn't even fought for her. She'd dumped his food, been a stonewalled bitch, and he'd let her get away with it like some kind of spoiled brat.

"It's not that I'm spoiled," she told the corner of the pillow that was under the covers with her.

Or had she hurt him so badly he wasn't able to respond? She didn't like that idea at all.

"Then what are you?" The tone of the voice, muffled by the blankets over her head, was so unexpected that, for a half moment, she thought just maybe the pillow was answering.

She lifted a corner to peek out.

"Emily?"

She couldn't account for how Mickey Hamilton had transformed into Emily Beale. Robin went back under the covers but figured that was too chickenshit, even for her. Tossing back the sheet and too-warm blanket, she sat up and dropped her feet to the floor, still clad in boots muddy from the riverbank.

"Crap!"

"You're a mess, Robin."

"Thanks for flying all the way to Alaska to tell me something I already know, Emily. Really helps."

"Tell me about the fire."

Robin eyed her for a moment.

No hint of sarcasm or humor. No...

"Shit! Next you're going to say *Tell me about your homeworld, Usul*."

"Fine, we can talk about the *Dune* books and the sandworms first if you'd like, but I'd rather talk about the fire."

Robin rubbed her face, trying to shake off the last vestiges of the nap. She felt thick, confused. "Because you know if you asked about Mickey, I'd throw your ass out of here."

"I will say three things to that. First, I'm not stupid. Second, I'm pregnant, soon to be bigger than a Russian Mil Mi-26 super heavy-lift helicopter, so please throw gently. Third, you may find that I don't throw so easily because I'm at least as nasty as you are."

"Yeah right." Robin went to the small sink in the corner of the brightly decorated room. It was her first good look at it—room decor hadn't been at the top of her list when she'd arrived—and she definitely wasn't ready for the results.

It was a room of Pooh. Not just in little ways, a stuffed animal here and a lithograph there. And it wasn't just cutesy touches like pinecone-shaped soap and towels with large, black bear paw prints as if they'd been muddy like the impressions her boots had left on the sheets. Nothing at all Disney about it.

A whole corner of the room had been reshaped to look like a tree had grown right into the side of the house, with a hole high on the side and a crooked sign that said "The Wolery." There was a spinney thicket in the other corner, mostly made of pussy willow branches, that had what might or might not have been a woozle peeking out from among them.

There was an actual round hole in the wall above the head of the bed with a small Kanga and Roo peeking out and an empty larder just visible inside.

"Please tell me your room isn't like this one." She kept her back to Emily as she braced herself against the sink and tried not to look in the mirror. She'd actually be happier if—ha! There was one Mickey hadn't come up with—Christopher *Robin* looked back out at her. She certainly wasn't ready to face herself.

"No." Emily spoke as if this was somehow a rational place and a rational conversation. "We're in the land of *The Little Prince* complete with baobab trees, a beautiful and rather vain rose under a glass dome, and most of an airplane. Tessa sleeps in the cockpit, and our bed is on one of the wings. Thankfully there is no giant snake that has swallowed an elephant whole."

"I can't imagine you being nasty." She grimaced a little at her early nickname of Queen Bitch Beale, but that had been before she knew Emily. "In what ways are you nasty?"

"One step closer, Henderson, and I will not be accountable for my actions." Mickey sat on the riverbank across the road from the aircraft hangars that used the way into town as a runway. The helicopters parked out back, and his key to the Twin 212 was in his pack back at the B&B.

Useless!

Mark stopped three paces away and Mickey refused to look up. He'd only see his own face reflected in Henderson's mirrored shades.

"You know."

Mark tucked his hands in his jeans pockets and turned to look out over the river.

Mickey had been watching a wolf slip silently through the thick stands of yellow larch trees on the other side of the river. No bridge across, the town was on this side and the steeply rising wilderness just fifty feet away on the other.

"I think you're only the second person to ever have yelled at Emily."

Mickey felt really lousy about that. She'd done

nothing to earn the rough edge of his tongue, but he'd needed someone to lash out at.

Mark finally sat two paces off, also facing across the water.

"What did she do when you yelled at her?"

"You think I'm a madman? That's the most dangerous woman I ever met. I'm not suicidal enough to think that yelling at Emily Beale is any kind of a long-term survival tactic."

"Then who was first?"

"Childhood friend named Peter Matthews. Now that's a seriously brave man."

"Peter Matthews." Someone that Mark Henderson considered to be brave must be something. "What? Like the President?"

"One and the same."

Mickey had meant it as a joke. A look at Mark showed that it wasn't.

"They grew up next door to each other," Mark explained as if this was somehow normal.

President of the United States Peter Matthews? "What did she do to *him*?"

"Married me. That seemed to upset him quite a bit. Though the yelling was back when they were kids and apparently had something to do with a brand-new pair of sneakers, the DC Reflecting Pool, and several policeman. She still calls him Sneaker Boy to this day."

Emily with a sense of humor was almost as hard to imagine as anyone calling the President that.

"First time I let her know my feelings for her, it went about as well as it looks like your attempt did."

Mickey was absolutely not ready to talk about Robin.

He tried to wait out Henderson as the wolf slipped away through the larches and out of sight. They were left with only the flowing river to watch.

Mark didn't explain and Mickey couldn't help himself; he finally took the obvious bait.

"So what did Emily do?"

"We were on an aircraft carrier when I kissed her. She slammed me facedown into a ready-room table, then stalked out, climbed into an F/A-18F Super Hornet, and catapulted out of my life."

"Yeah," Mickey agreed, never having even seen an aircraft carrier except on TV and in the movies. "I hate it when that happens."

~~~

Robin moved to the bed and sat on it facing Emily. She did her best to ignore the small piglet peering worriedly up at her from under Emily's chair.

"You really did that to him? Planted his face hard?"

Emily nodded.

"Damn. Knew there was a reason I liked you."

And Emily smiled at her.

Somehow that was all it took for all the pain and anger and hurt to just wash out of her.

"I like you too, Robin."

"Well…" Robin looked for something do with her hands. She took one of the small Pooh pillows that she'd strewn to the floor—this one was hexagonal and made of honeycomb material that looked as if it was really dripping with honey—and gestured for Emily to lean forward. Robin slipped it down behind Emily's back. "Don't get all mushy on me, okay?"

"That's not the sort of women we are."

We? "How did you just do that?"

"Do what?"

"Uh-huh. No Emily games. How did you just make me feel so goddamn important? No, important is the wrong word. So...pleased with who I am."

"That's what I expected you to find in the fire." Emily shrugged. "That's part of why I wouldn't let Mark fly with you. You were supposed to discover that for yourself. Reconnect with the soldier in you who knows who you are."

"Well, it was working until I was a total shit to Mickey this morning." Which she so wasn't going to talk about.

Robin shed her boots, made the bed after brushing out the worst of the mostly dry dirt, and propped up some pillows of her own to lean back against the headboard. There was another chair she could have dragged over, but she didn't want to disturb Eeyore, who was sleeping curled up beneath it. She reached up a hand to tickle Roo's nose where his stuffed head poked out of the hole in the wall. She really was a basket case.

"Maybe I did learn some things. The fire was harsh; the bastard fought us for a week. But the team, damn, Emily, the team you've put together. There's nothing they can't do."

"I know."

"She knows." Robin eyed her carefully but could detect neither sarcasm nor smugness.

Simple fact. If Emily Beale said it, what more was there to question?

"Mickey"—she managed to say his name without

wincing this time—"thought you wouldn't let Mark train me because he wasn't a natural pilot and I was."

"And what's your assessment?"

"Mickey is perceptive in a lot of ways." And she needed to change the topic fast. "But if anyone's a natural, it's him. He's almost as good as you are. And me? I'm not a natural anything. I'm not buying that explanation, even if Mickey did."

"Knew you weren't stupid." Emily settled back in her chair and rested her hands on her belly.

"Oh no, I'm eight kinds of stupid. Maybe I'm just not totally dumb."

"What did you learn during the fire?"

"Back to that again? Fine." Robin started to describe the tactics and—

"Let me rephrase. What did you learn about yourself during the fire?"

That stopped her. Emily's eyes were as pure blue as Mickey's, perhaps a few shades lighter. But there was an edge there that Mickey didn't have. Emily Beale could control an entire company, perhaps an entire regiment, with a single glance. Mickey's eyes were windows to the man within.

Robin considered lying back down and pulling the sheets over her head again. Seriously considered it. Instead she hugged a pillow in the shape of a clay "Hunny" pot.

"Me? What did I learn about me fighting that fire? How little sleep I can go on?"

Emily sighed and Robin hoped it had to do with an ache in her lower back but knew that it didn't.

"Seriously?"

"Seriously."

Robin tried to think of something, she really did. "I know I'm not the best pilot, but I figured that out the moment I climbed into that helo for an interview with the monstrously pregnant Queen Bitch Beale."

Emily laughed with delight at the description.

"But on the fire I learned that I wasn't a bad one either."

"What else?"

Robin shrugged and couldn't think of a thing.

"Okay." Emily stared up at the ceiling painted with green leaves of the Hundred Acre Wood and blue sky beyond. "Let's try this. What did you learn about the other pilots?"

—◦◦◦—

"You weren't planning anything stupid, were you?"

Mickey looked at Henderson. "What, like throwing myself in the river? No, it's too damn cold."

"No. Like thinking about leaving MHA for another outfit."

"Crossed my mind."

"Come on, man. Use that brain of yours."

"Hasn't done me much good so far." Mickey picked at some of the small stones along the riverbank. There weren't any good skipping rocks. He chucked a river-rounded pebble out to midstream; it disappeared into the smooth-flowing water with a tiny *plink* and a small ring of ripples that was washed away almost before they formed.

"Mickey, you're a top wildland firefighter, one of the best. You didn't get here without a lot of hard work."

"So what? A relationship is supposed to be a lot of hard

work? Doesn't that sound like fun?" He chucked another pebble. This one entered with no ripples at all. "Besides, I think Robin already proved the pointlessness of that."

"What *did* you do to her anyway?"

When Emily had asked the question, it had pissed him off royally.

Pissed him off because he only had one answer and didn't know what else he could say. He'd already tried blowing up with heart-of-fire fury…maybe he'd try confessing the truth. He gave in and went with it.

"I fell in love with her."

"And you *told* her?" Mark sounded aghast.

Mickey stared at him.

Mark had slipped his mirrored shades up into his hair and was staring at him like he'd totally lost it.

"Uh, yeah. I did. What was I supposed to do?"

"Aw, shit, Mickey."

━━━◇◇◇━━━

"I also learned how good a leader Mickey is. He doesn't see it, but he is."

"That"—Emily nodded—"is the real reason I wouldn't let Mark fly with you."

"What so that I'd become…" *What? Enamored? No!* "…uh, attracted to Mickey? Pretty bitch-manipulative matchmaker of you, Emily."

"No, you silly goose. I wanted you to understand that you see things as they are, soldier clear. You have just described exactly the strengths and weaknesses of every person on the MHA team. If Mark had flown with you, you wouldn't understand the rarity of that clear vision because he'd have explained it to you. That's why I put you in the lead seat on Firehawk One; you totally pegged me as the Queen Bitch."

"QBB. Queen Bitch Beale. It's a complete phrase," Robin told her. "Though I eventually changed it to Queen Bee Beale, just so you know."

"I appreciate that. They're both accurate, but you already know why."

Did she? Robin thought about it. "Because I'm the same." The words came out slowly as she hunted her way toward the idea. "And it's not that I wield it against others. It's that I, that *we*, demand it from ourselves before all others."

"Head of the class, Harrow."

Robin looked down at her hands. They made sense when she was holding on to collective and cyclic. Even when she was being a waitress, she'd understood her place and what she was doing.

"What is it?" Emily must have seen the confusion that wrenched at Robin's gut.

"If all this is so good, why do I feel so out of control?"

"You mean why did you come and hide under the covers on a beautiful summer morning?"

"Head of the class, Beale." She tried to make it funny. But it wasn't.

"Well, I'm not the one who's in love with Mickey Hamilton, so I can't answer that."

Robin checked Emily's expression.

No teasing.

No sarcasm.

No joking.

Robin really would have preferred if there had been some sign of joking.

She took the Hunny-pot pillow and moved it up to bury her face.

—◦◦◦—

"What did you do after she slammed you into the table for kissing her?" Mickey tried to imagine anyone doing that to Mark Henderson. Then he pictured Robin smacking him on the helmet with her paddle and maybe it wasn't so impossible.

"Went away. Licked my wounds for a while."

"How long a while?"

"Couple days. Maybe even three. I nearly screwed up waiting so long."

Mickey laughed even though he didn't feel like it. "Then?"

Now Mark was the one tossing pebbles. Each one arced high, dug into the water with a sharp *Thwup!* and left a big set of clean rings.

"What?"

"I had a different set of problems to solve than you do." Mark arced another one high.

"What did *you* do?" Mickey tried throwing his own pebble high, but still it entered the water with a quiet *plink*.

"I got emergency leave, flew halfway around the world, and showed up at White House security saying I was her jet-setting, playboy boyfriend. Secret Service was not the least bit happy about it, let me tell you; Frank, the head of the President's Secret Service Protection Detail, still hasn't forgiven me for slipping through his security even with the extra help I had. I think I told them that I piloted those high-powered ocean racers for a living…or something like that." His smile spoke of much more as he continued throwing his pebbles.

"Yeah," Mickey agreed. "Different set of problems."

Chapter 13

MICKEY WAS STILL PUZZLING AT HIS OWN SET OF problems when Mark's phone rang.

"Henderson." His voice was no longer that of a guy throwing out pebbles and advice. Nor was it the leader of MHA. It had a sharp, military snap. And not that Mark Henderson ever slouched, but now he sat bolt upright.

Then he keyed in some sort of a code.

Mickey tried throwing a few more pebbles at different angles to pretend he wasn't eavesdropping, but they all merely *plinked* into the water.

For his efforts, all he heard was a couple of "uh-huhs," one "okay," and a bunch of "yes, sirs." A glance at Mickey, then a "Lola and Tim would be good."

Then, "I'll let her know. I'm sure she sends her best right back to you. She's talking about going to visit her parents since she can't fly to fire. I'm sure she'll drop in on you."

Another pause while he listened.

Another pebble going *plink*.

"Right, thank you, sir. I'll keep you posted." And Mark hung up the phone.

"Where do Emily's parents live?" Mickey had a guess as to who that had been and was trying to find a tactful way to ask.

"DC." Mark was watching him with a sudden intensity.

DC. Someone that made Mark go all military and would be seeing Emily soon. "Was that—" The President? "Sorry, not my place to ask."

"What's your assessment of Robin Harrow?" Mark changed the subject, which was answer enough.

"You mean other than being in love with her and all?"

Mark merely nodded. Once. Sharp and definitive.

"An exceptional pilot. And a good leader. Who"— Mickey pictured the triumphant joy shining on Robin's face as she shot off the Class III Tea Cup in textbook-perfect form—"doesn't know that about herself."

"Doubt? I don't need someone who doubts themselves."

Mickey studied the flowing water. He might have seen a bit of pancake flow by but did his best not to think about that.

Doubts? No, Mickey had been feeling plenty of those himself all morning, mixed right in with the anger and frustration. But not his Ro—

His? He'd hoped but apparently she wasn't.

But not...Robin.

"No. She doesn't doubt her decisions for a second." Or she couldn't have shut him out so fast and so thoroughly. "She's an incredibly driven woman and it's all about excellence for her. Robin just doesn't see that she has already achieved it."

Then Mark reached across the gap that had separated them and rested a solid hand on his shoulder.

"But you do see it, don't you? Loud and clear."

"It's why I fell in love with her." And having said it, Mickey knew it was true. He loved that desire, that need of hers to always strive to be better than who she was in this moment. It was a need he'd taken a long time to recognize in himself.

"Know the feeling. Remember that when she's pissing you off next time, it will stand you in good service. Last question: Do you trust her?"

Mickey had to stop at that one.

What the hell was Mark asking?

And the pieces began falling into place.

He'd just spoken to the President on the phone—a phone that required a special code for security. They were on an unexplained break in central Alaska while fires were burning in the Lower 48. And the team was split, just as it had been before, with some MHA personnel sent to Australia and some…he'd never found out where Mark and Emily's half of the MHA team had gone last winter or the one before.

Mickey suspected that this time he stood on the other side of the split.

"When did I cross over?"

"A couple days ago when I received a Standby Alert, or three years ago when I came to MHA and got to know you but didn't need you to cross over yet. You choose. Can I trust Robin?"

"You need her on whatever this is, but you haven't had time to know her well enough?"

Mark hesitated, then nodded.

Well, whatever else he did or didn't know about Robin, Mickey did know one thing about her that was absolute.

"Yes, you can trust her. Hundred percent."

Mark's nod of acknowledgment was immediate. No time to consider or to weigh Mickey's words in the balance. Mickey had said it, so it was fact. It was an almost giddy sense of power.

But there wasn't any doubt—not with the way she drove herself to fire.

Besides, he'd trusted Robin with his love. And even if she'd battered at his heart, she'd also used her paddle to batter at his head and he'd survived that just fine.

Mark rose to his feet and Mickey followed.

Mark was right. There was a time to lick your wounds; there was a time to stop. He loved Robin. And he'd just keep that clearly in his sights until she realized that she was in love with him.

Hopefully he'd survive her wrath until she got there.

"Come on." Mark nodded toward the blue pickup that Tim's wife, Macy, had loaned him. It had two bumper stickers that said, *My other car is a Bell LongRanger* and *Auntie Em, There's No Craft Like Rotorcraft!*

Well, *There's no woman like Robin Harrow*.

At least not for him.

Maybe he should get it on a bumper sticker for his Twin 212.

He chucked his final rock high but didn't wait around to hear what sound it made striking the water.

Chapter 14

"This has always bothered me. I hate when they put my helo on a plane as if it isn't good enough to get there on its own." Robin stared at the monstrous Boeing airliner. It and the MHA team were currently parked in the 2:00 a.m. darkness on Ladd Army Airfield, Fairbanks. "Can't we fly wherever we're going?"

"Boss says no. Too far." Denise flitted by with Vern in her wake. "I love it. Fold the blades and we're good to go with this sweet little craft. This is the only plane that can do that."

This "sweet little craft" was huge—one of the four Boeing Dreamlifters. It was a Boeing 747—which was most of a football field long—but the fuselage was twice as big around as normal. They'd been specially built to haul prefabricated sections of 787s all over the face of the globe.

Robin had traveled to Afghanistan with the National Guard and her helo aboard a C-5A Galaxy, and this was bigger. At the moment, it was broken open at the tail and they were using cranes to lift the Firehawks twenty feet into the air and then slide them into the cavernous hold.

"I thought these planes *only* carried 787 parts. What is one doing in Alaska?"

"They're doing us a favor," Mark said, coming from behind her.

She'd been trying to ask Mickey. He was standing

nearby, but he still hadn't spoken to her except a perfectly civil "Hi." Two whole letters. Okay, maybe she deserved it. Crap, she did. But she wasn't quite ready to face him on it either.

And his expression, which she'd only looked at once during their last two hours on the river when it had been twisted in agony, was now open and content. She'd always been able to read him, but not at the moment. Open and content, almost friendly, didn't seem possible.

Had he figured out she was unlovable and come to peace with it in a single day? It didn't say much for the depth of his feelings.

Or had he decided that she really did love him and she was just too much of a doofus to figure that out yet, so he'd wait? In which case he was a fool... Wasn't he?

"We have to arrive absolutely cleanly." Mark continued his lecture while Mickey continued his silence. "No hint of military, not even for transport. Boeing would normally deadhead from Everett, Washington, to Nagoya, Japan, to pick up parts. We're just giving them a load while getting us there. We're only a few hundred miles out of their way."

"Japan?" Robin had only been overseas twice in her whole life. She'd spent all of that time either locked exclusively in highly protected Afghan air bases or racing as fast as possible past Afghan bad guys with the shit scared out of her for every single flight.

"Briefly" was all Mark said. "Then Korea."

"Why?"

"Think, Harrow. What does Mount Hood Aviation do for a living?"

"Fight wildfire."

"Good girl." And he walked away.

"You're lucky this Robin of the Hood doesn't have a bow and arrow." She raised her voice as she called toward his retreating back. "I've never shot one, Henderson, but you make me willing to try beginner's luck."

His laugh carried back to her, a wholly unsatisfying sound.

"I could teach you." Mickey's voice was soft, barely loud enough to carry the few feet between them.

She finally turned to really look at him for the first time since he'd cooked her pancakes eighteen hours and a whole lot of agony ago. The night was dark enough that the brighter stars could have forced their way through if not for the loading apron lights in front of the Alaska Fire Service hangar that blotted out even those. They were standing well clear of the operation that was up to Denise and the Dreamlifter's loadmasters, but enough light reached their position for her to see Mickey clearly.

He was looking right at her with those gorgeous blue eyes of his. She could see traces of the pain she'd caused, but mostly she simply saw Mickey, a man who could make her nerve endings scream and her body sigh. A man who she could trust. That alone was a whole new experience for her. The fact that he could also teach her to shoot a bow and arrow spoke all the more to who he was, a man perhaps patient enough to survive even her.

"I'd like that," she offered back just as quietly.

They traded tentative smiles that felt pretty good.

―⁓―

Six hours later, Mickey had decided that the entire planet and every stinking soul on it was conspiring against his talking to Robin—especially his friends.

The Dreamlifter was essentially the first-class nose of a standard 747, with a massive cargo hold bolted onto it. The flight crew was upstairs, as was the relief crew. The FAA had only recently authorized sixteen seats to be installed in pairs and a small grouping of chairs around a low table in the main deck of the nose section.

Mickey had dropped into the outside of an empty seat pair when he boarded, only to have Vern drop in next to him instead of Robin.

"Sorry about…you know." Mickey made a shoving motion.

"A couple aspirin." Vern rubbed the back of his head where it had pounded against the wall in French Pete's. "We're fine."

"Thanks, buddy."

He nodded.

They were good and chatted through the takeoff and climb to cruising altitude.

Yet when Mickey had gotten the two-at-a-time tour of the 747 cockpit—which made him suddenly glad for the humble controls of his Twin 212—Cal had been his shadow. On his return, Denise and Jeannie were gathered around Robin's seat.

He wasn't quite sure who to be angry at for all this kerfuffle. Mark and the guys for trying to protect him, or the women for trying to protect Robin from him. He had only himself to blame for his outburst of frustration in front of everyone at French Pete's restaurant, which had made them all overly watchful.

"Whatever," he mumbled as he dropped back into his seat.

Vern stretched out his long legs, once more

effectively blocking Mickey in. "Know exactly what you mean, buddy. Last winter, you would not bee-lieve what Denise did to me once I fell for her. I mean there we were in Honduras and—"

"Honduras? Is that where you guys went?"

"Shit, shouldn't have said that," Vern whispered in a hurry. "You better keep that one strictly between us."

Mickey nodded and slouched lower in his seat and tried to think what he knew about Honduras. Nothing except it was in Central America and had good coffee. And he only knew the second part because Vern had come back from last winter talking about the wonders of Honduran coffee. A clue that Mickey had completely missed. He wanted to ask a thousand questions but knew they wouldn't be welcome. And if Mark found out he was asking questions, he just might not be included in whatever was about to happen. He really didn't want to be moving in a different direction from Robin.

"What did Denise do to you?" He tried not to descend back into bitterness about his own recent experience. They were still one of the oddest couples imaginable, though Denise had come a long way out of her shell since the two of them had married. She was cute as all hell, but he'd never imagined her as even being available. All she cared about was her helicopters. "You two are happy enough now."

"Madly," Vern agreed with a smile that couldn't be denied.

"But what did she do?"

"It wasn't so much what she did…" Vern drifted off into happy-memory land. Mickey had seen it on enough faces of married MHA men to wonder what happy drug they were dosed with during the wedding ceremony. Or maybe it was administered along with getting your marriage license.

"Okay, so what *didn't* Denise do to you?"

"It wasn't that either."

"You're not being helpful, Vern." Mickey tried slouching lower. Too bad the Dreamlifter didn't have any amenities like an old-time stewardess in a short skirt serving from an open bar. Instead, like military flights, there was a small refrigerator stocked with juice and sandwiches. Strictly self-serve. Maybe he'd get some in a minute and see if he could run into Robin there.

"Sorry, man." Vern shrugged. "But that's exactly what she did to me. I felt like I was twisting in the wind. Everything I knew about women just went out the door and didn't matter anymore. Suddenly this little blond demon took over and occupied all my thoughts."

"Demon. I like that." Denise appeared out of nowhere and leaned in to kiss Vern. "I always wanted to be a demon." Then she dropped a couple sandwiches and juices into their laps.

Mickey took his reluctantly, so much for that ploy.

"Damn," Vern drawled. "Aren't the stews on this flight just the cutest thing ever?"

Mickey opened his mouth.

Denise pointed a finger at him. "Careful there, Mickey." And then she was gone.

He closed his mouth, unsure what he'd been going to say anyway. Something about agreeing...if Robin was one of them.

Mickey opened his mystery-meat-and-white-bread sandwich and concentrated on *not* thinking about Robin.

Vern was right.

It wasn't working.

———※———

"Of course they're talking about you," Denise reported as she brought sandwiches over to the low table they'd gathered around.

Robin wanted to go look for herself, wanted to see Mickey's face so that she could gauge it. But that wasn't going to happen anytime soon.

Emily and her daughter, Tessa, had flown back to the Lower 48 on their way to visit Emily's parents back east somewhere. Jeannie had her penned in to one side, Carly on the other. Now Denise sat across the table.

Egg salad on whole wheat, not bad. Except it was five in the morning body time, and they were fast approaching Japan.

Well, now she knew what Mickey and Vern were talking about, even if she didn't know what they were saying. If she did the same, she'd be far too conscious of him. And, no matter what Emily said about her being in love with Mickey... Robin tested the feeling like a sore tooth, gently. But she didn't know what she was testing for. Was her desire to get back to where they'd been the moment before he fed her pancakes moving forward or was it a retreat? And from what? Thinking about it didn't make her head hurt, instead it gave her an ache deep in her chest that was so cliché that it was just stupid.

Someday she'd have a kid, a girl, and the long line of single Harrow women would continue. Maybe even with Mickey if he was willing to do it without strings.

Robin almost laughed. The answer to that one was easy to guess; Mickey simply wasn't a love-'em-and-leave-'em kind of guy. Too bad, because that's all she was interested in. No matter what Emily said. This whole line of thinking was just making her feel miserable and she was sick of that.

"Fine," she said aloud, which stopped the quiet conversation among the other women about what few words Denise had overheard.

Time for a subject change.

"Any guesses on why we're going to Korea? Don't they have firefighters?"

"Don't want to talk about men that badly?" Jeannie teased her.

"No."

"Not even a little?" Carly nodded forward.

Cal, Mark, and Carly's husband, Steve, had gathered up at the very nose and were standing together looking very fit and handsome.

"Not even a little," Robin grumped.

"Killjoy." Denise offered a smile with her insult.

"You should have seen him." Jeannie bit into her sandwich.

"Who?" It slipped out before Robin could stop it.

"Him who." Denise waved her sandwich toward where Vern and Mickey sat across the cabin and forward.

She could only see Vern at the aisle. Mickey was completely hidden from view.

"I've never seen anyone yell at Emily before." Carly shook her head. "Can't even imagine it."

Robin choked on her egg salad. "Mickey yelled at Emily? About what?"

The three women went quiet.

"What?"

"I don't know what she said that set him off, but man, oh, man did he blow, mate." Jeannie giggled.

"Emily asked him what he'd done to *her* pilot." Denise would of course be the one to get close with no one noticing. "I can only correlate that she was speaking of you because the rest of us were there. She's very possessive about us, you know?"

"You too even though you aren't a pilot," Robin assured her.

"I am now." Denise fished a card out of her wallet and handed it around. "Just got my ticket, though I'll never be as good as Vern."

"Wow!" High fives happened around her.

"Though Emily always made sure I was okay even as one of her mechanics."

"Head mechanic."

"Emily's great."

"She's the best," the others agreed.

Robin's attention drifted back to where Mark was signaling for Vern to come join them. Maybe, if Robin could get free of this circle, she could go and take Vern's seat and have a talk with Mickey.

"Mickey told her to go to hell," Denise stated.

"Wait! What?" Robin tried to imagine such a thing and looked from one face to the next of the three women. They weren't making this up.

"Not just Emily," Denise said matter-of-factly. "You too."

Robin dropped back in her seat. She tried again to make sense of Mickey being angry and it just wasn't coming together. She'd dunked him and he'd explained why he hadn't taught her to Eskimo Roll. She'd hit him on the helmet and he'd laughed. She'd slashed at his heart and he'd just sat there and taken it.

"He told me to go to hell?" She could barely whisper it around the tightness once again lodged in her chest.

"'To hell with her and to hell with you.'"

"Denise!" Jeannie admonished her.

"What? Those are the correct words. You all heard it because he shouted it loudly enough to—" Then she stumbled to a halt. Denise blushed brightly and then rested a hand on Robin's arm. "Sorry, sometimes I'm not very good with people. Vern is trying to teach me." She bowed her head and a curtain of hair covered her face.

Jeannie gave her a side hug. "You're doing great, honey. But I thought it was us making all the difference in your life."

Denise shook her head and mumbled, "Vern" from behind her blond shield. Then she peeked out as Jeannie and Carly burst out laughing and offered a soft smile of chagrin.

Then she looked tentatively at Robin.

"I'm not great with people either, Denise, so we're fine."

"Oh no." Denise shook her head and then had to pause as she shoved handfuls of hair out of her face. "You're great with people."

"Then tell me why I don't have any friends." And Robin knew it was wrong the moment the words were out.

The three women looked at her in shock.

"Told you I was lousy with people. I'm just not used to having friends yet." She reached out and took Denise's hand, unsure of which of them she was trying to reassure. "It's not something I have any experience in."

"Okay." Jeannie's easy laugh resurfaced. "You're really good with people when they aren't your friends."

That got a round of snorts and giggles.

"Did he say anything else?" Robin asked once they'd all returned to their sandwiches.

Vern had clambered out of his seat, pulled Mickey after him, and they'd both moved forward. So much for plan C. What was plan D going to be? Jumping out of the plane and hoping that he did too so that they could shed their guardians?

"I don't want to hurt you." Denise was looking at her and Robin forced her attention back to the women.

"It's okay, Denise. We all heard it." Jeannie set down her sandwich and looked straight at Robin.

Uh-oh! She already knew she wasn't going to like this.

"He said, 'I tell her I love her and this is what I get?'"

"He said that to all of you?"

"More the entire bar," Denise noted. "He seemed quite upset and he was shouting rather loudly."

Robin felt ill and wished she'd eaten less egg salad. Perhaps taken some hemlock or arsenic instead. A man tells her he loves her, the first one to ever say it for reasons other than getting her into bed, and what did she give him?

"Was it romantic?" Jeannie asked.

"Mickey always struck me as having a romantic side," Carly put in.

"I guess." Romantic had always made her gag.

Looking at their faces, she could see that it wasn't enough. She had to tell them the story. One of the things she was learning about having friends, sometimes you owed them.

No, not sometimes; you always owed them honesty. Well, they'd been honest with her…so she took a deep breath, managed not to look at the man standing with his back to her, and began. "He made these great pancakes on the campfire beside the river…"

"Good choice of setting," Carly noted.

"I told him they were amazing. He said the recipe was a secret…"

"So he could give it to you but he'd have to kill you?" Denise tried to guess ahead.

"That was my guess too. He said that it was a family secret and he'd have to marry me." Robin's voice felt lost and dreamy even if she didn't want it to be.

Denise nodded matter-of-factly. "Would have melted me."

Jeannie sighed, and Carly rested her hand on her heart.

"Then I told him it was never going to happen. I'm not the marrying sort."

"What did he say next?" Denise asked as the other two held their breaths.

"He said, 'I love you, Robin.' Just that simple. Said it like he meant it."

Mickey stood with the others. His back was to her, but she could feel his attention on her.

There was no collective, girlish sigh.

Robin would have found that easy to discount.

Instead the three women looked forward to the men who had said those words to them. They were soft, quiet, ridiculously mushy looks.

Robin hoped to hell that her face didn't look like

theirs but decided that no form of honesty required her to say that.

"What the—" Cal was looking back over Mickey's shoulder.

One minute they'd been talking about whether or not an investment in more advanced night-vision gear would create any significant advantage, and the next minute everyone was turning to look at the women and putting on their goofy-happy expressions.

Mickey turned slowly to see Robin watching him.

There was something at war on her features. A softening, for a moment, that wasn't really her in some way.

Then it was erased and there was the Robin he knew. Ready to do battle with all comers. Ready to do battle but with a smile that welcomed him as well. Maybe they didn't need to talk. Maybe they just needed to give themselves a little time and space.

He looked at the guys around him. Goners, every one. Except Mark, whose spouse was on the way to visit her childhood friend the President of the United States. Mark just looked at the ceiling and shook his head sadly.

Mickey turned back in time to see Robin completing her assessment of the three women and shaking her own head. Then she looked right at Mickey.

They rolled their eyes in sync and totally busted up the tableau with their laughter shared across the length of the cabin.

It was a good moment.

Mickey hoped that there were a lot more of them to come. But there were going to be some serious talks before they did.

Chapter 15

"KOREA." MARK OPENED THE MEETING. THEY'D gathered in the nose of the 747 Dreamlifter cargo jet as it flew out of night and toward morning, still high over the Pacific.

Robin moved up close beside Mickey. Not close enough to brush shoulders, but close enough that, she supposed, if someone was looking at them from the outside, they might appear to be standing together. She wanted to test her comfort level around him. And it was pretty damn comfortable despite the last twenty-four hours. Enough so that she wished she hadn't tried the experiment to begin with.

Mark looked at her the same way he had when she'd showed up late to the line on that first fire-call morning. Like he was trying to assess quite why she was worth the trouble. *Crap! Back to square one? Fine!* She could deal with it.

"There's a wildfire that first swept southward out of North Korea across the DMZ and into the South." Mark tapped a tablet computer. A map of the Korean Peninsula showed once he'd logged and retinal scanned in.

Robin hadn't seen that kind of security outside of... the military. Suddenly those nondisclosure forms and government clearance checks she'd filled out just a few weeks ago took on another meaning.

"An attack?" Vern was the only ex-military here other than Mark and herself. Emily had said something about him flying U.S. Coast Guard helicopters.

"Not unless they sacrificed three villages of their own to do it. It's in the Taebaek Mountains, which run along the eastern, Pacific-side seaboard of both countries. Maximum height is only five thousand feet with an average around three, but very rugged country. Thankfully with low populations."

They all were quiet at that. They'd just come off a weeklong battle in an open stretch of forest that had few places for fire to hide and even fewer cliffs to accidentally run a helicopter into. And it had been a total bitch. A big fire in this kind of terrain was going to make the Dawson City Burn look like a cakewalk.

"The winds have gone through a shift due to a major low-pressure system moving up from Southeast Asia."

"How major?"

"Not bad, just a Category Three."

"That's called a hurricane, Henderson." Robin felt ill. She joined the AANG well after Katrina, but that disaster was scorched into the stories told by all the people who had been in the service at the time. The Arizona Army National Guard had been heavily deployed in the aftermath.

"They call it a typhoon in the Pacific," Denise put in.

"Doesn't make me feel any better about it," Robin told her.

"Category Three is well over half the speed our Firehawks can fly." Vern was still taking the lead. "Oh joy."

"That's right up near my never-exceed speed," Mickey noted about his slower Twin 212.

"The problem"—Mark's tone made it clear that it was time to stop interrupting him—"is not the storm. It's the wind shift that is preceding the storm by several days. They're predicting that the typhoon will turn inland across China, so that's not our issue. The problem is that the northerly winds of the approaching storm's east flank are driving the fire back across the border into North Korea."

"Great, now it's their problem again. Perfect." Robin dusted her hands together. "Our mission is complete." She couldn't let Vern have all the fun of poking at Henderson. Maybe if he hadn't demoted her back to square one, she'd have cut him some slack. But maybe not.

"There are two areas where South Koreans were allowed into North Korea," he ground on as if she hadn't spoken. "One is a North Korean industrial enclave manned by South Korean labor, which is still legal. That is to the west of the present fire and was briefly closed by a cross-border wildfire in 2015. The other is the Mount Kumgang Tourist Region, a massive park which extends up to the scenic Diamond Mountain." He traced a large area of rough mountains on the screen. "This area attracted over a million South Korean tourists before the North Koreans shot a tourist and the South closed that border."

"Fussy," Mickey shot for the joke. His timing was good, but it still fell a little flat. She'd had been on the verge of saying something similar, but her timing would have probably been worse, so she appreciated Mickey beating her to the punch.

Then Robin figured out that was exactly *why* he'd

done it, to save her from…herself. Should she be thankful and angry? Or should she be creeped out that any man could read her so well? But if he could do that, then how come he didn't know that she was not the marrying, one-man-forever kind of woman? And her unmarried mother had raised her just fine, thank you very much.

"That"—Mark did not sound amused—"is a lot of South Korean tourist dollars that dried up. However, the North continues their attempts to reopen the region in the hopes that the South will come back. However, if that region burns badly, then there will be no draw at all. UN sources fear that it could destabilize the Korean situation even further. The North Koreans need that tourist income desperately and have made several offers to the South Koreans to reopen it. They're staunchly refusing ever since the shooting. But again, if it's burned, then any chance for that extra bit of connection will be erased. That's why the UN is bringing us in to stop it."

"Still seems like a weird call, going to so much trouble to get us there." Robin shrugged. "But if they want someone to kick this fire's ass, I'd say that we're the ones to do it."

———

We are, Mickey acknowledged. But it still didn't make any sense, so why was everyone else buying into it? They were dispersing back to their seats. He leaned up against the small counter over the refrigerator and trash bin, staring out one of the round windows.

A haze of green far to the west would be Northern

Japan. They'd be descending soon onto the central island of Honshu.

The problem with MHA going to protect a North Korean economic zone as a favor for the UN was...the instructions hadn't come from the UN. They'd come from the President himself. The President didn't order firefighters into foreign countries. He especially didn't order former Night Stalkers to...

Mark and Emily *weren't* Night Stalkers anymore. Or were they? Undercover as firefighters, they could go almost anywhere...even North Korea.

What had sounded like a lark on an Alaskan riverbank suddenly sounded less so. There were strange things that happened when people were on the "other missions" separate from the bulk of the MHA's forces. Things they didn't talk about or even hint at.

Vern—no. Vern *and* Denise in...Honduras?

If those other teams had only flown to fire, it wouldn't have been an issue. They'd have talked about the fires.

Mickey scanned the forward compartment. Last winter he'd gone to Australia to fight bushfires, but everyone else in this aircraft cabin had been in Honduras. The year before that, Jeannie and Cal, Carly and Steve, and Mark and Emily had been sent off somewhere else for a month. And Jeannie and Cal had come back a month later than the others.

That meant that she and...

Robin was standing right in front of him and eyeing him in curiosity.

"Looking pretty thoughtful there, Mickey 'Blue Eyes' Hamilton."

"Looking pretty enough to be thinking about, Ms.

Robin Harrow." His mind had clearly decided that backing down wasn't an option.

Her smile was soft, acknowledging the challenge, but he wasn't up for a battle at the moment.

"Mickey?" That wasn't her battle voice.

"Yeah."

"It's the sweetest thing anyone has ever said to me."

"That I love you?"

"Yes, that."

Mickey nodded. It was there between them now. He wished it was as easy as trying to crash the gate at the White House like Mark had, but this was Robin Harrow. He longed for some action to take, but for the moment, there was nothing he could do but wait.

"I don't know what to say to it."

"There's nothing you have to say." Though he ached to hear it back. Wasn't it supposed to be the woman who said such things? Yeah it had been, in the past, and he'd never believed a one of them. Even still he didn't. The women in his past had said it too easily. Saying it to Robin had torn out his soul to flop like a dying fish on that riverbank. "It's simply there."

She studied him for a long moment, then nodded, as much to herself as to him.

"You ready for this, Robin?" Mickey wasn't sure if he was asking about his being in love with her or the upcoming wildfire.

"You know what they say?"

"Born ready." They spoke in unison, but there wasn't much joy in it.

"There's something odd going on here, you know," he said.

"You mean other than you saying…what you said?" Robin narrowed her eyes. "There's a fire, surprising locale, we're going to fight it. What am I missing?"

Mickey looked up over her shoulder. Henderson was shaking his head in a clear, *Don't!*

Crap! "Never mind."

Robin glanced over her shoulder at Henderson's retreating back. Then back at Mickey.

What? she mouthed.

He shook his head. Henderson didn't even bother to turn to double-check, that's how much trust he was giving Mickey. If he had turned to double-check, Mickey might have found the nerve to tell Robin what he was thinking. But facing the trust that Mark had shown him by the river, he couldn't betray that.

Unable to help himself, he reached out and took Robin by the upper arms and pulled her in. She didn't resist. She even leaned into the kiss he placed on her forehead.

With his nose buried happily in her bangs, he mumbled just a tiny bit louder than the engine noise, "Just because it's a Tea Cup doesn't mean it isn't also an MFDD."

Then he headed for his seat by Vern before he could do something neither of them was ready for. How was it possible to want a woman so badly?

———∿∿∿———

When is a Tea Cup also a Mighty Furrow of Death and Destruction? Robin wobbled a little bit before turning back for her seat.

Jeannie had saved a place beside her and Robin slid in.

"That looked like progress." Jeannie kept her voice soft.

"Huh? Oh, Mickey." She'd almost forgotten that

tentative bridge reborn between them, her mind now filled by the back blast of what he'd just said. There was some secret that Mark was holding on to that Mickey was in on, and he'd just done his best to warn her about it. Or at least he thought he had, but she wasn't getting it.

Then she tuned back to what was behind Jeannie's well-meant question. Being held by him for a moment and that kiss upon her forehead. She wanted to curl up against him and just hide there to wash away all the pain this day had brought—actually yesterday because dawn was breaking outside the windows and she'd barely slept on the flight. Pain that they had caused each other, so how was it possible that her chosen sanctuary would be curling up against him of all people?

"Yes," she answered Jeannie. "Yes, I think it was progress. I still don't know what to do about it or what I want to happen, but at least we spoke to each other."

Jeannie rubbed her upper arm as it if was paining her. "Just wait until he saves your life. It puts a whole different spin on things."

Robin looked at her, but Jeannie was off in memory somewhere.

Cal had saved Jeannie's life; that was something Robin hadn't known.

Mickey had just warned her that sometimes something that looked as smooth as a Class III Tea Cup could actually *be* a Mighty Furrow of Death and Destruction.

"Shit!"

"What?" Jeannie turned to her.

"I just figured out that we're not going to Korea just to fight a wildfire."

Jeannie smiled and patted her arm. "Welcome aboard, Robin. I'm glad you're with us."

"Right. But by the end of this, will *I* be glad?"

"By the end, sure." Jeannie spoke with the supreme confidence of a survivor as the captain announced they were beginning their descent.

Jeannie dropped her hands back into her lap to check her seat belt and Robin managed a good look at the spot Jeannie had just been rubbing on her upper arm.

"Great." Robin offered all the sarcasm she could muster.

"During," Jeannie continued as she settled back in her chair and folded her hands tightly in her lap, "maybe not so much."

Maybe not so much, Robin reiterated to herself but found little comfort as she looked away from the distinctive scar on Jeannie's arm.

Robin knew what a bullet wound looked like.

Chapter 16

"Only the pilots," the officious North Korean representative insisted. "No others may have permissions to fly into the great Democratic People's Republic of Korea."

Mickey was nearing his limits. The last time he'd slept had been along a small river upstream of Larch Creek, Alaska. He'd just flown seven hours to Japan and—once the helos were unloaded and Denise had certified them for flight—three more hours across the Sea of Japan to reach Korea.

It was now lunchtime the next day and Mickey's patience with Emily, Mark, and everyone else was hitting its absolute limit. Or maybe it had already passed it.

They'd clearly been relegated to the Korean equivalent of Podunk and it was named Yangyang International Airport. The one-runway field had a beautiful three-story, glass-fronted terminal building with three Jetways, a small plane parking area, and a soaring air control tower sufficient for a decent international hub. The four MHA helos were parked out on the unmowed grass beside the narrow, paved taxiway between the concrete runway and the terminal.

The airport's lone fuel truck had raced up at their arrival, its driver thrilled at having something to break the tedium of his days.

"You are the first flight in two months." He bounded

joyously to and fro, hooking up grounding lines and running out the hose from his truck. "Yangyang not have commercial flight for three years. High-speed train very bad for new airport. No planes. No people."

The terminal looked only a few years old. The fuel truck driver appeared to be the sole employee.

"Only pilots," the little North Korean man in his brown Army uniform insisted again, clearly displeased with the interruption to the sound of his own voice ringing across the empty airfield.

Mickey wondered if the five-person South Korean "honor guard" dressed in green uniforms was there to make sure that the North Korean was fully escorted, or to make sure that he wasn't beaten to a pulp by an irritated American pilot.

The inspector started with Mickey. Spent a long time on his pilot's license as if it wasn't about the easiest thing on the planet to forge. Then he inspected the helicopter, apparently shocked at not finding dual-mounted nuclear missiles and a half-dozen miniguns. That lack got Mickey off the hook fairly easily.

Vern also passed muster, though the official didn't know quite what to make of Denise, who was even shorter than he was.

"I am *not* letting my husband fly into North Korea without me," she'd told Mark and Vern earlier in no uncertain terms.

"You are a woman." The official inspected her license.

Duh! Mickey wanted to say. He knew he was overreacting to what was occurring around him, but he couldn't seem to stop his urge to do so. It had started with shouting at Emily and it had yet to settle.

"Many proud women fly our fighter jets in the great Democratic People's Republic of Korea."

If the inspector said that whole phrase one more time, Mickey just might do a little destruction of foreign relations himself when he throttled the man.

But the official kept looking at Denise's long, blond hair as if it might attack him at any moment. Between Robin's white-blond chop, Carly's elegant, straight fall of gold to her jawline, and Denise's bountiful waves down to the middle of her back, he'd probably never seen so much blond hair in his entire life, and Mickey did what he could to keep his smile down.

"You." He'd moved on to Cal at Firehawk Two. "No cameras. You may not go to our country."

He started to move by, but Cal stopped him. "Don't you want pictures of the great battle of the Kumgang wildfire? Our helicopters in the air and your people on the ground, fighting together."

The official scoffed.

"I often take pictures for the cover of *Time* magazine, *National Geographic*, and many others."

"*National Geographic*?" His dark, piggy eyes that had spent entirely too much time dwelling on Robin's bosom lit with sudden interest. "Prove it to me."

Cal pulled out his tablet computer and pulled up a copy of his latest cover for the magazine. The two of them were soon negotiating over what he could and couldn't take pictures of.

"I promise to be most careful," Cal assured him.

"You may go." The official granted royal dispensation, so Cal was in. The official moved on to Firehawk One.

That's when the explosion occurred.

"What is this? And this? And this?"

It was Steve's computers for controlling the drone—though they didn't mention that—and Carly's special screens in the copilot's position to receive those feeds and perform her fire behavior analysis.

At Mark's suggestion, they had left the launcher and drones under lock and key at a nearby safe house. Mark had declined to mention why it was safe or who it was safe from—though that was now apparent.

They tried calling all of the gear "fire monitoring equipment," but that didn't help.

"No! No! No!" He wasn't satisfied until everything had been removed. He walked back and forth between Firehawk Two and Firehawk One to make sure there was no extra equipment he didn't recognize.

When Carly held up her license, the little man repeated, "No! No! No!"

"But I have to see the fire to fight it," Carly protested as Steve stepped up to rest a hand of restraint on her arm. She was far taller than the inspector and was looming over him enough to have him stepping back with nerves.

"You try to bring spy equipment into our country. If this were the native soil of the Great DPRK"—he barely dodged the bullet of repeating his country's full name again, but the name stiffened his resolve—"I have you both arrested as CIA spies. No! No! No! You!" The little man went toe-to-toe with Mark though he was a foot shorter. "What do you do? I can smell spy from across the border in my own country of the great—"

"I'm the fire boss," Mark interrupted him, but kept his temper in check. "I fly overhead in a small plane and tell these pilots what to do."

"You no fly firefighting helicopter, you no fly!" And the man walked away.

Mickey sidled up to Mark. "You know, it's almost worth the trouble that's going to cause us just to see your jaw hanging loose in surprise."

Mark recovered his jaw and replaced it with a grim expression. "I am this far"—he pinched a finger and thumb close together—"from pulling the goddamn plug." He practically shouted the last of it at the inspector's back.

Mickey looked at him. Then up at the sky graying with the high, thin clouds of the storm passing far to the south, at the plume of fire smoke to the north, and then back to Mark.

"But you can't, can you?"

Mark bit his lower lip, then shook his head sharply no. But it looked as if he was trying to hide a smile, which didn't make any sense at all.

"You need to fill the others in."

"I was going to—"

"No, now." Mickey had never confronted Mark in the three years they'd flown together. But what the hell. After yelling at Emily yesterday, maybe he was getting good at it. Or developing a death wish.

"Not just yet."

"I won't let them go aloft." Mickey braced to take him on. "All I have to do is tell Robin to say no and none of them will—"

Mark raised one finger and then pointed it south toward the far end of the terminal building.

The high whine of a racing car engine caught on the wind and blew toward them. Moments later Mickey

spotted a white SUV hauling ass around the corner of
the building, shooting under an extended Jetway with
only inches to spare and racing in their direction.

Aircraft by aircraft the other pilots had followed in
the official's wake until they were all gathered around
Firehawk One. Even the official had stopped being officious over his individualized authorization forms to see
who was coming at such a speed.

A rental-white Kia SUV slammed on the brakes at the
last second and skidded in sharp chirps of rubber on dry
concrete, leaving long, black marks on the pristine sun-
bleached surface. It drifted sideways toward the North
Korean official for a long moment before twisting to
a halt close behind Firehawk One. A wave of burned-
rubber stench rolled over them.

Mickey, at first, thought it must be a lunatic, but then
he saw the driver's grin flash through the windshield and
decided that he was a very skilled lunatic and had known
exactly what he was doing.

A couple piled out of the car. The driver would be
a small man if he weren't so broad and muscular—he
looked like one of those guys who could bench-press the
car he'd just been driving. His black Foo Fighters T-shirt
was stretched tight over his chest and clung around his
massive biceps. His eyes were hidden behind wrap-
around shades that might be appropriate on a Florida
beach during spring break. He wore his dark hair short
and his smile broad.

The woman was something else entirely. Her long
form emphasized by the Maroon 5 T-shirt that was as
tight on her lithe form as the Foo Fighters one was on
her companion's expansive one. A tumble of mahogany

hair down past her shoulders framed tanning-cream-ad skin and mirrored aviator sunglasses just like the ones Mark wore.

"Sorry we're late, Mark," she called out merrily. "So who's stuck flying solo?"

Mickey looked at Robin, and they both tentatively raised their hands.

"Aw, he's a cute one." She strode over, looking him up and down. Then turned to Robin. "You and me, babe. 'Cause women rule." Then she held up a hand for a high five. When Robin raised her own, the smack the woman delivered was so loud it almost hurt Mickey's ears.

"You and me, pal." The guy came up and gave Mickey's hand a crushing handshake. Mickey returned it and came out about even.

He could see that Mark was not showing the least surprise, so Mickey played along. "We've been waiting on you."

"I need your licenses." The North Korean inspector came up to them and they each dug out FAA cards.

Mickey managed to spot their names. "Lola and Tim Maloney," he whispered to Robin when she looked at him inquiringly. The names Mark had given to the President.

"So, Tim, buddy…" If Mark wanted him to, Mickey could play the game as well as anybody. "What kept you?"

Tim just hooked a thumb toward Lola and leered happily.

Mickey bought it and also didn't believe it for a second. Their arrival had been as well-timed as it had been orchestrated.

"You are not military pilot?" the North Korean asked them both.

Lola snorted out a laugh. "Do I look that stupid?" Yet she'd greeted Mark like an old friend. Like...a fellow Night Stalker.

He glanced at Robin, who nodded.

—∿∿—

Robin recognized military even if the North Korean didn't.

"Way more money in firefighting than the military." Lola continued her expert razzle-dazzle of the official. Which was true. Robin's present pay scale wasn't even on the same page as her Army National Guard income. Even the overseas hazard pay in a war zone didn't match...

Robin coughed to hide her surprise. She'd just figured out what the "Special Projects" pay-rate column had meant on the MHA paperwork. This. Doing something as stupid as flying across the Pacific to fight a fire in North Korea for reasons unknown.

Well, she'd certainly be able to afford a hot motorcycle sooner rather than later. Though she could hear Mom's advice to bank it against a lean season. Mom was usually right—thrifty was a major Harrow-woman trait—but Robin would worry about that later.

The other thing that Robin appreciated about Lola's arrival was that her own chest was no longer the only one snagging the official's attention. That he was short enough for Robin's breasts to be close to his eye level didn't make her any less tempted to pop him in the nose—which she guessed would be bad for business, even if it had increased business at Phoebe's Tucson Truck Stop.

If Lola and Tim were military...and they knew Mark...and Mark knew them—

MFDD. When is a Tea Cup also a Mighty Furrow of Death and Destruction? When two unknown military pilots show up using false identities as firefighters. When two…Night Stalkers! That's what Mickey's look had meant.

Lola was as different from Emily as could be, loud and boisterous versus calm and cool. But it was also easy to see the simple assumption of power that both women carried. *I'm just that good* radiated off both of them. Not bragging. Fact.

And if top military pilots were joining their firefight, then something far bigger than fire and smoke was in the air.

Robin wasn't a big thinker about herself, but she could feel Emily waiting off to the side just dying to ask her question: *What did you learn about you?*

What she was learning in this moment was that her feet felt more firmly planted on the Korean concrete than they had on the Alaskan tundra. Suddenly, more of her was going to be needed than her ability to fly a helicopter. She'd been a soldier for six years, and with the arrival of Lola and Tim, she suddenly was again. Another piece of the multifaceted riddle of why she'd been hired so quickly and landed in Emily's command seat.

She wished she could tell Mickey, but saying *I'm a soldier* in front of the Korean official currently handing back their FAA licenses would be a bad choice. Even out of the Guard, it was a part of who she was.

She wished she could tell Mickey though.

That too was a new thought. There was someone in her life that she wanted to share things with. Things about herself. Weird.

Robin looked at Mickey, really looked at him. He was as solid in being a firefighter as she was in being a soldier. There was a completeness to him standing there beside her. All afternoon, he'd remained a half step in front of her. Ready to jump in to protect her from the North Korean, even from Mark.

Yet he wasn't judging her as weak or unimportant. She'd heard his whisper to Mark, "All I have to do is tell Robin to say no and none of them will—"

Mickey believed in her. The only other people in her life to ever do that were the Harrow women and Emily.

Robin knew that wasn't love, but she knew it was something special.

As Lola and Tim continued their play at the North Korean's expense, Robin took the half step forward to stand close beside Mickey.

She took his hand. That was something that Robin had never been big on, holding hands. But Mickey's palm felt good and right against hers.

He looked over at her in surprise, those brilliant blue eyes filled with such hope.

"No promises, Mickey."

He watched her for a long moment, squeezed her hand in acknowledgment, and turned back as the official finally gave in and began issuing certificates to fly over the soil of the great Democratic People's Republic of Korea, but *not* to land there unless it was a true emergency…and maybe not even then.

Robin took her clearance in one hand but continued to hold on to Mickey's with the other.

Something else I just learned, Emily. I could get to like this.

—◦◦◦—

Once the inspector was done with them, he pointed at the terminal.

"I will be right there, sitting in your empty, decadent South Korean terminal, yet another sign of the failure of the capitalist state. I will be watching everything you do, every day. I keep records, I keep track, so no underhanded American strategies."

Then his five-person South Korean "honor guard" escorted him away to the building.

Mark led the team well out in front of the helos so that they could see anyone coming their way.

"Okay, that went better than expected." He winked at Mickey.

"That's what your smile meant." Mickey smacked his forehead.

Of course Henderson had anticipated not being allowed aloft. One of these days he'd get a step ahead of the man. Though a man quick on his feet enough to be happily married to an elemental force like Emily... Yeah, it would take some serious footwork to catch up to Mark.

"*That* was better than expected?" Carly nearly screamed and Steve shushed her. She continued only a little more softly, "How am I supposed to analyze a fire I can't see?"

"Once they're aloft, you, Steve, and I will return to that safe house and launch Steve's drone. You'll have to run remote. Sorry, Carly, best I could do."

"What's Steve got?" Lola asked.

"A little ScanEagle with visual and infrared cameras and a high-end communications package."

"Shit, Mark. The North Koreans will spot that in a second. They have the most paranoid radar coverage of any country, and an awful lot of that is wired directly into the largest antiaircraft emplacements anywhere."

"He knows that, honey," Tim said softly. "We've been there, done that."

Lola looked at her husband in surprise.

Mickey knew the Night Stalkers were Special Forces helicopter pilots. And if Mark had flown into North Korea, that meant he was probably one of the best ones, because it would be risky as hell; one false move could have started a war. No longer a real surprise that Mark was the best when Mickey considered that Mark was the one the President had called when he needed help.

"We have been there." Mark looked around the circle and especially stopped at Mickey and Robin.

"Top secret," Robin huffed out in frustration. "We got that already. Signed the confidentiality documents and shit. Get on with it."

Mark offered her one of his half smiles.

Mickey finally understood that was one of his signs of approval.

"Steve has a special drone that's full stealth. Composite frame and hull. Quieted engine. It has the radar signature of a peanut. Vision is good enough that it won't need to cross the border, though comms will be spotty in the deeper canyons and the view of the fire's leading edge will be nonexistent."

"Oh, like I don't need that," Carly complained, but was mostly mollified.

Mickey had never heard of or seen such a drone, but

it was no surprise to the other MHA pilots, so he simply accepted it.

"Robin, you're lead flight. I know Alaska wasn't much prep—I tried to give you as much as I could—"

"Another reason you wouldn't fly with me," Robin stated.

Mark nodded. "Em and I wanted you to get as much *in command* time as possible. Mickey and Jeannie, you have the most hours on fire, so you're Carly's eyes on the front line. Keep high, keep safe."

Everyone was nodding.

Mickey waited. He stared at Mark's silvered shades until the man turned to him.

Then Mark laughed.

Mickey had had enough shit. He'd taken it from Robin, from Emily, and now he'd found exactly where to unleash his frustration. There was no way in hell that Mark was going to send the team aloft without everyone knowing what they were up against. If he had to god-damn beat it out of Henderson, that's exactly what he'd do. He—

"Whoa!" Mark raised his hands in a placating gesture.

Mickey stayed up on the edge of his toes, only marginally aware of Robin and Vern holding on to him from either side.

"Easy, Mickey. Easy." Mark stayed in place, in easy striking range.

Mickey yanked, but Robin had a powerful grip. He tried to remember the last time he'd wanted a go at someone and couldn't. But that didn't stop him from wanting a shot at Henderson.

"I don't know either," Mark lied. No half smile; no knowing wink. A bald-faced lie.

"Don't know what?" Robin's voice cut through the buzzing in Mickey's ears.

"Why the President sent us here," Mickey ground out.

"The President? Like our President?" Robin's eyes had gone wide, probably as wide as his had been when it happened.

Mickey nodded. "I was there when he took the goddamn call. Received the orders that brought us here. He knows exactly—"

"He didn't tell me." Mark's flat statement stopped Mickey cold.

"What do you mean he didn't tell you? The President just said, 'Mark, buddy, why don't you go fight a fire in North Korea for me. I'll send along a couple of Night Stalkers to keep you company'?"

"Pretty much."

Mickey blinked. First man to blink loses, even if the other one is wearing mirrored shades. Mickey settled back on his heels, still feeling the strength of Robin's hands clamped on his arm and shoulder, though Vern let go. She was no longer holding him back; now she was holding on to him. Well, he wasn't going to let her down.

"What the hell, Mark?" But Mickey wasn't able to find much heat to put in back of it.

"It's how these things sometimes work. Some missions are heavily planned, right down to full-scale models and practice raids. Bin Laden's compound was built four times, you know. The original in Pakistan, a full replica in North Carolina, a partial in Nevada, and the one they used in the movie in India."

Mickey had sometimes wondered if Mark had been on that mission but knew there was no way to ask.

"In a dynamic zone," Mark continued, "like the two wars in Southwest Asia, we were making it up minute to minute. Today's scenario is far more typical."

"And what's that?"

"Get our asses in place," Lola answered for him.

"Put our thumbs *up* our asses," Tim continued.

"And sit on them until someone tells us if anything is even gonna happen," the tall brunette finished with a snort of disgust.

"Sorry for laughing at you, Mickey." Mark was still smiling. "But they're exactly right. I've been forward deployed hundreds—"

"Thousands," Lola declared.

"Millions," Tim moaned.

"—of times," Mark continued, "and nothing has come of it. And then one time it does. That one time is why we set up for all the other ones."

"We"—Denise pointed at Vern—"had to get kidnapped to find out anything was happening."

Jeannie merely shuddered and rubbed her upper arm where she had an odd scar that Mickey had never given much thought. Cal pulled her in close and kissed her hair.

"Seriously," Mark continued, "almost always in these situations the answer is, nothing happens. Then we stand down none the wiser for why we were called out in the first place. I will not be disappointed if all that happens here is we do our job—fight this fire and go home."

"At least we have something to do while waiting." Tim clapped his hands together. "Never fought a fire before."

"Can't wait," Lola agreed.

Mickey couldn't think of anything to say.

"So, at the risk of repeating myself…" Mark offered Mickey a smile that he could now see was understanding rather than condescending. "Keep high. Keep safe."

Chapter 17

ONCE THEY'D DECIDED ON A BASIC ATTACK PLAN, safety protocols, and done their Preflight Inspections, Robin got Firehawk One aloft and watched as the others climbed into the air beside her. All that remained at Yangyang field was Mark, Carly, Steve, and a white rental SUV. The North Korean and his South Korean escort were long gone into the terminal building, probably for a *non-decadent* nap.

"Wow!" Lola said from beside her. "I haven't flown left seat since the last time I lofted as Emily's copilot."

"You flew with her? In the Night Stalkers?"

"Emily's the best goddamn pilot on the planet." Lola rode the controls lightly.

Even from a low hover, Robin could see the golf course tucked up tight against the airfield. It had a lot of water hazards and few trees, which made it ideal. She lead the flight over to pick up their first load of water for the day.

"More people here than the whole airport." The four helos descended over the various ponds, lowered their snorkels, and fired up the pumps. All over the golf course, people were holding on to hats and more than one golf umbrella went skittering across the fairway.

Robin explained how the simple snorkel and pump controls worked as she completed taking on the load, then eased forward and up. A group came out onto the first tee just as she approached it—a very distinctive group. One man in a brown uniform surrounded by five in green.

"Oh, this is too good." Robin could feel herself sideslipping the Firehawk even as she told herself she really shouldn't.

Lola's laugh was low, evil, and matched her own.

"Don't even," Mickey transmitted, though she could hear the laughter in his voice as well.

"Bad idea, huh?" And it was if they wanted to continue to have permission to fly into North Korea.

The North Korean cowered suddenly as he figured out what was about to happen. Robin peeled aside at the last moment and didn't hit the dump switch.

By Lola's groan, it was a good thing that Robin was presently pilot in command rather than the Night Stalker.

"Been done," Jeannie commented drily as the entire flight peeled away, which took all the fun out of it. Though she looked forward to hearing the story. That Jeannie had thought of it and followed through made her like the Aussie pilot even more.

Robin turned north and led the way up the beach. Mickey fell in close behind her. Jeannie and Vern veered off to the west to approach the other side of the fire so that they could get a feel for it. The closest point was twenty miles and ten minutes away and the drone wouldn't be in the air for a while yet.

Robin could feel her through the joined cyclic and collective. Lola's feet on the rudders mirrored her own, not correcting as Emily had, but rather adapting to Robin's own style.

"Wow! That's different, but I like it. Where did

you learn to fly like that?" Lola didn't slow down long enough for Robin to squeeze in an answer, never mind think of one past her surprise. "Even Mark says Emily's the best and he's bloody amazing. I try, Lordy knows, but those two fly on some whole other plane of reality."

"What craft is your specialty?"

"Oh, we're sitting in it. Actually, just like Emily and Mark did, I've flown the DAP ever since I hit the Night Stalkers, but this Firehawk is the same airframe, just with less power and fewer weapons."

"And fewer people shooting at you."

"Can always hope," Lola agreed cheerfully over the intercom.

Away from the empty airport, Robin cut east to the coastline. The midday sun lit the high clouds so bright that it hurt to look upward. They, in turn, were reflected off the Sea of Japan, blurring the line of water and sky. She turned and followed the sandy beach north.

Robin had never seen a Direct Action Penetrator version of the Black Hawk, but she'd heard about them. The Army National Guard pilots would sit around the barracks between exercises and tell stories they'd heard, mostly spreading rumors, but it was as close as they ever got to one.

The list got pretty wild at times.

One: The DAP was one-hundred-percent pure weapon, redesigned from the ground up—exclusively by the Night Stalkers and for the Night Stalkers—to be the most lethal rotorcraft in history (they were pretty sure that one was true).

Two: The people who flew them were cyborgs wired directly into their ships (a bit less likely).

Three: They (no one was quite clear on whether "they" referred to the rotorcraft or the pilots) were built out of Area 51 composites scraped molecule by molecule off all of the alien spaceships stored there.

Four—a little closer to reality: There were maybe twenty DAPs in existence.

And five: No one doubted that they were all flown by the Night Stalkers' very best pilots.

That made Emily and Lola…

She'd known Emily was good. But "The Best" by a DAP pilot's standards? That was a little spooky.

"Did you fly into bin Laden's compound? Oh, never mind, you can't tell me even if you did."

"No, I didn't. I was still flying Army Combat Search and Rescue back then, fresh out of the Louisiana Army National Guard."

Robin looked over, startled. If Robin had chosen a different path, from Guard to Army, might this be who she'd become?

"But I think Mark may have been on the bin Laden run. I'm guessing, but I think so."

Robin was feeling hopelessly outclassed as they continued up the coast.

Yangyang International lay south of Sokcho—at eighty thousand people, it was far and away the largest city in the area—but they passed by it in just a few minutes. Soon they were running along a wide, sandy beach, only occasionally interrupted by small towns and low, depressing resort hotels. It could have been a stretch of Lola's Louisiana Gulf Coast except for the occasional standout building with the classic red-tile roof and upward curving corners. For the most part, it was anywhere, USA.

In just a week, Robin had grown used to having the data from Steve's drone and Carly's analysis ready to hand, Carly often muttering audibly over the data as she strained to outsmart every last finger of flame. Robin missed them.

"Jeannie," Robin called the other team, "how is it looking?" Vern had bowed back to let Jeannie lead their separate flight. Vern had no ego at all about his skills, just as happy in the back of the flight as in front. Like Mickey, he was just solid and he clearly loved Denise. Like Mickey said he… *Crap!*

"Not much yet," Jeannie answered. "A lot of smoke in the distance. I'll know more in a few minutes."

"Cloud plume on this side is indicating a lot of heat," Mickey radioed in.

"What makes him say that?" Lola asked over the intercom.

Robin felt a little better. She could see it, now that Mickey had pointed it out.

"Look at how the smoke is changing colors as it climbs. The black at the bottom is still thick with ash. At the top, where it's white, most of the ash load has been dropped. The silvery top is as much cooling water vapor as it is smoke. We know that it's hot by the fact that the line where the black shifts to gray is well up the smoke column. Takes a lot of heat to push the ash that high."

Lola leaned forward to squint out the windscreen and upward. "Tall sucker too." Even five minutes and a dozen miles out, it was still enormous.

"That tells you the fire's size. It's not just a leading edge that's burning; it's the entire area because the whole column is reaching right up into the jet stream. See how it's getting flat-topped to the north?"

"Uh-huh."

Robin did have skills—hard-won ones—she just needed to remember that.

"I thought we were going to come at this fire from its tail. Guess we missed it. Mickey?" She keyed the radio.

"Here, Robin."

"Swing south, survey only. Find out what happened to the tail. I'm going to follow the smoke line north and see if I can find the head of this beast."

"Roger. Don't go too far alone."

A nice way to remind her that the North Korean border didn't lie far away. "Roger that."

"We'll trace a circuit around it," she told Lola, "in the direction of building flame to find out just what it's doing before we set up a plan of attack."

Reports began flowing in from Jeannie and Vern. She had Lola start recording GPS coordinates of the fire so that she could get some idea of what was happening when one of her data radios began flashing red. It was a radio she hadn't used before. It was encryption capable, military grade.

"What's the password?" Lola asked.

"How the hell am I supposed to know?" She'd always meant to ask what it was doing on a civilian helicopter…and now she knew. It was blinking at her. Real damn useful.

"Typical," Lola muttered.

"Hey!"

"Not you. Henderson. He always thinks he's being so smart. If he was right a little less often, it would be a source of some comfort to this Southern gal."

Robin considered. She'd used encrypted radios in

Afghanistan, everything was encrypted there. Cipher codes varied, basic ones were four characters.

"He said, 'Keep high. Keep safe.' Try *high*."

"No letters on these models."

"Think cell phone, hit four 4s. H-I-G-H."

Lola laughed, keyed it in, and the radio flashed to green.

The copilot's screens were immediately filled with Carly's typical array of information.

"What the hell?" Lola leaned so far forward that she bumped the cyclic as she tried to understand the information on the displays.

Robin had to pull back on her control to nudge Lola in the solar plexus as a reminder to stay off the controls. She was feeling better by the moment. Of course Robin also wouldn't put it past Lola to do it as a tease.

Another radio flashed red.

"Try *safe*," they said in unison and shared a laugh.

Moments later Mark's voice came over her headset. "How do you read, over?"

"Five by five," she and Lola said in unison.

"Sorry." Lola made a show of taking her finger off the mic switch on the back of the cyclic control. "Old habits."

"Tell me I'm not going to be dealing with a Greek chorus for this entire fire," Mark whined.

Robin glanced over at Lola and mouthed *Two, One*, and keyed the mic. "Nope," they managed in unison. "Not gonna happen," collided with "Not a chance," and gave them both the giggles.

Mark groaned over the air. "Okay. I'll keep this short to avoid detection of our encrypted signal. Robin, I'm only connecting to your Firehawk One. I'm bouncing a signal off the drone and don't want the North Korean air controllers getting worried when our aircraft all stop talking to each other. I don't even want them reacting to an order that they can't hear. So I'll hit you and you'll be calling the Incident Commander—Air instructions that I feed your way. You're going to be busy as hell, so get the Stripper up to speed as fast as you can to help you with the firefighting. I don't want you ramming any cliff walls. That would completely ruin my day." And Henderson was gone.

"*His* day?" Robin asked the radio without keying her microphone.

"Sure. He'd have to give the news to my husband, who would beat the shit of Mark for killing me. What would your SO do?"

"My what?"

"Your significant other. Get a clue, girl."

Robin knew what an SO was. "He wasn't…isn't, uh, won't be my…" But what was he?

"Get a clue. Couples don't stand the way you two were unless they're way past the 'mere heat' stage."

Robin couldn't think of what to say. *How had they been standing together?*

Lola began toggling through various modes on the screen displays, ultimately scrambling all of Carly's careful settings.

Mickey was what? She didn't even know what to call him. It certainly wasn't significant other, but Lola was right; they were way past fuck buddy. Had been past that since the first time that they'd…what…shaken hands?

"I'm going to have to kill him." It was the only obvious way to deal with the situation.

"Works for me." Lola kept working the displays. "Neat, simple. Glad to help if you need it, but can we do it after we beat the fire? I came close enough to offing Tim a couple of times along the way too. Almost took him out with his mom's favorite kitchen knife one night. But what with the head of the President's Protection Detail breathing over my shoulder, I thought better of it. Frank gets antsy when you're wielding an eight-inch chef's knife anywhere near *the Main Man*."

Robin focused on the fire. She could deal with the fire. Sitting next to a chatty DAP Hawk pilot who had eaten with the Commander in Chief…Nope! Couldn't deal with that.

"After the fire is fine," she managed around a throat gone drier than fire smoke. Significant other? Mickey sure as hell wasn't that. But then what in the wide, wide world of helitack firefighting was he?

Subject change!

"Why did Mark call you the Stripper?" Robin found the leading edge of the fire and moved to circle ahead of it.

"My maiden name was Lola LaRue. I used to have this line about how Daddy must have wanted me to be a stripper. Mark still teases me about it sometimes."

"You two close?" Robin looked again. The only way to survey the leading edge was to fly right into the ash cloud streaming off the fire. She'd stay low and duck under the worst of it.

"To Daddy? Not very. He's doing forty to life of hard time in a Louisiana pen, not real happy about it."

"I can only imagine." Robin considered shooting far enough ahead of the fire to get the lay of the land, but her grid map display showed her fast approaching the North Korean border. She eased back on the cyclic, not quite willing to cross the DMZ on her own.

"Might help if I hadn't been the one to put him there." Lola shrugged and went back to studying the screens. "You close to your old man?"

"Gone before his sperm got to the egg. Mama was kinda wild when she was younger."

"And you're all mature and settled?" Lola scoffed.

"Not a chance. A girl's gotta have some fun. I'm gonna be just like Mom. No man for me."

Lola gave her a look that Robin did her best to ignore.

Damn, but this fire was eating up terrain. "Go back a screen," she told Lola.

"This one?"

"Go back another. There. Keep that one on the middle screen between us."

Lola flipped it into place so that it showed on the center of the console. It wasn't Steve's usual sharp view of the fire from directly overhead, and it took Robin a few moments to adjust to the angle of the view. The drone had to do its best from safely deep in South Korean airspace.

"What's the scale?" Lola was still tinkering with it. "It doesn't look like terrain contour lines."

"Temperature in hundreds of degrees. See along the left edge, it's down in the six to seven range. They must have the drone up over that section of the fire."

"Six or seven hundred? Please say you're shitting me."

"Would I do that to a fellow heli-gal?" Startling a Night Stalker! Robin was thoroughly enjoying herself. "What that tells me is that the fire is retreating from the southwest. Have to be for the fire to be that cool," she managed with a straight face. "No readings up in our area yet, but I'm guessing fifteen to eighteen?"

"Hundred?" Lola breathed it out on a gasp.

"Hundred," Robin confirmed, then keyed the general frequency that would reach all of the aircraft. "It's hot on our side. Jeannie, Vern, do you have any readings?"

"Just edge temperatures," Jeannie called back. "We didn't want to fly over the fire without your say so. But we're flying in clear air within two rotors of the active flame—tells me it's heading away from us."

"I can't even see orange," Robin reported back. "All I'm looking at is hot black smoke. Definitely moving north and east."

On their cockpit screen, a series of broad green lines appeared. Carly often drew on her tablet to indicate the lines of attack.

Robin had seen enough of her onscreen notes during the Dawson City fire that she could make sense of what Carly was recommending, at least she hoped so. "Start cleanup on your side, Jeannie. You and Vern start chasing the fire back into the Black and kill the boundary with a wet line. Make sure it can't escape. Swing south first to secure the tail, then sweep north along your western side."

"Roger that. We're on it."

"Talk to me, Mickey." At some point they had to have time to talk…didn't they? National Guard was called out a half-dozen times a fire season. Robin had the feeling that Mount Hood Aviation's operational tempo was way higher than that. Waiting until the autumn to have a conversation when they weren't exhausted, ticked off, or surrounded by others was not going to work for her.

"Found the tail here," he called from the south end of the fire. "We can work this, but I think the strengthening northerly winds will make it a nonissue."

"Roger, get back up here. The North Koreans didn't give me any ground team frequency, but I'll bet they're down there and this monster is headed straight into the DMZ." Robin hoped that Steve heard that and could find some way to get her an infrared view of bodies on the ground.

She decided that Carly's scrawled advice wasn't the best option. It was strange talking to Mickey and, at the same time, asking a question of Carly on the open air, which she would hopefully answer with a revised encrypted drawing.

"I think we need to flank the head," Robin said. "We'll watch for it curling around behind us, but we need to start narrowing this thing before we can trap it."

"Makes sense to me," Mickey acknowledged. She could see him on her radar coming up fast out of the south.

Carly erased her initial attack lines and began altering them for how to take best advantage of the terrain.

"Slick," Lola said. "That was well done. You do have fun up here."

"Thanks."

"Of course," Lola continued in her cheerful tone as Mickey lined up behind Robin and they began the first dive on the fire. "I was all about having fun for me too. But Tim kept showing me that it was more fun to be with him than without him."

"Not gonna happen to me."

Robin slid down toward the flames and tried not to remember the feeling of flying into space off the Class III Tea Cup with Mickey's joyous smile awaiting her below.

———

"That woman, man, she's making you crazy, isn't she?"

"Some." Mickey wondered where Tim had come up with that idea. They were flying to fire. Something they'd done hundreds of times a day for the entire week of the Dawson City fire. For Mickey this moment was no different, yet Tim had picked up on something.

"Yeah." Tim sighed happily over the intercom on the Twin 212. "Lola did the same to me."

Mickey could feel Tim's hands were unsure on their joined controls. Tim had admitted it was his first time flying something other than a Black Hawk and the Twin 212 had a very different feel. Though the Night Stalker was learning very fast, smoothing out even in the short run down to the fire's tail and back.

"What's she doing now?" Tim cocked his head forward to see where Robin had gone. She'd dived down to lay down the first line of attack.

"You can't fight a fire from a thousand feet up; all of the water will evaporate before it reaches the ground."

"I'm used to fire*fight*, bro. Not fighting fire…except from Lola."

Mickey really didn't want to talk about women, especially not Robin, with this stranger suddenly planted beside him. He dove the Twin 212 to follow in Robin's wake. At two hundred feet, she ran a canyon line and doused a series of spot fires that were threatening the next canyon over. Mickey dumped his load on two more.

Tim was looking out the side window as they turned away from the fire to fly to a lake in the next valley over for reloading. "You actually fight a monster like that with four little helicopters? Shit, man. I thought we were the crazy ones."

"Between the four of us, we can dump a million gallons of water a day if we have a decent water supply. Doesn't appear to be a problem around here." Mickey had fought fires where the nearest water was a ten- or fifteen-minute flight to reach a dipping tank fed by a line of pumper-truck fire engines.

Until now, all of Mickey's attention had been on the fire and the intruder in his cockpit. Mickey had grown so used to flying alone that having a copilot was a visceral shock. He still wasn't sure why the man was here, just as Mickey still wasn't completely convinced that Mark knew as little as he claimed, but neither choice had been left in his hands.

Now he started to pay attention to the terrain, assessing the challenges. The Taebaek Mountains weren't high, but the fire was entering a rough area of valley and ridge that would be brutal work for a smokejumper or other ground crew.

In the structure of how each spot fire burned, Mickey could see that the growth was a worst-case mixture.

There was a low, bushy tree that reminded him of a Japanese maple that ignited hot and burned long.

The big trees had two primary forms. One appeared to be a big-limbed oak that started low and reached up to a hundred feet high—lots of foliage to catch and lots of hardwood to burn. Its low branches would naturally lead the fire upward into the crowns of the trees where it could move as fast as the wind and be ten times as hard to kill.

These two would have been okay together, a fire would have to struggle to progress through such a forest, so it would move slowly. But the third major tree was obviously a pine. It grew tall and dark green, and at the least hint of fire, it turned into a hundred-foot spire of burning sap, which shot bolts of flame like Roman candle explosions upward to twice that height.

The fire fought and spit. Each load of water they fired against it only seemed to make it angrier.

"Don't we have any ground teams down there?" Mickey's complaint to Robin wasn't answered right away. He was getting the hang of her pauses. She wasn't the sort to think about things or withhold information, which explained her reaction during their kayaking trip. Robin didn't hide her emotions away or make any pretense about them; they were right on the surface—even if they were a slash at the heart.

So, for her long hesitations to make sense…she was in communication with Mark and Carly. That had to be it. Well, he hoped it wasn't a pattern that the North Koreans, who were sure to be monitoring their frequency, could pick up.

"There are no ground teams in the area," Robin finally responded.

"None? How are we supposed to—" Mickey bit down on his frustration. Beating a big fire took a coordinated effort of ground and air teams building and protecting firebreaks. Beating out a small spot fires was done far more efficiently by someone on the ground with a five-gallon backpack pump and a rake than a helo at two hundred feet. Cutting down a dozen strategic trees could make more difference than a dozen loads of water.

"I'm guessing nobody wants to work in the DMZ." Tim pointed ahead.

"I don't want to either." Mickey was rapidly become less and less happy with the situation. Even more than not wanting to go himself, he didn't want Robin going there. Then he looked down at his navigation display and cursed.

"That's what I'm talking about, bro," Tim agreed.

Mickey had been following Robin's flight pattern. They weren't nearing the DMZ—they were hard against it. No wonder there were no ground teams. With over a million land mines in the 250-kilometer by four-kilometer strip of land, it was the most dangerous no-man's-land anywhere.

After two hours turned into three, they still hadn't crossed into the zone, but that's where they'd be next.

The whole flight raced back to Yangyang airport for more fuel and a quick sandwich. They talked with the other pilots for the ten minutes the refueling took, all about burn fuels, relative humidity, and ignition points. Jeannie had some good suggestions based on the tree species. She was the only one among them—other than Carly who was still working only over the radio—with a master's degree in fire management.

Robin had looked great, so completely in her element.

"Firefighting suits you," Mickey said in a stolen moment before they returned aloft.

"I guess." She bounced on her toes for a moment. "I guess it does."

"Looks damn good on you, Ms. of the Hood."

She grinned at him, grabbed a sandwich, and hustled over to find out how much longer until they were all refueled.

It looked beyond good on her. Made him want to be close and stay close and... Now wasn't the time. But Mark was right, it wouldn't do to wait too long. Next time they were on the ground for more than a few minutes, Mickey was done with waiting.

Back in the air, they worked north along the fire's edge. The lake they'd initially been using as a water supply was now farther behind them than a river was ahead.

But it wasn't just any river. As the two helos flew down to it, his navigation display—which automatically shifted with his movement—scrolled the river onto the screen. Along with it scrolled a bright red line that said South Korea on one side and North Korea on the other.

Robin must have spotted the same thing at the same moment because they slid to a side-by-side halt and looked down at the terrain together.

"This looks like fun," Mickey managed over the radio against a dry throat.

"Not my idea of a good time."

"What about them?" There was no need to explain who he meant.

Four kilometers away—on the northern side of the Demilitarized Military Zone—Mickey's radar showed a pair of helicopters patrolling back and forth, circling directly opposite them.

Robin didn't reply for a long time. "Someone please tell me there is another option."

"Attention, American firefighting helicopters."

Mickey looked down at the radio. The North Koreans were hailing them on the general frequency. He'd known that they had to be monitoring the open firefighting channel, but it was the first time they'd said a word all morning. Their English was clear, though heavily accented. Did the Korean People's Air Force all speak English to prepare them for the Great Future Invasion? Or were these the only ones who were even allowed to learn the language? No way to tell.

"Firefighters here," Robin answered with her voice sounding all casual as if this was business as usual. Damn, but she was good.

"We are your escort to make sure that no harm comes to your craft in our airspace. We are not firefighting aircraft but military escort. What are your plans, that we do not mistake your actions?" Their tone was very polite, rotorcraft to rotorcraft camaraderie. Though he'd wager they were in turn being monitored by layers of military and politicians who would watch every word. So, polite but not too friendly.

"No harm?" Tim groaned. "Like, *we want to make sure we don't shoot your asses by mistake*. Why am I not liking this experience? Where the hell's my DAP Hawk?" He managed to make it funny.

"Don't say that one on the open air, amigo." Though Mickey wasn't going to argue with the sentiment.

"Roger that," Tim agreed.

"We need to get to a water source." Robin made it sound like the most normal thing on the planet to be talking to North Korean military helicopter pilots across the width of the DMZ. "We will always utilize the closest supply. At the moment, it's that river between us. We need to hover at five meters over the water for approximately one minute each time we refill our tanks. We will circulate rapidly between the fire and the water supply, except when we are returning to our airport for fuel or needing to survey the fire line."

"There will be no surveying."

"There has to be. We will inform you when we do so and we welcome your protection."

"Damn straight," Tim muttered.

Nobody wanted standard border patrol forces trying to fry their asses.

There was a long silence before the North Koreans answered, "It is permitted." And they were gone off the air.

Robin turned her helo and Mickey followed suit so that they were face-to-face, hovering a hundred feet apart. Not knowing what else to do, he offered her a nod of support.

He was pretty sure she shrugged a "What the hell!" in return.

In unison, they turned and rolled down into the Demilitarized Zone, the most fiercely armed and contested strip of soil in the world, to load their tanks from forbidden waters.

Chapter 18

"Let's never do this again." Mickey sat beside her in the main restaurant of the Sol Resort. The massive resort in Yangyang was close to the defunct airfield. They sat in a neat spread of tables lined up in orderly rows. A three-story-tall wall of windows shining with the last pinks and oranges of the ending day curved along one side of the room.

And Robin knew that, despite sitting inside air-conditioned helicopters all day, they stank. She couldn't care less.

This stretch of the beach was only officially "open"—whatever that meant—for forty-two days of the summer, and this wasn't one of them. That meant that the resort's main restaurant was echoingly empty at eight at night. Five of the fifty or more tables were occupied by small, quiet groups.

Which was good, because MHA's whole team stank and were too tired to worry about polite noise levels. They smelled of wood smoke and they smelled of exhaustion.

"Beat's Denny's," she teased Mickey.

"I meant let's never fly in formation with a dozen tons of North Korean attack helicopters manned by the severely paranoid." He was so tired he'd taken her statement at face value. "They stayed so close, except when we were actually dropping on the fire, that I swear I could see the bullets in their guns. My knuckles are still white from fear I was going to ram one of them."

"I hear ya, bro." Tim thumped Mickey hard on the back. "We, I mean, the, you know, U.S. military guys, don't fly formations that close."

Robin wanted a burger and fries but had settled for fish and chips. There was a lot of seafood on the menu, very little meat. Mickey was splitting a pepperoni pizza with Vern from which Robin stole a slice.

"At least there's a decent amount of darkness here. Nine full hours," Jeannie groaned, almost nodding into her chowder. None of them had slept since Alaska.

"Certainly beats three hours of twilight we just came from." Cal rubbed his wife's back.

"And the North Koreans said no nighttime flying, which I'm not gonna argue with," Tim agreed and worked on the steak that Robin hadn't seen anywhere on the menu. Of course she was so tired, it might have been on the middle of the page in bold type and she wouldn't have seen it.

"How many people would normally be needed to fight a fire this huge?" Lola asked from Tim's other side. She had a surf 'n' turf, of which Robin was also quite envious.

"This one is running around twenty thousand acres," Mark replied. "Which is low-end average by our standards." He too had ended up with fish and chips and was eyeing Tim's steak.

That made Robin feel a little better. She was wolfing her meal down anyway, her body wanted the calories, but they would have tasted so much better as red meat.

"I'd like another two helos, a pair of air tankers,

and at least one full load of smokejumpers—twenty of them would be very handy right now," Mark continued. "Though I bet even they would hesitate about jumping into a mess like the DMZ. Normally, because the terrain is so rugged, we'd also have a half-dozen wildland fire engines on the ground and maybe a hotshot crew."

"Based on what I can tell from the limited feed from the drone"—Carly sipped at her tea—"and the little that I can pull off the helo's cameras, the only assets they have are a couple hundred peasants out on the line beating at the fire with pine boughs."

"Damn." Mickey sounded pissed.

Robin wondered at his irritation and then imagined some poor, underfed farmer without any Nomex gear beating at a forty-foot flame with a highly flammable tree branch. They'd have no training about entrapment or escape routes. Now she was getting as angry as Mickey, not that they could do anything about it. "They lose any in the fire yet?"

"Can't be sure," Carly said quietly enough to make the answer a clear affirmative. "I'm sure they will as the fire progresses. They don't even have a crew boss based on how they're deployed along the line, at least not one that's ever faced a big fire."

That killed any lightness to the mood. What had been…not celebratory, because they were too exhausted for that, but positive, had just been swept under the table.

Robin looked at the faces around the table and not a one of them didn't look hammered down and hurting after the long flight from Alaska, the crossing from Japan, and eight hours on the fire.

"Any word on anything else?" Robin asked Mark.

He shook his head and didn't look happy. He still didn't know why they'd been sent here.

Fine.

"Tonight, sleep." Robin looked over the weary and discouraged crew. "Tomorrow, we're in the air at dawn. If we beat the shit out of this fire, it won't have a chance to burn anybody. Deal?"

One by the one, everyone looked at her and nodded, resigned but in agreement.

There were two exceptions.

Mark was looking at her as if Robin had just fulfilled all of Emily's plans for her. They'd been looking for someone to lead. Why else would they have given her command of Firehawk One? By all rights she should have been copilot in someone else's bird for a few months first. But Mark's smile looked terribly smug and self-satisfied. Well, they'd pushed her into the position and she'd pulled on her big-girl boots and stepped into it. He made as if he was tipping his hat to her, if he'd been wearing one.

The other exception was Mickey. He was looking at her like...like she'd be an idiot if she didn't drag him straight to bed.

Robin was many things, but she wasn't an idiot.

"Excuse us." She pulled Mickey to his feet, reached over to steal another slice of pepperoni pizza, and led him out of the restaurant.

—⁓—

Mickey didn't wait for the elevator doors to close.

He didn't give Robin Harrow a chance to take a bite of her pizza.

She stepped into the elevator, punched in for the fourth floor, and he drove her back against the brass rail and mahogany veneer of the elevator wall. He pinned her there and she didn't complain when he drove his mouth against hers. He scooped her butt and pulled her hard against him, frustrated by the layers of clothes that separated them, but unable to control himself.

He had her untucked and totally disheveled by the time the elevator door opened. The transition from elevator to room was a blur. She kept slowing him down by tossing articles of her clothing in his face as she scampered down the hall just out of his reach.

She arrived at the door, carrying a key card and a half-eaten piece of pizza, and wearing a smile.

Robin unlocked the door and dodged inside—it was a good thing the key card worked on the first try, or he'd have taken her right there. She made as if to close it in his face and leave him out in the hall with nothing but her clothes.

He jammed a palm against the door as she laughed, and he forced his way into the room.

"Oh my God, Mickey." The wonder in her voice was enough to stop him, though she was in easy reach.

"What?"

"A bed. A real bed. We get to make love in a real bed."

No way could Mickey wait that long. It was at least a dozen steps away. He also couldn't wait to take off his own clothes and find some protection.

Not with Robin Harrow standing naked in front of him. A part of him wanted to hold her, cradle her to him, take his time—and that was just one more thing he discarded as he tossed his armful of her clothes aside.

As he pushed her back against the wall and took her, she dumped her pizza slice on the entryway table. He took her with his mouth, with his hands, with kneeling down and rubbing his cheek against her, like Adam must have as a supplicant the first time he knelt before Eve.

Robin protested.

Writhed.

And wholly cooperated, finally ending up with her back against the golden wallpaper and her legs over his shoulders as he held her aloft and sent her flying.

Only when she was done, when her hands had eased their purchase in his short hair, did he finally come back to himself and rest his head on her belly.

"So, I'm guessing you want me, Hamilton?" Her tone was teasing, though her voice was husky and her breathing hard. But her hands were gentle as they stroked and smoothed his hair back into place.

"Seem to." *Want?* He didn't *want* Robin. He *needed* her like a drug. He tipped his head back to look up at her. "And I'm nowhere near done, my Robin of the nice breasts. Just warning you."

"Good!" She untangled herself from him. "Strip 'em down, Mickey me boy. We both need a shower desperately."

Shower was not on his list of priorities. Bury himself in this woman was his entire list at the moment.

She held out the pizza for him to take a bite as he stripped, teasing him forward as if he needed more encouragement. They split the last of the crust as they went into the bathroom.

"I want to cry," Robin cooed. There was a big soaking tub and a glassed-in shower that would easily fit several people.

"Never had a base camp like this one before." Not in all of his years of flying to fire.

"Maybe we should fight fires for an unfriendly foreign power more often."

"Pass."

She strode across the room and entered the shower.

Mickey stood there unable to move. Robin in motion was a powerful wonder. It was the way she flew, powerful movements that didn't doubt themselves. Graceful— not because they were delicate, but because their purpose was so consistently clear.

Robin striding across the silver-and-black tile without a stitch of clothing on left him helpless to do anything more than watch.

She had the shower going, the temperature set, and had stepped under the falling water, and still he couldn't so much as blink or wiggle a toe.

Robin turned to look at him through the glass. Her hair so light that it barely darkened in the water. Her eyes so bright. Her form ever so slightly blurred by the water sheathing over her.

She moved, back out of the shower until she was standing close before him, dripping on the tile floor. Her blue eyes looked up at him and waited, but he couldn't think of what to do.

—◦◦◦—

"Oh boy. What am I going to do with you?" Robin took Mickey's hand and pulled him toward the shower.

Men had looked at her with need before, with hunger, with avarice, and even with a desire for vengeance— perhaps against their past, perhaps against all women. She was plenty capable of protecting herself, to many a male's dismay she'd left on the ground in deep physical pain.

She was less sure how to protect herself against the look on Mickey's face. She wasn't even sure how to interpret it.

Deal with what you do know, honey had always been Grandma Phoebe's advice, along with one of her whiskey-rough laughs.

Well, she knew that Mickey had just given her exactly what she'd needed. She picked up a bar of soap as she nudged Mickey under the water and closed the shower door behind them. She also knew that Mickey had a body that could make *any* woman happy, and she was really going to enjoy giving him exactly what he needed.

He stood unmoving beneath that hot water, head tucked down as the water streamed down his neck and over his back. She soaped up a washcloth and began scrubbing at his broad shoulders.

He moaned in pleasure.

Oh yeah—she worked her way down his back—he'd be moaning but good by the time she was done with him.

―――

When Robin finally slipped in between the sheets beside Mickey, she knew that their record of not having sex in a bed was going to remain unbroken. He'd already crashed into exhausted sleep and she was only a moment behind him.

What she hadn't counted on was Mickey. Somewhere in the dark of the night, Mickey kissed her awake as if she was a princess and he was absolutely the charming prince.

She'd expected to be woken by the firefighter with

his insatiable fire-hot need for her or perhaps the sly Mickey "Blue Eyes" Hamilton. Prince Charmings were outside of her experience, so she didn't recognize that's what he was until she'd been swept up by this one.

He cradled her against him, brushing his hand over her, sometimes getting lost in the curve of her hip, sometimes the arch of her eyebrow. There was no question what he was doing to her, memorizing her as if she were worth more than a passing fancy.

She felt a moment of panic that his powerful hand brushed away as if it were a fire in full retreat.

Then she felt that it was a cheat to accept something like Mickey was offering, but when she said his name in a warning tone, he kissed it away, whispering into her ear as he continued to nuzzle it, "No promises. I know."

And with that, she let go and for the first time in her life, chose to let a man make love to her.

There was nothing else she could call it, nothing less that she could pretend it might be.

Mickey didn't take a single moment for granted as he made love to her: not a single bit of curve, not the least reaction, not any of who Robin was. Sex was always about giving and taking and hopefully having a good enough time to make it worth remembering the next day after reality had come crashing back in.

In Mickey's hands and the darkness of a South Korean hotel, Robin became more of who she was than perhaps she had ever been.

Rather than making a thing of her unusual strength, he dug strong fingers into tight muscles until they went liquid.

When he kissed the inside of her palm, he left behind

a memory that she knew would return every time she wrapped her hand around a helicopter cyclic.

And when he at long last entered her, it was a long, slow slide. No pumping fire, no pounding her down into the broad support of a soft mattress. It was a gentle climb of unstoppable power.

How he held on as long as he did, she couldn't imagine, but she enjoyed every single moment of it.

What she could imagine as she locked him against her afterward was never, ever letting go of him again.

And for some reason, that thought didn't scare the shit out of her.

Chapter 19

Day Two of the fire had been brutal, there was no other way Mickey could think to describe it.

Robin had pulled all four helos to the head of the fire to try and protect the ground crews, which meant flying in and out of narrow holes in the smoke through rough, superheated air. And not hitting each other.

For perhaps the first time on a fire, Mickey knew he couldn't have managed the flying alone. He did the firefighting, but when Tim shoved at the controls, Mickey let him have his way, because Tim was monitoring the air traffic. With no ICA up in a control plane and the North Koreans hovering so near, it was barely controlled mayhem.

He had no idea how Vern was coping because Denise had been grounded so that she could service the helicopters as they rotated out of the fire and back for fuel. Air filters, pump problems due to the silt-laden water, windscreens so coated with sticky ash inside and out that they might as well been night flying for all the visibility they had. Strained air-conditioning systems fought ash and heat to make the cabins at least tolerable, but still they were constantly restocking liter bottles of water.

MHA's efforts kept the wildfire from blowing up and devouring a hundred thousand acres, but they weren't able to hold it at bay either.

When they woke up for Day Three, Mickey figured

they had twenty thousand acres of Black, mostly, and ten thousand of fire—fifteen square miles. Ten of that was merely burning, but five of that was hot and looking to spread. If they didn't stop it today, it would be solidly into the Kumgang Tourist Region. Unlike so much of North Korea, Kumgang had not been clear-cut for firewood and stripped of all game. It was one of the few stands of timber remaining in a country that had harvested sixty percent of their forests in the last dozen years and lost much of the rest to uncontrolled wildfire.

"What the hell are we doing here?" Mickey yanked on his Nomex pants.

Robin just shook her head as she dragged on the clothes she'd been wearing yesterday. They had some fresh gear in their packs, but it just didn't seem worth the trouble of digging it out.

"Shit!" Robin's curse had him looking over. "I didn't even get any wake-up sex."

"Hell, Robin, we barely made it through going-to-bed sex last night." It had been fun, way too fast, and they'd fallen asleep within moments of rolling apart.

"I've been robbed," she protested as she continued dragging on her clothes. "A girl goes and lets herself get all soft and mushy on a guy and she doesn't even get wake-up sex!"

Still just three-quarters dressed, he pulled her into his lap.

"What? We don't have time, Mickey. I was just whining."

He kept her across his legs when she struggled to free herself.

"What's with the cat-ate-the-canary grin?" She

squinted those startling blue eyes at him and inspected his face from inches away. "Did you get wake-up sex and I didn't? Who was she?"

"You got all soft and mushy about me?"

She looked at him aghast. "No, about Hugh Jackman. He's the guy I want wake-up sex with. Now unhand me, you cad."

And he had to. They didn't have time no matter how fast they were, so he kissed her and she melted against him with a "Damn you!" that was very satisfying and offered him great hope for the future.

But when they hit the air twenty minutes and a folded-over stack of pancakes with bacon "sandwich" later, he couldn't find much to be cheerful about.

"I have a new strategy," Carly had said at the morning briefing—the three-minute car ride from hotel to airport.

"Bring it on," Robin said with more enthusiasm than Mickey could find.

"It looks like the *other* mission"—she was circumspect even in the privacy of the car—"is a flameout. There's only the fire now and this has to be our last day on it."

Robin glanced at Mickey, Jeannie, and Vern. The lead pilots had all crammed in with Carly for the drive over.

"The storm system, once upon a time—like yesterday—was headed for China. Overnight it has decided to stay at sea. It's barreling down on the southern coast already. In a dozen hours, we'll start feeling the effects up here at the DMZ. Full-blown by sunset. Category Two to Three, so figure hundred-mile-per-hour winds."

"That's a strategy?" Mickey protested.

"That's a goddamn nightmare." Robin backed him up.

"No. The strategy is no longer to kill the fire. I just need you to delay it. Delay it until the rain front that's coming ashore with the typhoon can get here and snuff this bastard."

Mickey knew there was nothing Carly despised as much as a wildfire that wouldn't lay down. Fire had taken her father and a fiancé who came before Steve. "Well, that is a new strategy," Mickey agreed. "Intentionally putting out a wildfire with a typhoon. I wonder if that's ever been done before."

"The challenge is," she continued as they pulled up beside the helicopters, "the winds will arrive before the rain. You have to hold the fire in place until the rain arrives, or it will drive the fire straight up to the Russian border."

"Oh joy," Robin commented drily as the car arrived, and she jumped out to head over to Preflight Firehawk One.

Mickey met Tim at the Twin 212 and filled him in as they climbed aloft.

"Well, bro. It's gonna be one hell of ride." Tim held the collective with his left hand and Mickey held the cyclic with his right. They high-fived with their free hands.

"Hell of a ride," Mickey acknowledged.

Like the emotional roller coaster of Robin Harrow. It was so good right now that he couldn't imagine it going bad again. But she'd made "no promises" absolutely clear and Mickey didn't doubt that Robin was a woman of her word.

—◦◦◦—

Robin could think of plenty of foul words to say but didn't have time to say them.

The early edge of the storm winds had hit them shortly before the break for lunch. Which meant no break for lunch. She and Lola had taken turns on the flight controls so that they could each wolf down a couple energy bars and a bizarre-tasting sports drink from Japan with the unlikely name Pocari Sweat.

The fire bucked and spewed.

The North Korean escort helos backed off as the winds picked up. Actually, they'd backed away after her third complaint yesterday. One of the pilots managed to slip in an apology of "orders" in the middle of one of his messages. Their shadows now flew a quarter of a mile away.

To make up for that, the North Korean commanders had added a monitoring plane—Lola identified it as a 1950s-era MiG-21. All Robin cared about was that it was a very nasty-looking jet fighter that raced back and forth along the line behind their helicopters. It often passed tipped to the side, so that she could see the four air-to-air missiles on its belly. That it occasionally made the pass at supersonic speeds and slashed by with a sonic boom easily audible over the sound of her own helicopter only made it worse.

Without Lola's steadying presence, Robin might well have ordered them all back to the south and to hell with the fire and to hell with the President.

Then the fire jumped the line they'd been holding and started a fresh blaze. It trapped a group of forty or fifty of the ground crew, burning from both sides at once.

Her request for permission to land and extract them was summarily denied.

So they fought the battle, dedicating all four choppers

to punching a lane for the ground crew to race along only moments before the jaws of the fire closed over their narrow space.

And while they'd been doing that, the northwest flank had jumped a ridgeline that they hadn't been there to hold, and the battle was now on there.

The scene grew more chaotic as they shifted deeper into North Korea. A dozen miles in, Steve's drone could no longer get a good angle on what was happening on the front. Carly began asking for particular flight lines so that she could watch through the helo's cameras. Robin did her best not to think about the mess Carly was facing: a wildfire, a poor-quality map of North Korea over uncertain terrain, and a scattering of dizzying images.

She had enough dizzying images of her own, thank you very much.

Mickey got right down into the flames to hit a particular spot fire. He wasn't actually in the flames, but it certainly looked as if he was. That he carried less than half the water of a Firehawk didn't appear to phase him in the slightest or decrease his usefulness. He slipped his helo into tight places and nailed burns that she wouldn't have trusted herself and her less-agile Firehawk to mess with.

She brought the hammer, but he often brought the finishing tap to make sure a particular spot was nailed down hard.

It was too much like their relationship to be comfortable.

I love you.

Total chaos from Robin Harrow's emotions that were never designed to process such a statement.

I'm going to be so steady and reliable that you trust me anyway.

And goddamn it, it was working!

Robin felt battered from a hundred directions, and her relationship with Mickey was oddly nowhere near the top of that list. But that was only because that list was so full.

Four helos she had to keep safe.

Four North Korean helicopters, one shadow for each of their craft, plus that stupid MiG-21 that kept booming by with alarming regularity.

An ineffective ground crew that she couldn't talk to—constantly in the wrong place and dangerously exposed.

Carly demanding imaging information and visual confirmations.

Mark's ICA instructions that she then had to alter as necessary and turn into flight instructions for her team.

Rotation schedules on the refueling back at Yangyang International so that Denise was never confronted with two aircraft that needed work at the same moment.

Oh yeah, an approaching typhoon.

Mickey was the least of her problems. Which only confused her all the more. How had the man become so important to her that she was constantly aware of where and how he was flying?

She used one of the rotation switches to shift the team around, shifting back to the helicopter pairing they'd used in Alaska: Vern and Mickey, Jeannie and herself. It didn't make her think any less about Mickey, but it did ease the workload some as Mickey took on whole sections of the fire with only the vaguest of instructions.

—⁓—

Mickey shifted his battle tactics as he and Vern beat against the northeast corner of the fire. If this was a holding action and they were merely waiting for the rains to arrive, then killing the fire was no longer the top priority.

Harnessing it, steering it, was what became the goal.

It didn't matter if the fire shot up a particular valley, as long as it was one with no village at the head of it. It could climb the ridgeline in northeast grid 3-17, but it couldn't slop over into 3-18 because of a particular scenic waterfall in the Kumgang National Tourist Region that drew many tourists. And tourist money.

The ground crews were concentrated to the northeast, in the direction of the park and Kumgang Mountain itself. So his method of driving the fire north and west also helped to protect them.

"Damn, bro." Tim was working mainly as a spotter, though Mickey could also rely on him to do an accurate drop when he himself was too busy with instructions from Robin. Tim still didn't have the complexities of fire chatter down when she kept asking for details of his area of the fire battle.

And then she'd come back with a brilliant line of attack.

Robin was an amazing pilot, but she couldn't read fires that well yet and was constantly asking for more information.

Hell, Mickey couldn't read this fire that well himself.

He could feel Carly pulling all of their strings and he was totally thankful for it.

"What?" Mickey finally found a moment to respond

to Tim's exclamation as they hovered low over a river and snorkeled up a quick 450 gallons.

"I think I'm looking forward to the peace and quiet of getting back to a battlefield, where just the people are shooting at you."

At the moment, they were fighting their way through a stand of sappy Japanese red pine. The highly flammable trees had invited the fire in, and once they were about fifty feet behind the line, they were superheated enough to explode. Typically they threw only clouds of sparks, but occasionally they launched branches or whole trees into the climbing column of fire-driven winds. Fighting the leading edge of the fire, it wasn't at all unusual to see fifty feet or more of a tree go shooting by.

"On a Montana fire last year, I was hovering outside of a mountain drop zone. A fire roller developed just as Vern entered it. None of us had never seen anything like it. Flipped him over in the air and punched a five-inch branch right through his fuselage. We still don't know how he came out of that one alive." Mickey double-checked escort helos, Vern's position, exploding trees, and cliff walls, then ducked in for another run at the fire.

"Definitely gonna feel lucky next time I'm flying in somewhere bad. Why didn't you ever go military? You really bring it, my friend." Tim triggered the load smack on target as Mickey listened to Robin's latest chatter, but it was all to Jeannie.

Mickey didn't have a good answer for Tim. "Never thought about military really. I got my helo license as early as I could. There was a two-year combined college-and-aviation program right in my hometown of

Bend, Oregon. I did the whole early start while I was still in high school thing. MHA swept me in right out of school."

"Well, you're good enough to have gone the distance." Then Tim called, "Goose!"

Like a game of Duck-Duck-Goose, Tim had taken to calling the racing North Korean MiG-21 "Goose" every time it ripped pointlessly by in the background.

Mickey snorkeled up a fresh load of water and returned to the fire while he thought about it.

The distance to someone like Tim meant that Mickey was good enough to have gone Night Stalker, because nothing else was far enough. He liked the way that sounded.

"Not too late, man."

"Naw, I'm happy doing what I'm doing." And Mickey was. He loved flying to fire. He couldn't imagine doing it with anyone other than MHA.

"Lady, huh?"

"Yep." Mickey didn't see any point in arguing. "There's that too." Flying with Robin had become the best part of a very good thing.

Mickey hit the next drop point. Vern slid in behind him and beat back a developing crown fire. Once a fire climbed high in the treetops, it could race along at the speed of the wind, outdistancing ground crews between one breath and the next. A lot of what they were doing today was getting the crown fire to lie back down as a ground fire.

They weren't attacked with any surprise tree-sap explosions on this run. They'd managed a clean drop with no problems. A whole lot of things were going right with his world.

They circled back for another load of water.

Mark was waiting for her on the ground the next time Robin rotated back to the airfield for fuel and inspection.

Denise was already checking the systems before Robin could finish shutting down.

Robin crawled out of the cockpit beneath the glowering sky. The wind felt good. She knew it would be causing them more trouble on the fire as it struck northward, but the air was fresh and had a decent humidity level, which would also help slow the spread of the fire.

Already thinking like a firefighter.

That's when Robin felt the first real pang. She'd barely started her first season as a heli-aviation firefighter and she was already dismayed that her contract with MHA was only for a single season. Which also meant her time with Mickey was only a single season, because it was far clearer than the muddy water they'd been sucking out of the North Korean rivers that these guys stayed busy. A relationship would only work if they were busy together.

That explained all of the MHA couples.

Though it didn't begin to explain why *she* was thinking about it.

Mark placed a bottle of Pocari Sweat in one of her hands and a roast beef sandwich in her other. She stuffed as much of the sandwich as she could manage into her mouth and closed her eyes to relish the taste. The mustard was odd and sharp, but the meat was great.

"You are a god, Henderson," she mumbled around another bite.

"I always thought so," Mark said complacently.

Lola, who had come up and been handed her own meal, laughed outright.

Denise scoffed as she passed by and then climbed up the kick-in steps built into the side of the helo to inspect something up on the rotors.

Robin was even getting used to the strange grapefruit-and-electrolyte taste of the soft drink. "This totally rocks!" And then her brain finally began working again. "And, Mark, you're here at the field instead of sitting beside Carly and Steve on the radio. Why am I guessing that totally *doesn't* rock?"

"Because you're a smart woman, Robin Harrow."

"He's complimenting me," she said to Lola as an aside. "It means we're fucked."

Lola nodded her agreement.

Robin tore off another ravenous hunk of the roast beef so that she could have one more moment to appreciate the taste, then spoke around the mouthful. "Give it to me."

"In exactly one hour, I need you to crash at the following coordinates." Mark held up a slip of paper long enough for her and Lola to read it twice. Then he dropped it into her half-empty bottle of Pocari Sweat. The paper dissolved.

Robin glanced up at him as she continued chewing.

"Rice paper."

"Duh! I already knew that." She swallowed down most of the last bite she'd taken and handed him the unfinished bottle of Sweat. "I was wondering about the *crash* part."

"There, with such assets as you deem necessary to mask your actions, you will wait on the ground for fifteen minutes. There may be further instructions at that time. Be sure not to attract the aid of the North Korean escort."

"Instructions from who?" Lola asked.

At that, Mark shrugged uncomfortably, which told Robin plenty. As far as she could see, nothing made Mark uncomfortable. Mickey going toe to toe with him on safety issues hadn't bothered Henderson for a moment. The North Korean official hadn't even been a radar blip on his plans, his half smile was such a giveaway.

This was something he didn't like.

Robin thought about the coordinates again. "That's well under the smoke cloud at the leading edge of the fire."

Mark nodded.

"And if the fire gets there first?"

"You need to make sure it doesn't."

"So you want me to control the speed of a fire so that I can crash in front of it…"

Mark opened his mouth.

"…out of clear view under the edge of the smoke."

Mark closed his mouth and did that smile thing again.

"Then I need to wait for fifteen minutes while calling for help—"

"But making sure that the North Koreans aren't the ones to respond," Lola mumbled, then swilled down some electrolyte and repeated herself so that Robin could identify the actual words.

"Right. And on top of that, you don't have any idea why."

"Roger that," Mark confirmed.

"Anything else while I'm at it?"

"Nope, that about covers everything." He was back

to being his normal business-as-usual, pleased-with-everything self.

For Emily's sake, she didn't break that pretty nose of his.

Then Robin heard a slight sound, like someone knocking for her attention and hers alone. She glanced upward at Denise still perched atop five tons of Firehawk.

The mechanic was looking right at her.

And in her look, Robin could see the fear, no, the terror that Denise had survived when she drew the wild card on whatever last winter's mission had been. But she could also see that Denise was proud of the outcome and her part in it.

And she wanted Robin to know that.

It was a curious mixture of emotions to witness. It was mortifying to think what might be waiting for her when she "crashed" in North Korea.

She and Denise, by some mutual, unsignaled agreement, looked away at the same time. It had only lasted an instant, but Robin knew they had just become closer than perhaps any other woman had in Robin's life.

She made comfortable acquaintances easily, but it always stopped there. In this moment, it was something more. More than it had been on the flight here. When she left MHA, she was going to miss the women desperately, and Denise the gentle-hearted mechanic most of all.

Robin also knew what Denise must be feeling about Vern being on the front lines and her being trapped here doing maintenance. She'd certainly felt that enough each time she'd watched Mickey dive on a particularly bad portion of the fire.

"I'm changing up the rotation," Robin said loudly enough for Mark and Denise to both hear. "Vern's rotation for service will be due right on the hour. I want him back early, checked over, and fully refueled before I, you know."

"Crash," Lola provided.

"Right."

"In a wildfire," Lola continued.

"Uh-huh." Robin did her best to shut the woman down with her tone.

"On purpose."

Somewhere above their heads, Denise giggled.

Robin threatened to dump her drink on Lola's head to squelch her.

Mark shrugged as if it made no difference to him. "You might want to pull Mickey *and Tim* back under your wing." He made it sound completely casual, but she hadn't missed the slight emphasis.

Right! Whatever might be happening, it was the reason they had two Night Stalker pilots aboard.

"Good idea. Actually, I'm going to pull the whole flight, all four helos, together before I land so that we're never more than a minute or so apart. And when Vern is refueled, I want Denise back up in his copilot's seat. If I'm going to 'crash,' I want to have her close by just in case I screw up and really do."

"Fine," Mark agreed. "All assets forward. Good idea."

She glanced up at Denise, who mouthed a quick *Thank you*. She, at least, understood the real reason for calling Vern back.

Chapter 20

MICKEY KEPT TRYING TO MAKE SENSE OF ROBIN'S attack plan, but he couldn't. It was as if she no longer fought the fire but now toyed with it instead.

When Vern had been ordered back to the airfield long before his current rotation should have arisen, Robin had once again shuffled the teams so that she and Mickey were flying together again, which was fine with him. Between the North Koreans, the approaching storm, and a wildfire, he preferred keeping her in his sights.

When Vern flashed by after his return from base, Mickey could see that Denise was aboard, which meant that when it was his turn to rotate back in about two hours, his mechanic would be off flying in North Korea. Vern and Jeannie were working the northeast flank.

And suddenly he and Robin were fighting the center of the main head. You didn't tackle the beast head on—that never worked. You harried it from the sides until you had it pinched off. He couldn't even see anything valuable that they were protecting; they were fighting the fire on an open valley between two ridges so low that they stood no chance of cutting it off.

He tried to explain the problem to Tim. He understood what Mickey was saying about the changed tactics, could see it once it was explained, but didn't have the background in fire to offer any insights as to what the hell Robin might be up to.

"Robin."

"Here, Mickey, go ahead."

Then he looked at the North Koreans circling close behind him as he dipped his snorkel into a pond and realized that he couldn't ask his question on an open frequency.

"Go ahead," Robin repeated when he didn't speak.

"Just thinking about our progress on the northeast flank."

"Roger that. I'm good with Vern and Jeannie's ability to hold that line."

"What does that mean?" Tim asked.

"It means"—Mickey shut down the pump and pulled back aloft—"that our four helos that could shut down the entire northeast head of the fire in the next two hours are going to remain split two and two."

"Sound pretty pissed about it, Mickey."

"It doesn't make any goddamn sense! What is up with that woman?"

"Are we still talking about the fire? It doesn't sound to me like we are." Tim took the controls and led them back up to the fire—the venter of the northwest head of it that wasn't particularly threatening anything at the moment.

Mickey scrubbed at his face and growled into his hands.

Robin was clearly in communication with Carly. Robin also had Lola Maloney—who had replaced Emily Beale in the Night Stalkers, which meant she was probably now the best pilot there was in the military—flying beside her. He should really trust what Robin was doing, even if he couldn't make sense of it. But it was proving harder and harder to do.

She was keeping him at arm's length with her

goddamn "no promises" policy, yet welcoming him all
the way with her body in a way no woman ever had.
And she'd given back—sex with Robin Harrow was
very much a two-way street. She'd been tender…and
loving. He'd swear that she had been, but—

"Shit!" He dropped his hands back onto the controls.
He let Tim remain pilot-in-command but floated his
hands along. They now flew so much alike that Mickey
didn't feel any corrections he'd make for Tim, nor that
Tim made to his flights.

"Welcome to my world," Tim practically chortled
with glee. "Woman practically humps me to death at
every chance and wouldn't let me anywhere near her,
not where it counted." Tim thumped his collective hand
on his chest before returning it to the control.

"Yeah" was all Mickey could think to say as they
ducked down under the screen of the billowing smoke
clouds overhanging the northwestern head of the fire.
The North Koreans fell back and continued to parallel
them from farther out. "How did you solve it?"

"Stopped her from killing her father with that DAP
Hawk of hers."

"Robin doesn't know who her father is. Her mom
runs a truck stop."

"Oh." Tim shifted smoothly to trace Robin's inex-
plicable attack line. "Yeah, not quite the same I guess.
Sorry, bro. Best I got."

Crap! Different people's problems.

The line of attack Robin had turned to made even
less sense than her prior headings. If she dropped water
anywhere down this path, it wouldn't achieve—

"Mayday! Mayday! Mayday! This is Firehawk One.

I have a flameout on both engines. I'm headed down. I have a spot in sight."

"You are forbidden to land on North Korean soil!" a new and thickly Korean-accented voice cut in.

"I'm declaring a goddamn emergency." Her voice was cool, steady, and nasty enough that Mickey sure wouldn't argue with it. "Deal with it!"

Mickey could only watch in horror as Robin headed down. They were inside a screen of heavy smoke. At least the North Koreans couldn't see her to shoot her.

But he was helpless to do anything other than watch as she descended toward the dense forest below. There was a small clearing ahead, but—

"It's out of reach," Tim confirmed Mickey's fear. "They can't make it there without any engines. An auto-rotate glide slope just won't…"

"Won't what?" Mickey had done plenty of autoro-tates in practice. Because he flew with MHA, the gear simply didn't fail short of a tree strike.

"Their angle is wrong. I know how a Hawk goes down. They should be falling faster."

They did seem to float for a moment before heading down into the clearing.

Mickey finally remembered how to breathe again as she landed with a good, solid thump, but she was down.

"You okay, Robin?"

"Better than when I was sitting in your goddamn eddy current, Mickey!" Her voice had a light laugh to it. Strained but with no edge of hysteria that he could detect.

"Roger that. Think fast, Robin." Mickey eyed the head of the fire, which raged behind a wall of black smoke only a few hundred yards from where she'd gone down. They needed to solve this fast or he'd need to extract her and lose the helo. "I estimate twenty minutes max until the fire overruns your position."

"This is Firehawk Two." Denise's voice sliced in right behind his. "Mechanic for Mount Hood Aviation. What is the problem, Ms. Harrow?"

"What the hell?" Mickey asked Tim over the Twin 212's intercom.

Tim just shrugged. The women of MHA were tight, seriously tight. What was with the "we're strangers" double-talk?

"Double-talk," he whispered.

Tim laughed. "Of course! Women. Man, I'm telling you. They're a very tricky gender."

Something was up and Denise knew about it. She'd found a way to tell him that everything was okay and not alarm the North Koreans that there was a reason for the odd communications.

That's why Vern had been sent racing back to the airfield, to make sure Denise was here to cover for the failure.

The *phony* failure!

Mickey heaved out a sigh of relief. Robin was okay. Okay except for the fast-approaching fire and being on the ground in North Korea in violation of their orders.

Robin was speaking. "Air intakes clogged maybe. I haven't had a chance to look yet."

"I have some spares aboard," Denise answered. "We'll come down and deliver them."

"You do not have permission to land," the Korean radio voice shrieked.

Tim jerked back on the controls at the same moment Mickey identified a fast-moving object on the screen.

Seconds later, a missile shot past not five rotors off his nose and plunged into the fire. It exploded with a great roar of fire so bright that Mickey could see it blooming upward despite the heavy smoke.

"This has been a warning." It wasn't the North Korean helicopter pilots. It was a command voice they hadn't heard before. "No one else is to land. We will send in a helicopter to retrieve the firefighters."

"No need," Robin sent back. "I can probably clean the filters myself."

"I can fly over and drop these down to you without landing," Denise offered.

Mickey held his position and waited for the North Korean response. It was a long time coming. Long enough that Mickey could see the fire in motion.

"This is authorized," the commander finally announced.

Moments later, Firehawk Two moved in above Robin's position. A package was dropped, then Vern and Denise were gone once more through the smoke.

"Damn, but your woman has a load of cool in her," Tim observed.

"Okay, Robin, honey." Mickey didn't key the radio but wished she could answer. "What's your next move?"

—⁓—

"What the hell are we doing here?" Robin demanded.

The clearing barely bigger than her rotor blades a dozen miles into North Korea. She'd half expected the ground to explode beneath her with a thousand land mines when she landed, even though the DMZ was far behind them.

"And what the hell was that thing they shot?" She looked toward the fire in horror. Whatever it was had exploded and blown the fire in her direction. Her carefully chosen and pampered clearing among the tall trees wasn't going to last for twenty minutes.

"I'm thinking it was an Vympel R-77 air-to-air missile." Lola spoke matter-of-factly. "At least that's what the MiG-21 was flaunting up and down the line. It also didn't have the feel of a 9M117 Phalanga. They tend to have a little less accuracy and a little less oomph. Someone is going to be ticked off; those are expensive missiles. North Korea doesn't fire Vympels very often, even in their bigger exercises."

Robin was suddenly very glad of her career choice. She was fine going through life not being able to distinguish Vympels from Phalangas from…her freaked-out brain had run out of the ability to metaphor…from flying zucchini bread!

Then she eyed the smoke wall and was less than sure of her present career choice. The missile really had driven an outward blast of fresh heat into the flames. Her twenty minutes had just become closer to five.

She twisted to look back and see if Mickey was still hovering up and behind her. He had a load of water still and might buy them another couple of minu—

Robin screamed!

A face was grinning at her from just outside her pilot's door window. A female face, holding aloft a package of Blackhawk cabin-air filters—like the ones she'd watched Denise change just an hour ago.

The woman knocked politely.

Robin slid back her earphones and opened the door.

The wood smoke was a hot slap to her sinuses. The fire was very close, but Robin couldn't look away from the woman to see how close.

"Hi, did you drop these?" The woman's English was perfect. Her face wasn't Korean. Though her skin was dark enough, her features were First Peoples American. Not Navajo or any of the other Arizona tribes, but maybe part Cherokee.

"Seem to have." Robin did her best to return the woman's smile, but her nerves weren't cooperating.

She'd been shot at plenty in Afghanistan, but her last tour was three years ago. The missile shot had snapped her war-zone-triggered fight-or-flight nerves back to a full roar.

But that wasn't what had her knocked back so hard in her seat. Instead, it was the totally incongruity of the moment.

She was parked on soil that she half expected to blow up if she stepped on it.

A wall of fire was minutes from incinerating them. Minutes, as in low-end single digits.

And to be greeted by someone so clearly American...

It was the last piece that tipped her mental balance all the way to overwhelm. It was just too much to process.

"You can put them in back," she managed with a vague croak.

The woman stepped out of view and slid open the Firehawk's main cargo bay door. They'd been sent here to pick up something to smuggle out of the country. "What else are you going to put..."

People began appearing out of the smoke like ash-covered wraiths. Men, women, children—over a dozen and more were coming.

"No, wait!" She started undoing her seat harness to go find the woman. The toggles didn't want to release as she bucked against them. "If they catch me with refugees, they'll fry my ass. If I return to the South with a dozen North Koreans, you could start a god-damn war!"

"We know that." A man who stood a head taller than the others brought up the rear of the crowd. He moved up to stand close beside her open door. No Korean, he was built practically on Mickey's scale, though his build was a little leaner.

"And?" she demanded.

"We have a plan." He offered her a brilliantly white-toothed smile offset by his ash-and-char-coated features.

"Great! That's supposed to cheer me up?"

"Sure. I think that it's going well so far. Don't you?"

Robin could only watch in bemused confusion as what she decided were two families and a couple of outliers came out of the heavy smoke and climbed aboard. Their clothes might be worn, even tattered, but there were giveaways that they wore borrowed garb. They didn't move like peasants or farmers, at least not poor ones. Their hair was neatly trimmed. One of the women sported polished fingernails and a very modern hairstyle. A man had an expensive wristwatch.

Robin twisted around to look at Lola. But by her nar-rowed eyes, Robin would guess that she didn't recog-nize anyone either, not the two Americans and none of those with them.

––––––

Mickey watched, aghast, as Robin allowed people to

climb aboard her helicopter. "What the hell?" He had no one he could call and ask.

"Got me, bro. I make it twelve locals, seven kids, and two military. Highly trained by the way they move."

"Ours or theirs?"

"No way to tell from here." Tim shrugged.

"Thanks. I feel so much better now." Then Mickey finally thought of something safe to ask. "Robin," he called over the radio, "how's that repair going?" There was a long enough pause that he called again. "Robin?"

"Sorry." She sounded breathless. "I was outside. Just finished the repair. Now to test it."

She'd never left her seat.

"Roger that. Standing by." Then Mickey looked at the smoke wall approaching them. The haze was so thick that in another minute, he wouldn't have seen her passengers climbing aboard. What he did see was that the smoke was turning deeply orange as the flame drew closer.

She'd just taken on a ton and a half of personnel.

"You might want to unload your water before trying to take off." If it were him down there, he'd probably be too rattled to remember the four tons of water she was burdened with. "Don't want you to strain any systems getting clear of the fire."

Another long pause. As if she was distracted by something else.

"Roger, thanks," Robin answered. Moments later, a bright wash of water spilled out from beneath the helo.

The water reflected the oncoming orange and made it look as if she was sitting in a pool of fire.

"Move now, Robin. It's almost on you."

"Lifting." No pause this time, which made him feel much better.

Firehawk One climbed easily.

Soon they were up over a hundred feet. It was no longer a matter of flying safely under the smoky haze—they were in it now. Visibility was barely a hundred feet; it would be strictly a radar-and-guts job to get out of here. Firehawk One was little more than a vague blur of black-and-flame-painted helicopter against a backdrop of black-and-flame-colored wildfire. Mostly flame.

Robin then turned her helicopter, hovering in place for a long moment, and then drove straight ahead.

———

Robin had tried to see Mickey as she dug for the courage she needed, but the smoke was too thick, and she could barely make out the blurred outline of his rotorcraft.

"Really hope I get to see you on the other side, sweet man," she whispered to herself.

"Big ditto on that one, sister," Lola whispered back.

Then they looked at each other.

Then the fire.

It towered outside the laminate windscreen. A rolling wall of orange hell, unreadable through the thick smoke.

Before she lost her nerve, Robin yanked up on the collective, shoved the cyclic forward, and plunged straight into the flame.

Chapter 21

MICKEY AND TIM SCREAMED TOGETHER.

"No. No. No." Tim kept repeating it like a mantra. "They did not just do what I think they just did. No. No. No."

Mickey hovered in place another three seconds before he acted.

He yanked up on the collective to gain another hundred feet and slammed the cyclic forward and to the left.

The smoke was blackout conditions at this altitude. All he could see was the red-orange heat below and the gray-black ash everywhere else.

But on the radar, he saw Firehawk One moving fast and low. At its upper speed, it was steadily pulling away from him. He retrimmed his flight, riding hard against the edge of his never-exceed speed and still losing ground.

The heat hammered at them. Tim kicked the air-conditioning on high, but still it felt as if the fire was right in the cabin with them.

The turbulence slammed at them and buffeted his helo.

Updrafts weren't an issue. There were plenty of them—sudden vertical express elevators that sent them shooting up two or three hundred feet before he could compensate, wrapped in a cloud of swirling embers.

The downdrafts were utter hell.

One moment he was well above the fire; the next moment he was fighting for every inch of altitude he could get as he looked straight at a line of trees burning dead ahead.

And Robin was lower than he was.

"Damn," Tim muttered, "she's good. And I don't think it's my gal doing the flying. Not her style."

"What?" Mickey couldn't spare a moment to look except enough to make sure the Firehawk was still aloft at all.

"Robin should compete in slalom skiing. She's hitting the gaps between trees at close to two hundred miles per hour. If a tree cooks off, they're going to be off to either side of her rather than directly beneath."

Mickey began to get a feel for her flight patterns as he followed her through the smoke. He made up a little ground because he was high enough to fly in a straight line above her twists and turns.

The question remained: What the hell was she doing down there?

Something the North Koreans were also demanding to know.

———

"American! Explain flight!"

"What do we say to them?" Robin asked.

"Hell if I know!" Then Lola keyed the mic. "We're unsafe to climb higher pending possible recurrence of failure. Seeking shortest route back to South Korean territory so that we do not risk upsetting those who have the honor of living in the great Democratic People's Republic of Korea." She clicked off the mic. "There, let's see if that holds them."

"How did you say that with a straight face?" Robin

slammed the controls left as she nearly overran a broad, hundred-foot oak that was sending a tower of flame far above their current flight level.

"I was laughing inside," Lola managed through gritted teeth.

Robin had done some freaky flying in the dust bowl.

Just because you came over as Army National Guard and were told that you'd only be used for cargo and troop transport didn't have squat to do with reality. She'd never been on any black ops, but she'd dragged more than her fair share of gear and people in, and injured out, of nasty-ass battle zones. Her helo had gone back to America with plenty of holes in it. Whether by skill, by God, or by luck, the only injuries among her crew had been bad scrapes and a mild concussion when Josiah ran straight into a HESCO barrier while chasing an errant Frisbee. Should have been wearing his helmet.

By comparison, this fire was Sunday preacher hellfire and brimstone, or at least hellfire and exploding trees.

The North Koreans were still puzzling over that last broadcast.

"Hit the encrypted radio, find out what we're going to be landing in."

The polite and overly cheerful Carla and Kyle—the two obviously military types had introduced themselves as they loaded—had provided a new set of coordinates to deliver their passengers to.

It made no sense. Robin had flown halfway around the world and then deep into the heart of North Korea.

And for what?

To move a group of people twenty miles across North Korea and still leave them on the wrong side of the DMZ?

Carla and Kyle had insisted it made perfect sense.

Well, not to her.

Lola had finally whispered over the headset intercom, "They're Delta Force. No one else acts like them in a battle situation. Didn't know they had a woman aboard. We absolutely do what they say."

So Robin had taken them aloft and done exactly what they said. "Go to these coordinates. Stay out of sight." She'd shot low and fast. The coordinates were two miles from the north side of the DMZ, but that was all the information they had.

"Mark," Lola transmitted on the encrypted radio. "Tell me about current conditions at," and she read out the coordinates.

"It's on fire. What did you expect? The rains aren't here yet, but the winds are forty knots and climbing. The whole tail of the fire has relit. Rain is two hours out. What's the issue?"

"The issue," Robin kept it to herself, "is that I have to land in the middle of the fire."

Mickey could feel the North Korean's tension building and knew that Robin didn't have time to deal with them. So, he'd take some of the heat.

"Attention, North Korean escort."

"Escort here. You must both return to normal flight levels immediately."

"That's what we've got to delay," Tim said. "Whatever Robin and Lola are doing down there, we need to buy them some time."

Firehawk One was still flying down below a hundred

feet, deep in the flames and smoke. He was following at two hundred. Few flames reached this high, but the smoke was pea-soup thick and he often couldn't see the outer edge of his rotor disk just thirty feet away.

"Escort, this is MHA Twin 212," Mickey transmitted. "Our sister ship is in trouble and must stay low in case they need to once again make an emergency landing. Because of present conditions, I am flying escort."

"That's gonna hold them for only like—"

"We have no radar contact with your Firehawk One."

"—about that long," Tim finished.

"No radar contact," Mickey confirmed to Tim. "That's what Robin is doing down there."

"Sure, if we weren't five hundred yards off her butt, we wouldn't have any either. And it's not a good contact even this close. She does something radical, we could lose her."

"Escort"—Mickey keyed the mic again—"you may track Firehawk One following my position. I have positive contact and will not be leaving my teammate."

That seemed to buy them some silence.

"Where the hell are you going, Robin of the Hood?" Mickey snarled down at the image skittering across his radar display.

"Three miles to DMZ," Tim announced. "She lands in South Korea with refugees aboard and gets spotted, they're going to shoot down Vern and Jeannie back there." Tim hooked a thumb northward.

"Then that isn't the plan." Mickey knew Robin would never take such a risk.

"Then what is her plan?"

And in that moment, Robin disappeared from the scope.

———

"Robin, talk to me."

Robin did not have time to talk to Mickey at all. They'd reached the coordinates and Mark hadn't been kidding—it was fully involved. The winds were ripping flaming embers off every tree. That was how she'd navigated in the gray-out conditions of smoke and ash. Every time her windscreen was blasted with embers, she'd know there was a burning tree straight ahead and she'd slip to the side. Sometimes the embers grew thick enough to become a shimmering whirlwind of sparks as she shifted, in which case she'd slam back the other way to find a gap between the trees.

She'd reached her landing point, but she couldn't have the North Koreans know she'd stopped here. If Mickey stopped, they'd know exactly where she'd landed.

"Stay clear of the Tea Cup." She risked the transmission over the general frequency and then went back to figuring out how to get down.

"He's moving again," Lola reported. "At this speed, he'll pass over us in about two minutes."

"Thank God."

Robin was hovering fifty feet over the end of a road; the road itself was clear of flames, though the woods to either side roared with fire. The only thing keeping the area around her clear of fire was the downdraft of her rotor blades driving the flames outward in every direction.

The problem, Mickey—damn, but she wished she could tell him this to his face—*is that I'm not in a Tea Cup. I'm truly in the Mighty Furrow of Death and Destruction.*

Two hundred feet straight ahead was a low building,

or the remains of one. The roof was gone and anything that had adorned the concrete-block walls had been burned away. And still it burned with towering flames that rotor wash would only fan higher.

"That's our target," Carla shouted, leaning forward between the pilot seats. "How do we get in there?"

Robin stared at the flames. "Damned if I know!"

—⁓⁓⁓—

"Shit!" Mickey took his feet off the rudder pedals for a moment so that he could pound his heels on the cockpit's floor in frustration. "I know what that is."

"What?" Tim shouted back.

Mickey had stopped when Robin had dropped off the screen. Then she'd told him to "stay clear of the Tea Cup." It meant she was only passing through her present position and he couldn't be in the way.

Or he couldn't be marking where she'd been for those watching his progress on the screen. So he'd continued ahead slow, but there was only so long he could delay.

As he passed over her, he was able to look down and see the hole she punched in the smoke with her rotor blades.

She hovered inches above a road that dead-ended in a burning building. But there wasn't some big parking lot—the road simply went right into the ground.

"It's one of the Tunnels of Aggression," he told Tim.

"Tunnels of what?"

"I read about them as a kid in school. North Korea dug infiltration tunnels along the border, right under the DMZ."

"There's a river just over there." Tim pointed to the river they'd dipped water from for much of the wildfire battle.

"They found this one in 1990 or something like that. It was four hundred feet down. I remember being fascinated by it because I thought it would be a great way to accidentally find buried pirate treasure."

Tim snorted.

"I was eight, give me a break. But that's how they're going to get the refugees to South Korea."

"They're not going to get fifty feet." Tim pointed at the burning building now coming visible to the naked eye as they cruised slowly over the hovering Firehawk One.

Not unless they wanted to burn to death.

Then Mickey had an idea.

———— ∿∿ ————

"Remember how to ride a Tea Cup, honey," Mickey's voice sounded over the radio. "Just keep your cool and move right down the middle."

Robin laughed.

"What the—" Lola sounded pissed.

"Get ready," Robin shouted back to the rear of the cabin.

"But—"

"Mickey's up to something. And I have a pretty good guess what. It's gonna be good."

She heard the cargo bay doors being slid open in the back. The heat from the fire to either side of the road poured into the cabin, but in moments it shouldn't matter.

And then rain began to fall in a smooth sheet not a dozen feet ahead of her rotors. Just far enough ahead to not risk flaming out her engines, just close enough to cool a narrow pathway through the flames. Mickey was dumping a smooth cascade of water that suppressed the fire right up the middle of the road. And, as with everything else he did, he was doing it perfectly.

Robin nudged the collective forward, keeping her wheels just clear of the gravel surface. She didn't want to snag so much as a twig.

Mickey's dump of his water load paved the way to the burning building and then put it out. He slowed there, dousing it heavily until it wasn't merely out, it wasn't even smoking anymore. The surrounding flames would relight it soon, but he had cut them a window of opportunity.

Carla's hands clamped onto her shoulder from behind and shook her hard enough for Robin to make the Firehawk wobble a little.

"Oh my God, you guys just totally rock. We owe you a serious amount of beer."

At forty feet away, as close as her rotors would let her get, Robin paused—the two Delta and their passengers poured out of the side doors.

Robin saw scorched helmets and rifles scattered along the ground in front of the destroyed gate. She only hoped the guards had gotten out ahead of the flames.

She again caught the flash of a fancy watch on one of the man's wrists.

"Take the controls," Robin shouted to Lola and yanked open the pilot's door. "Carla!" she shouted over the roar of the rotors and the hungry fire burning to either side.

"Yo!" The woman trotted over as if they were just doing drill duty on a quiet Arizona airfield.

"That guy's watch. Is it uniquely identifiable?"

Carla raced ahead a couple of dozen steps, stopped

the man, and spoke with him for a moment. She came
back and slapped the heavy watch into Robin's hand.
"Personally inscribed from the Supreme Leader himself
in thanks for service as the head of the North Korean
rocket program."

Holy shit! No wonder MHA and Delta were here!

Carla shot her a huge grin. "Do something fun with
it. We have a tunnel to run through!"

"A tunnel! Of course." Lola laughed over the headset.
"High level defectors smuggled by Delta operators out a
tunnel that the North Koreans dug themselves. It's perfect."

Carla raced away and slapped her fellow Delta opera-
tor on the butt in a way that looked far more than com-
radely. Together they herded their crowd of defectors
toward the building and the tunnel's entrance.

"Not just women in Delta," Robin noted.

"Awesome women who marry very hot men," Lola
concurred. "Damn, but I love this life."

Robin hovered a moment longer until Kyle popped
back up from the tunnel's entrance and waved a hand in
their direction that they were in good. Then he ducked
out of sight and was gone.

Robin closed her door, lifted back into the smoke,
and raced south until she was once again flying under
Mickey's watchful eye.

Awesome women who marry very hot men.

The hottest man she'd ever been with was Mickey
Hamilton. And not only in bed. With almost no clues, he
had found the perfect solution to her dilemma.

And, just as he did with every single action he'd ever
taken, he delivered it straight from his heart.

Chapter 22

TOGETHER THEY RACED SOUTH. WHEN THEY WERE finally over the DMZ, Mickey started to breathe again, though not for long.

Once clear of the smoke, he could see that the afternoon sky had gone black with massive storm clouds. The wind was kicking at thirty to forty knots, which was a third of his Twin 212's limits. It took them almost ten extra minutes to reach the field at Yangyang.

They hit the concrete just as Mark raced up in the white SUV. They filled him in quickly.

Mark nodded. "I'll get the rest of our people pulled out. Tell them we've done all we could before the storm."

Robin held up her wrist. She was wearing a men's heavy silver watch that Mickey had never seen before.

"Not yet. We're going back in," Robin said.

Mickey's heart just about stopped. "You are not going back in using that aircraft. Not until Denise has a chance to go over every inch of it and makes sure you didn't melt any critical systems."

They all turned to look at Firehawk One. The black paint was gray with ash, as were the yellow-orange-red flames. All along the underside, there were large blisters where the finish had been overheated by the passage through the fire.

Robin had the decency to pale a little as she inspected her aircraft. She finally patted it on the nose cone over the forward radar dish. "I'm so sorry, baby, but you done good. Real good."

"Well"—Lola and Tim came up with packs slung over their shoulders—"I'm guessing that we're about to receive orders to go meet up with a couple of Delta operators as soon as they're done pretending that they're gophers."

Mark smiled and handed over a thin slip of paper. Mickey could see a set of coordinates scrawled on it. He saw enough to know that it was south of the DMZ, and he figured it must have been where the tunnel let out.

The North Korean official emerged from where he'd kept watch at the terminal building's windows. He looked at Firehawk One, looked inside through the still-open cargo bay doors where there was nothing to show that it had been crowded with defectors less than thirty minutes ago.

"As this aircraft is no longer serviceable," Mark informed the official, "we're going to be changing up pilots. I will be sending Ms. Harrow and Mr. Hamilton back to fight the fire in the Twin 212 and standing down the Maloneys."

"This is acceptable." The official made a note and glanced uncertainly upward as the first large drops of rain spattered out of the sky, leaving dark circles on the dry concrete.

"Yes," Mark told him. "We're going to do everything we can for your great country, but the storm will drive us out soon. We have done all we can."

"Understood." The official made to hurry away but then turned back. "We have uncertain times." His eyes shifted left then right. "I do not know if our country's leader will thank any American for help, but I have seen. I will say thank you." Then he hurried off without any offer to shake hands or otherwise acknowledge them.

"Well, if that don't beat all." Tim chuckled. Then he wrapped Mickey in a brutal hug and lifted him off the ground even though Tim was several inches shorter. "Wasted in civilian life, I'm telling you. Totally wasted."

At a loss for words, Mickey let his good-bye be a solid handclasp. Tim hugged Robin barely more gently while making *oh-la-la* eyebrow motions at Mickey over her shoulder, slapped Mark hard enough on the back to stagger any lesser man, and moved off to the SUV.

Lola's hug with Robin was soft and sincere. "You kicked ass, sister." As she hugged Mickey good-bye, Lola whispered, "Don't you let her out of your sight or I *will* kick your ass." Then she turned to Mark. "An honor as always, Mark."

"Likewise, Lola."

"Oh my gawd!" Lola placed the back of her hand against her brow. "He used my first name. I think I'm a-goin' to have me a spell."

"Get out of here," Mark growled happily.

Lola shot him a grin and went.

"So"—Mark turned back to them and pointed to the watch still on Robin's wrist—"what's the plan?"

~~~

Refueled, they lifted into the teeth of the rising storm and turned once more for North Korea, Robin aboard the Twin 212 as his copilot.

"This had better be the last time." It had given Mickey the creeps every time they'd crossed the border, but with Robin this close it was ten times worse. He'd flown beside her across the DMZ in separate helicopters, but this was their first time flying together and his awareness of her was huge.

Wow! There is a totally lousy adjective. But it was huge. In two weeks she'd come to fill so much more than his bedroom fantasies. Her bravery, her dedication, her performance under pressure…the whole package just…

"I love you, Robin."

"You aren't supposed to be saying such shit," she replied over the onboard intercom, but her voice was a caress not a slap.

"Can't help it, lady. You're just that amazing."

"Tell me that after we pull this off."

"Okay," Mickey agreed easily.

"That was far too amiable a response." He could feel Robin looking over at him.

"After what you just did, Robin of the Hood— stealing people from the North Koreans through the heart of a wildfire—I'm supposed to doubt that you can do absolutely anything you set your mind to?"

"Well, no. A girl wants to keep her man totally dazzled. I think that's a good policy and I have no plans to change it."

"Dazzled," Mickey agreed. "That's the word I was looking for. You dazzle me, Robin."

"That's a lot easier to swallow than you saying you love me."

Should he point out what she'd just said? What the hell, why not? "You just said the *L* word."

"But I didn't *use* it." She stumbled out her reply a little too fast.

"Okay, just checking."

She grumbled to herself as they crossed the DMZ. Even twenty miles from Yangyang, the winds had dropped back under twenty knots and the rain hadn't arrived yet. Despite the filters and closed doors, the air no longer smelled of rain but once more of wood smoke and char.

Their North Korean escort picked them up on the far side of the DMZ.

"The other helicopter was too damaged to return," Mickey reported to the escort. "We also have a change of pilots that was reported to your official on the ground."

"Understood," the North Korean helicopter pilot replied.

"Also, we anticipate being able to fly only one more hour before the storm forces us down."

"Understood."

Mickey and Robin shared a laugh at the sound of relief in the pilot's voice. He didn't want to be aloft when the storm hit any more than they did.

They rejoined Jeannie and Vern and began working the fire. Mickey flew his 212 and Robin acted as the Incident Commander—Air. She had learned so much that he only found it necessary to give advice on occasion.

She led them back to the northeast section, but per the plan they'd worked out on the ground, they only made a partial show of fighting the head of the fire itself.

Instead they began steadily slicing into the body of the fire. Direct attack, a very rare tactic that took them straight into the heart of the fire. Vern and Jeannie followed after only token protests. They understood that whatever they'd come for had happened, so if the new tactics made no sense, they knew better than to complain.

"Separating the head from the main body" is what

they would have given as an explanation if the North Koreans had asked. No one did. Not once during the long days of the firefight had they questioned MHA's tactics. Their escorts were military, not wildland firefighters.

They had warned the North Koreans of the coming storm-driven flare-up that would occur before the rains arrived. It was out of their hands now as to whether or not the remaining ground crews were pulled back; they'd done all they could.

~~~

Robin braced herself. They were getting close to the area that Carly had pinpointed when she asked.

Her stray comment over dinner about a lost ground crew had stuck in Robin's mind as she'd hovered over the devastation at the tunnel's entrance and stared out at the scattered guards' helmets.

Because it was a given that the North Koreans wouldn't tolerate it if the MHA helicopters strayed off the reservation again, they'd just spent the last thirty minutes trying to slice a path to that location in what at least appeared to be a constructive, planned fashion. It was an area they hadn't flown near during any part of the firefight, but Steve's far-seeing drone had spotted it early on in the battle.

What would they find?

Nothing, a part of her hoped. Maybe Carly's interpretation of the distant image was wrong and the ground crews had gotten away.

But a part of her knew they really needed to find the burned-over firefighters.

The North Koreans would know that the head of their

rocket program had come to this area along with his family. Maybe he'd used an excuse of being born here...no, he'd probably taken his family to see Diamond Mountain at the heart of Kumgang National Tourist Region.

Then the opportunity of a devastating wildfire had reared its ugly head and the U.S. Special Operations had seen it as an opportunity and sent in Delta.

He and his family had disappeared into the ranks of the peasants sent to fight the fires and had, courtesy of MHA, vanished without a trace. It was time to make sure there was a trace.

"There." Mickey pointed.

She couldn't see it at first.

Robin had once seen an entire herd of sheep that had taken refuge in a low swale before dying from a fire's heat. Other than being covered with a thick layer of gray ash, they had looked like they were sleeping.

That wasn't the case here. There were also no foil fire shelters.

Blackened lumps and exposed bits of skeleton. Twenty people huddled together in desperation when the fire took them.

"They must have been completely surrounded," Mickey said softly. "No one ran."

Robin looked down in silence as Mickey hovered over them and Vern and Jeannie beat at the flames to either side that were on the verge of running over the area once more.

"Let me do this, honey. Please."

Robin wanted to let him, let Mickey deal with it so that she wouldn't be stuck with this image in her head. But even more she didn't want to have it in his memory either.

"No." She began unbuckling. "This is your aircraft. I could fly it, but I'm not trained on it if something goes wrong. I'll go."

"Make it fast, try not to look."

As Robin climbed out between the seats toward the rear of the hovering aircraft, she paused and kissed Mickey hard. She kissed him for what a good man he was and for how he made her feel.

But most of all, she kissed him for how they felt together.

Then she stumbled into the back, slid open the cargo bay's side door, and snapped the winch cable onto the front of her safety harness.

"Do it!" she shouted and stepped out into space.

They didn't dare land again, not with the North Koreans hovering just outside the walls of tearing smoke and flame. So she rode the winch cable down to the charred forest floor. Winds buffeted and spun her until she was nauseous. The heat was a physical slap far worse than at the tunnel's entrance.

Still plenty of fuel here for the wind-driven reburn.

Gods, she really was thinking like a firefighter now.

Her feet hit the ground and she did her best not to think. She ran over to the gathered corpses. Found a man and woman holding hands—though they were barely identifiable as such—and snapped the watch over his charred wrist. She didn't look at their faces but simply turned and ran back to stand below the helicopter.

Mickey reversed the winch.

And only as Mickey lifted her back into the sky did Robin really look at the devastation around her. The Black was charred and gray, all color had been leached from this part of the world. All beauty was gone. They hovered in a narrow hole made of smoke and flame that would overrun the area the moment they were gone and char the silver watch to match its deceased owner. The poor ground crew member would probably have a state funeral, one of North Korea's greatest scientists died fighting a wildfire to save the Diamond Mountain, the visual and spiritual treasure of Kumgang.

Once she was back aboard, they continued fighting along the same line of fire. Not that it mattered anymore, but it would look as if they had only paused and continued on.

For thirty more minutes, they kept up the pretense before finally calling an end to operations and turning south.

During that entire time, Robin did not look up once from where she leaned across the console and kept her face buried against Mickey's shoulder.

Chapter 23

IT TOOK THEM OVER A MONTH TO MAKE IT BACK TO Hood River, Oregon. Once the storm had cleared Yangyang Airfield, which Robin deeply hoped to never see again, they flew back across the Sea of Japan. Rather than going to Nagoya, because the Dreamlifter always traveled fully loaded on the return flight to the U.S., they turned south for Kadena Air Base on Okinawa.

From there, a C-5 Galaxy Air Force transport had delivered them to Joint Base Fort–Lewis McChord in Washington State. At McChord, Denise scrounged up the last of the parts she needed before she'd declared Firehawk One fit to fight fire once more.

Instead of heading two hundred miles south, they first had to fly north and over the Cascade Mountains to rejoin the rest of the MHA crew. The Leavenworth fire had been beaten, but a new fire was slashing its way west out of Ellensburg and up into the North Cascades.

After that, the entire crew had fought a fierce battle in the Bitterroots of Montana and finally a nasty little burn outside of Reno, Nevada.

Robin collapsed into bed with Mickey when she could. Sometimes a tent, sometimes a crappy hotel, sometimes nothing more than a sleeping bag beneath the stars. It didn't matter, it was enough.

Somehow that flight through the fires of the Kumgang National Tourist Region had burned away the past between them. For a month, they had flown and lived only for the present. Fly to fire and sleep.

Mickey held her when the nightmares hit, which thankfully tapered off quickly, and made love to her when they could stay awake long enough.

Robin no longer questioned that's what they were doing. Making love. Not that she ever said it, but it was definitely what they did. Making love didn't necessarily mean *in love* anyway.

She couldn't afford that.

No promises.

That line remained clear between them, but it was the only one that remained.

It had been June when she'd been hired and they left Oregon. Now it was August. Her contract would be done by October and she certainly wasn't going to sign on to hang out back at the base camp as a waitress for Betsy the cook.

But they were living in the present, so Robin would take in all she could of this moment in time. This would always be the best summer of her life, just as no one would ever replace Mickey as the best lover.

It was a warm summer's day when they finally returned to the Mount Hood Aviation base camp in the Oregon foothills near Mount Hood. The sky was a beautiful blue, and once again all of the helicopters and jump planes were neatly lined up along the far side of the grass-strip runway.

She was done in. The other heli-pilots were in no better shape. The smokies were stumbling about like sodden drunkards.

"Two days dark," Mark announced once they had all

the gear unloaded and cleaned up. "I don't care if it's our own damned camp that's on fire, MHA is offline for this afternoon and two more days. You folks earned it. Now go sleep."

Robin sagged with relief.

The crew, which had been dead on their feet moments ago, lit up like they'd just mainlined super-caffeine. Shouts of "Doghouse!" echoed from all quarters.

Mickey was shouting right along with the rest of them.

"Doghouse?" Robin asked him as everyone began racing for their vehicles.

He gave her a shove toward her quarters that forced her to run or face-plant. She managed to save herself with a shambling trot.

"Don't ask. Grab a warm jacket and sunglasses. Meet me over there." He waved vaguely toward the mayhem of the parking area and raced away.

Robin had been on the ground here for an interview six weeks ago. She couldn't equate who she'd been so long ago. It actually took her a couple of minutes to even locate the bunk where she'd lain awake, awaiting her first fire call. The sheet and blanket were smooth; her National Guard training had made sure they were before she'd headed out to the line.

Was Mickey neat or a slob? She didn't even know that about him. Was he… She didn't even know what questions to ask. Mickey was…Mickey.

Feeling a little frivolous, Robin shed her work shirt. She didn't dig out the bit of black lace that she wore sometimes as a treat for a guy who was being especially nice to her. Instead, she dug around among the few clothes she'd left in the small room. She pulled on the robin's-egg-blue—labeled as sky blue by some clueless marketer—silk that always felt so good against her skin and really made her eyes look good. Her one good silk blouse that would feel just as good when Mickey took it off her later as it did when she pulled it on now.

Over that, she shrugged into a brown leather WWII bomber jacket. Grandma Phoebe had given it to her in a fit of sentimentality on the day she joined the AANG. If it had a story, Grandma was keeping it to herself, but there was no question about its authenticity. A line of sixteen Luftwaffe crosses had been inked down the inside of the jacket. Most of the dates were blurred out, but there was no doubting that this had been an ace's jacket, however her grandmother had come by it. Maybe her grandfather?

The parking lot had quieted by the time she returned. About half the vehicles were gone. Some had apparently looked at their bunks and seen no farther. Others had hit the showers.

In the bright August sunshine, Mickey stood in a sleek, black leather jacket and black jeans. In his hands he held a pair of motorcycle helmets.

And parked close behind the smiling goofball was…

"No way, Mickey! No self-respecting girl would ever ride on such a thing." The Gold Wing motorcycle was painted in the MHA motif, black with flames. And he looked so damn good standing in front of it that her knees threatened to go weak.

She took a deep breath. Robin Harrow went weak in the knees for no man, especially not one whose ride was a Honda Gold Wing.

All he did was give her one of those big smiles that

always stopped her in her tracks. Then he walked up, kissed her like he really meant it, and used that as a distraction to pull a helmet down over her head and buckle it in place.

"Hey! I mean it."

"Robin of the Hood. You cannot possibly look as good in that jacket as you do and think that you belong in a twenty-year-old Toyota."

The fact that her Toyota sedan was parked behind a truck stop in Tucson seemed to make that statement a little irrelevant.

By the simple expedient of scooping her paralyzed-in-dismay form into his arms as if she was weightless, he dropped her into the pillion seat. It *was* cushy. It had a comfortable backrest and a very handsome man slid in front of her.

"Okay, but just this once."

He nodded that happy, it-ain't-nothing-but-a-Class-83-Tea Cup nod of his.

She jab-punched him in the kidney, lightly, and then wrapped her arms around him and held on tight.

"I haven't even started the engine yet."

"You just feel that good, Blue Eyes."

He rested his hand where her arms crossed over his chest and pressed them more tightly against him.

Then he fired off the engine that awoke with a soft throb rather than a mighty roar, and they were rolling out of the gravel parking lot. A Ninja would have ripped gravel, spewed a rooster tail cloud of dry earth, and shot off down the road. Mickey driving a Gold Wing was like riding on the back of a limousine. The comfort was whole levels above the seat in her Firehawk, the view of the surrounding countryside from the raised pillion was spectacular, and she could feel that the man between her knees and in her arms was strong and sure in every action.

They swept down out of the high camp, descended through forested foothills, and rolled along country roads thick with apple orchards and vast blueberry fields.

There was something going on inside her that she had trouble identifying. For the length of the half-hour ride, it remained as elusive as that key water drop that would finally break the back of a fire and put it on notice that its end was near.

Robin finally let it go with a shrug and let herself simply enjoy the ride as they flew into the small town of Hood River, perched on the edge of the Columbia Gorge.

Mickey rolled up to a ramshackle bar on the edge of town. The sign said Doghouse Inn, so it must be the place, but Robin couldn't understand why it was so popular. The building looked like it shouldn't even still be upright.

But the street and a nearby parking lot were thick with the trademark vehicles of firefighters: hot cars and battered pickup trucks. Plenty of bragging bumper stickers to make sure everyone knew just how cool they were. *Wildland Firefighter! Smokejumpers like it HOT!*

An immaculate quad-cab Ford pickup pulled up as Mickey was locking their helmets away in the bike's side carriers.

Robin hustled over as soon as she saw who it was and held the door for Emily.

"Oh my God. You're huge!"

"Why thank you, Robin."

"And you look fantastic," Mickey said, walking up.

"Good choice," Mark said protectively as he came up beside his wife and scooped an arm around her waist like she was an invalid.

Emily rolled her eyes at her oblivious husband.

"Shoo!" Robin unwrapped his arm and gave him a little shove. "She's mine. Go away." And she slipped her own arm around Emily's waist. "Go fetch Tessa or something."

"Our daughter is visiting her grandmother in Montana for a week," Mark protested but finally gave way.

"Because her mother really needed a break." Emily sighed. "The Terrible Twos, they certainly were not kidding."

They walked side by side toward the Doghouse.

"Mickey's right, by the way," Robin whispered to her. "You really do look fantastic."

"Month eight. I forgot about month eight. I'd never have let him touch me again if I'd remembered month eight. Terrible Twos and Month Eight. Don't give in, Robin. Men will implore and you'll regret it forever."

"Sure, like I believe that." They shared a smile. There was something else Robin had to say, but she wasn't sure how to do it.

"What?" Of course Emily would see right through her.

"I get it now."

"What?"

Could Robin be more obtuse? How was she supposed to speak to someone she respected so much?

Just do it!

"I get why you left the military. I didn't understand how a soldier like you could do that. Before MHA, I spent a lot of time thinking it was a major mistake on my part…because I'm sure a crappy waitress. But I understand now."

"Oh." Emily's tone was carefully neutral, but her smile gave her away.

"Because you didn't, not really."

Emily's smile was radiant. "Head of the class, Harrow. MHA was a way for me to raise a family and keep a hand in."

Robin decided she had a new goal. She was either going to rejoin the Army and track down Lola Maloney, or she was going to stick until MHA decided they had to hire her long-term.

Two handsome men jostled to hold the door open so that she and Emily could enter the Doghouse together.

Robin had worked both the restaurant and the bar at the truck stop back home. And she'd definitely been to her fair share of others. Nothing had prepared her for this.

The seedy outdoors disappeared at the threshold. Warm light washed in through big windows tinted just enough to make them look dark from the outside. The walls and ceiling were covered in a mixture of cedar and white pine. A long bar of bright oak occupied one side of the room. No hard liquor, but enough draft beer taps to keep the most itinerant drinker content—and she didn't recognize any of the names; they must all be from microbreweries and craft beers.

The main area of the room was packed with tables. Robin knew the spacing; it was for socialization of the customers between tables, not for the ease of the waitresses or the maximum packing for profit. It was the same table spacing Grandma insisted on at the truck stop. It gave the crowded mayhem a friendly, homey feel.

And then there were the walls.

Every inch of the walls and much of the ceiling were

covered in photos of dogs in their doghouses. Miniature dachshunds in a child-painted shoe box, a Saint Bernard in the classic white-clapboard-and-red-roof home complete with a pussycat weather vane atop a tiny cupola, a miniature pink poodle in ribbons curled up on the plush mattress of an equally miniature four-poster bed complete with heat lamps.

They went on forever, thousands of them.

Looking for somewhere to focus, her gaze finally landed on the far wall. A giant Snoopy had been painted directly on the wall. He sat atop his doghouse in full WWI flying ace regalia ready to battle the Red Baron.

The smells of rich bar food were not lost among the low roar of happy people.

"A little overwhelming at first, isn't it?" Emily was the one guiding her rather than the other way around as they headed for an open table. At a big table in the center, pilots and smokejumpers had gathered and were already being loud over platters of nachos and pints of beer. There were other tables packed with Columbia Gorge windsurfers—and the smokies were clearly evaluating the fresh targets as they scanned the women among them. Akbar was right in the middle of it but with his hand clasping that of an elegant brunette wearing a wedding band—the trail guide spouse he talked about every time he had the chance.

Robin rested her hand on Jeannie's shoulder to get her to scoot in closer to her husband, so that Emily could get by. Denise leaned over and whispered something to Vern.

In moments, their end of the room had been reorganized so that an empty table was pulled up with the other pilots. Robin ended up between Denise and Mickey, across from Emily and Mark.

"Oh. My. God," she finally managed.

Emily laughed.

"I'm moving in." She turned to Mickey, though she wasn't quite sure why. "I mean it. Right here. This table. I'm never going to leave. It's almost as good as…well, you know."

And his smile agreed. The meadow by the lake on Larch Creek would always be their special spot.

"That was great, but this is where I'm living from now on." She needed to shake off the amazing memories so that she could even breathe. The best moments of her life had been along that wandering river with Mickey, and the worst, but they seemed to be over that now. "I'm never leaving this place," Robin insisted to bury the last of that bad feeling.

"Good, that's settled." Mark turned to the redheaded waitress who came up. "Hi, Amy, looks like you're hopping. We'll start with potato skins and buffalo chicken wings. Em is after ice tea, decaf, or the baby will kick the crap out of her, and I'll have a Black Butte."

"He gives restaurant orders the same way he gives fire orders," Robin couldn't help observing.

Emily laughed and nodded. Then she kissed Mark on the cheek when he looked chagrined. "That's my man."

"What do you like?" Mickey had to ask her twice before Robin realized the question was for her.

"Dark" was all she managed. It was one of those questions she should know the answer to about Mickey but didn't. There wasn't a whole lot of drinking when you spent every waking minute on the fire line.

"Walking Man Cherry and a Walking Stick Stout," he ordered. "I'll take whichever you don't want," he told Robin, then turned back to the waitress with that amazing smile he'd used on Robin any number of times. "Thanks, Amy. You're the best."

"She's cute," Robin said as soon as she was gone. Jealous that Mickey would share that smile with another pretty woman? Maybe jealous that he'd been with her in the past? Maybe losing her mind because she had no hold on Mickey, no ownership invested in him. *No promises*, she'd insisted.

"She is," Mickey agreed amiably. "She also owns the place and is married to the cook."

"Shutting up now," Robin informed him, and this time his radiant smile was aimed at her. Which was equally disorienting.

"She didn't get it," Emily said to Mark but was looking at her.

"I didn't get what?" There was a whole lot that Robin wasn't getting at the moment.

Mark was wearing that half smile that always made her want to take a poke at him.

"How do you live with him?" she asked Emily.

"He knows better than to use that look on me. Besides, I'm the mother of his children and the man is secretly a total mush."

"Not so secret." Robin gave it her best sneer.

Mickey and Emily laughed while Mark did his best to make an unhappy face. He totally failed.

"So, *Emily*"—Robin emphasized who she was talking to hard enough to keep Mark quiet—"what did I miss?"

"You agreeing to sign on long-term with Mount Hood Aviation."

Robin checked Emily's face, then Mark's, then Mickey's. Mickey was as surprised as she was, so she squinted her eyes and turned back to the other two.

Then she happened to glance at Denise on her other side.

Denise's nod was in such an emphatic agreement that she momentarily disappeared behind a shield of hair.

"When did I…" When she'd said she was moving in right here and was never going to leave.

And…what had Mark said? *Good, that's settled*.

"Okay, I guess I did."

"You did?" Mickey asked her. "She is?" he asked Mark. "Really?" he asked the table in general. His voice rising.

"Yeah, I did. Why?"

Mark's eyes crossed at her apparent non-reaction.

Emily just smiled and left Robin to play her game.

Denise nudged her shoulder against Robin's. Of course she hadn't missed a word of anything that happened around her.

Robin casually leaned back and wrapped an arm around Denise's shoulders in a comfortable embrace. That her new friend would now be an ongoing part of her life was a huge bonus.

"*Why?*" Mickey's voice practically broke with excitement. "Because for weeks I've been trying to figure out how to tell Mark that I was going to quit this job so that I could follow wherever you needed to go at the end of the season."

All of the teasing evaporated in that moment, washed away by Mickey's offer.

"You wouldn't," she managed on a croak.

"To be with you? Of course I would."

This time it was Emily who looked flabbergasted and Mark who was looking pleased.

"What?" Robin snapped at Mark.

He just pointed at Mickey. "His set of problems, not mine."

"What?" Robin tried again but didn't know where to aim the question.

Mark pointed again, forcing her to turn back to Mickey.

"You wouldn't dare quit MHA." Robin saw that he would. "You were born to do this. You love doing this." She wound down to a whisper against that look of perfect surety. He'd leave everything he loved in a heartbeat because he loved her more. "Holy sh… I don't know what to say."

"You say—" Denise started to whisper in her ear.

"Shush, Denise," Emily told her. "Let her find it on her own."

You say… Denise was right and so was Emily.

Robin had kept a small part of herself shut away, locked off in a corner because she knew that she couldn't stay. Because she knew that Harrow women had men, not husbands.

But the question that a Harrow woman never seemed to ask was what if she met the right man. The man that she could never imagine being apart from. The man who would be such an incredible father to their children.

She took Mickey's hands and held them in hers as the happy mayhem of the Doghouse made a somehow perfect backdrop. She looked into those beautiful, blue eyes and spoke the words that were finally so clear in her heart.

"I say…for as long as we both shall live. Yes."

Denise squeaked with joy, Emily wiped at her eyes, and Mark reached across the table to pound a fist against Mickey's shoulder.

News swept the Doghouse faster than wildfire.

But all of the cheers, hugs, and congratulations remained in the background.

Front and center was the best man she'd ever known.

Her man.

"I love you, Robin of the Hood."

"I love you, Mickey. For as long as we both shall live, I do."

Then she leaned in close because there were some words that were too precious to share with more than this one man.

"That's the version *with* promises."

Read on for a sneak peek at *Heart Strike*, the second book in the explosive Delta Force series by M.L. Buchman

RICHIE GOLDMAN EASED BACK INTO THE DARKNESS.

Most of the Bolivian farmworkers were sitting around the nightly campfire, eating their *salteñas*—meat-, veggie-, and quinoa-stuffed pastries. He'd learned to pretend that their food didn't agree with him. It gave him an excuse to duck into the trees frequently, though he'd actually learned to enjoy the local food almost as much as a good New York pastrami on rye.

Some of the farmhands were idly chewing on a strip of *charque de llama*; the llama jerky lasted forever despite the jungle heat. Others chewed on coca leaves— little more than a low-grade stimulant in that form, and it grew in lush abundance all across the hillside above their camp. Refined cocaine was too valuable for mere farmers, but chewing the leaves was practically a national pastime. Street vendors had piles of them in all the cities.

Richie had tried it, thinking it would help him fit in, but found the taste so astringent that he had no problem just tucking it in his cheek and only pretending to chew. Others on his team had found similar tricks. Only Duane had flat-out declined, but his formidable silence made it so that he wasn't an easy man to question. The locals let him be.

Once out of the firelight, Richie met up with Duane. That left the other three members of his Delta Force team— Chad, Carla, and the team leader, Kyle—still at the fire making sure that no one followed them into the darkness.

He and Duane spoke softly in Spanish about nothing in particular as they strolled along the edges of the coca fields they'd been working for the two weeks since their arrival. A thousand hectares, almost five square miles of coca plantation in this farm alone. They'd been building up to this one for six months; it represented almost five percent of Bolivia's coca production. They'd be gone in a few more days.

And that would be the last day of this farm's existence.

Only two more measurements to take. They strolled the edge of the field like a pair of *hombres* walking off the day. Their feet were nearly silent on the rich dirt. To one side was thick jungle, with no two trees alike. A massive kapok, a spindly palm, a fig tree that was bigger than the Goodyear blimp sitting on its butt were crowded together. Beneath them were banana, rubber, and a hundred other small trees he couldn't identify in the dark, but the rich, loamy scent was lush with life. The leaves rustled, whether on the light breeze or due to some passing band of monkeys, he couldn't tell. To the other side, there lay row upon neat row of man-tall coca bushes with their thick leaves ready for harvest.

When they reached the southwest corner of the main field, Richie ducked down low while Duane kept watch. He pulled a GPS tracker out of his boot, checked that he had a valid and stable reading, then recorded the numbers. He slipped it back into his boot and once more they were just two shadows strolling the line.

The two of them had originally bonded during the six-month training course for The Unit—as Delta Force operators commonly referred to themselves. They had discovered a shared inner nerd over various triggers for different types of explosives, which was Duane's specialty. *Being* the team's chief nerd was Richie's specialty.

Duane's deeply laconic nature made for a very lazy conversation, a rhythm which Richie had come to rather enjoy. It felt as if they blended better into the night that way—the occasional bat winging by with a quick *brrrr* of wings, the dry grass rustling against their calves, and two guys down on their luck sharing quiet commiseration.

Kyle and Carla were a couple now and it was rare to have a conversation with one and not the other. And *any* conversation involving Carla was more like a debate match than a conversation. The lady was intense. Amazing, beautiful, and incredible…but intense. And Kyle and Carla's relationship was like that too. Richie had never seen anything like it, had never imagined it was possible. When the two of them were together, the day became brighter. His parents had always been his ideal of a good relationship, which was solid and stable, but Kyle and Carla made it look like a heck of a lot of fun too. For the first time, Richie was forced to recalibrate the standards of what he hoped for from his own future.

Chad, on the other hand, talked about women and nothing but. He thought women were great sport, and if he hadn't been so successful with them, Richie would have discounted half of what he said. Chad somehow always ended up with the hot women and seemed to leave every one of them smiling; his successes were short-lived and he claimed that's the way he wanted it. He just didn't have the greatest conversational range on other topics.

Duane was the one most like Richie on the team. They came from professional backgrounds; they both had grown up in nice neighborhoods with good schools, corporate executive fathers, and involved mothers— Richie's was a housewife who did a lot of entertaining in support of Dad's job; Duane's was a family-law attorney. It was almost like he and Duane were related, separated only by New York versus Georgia respectively and an entirely different hereditary line.

"I don't know, brother," Duane was saying. "How did Chad sweep up Mayra?" They spoke Spanish for both the practice and to protect their cover story.

It wasn't typical of them to discuss women, but Mayra was the hottest, most-built Bolivian beauty they'd seen in the eleven coca farms they'd worked over the last six months. Their Delta team had been quietly roving the countryside, posing as itinerant workers—ex-pat Americans down on their luck. Their assignment had been to blend in, precisely map each field's location, and then move on with no one the wiser.

"Chad makes it look so easy." Richie didn't exactly envy Chad's insane success with women. It was too slick, too casual, and too easily forgotten. But he wouldn't mind having at least a few of those skills himself for when the right woman came along—so she wouldn't pass on by before he could untie his tongue.

"Maybe he is hung like horse," a voice said out of the darkness. Rolando faded into view, a battered AK-47 over his shoulder catching the moonlight and an even more worn radio at his hip.

"You got patrol tonight. Sorry, *amigo*," Duane said more easily than Richie could have. Rolando was one of the most dangerous of the coca farm's guards. The others joked that he loved his gun more than his mother.

"No big deal. But I was *mucho* close to spreading Mayra." He held up two fingers so close together the moonlight couldn't slip between them. "Like so before he come along." Then he shrugged. "Maybe when he gone."

With Rolando it was hard to read if that meant he was expecting them to just leave or if Rolando was planning to accidently shoot Chad some night soon. Richie reminded himself to tell Chad to watch his back around Rolando—not that Chad was easy to surprise. He might be a complete womanizer, but he'd also grown up on the wrong side of the Detroit streets.

The first option was unlikely, because once a person came to work on a coca farm, it was very hard to leave. There were hundreds of booby traps set around the perimeter of the fields. They were intended to keep raiders and government men out, but the lethal wall was not far into the jungle and it did just as effective a job of keeping the workers in. The main road in and out was always heavily guarded, except for a few minutes around sunrise a couple days from now, which is when the Delta team would be leaving.

They traded some more sympathy with Rolando, all agreeing that it would help if Chad wasn't such a good guy as well.

Richie knew better.

Chad was one of those guys who was everyone's friend and most people assumed that's all he was. But he had also come by his nickname, The Reaper, because he was a stone-cold killer when he needed to be.

Richie and Duane continued their walk, leaving Rolando to watch the night. They stopped and chatted with two more guards before reaching the one corner of the field they hadn't had a chance to exactly locate yet.

"Anyone?"

He and Duane stood for at least ten minutes, talking about the backbreaking work of tending the vast plantings—which in truth wasn't as tough as a typical day of Delta training—and watching over each other's shoulders.

Duane finally shook his head in answer to Richie's earlier question. They were alone.

Richie knelt quickly and pulled out a small, high-powered radio, unfolded a tiny parabolic dish antenna, and aimed it upward. He checked his watch, shifted the antenna to point toward the constellation Virgo, and pinged their full set of GPS data coordinates up to a satellite that should be in that vicinity. By using a directional antenna and sending all of the data compacted into a single short burst of information, their signal should be undetectable.

Many coca fields were heavily protected from above as well; acre after acre of camouflage nets hid the cash crop. Others, like this one, were hidden so deep in the mountains that it was easier to find them from the ground, following leads and tips rather than aerial photos.

Ten seconds later a "squirt" pinged back from The Activity—America's most clandestine military intelligence agency in Fort Belvoir, Virginia. Another coca field had been accurately located and recorded.

Richie glanced at the return message quickly, checking that it unscrambled cleanly. Then swore when his eye caught on the last line.

"What?" Duane whispered.

Richie sent the "message received" squirt back, collapsed his little setup of equipment, and scanned the message fully before putting away his gear.

"Six hours," was all he said. "All the way out."

"Aw, *mierda*!" was Duane's response.

About the Author

M. L. Buchman has over forty novels in print. His military romantic suspense books have been named Barnes & Noble and NPR "Top 5 of the year" and twice *Booklist* "Top 10 of the Year," placing two titles on their "Top 101 Romances of the Last 10 Years" list. He has been nominated for the Reviewer's Choice Award for "Top 10 Romantic Suspense of 2014" by *RT Book Reviews*. In addition to romance, he also writes thrillers, fantasy, and science fiction.

In among his career as a corporate project manager he has rebuilt and single-handed a fifty-foot sailboat, both flown and jumped out of airplanes, designed and built two houses, and bicycled solo around the world.

He is now a full-time writer, living on the Oregon Coast with his beloved wife. He is constantly amazed at what you can do with a degree in geophysics. You may keep up with his writing at www.mlbuchman.com.